Emerald Germs of Ireland

PATRICK McCABE was born in County Monaghan, Ireland, in 1955. He has published a children's story, *The Adventures of Shay Mouse* (1985); five adult novels, *Music on Clinton Street* (1986), *Carn* (1989), *The Butcher Boy* (1992), which was the winner of the *Irish Times*/Aer Lingus Literature Prize, was shortlisted for the 1992 Booker Prize and was a highly acclaimed film directed by Neil Jordan, *The Dead School* (1995) and *Breakfast on Pluto*, which was shortlisted for the 1998 Booker Prize; and a collection of interrelated stories, *Mondo Desperado*, which was widely acclaimed on publication in 1999. He lives in Sligo with his wife and two daughters.

Patrick McCabe

Emerald Germs of Ireland

PICADOR

First published 2001 by Picador

This edition published 2002 by Picador
an imprint of Pan Macmillan Ltd
Pan Macmillan, 20 New Wharf Road, London N1 9RR
Basingstoke and Oxford
Associated companies throughout the world
www.panmacmillan.com

ISBN 0 330 39375 8

1 3 5 7 9 8 6 4 2

A CIP catalogue record for this book is available from
the British Library.

Typeset by SetSystems Ltd, Saffron Walden, Essex
Printed and bound in Great Britain by
Mackays of Chatham plc, Chatham, Kent

Emerald Germs of Ireland

An Introduction

THESE FEW WORDS are written so that we might understand why Pat McNab, the main character in this book, behaved in the way he did. What they definitely are not is an attempt to excuse him, for Pat is guilty and everybody knows it, but at least, with a bit of luck, they will go some way towards explaining why he grew up with the reputation of being a complete '*loo-la*' and a '*headbin of the highest order*' as Timmy Sullivan, the proprietor of Sullivan's Select Bar, described him one night. You see, for as far back as he could remember, Pat had always wanted to be in a '*pop*' or '*show*' band but his mother wouldn't countenance it. Almost losing her mind, in fact, if it was even so much as mentioned! 'Band!' she would snap, glowering at her son, 'I'll give you band! Think you're going to end up like that other lug, do you, that father of yours, disporting himself in his great big Captain's uniform for every trollop and painted hussy that went walking the road, and ne'er so much as a copper sent home to buy a crust of bread! Band! Pshaw! Get down on your knees this very instant and scrub them tiles before I put this brush across your back and don't think for a second I wouldn't!'

Which Pat did not doubt in the slightest, for many's the time he'd had to endure her doing just that, and for offences far less serious than bringing his father up in the conversation. He had left them not too long after Pat reached his ninth birthday and all that was heard tell of him subsequently was that he was seen in Dublin with two girls in flowery dresses, one dangling on each arm. After that, all that had to be said was D—, never mind his whole name, and she would 'freak', as Honky McCool might put it, throwing jugs, plates and anything else that might be to hand, calling him the most outlandish names. Names unrepeatable in any civilized company. One day, Pat, without thinking, had the misfortune to muse aloud: 'I wonder will Daddy ever come back' – without hardly realizing he had spoken at all – his mother, before he knew it, pounding him across the head with a plastic basin, crying: 'I warned you! I told you not to say it!', after which he was more than careful about what he pondered aloud, and '*then some*', as the Americans say. But then, to make matters worse, other days you'd come across her sitting in the dark clutching his father's photograph and wiping her eyes as she sobbed: 'I wish he'd come home, our Daddy.' An eventuality which, sad to say, was never to come to pass. There were rumours that he got hit in the chest by a stray shell and died right there on the spot. But then there were the other rumours that he'd deserted and ran away to hide in Belgium with a woman so it's very difficult to say.

In any case, it doesn't matter, for what we are primarily concerned with here is Pat, his mother and this band business, as she called it. The band that never was, of course, for what with his mother's persistently unhelpful attitude how could it ever have possibly been – when, literally, you weren't permitted to open your mouth about it. Just as Pat daren't open his mouth to his mother about most things, for somehow no matter what you said to Mammy (as he had always called her, for as far back as he could remember) she always seemed to take it up as you saying: 'Well then! That's the end of our relationship, I guess! I'll be off to live my own life! Toodle-oo!' Even if it was in reality about a million miles from what was truly in fact going on in your mind! And which became very exasperating for Pat, as I'm sure you can imagine, the simplest declaration such as: 'Well – I think I'll just pop down to

Sullivan's for a bottle of stout – I've a bit of a thirst on!' being greeted with a foul glare and the words: 'Oh, have you now! A bit of a thirst on, eh? Well – go on, then! Go on then with your thirst, Pat McNab! But don't think I'll care if you never darken the door again as long as you live!'

Sometimes she might even start to cry until in the end it would get so bad that Pat would say: 'I won't go, then! I'll stay here, Mammy! I'll stay here with you, then, if that's what you want!' Particularly if he had been doing some reading or practising his acting skills.

But not without being furious with himself for doing it, for at times his late-evening thirsts could be almost unbearable.

A lot of people, if they could gain access to Pat (which, admittedly, can be difficult, for he rarely answers the door now), would probably be hard pressed not to look him in the eye and say: 'Pat – what made you go and do the like of that – clobbering your poor mother – not to mention everything else you got up to, God knows how many unfortunates fertilizing the daisies in your garden. What on earth were you thinking of?' As if to suggest that Pat is some big mysterious psychological puzzle, instead of the most ordinary fellow you could ever hope to meet. An ordinary fellow who just happened to want to have a few drinks at night-time and maybe join a band to sing a few songs. Without always having a shadow falling across him and a dumpling-shaped parent snarling: 'Where do you think you're going?' every time Pat opened the front door. After all, as Pat often pointed out, he *was* forty-five years of age.

Still and all, there were times he missed his old Mammy and there is no point in denying it. Times when he would think of her chopping up fingers of toast and coming out with a plateful of them and handing them to him proud as punch, all in a line with the butter running through them. Times when she'd dress him up in his pressed soldier's uniform and say: 'Be my little Captain for me, Pat!' as off he'd march up and down the kitchen with his mother beaming, thinking of all the good old days she'd once had with his father.

He would feel lonely whenever he thought of those times, seeing his life stretching out before him like some deserted highway, his bed at night now hopelessly bereft of her big warm rolls of fat and those comforting occasions when she would respond, in answer to his anxious night-time query: 'Are you there, Mammy?', 'Yes, yes of course I'm here, son! As I always will be!'

Which was no longer the case and never would be again, for as long as he lived, as Pat knew, the saddest part of it all being, of course, the fact that she had herself been responsible for the situation which had brought so much unhappiness to them both. As indeed had a lot of other people who couldn't find it within themselves to mind their own business. People who found it difficult to go through life without saying: 'Look! There goes McNab! Odd as two left feet, that fellow!'

But there is something special about the relationship we all have with our mothers – and Pat, in moments of reflection, would feel a wave of melancholy sweep through him as he thought how if he had to live through it all again he wouldn't have laid a finger on her. Often, he would wipe a tear from his eye and, seeing her before him large as life with her two eyes twinkling, whisper the words: 'Mammy. This time let us do it right and when I ask you can I join the band or have a bottle of stout, you just say: "Yes, Pat, you can. Why, of course you can. You don't even have to ask."'

And when in his imagination Pat McNab hears his mother uttering those words, there is no happier man on this earth, and all he can think of is throwing his arms around her neck and giving her a great big 'gooser' (their private name for a kiss) on the cheek as he cries: 'Do you know what I'll do, Mammy? I'll join no band! I'll say to the band – go to hell, band, for what do I care about you! And then I'll stay home all day with you! That's what I'll do! For you're better than any band! Band bedamned! I care about no band!'

Obviously, Pat was aware that many people might think it foolish and, to say the very least, inappropriate, for a forty-five-year-old man to seat himself on his mother's knee, the pair of them singing away as though they were some ridiculous kind of two-headed human jukebox. The truth is, however, that Pat didn't care, literally squealing with delight at times as he cried: 'Come on, Mammy! It's your turn now! Sing one we all know!' as she would hit him a playful slap and cry: 'No! You, Pat! It's your go!' and between the pair of them they would be as happy then as that very first day he popped out from between her legs so many years before that final day when her son swung a saucepan and pitched Maimie McNab into the black unending pitch of all eternity.

*

Which – and let us not mince words here – makes Pat McNab a perpetrator of that most heinous of crimes, the taking of another person's life, and earns him the reprehensible, odious appellation of 'murderer'. But not just any ordinary murderer, either, for quite how many people ended up covered in a carpet of leaves in the environs of Pat McNab's garden even now it would be impossible to state with any degree of accuracy. Suffice to say that a conservative estimate might be around the fifty, fifty-five mark. That is not, however, to include the various fly-by-nights and assorted drifters who turned up unannounced at the McNab household (a grey, parsonage-type edifice two miles outside town), never afterwards to be seen again, the only evidence of their ever having been in the vicinity the faint strains of an Irish ballad or obscure 'pop' or 'show' tune with which Pat commemorated their untimely passing, a new vitality entering his life as he, by dint of sheer experience and a sense of 'warming to his task', gradually found himself becoming as efficient in this heretofore undiscovered arena as any 'Cleaner' or 'Regulator' one might encounter in the world of Hollywood action pictures.

It was, perhaps, inevitable then that Pat might – simply through the sheer force of his new-found excitement and sense of achievement, something previously utterly unknown to him – gradually begin to perceive himself as one of these individuals – a sort of long-coated, mysterious loner whose dedication to his career ('termination with extreme prejudice') was fierce and shocking in its simplicity. Even to the extent, for a time, of finding himself convinced that he was bearing with him throughout the village of Gullytown a special, custom-made briefcase which contained the precision instruments essential to his trade, including a Walther PPK pistol and a sleek night-rifle which could be assembled in a mere matter of seconds. This was all sheer nonsense, of course. Pat was the possessor of no such instruments, or briefcase, for that matter. The only similarity between his persona and that of the cinematic regulators might be said to have been located in his coat, being as it conferred upon him, in its blackness and inordinate length, a mysterious, shadowy quality – although, in the case of the fictive regulator, the garment would almost certainly have been expertly tailored and unlikely to hang baggily about his frame, flapping disorientedly, almost apologetically around the knees. Indeed, to be honest, Pat's garment appeared not so much as something that had been purchased in a leading Paris fashion house at absurd cost to the professional assassin, but something hens might have slept in, and in fact, if the truth be told, most likely had.

This is all of little consequence, however, for these early fancies and delusions thankfully did not persist (Pat was intelligent enough to know that he was simply attracting unnecessary attention to himself), and within a matter of weeks he was more or less what you might describe as 'back to himself' – the perfect disguise, of course, for any regulator! – smiling away to his neighbours and greeting them with salutations such as 'Not a bad day now, Mrs O'Carroll!' and 'There you are now, Mrs O'Hare! And Barney! Turned out nice again, thank God!'

Thus proceeded the first 365 days of what might be called Pat McNab's 'post-matricide' year. Pat, who, it seemed, now spent many of his waking hours sitting by the window of his old dark house and nibbling abstractedly on fingers of toast. Every so often experiencing a slight twinge of remorse as he considered: 'Why did I have to do that – go and murder my own mother, the woman who looked after me and attended to all my needs for almost forty-five years?' But it would pass, almost as if it had never existed, and as he finished the last of his toast, a small smile would begin to play on his lips and he would find himself consumed by the strangest warmth, as if he had just been informed that he had won a much-coveted prize, the pearly-toothed presenter (for that was how he imagined him) grinning from ear to ear as he informed the blushing Pat that he, in the opinion of the judges, had shown himself to be the best, in his particular field (that of what might be termed 'efficient despatch'), 'by far'.

*

All of which a certain Mrs Tubridy knew nothing about – and it was tragic that she didn't – as she went about her business one fine day making her way to Tom Donohoe's shop where it was her intention to purchase some carrots for an Irish stew, and which she would have been much better advised to concentrate on, instead of making it her business to enquire of Pat as to the 'purpose of his business' on this particular day and as to 'where he might be off to'. Quite apart from making impertinent suggestions as to the nature of Pat's drinking habits and his 'fondness for Sullivan's Bar' – asides, which, had she seen fit not to make them, might have seen her alive and healthy and well to this very day. But make them she did, and, in the process, sealed her fate.

What is especially poignant, perhaps, is the fact that Pat – as he reposed in his armchair after what was now, of course, his 'second performance' – quite unexpectedly found himself recalling a night when Mrs Tubridy had come around visiting – it was around Christmastime, and his father was home! – and had spent the evening doling out punch and singing ballads ('Who Put The Overalls In Mrs Murphy's Chowder?' was her party piece), lifting her skirts as his mother and she danced away around the flagstones like there was no tomorrow!

And which, for her, sadly now had proven to be the case, as Pat stared at her stretched full out on the table, silent as the morgue now, all because she had to go asking questions about people's mothers and drinking whisky and all these things that should have been no concern of hers at all, their only benefit to anyone being that what could have been the happiest ballad-story of all time had now ended up like this, with Mrs Tubridy's furry boots rigid as sticks sticking out from under her coat and her hand hanging down like some sad and lonesome glove of wax. It was sad, there can be no doubt about it – and this, our first song, tale, 'Whisky On A Sunday', tells exactly how it happened.

CHAPTER ONE

Whisky On A Sunday

Whiskey On A Sunday

He sat on the corner of Bevington Bush
'Stride an old packing case
And the dolls on the end of the plank went dancing
As he crooned with a smile on his face.

Chorus:
Come day, go day.
Wish in me heart for Sunday
Drinking buttermilk all the week,
Whiskey on a Sunday.

His tired old hands drummed the wooden beam
And the puppets they danced d'gear
A better show than you ever will see
At be Pivvy or New Brighton Pier.

But on some stormy night, down Scotty Road way
With the wind blowing up from the sea
You can still hear the song of old Seth Davey
As he croons to his dancing dolls three.

PAT WAS COMING WALKING down the road whistling when he saw Mrs Tubridy up ahead in her headscarf. 'Hello there, Mrs Tubridy!' was the salutation with which he greeted her as a dandelion clock, quite insignificantly, went blowing past his nose. 'Oh God love you, I didn't see you there, Pat,' she replied, 'I think I was lost in a world of my own. How are you at all, Pat? It's not that often we see you rambling about the byroads! Are you in good health then, if you don't mind me asking?'

'Oh, I'm not too bad, Mrs Tubridy, thank you,' replied Pat.

Mrs Tubridy nodded and gave the knot of her headscarf a little tug.

'I'm just on my way this minute from Benediction,' she continued, 'Father Swift said it. God but he's a great speaker. A lovely speaker. I hope you're not on your way to it, Pat, are you, for if you are you're late.'

'No, I'm not, Mrs Tubridy,' Pat responded, 'I'm just on my way down the town. I thought I might drop into Sullivan's for one.'

There was a catch in Mrs Tubridy's voice as she spoke.

'You thought you might drop in where, Pat?' she said, the tip of her tongue appearing out from between her two lips. It was – surprisingly, Pat reflected – curved rather than pointed. He was also surprised to find that there was a catch in his own voice as he spoke.

'Sullivan's. I might just drop in and have one and then go off about my business.'

Pat winced – imperceptibly to Mrs Tubridy – as he felt her gloved hand touch the sleeve of his coat.

'But sure Sullivan's,' she proceeded, 'everybody knows . . . Pat, what would take you in there?'

Pat shook his head and began to laugh as he said to Mrs Tubridy:

'Do you hear me, Mrs Tubridy – Sullivan's! Sure I'm not going there at all!'

Mrs Tubridy nodded as if she had known this all along.

'Don't I know you're not, Pat!' she said, adding: 'For your mother'd go mad if she thought you went anywhere near that place. Wouldn't she, Pat?'

Pat's grin – for he was grinning now – broadened.

'Oh she would!' he cried. 'Her and Timmy the barman! Sure they don't get on at all!'

Mrs Tubridy pulled at one of the fingers of her glove.

'I know,' she said, 'didn't she tell me all about it. How is she anyway, Pat? I don't remark her at the bingo this past couple of months.'

Pat looked away momentarily. There was a sheep eating a leaf not far from the five-barred gate which was directly behind Mrs Tubridy.

'No,' he said, 'she says it's a waste of money.'

Mrs Tubridy frowned for a second. Then she looked at Pat and said: 'What? And her after scooping all before her only last Christmas?'

'Pshaw! Do you hear me!' interjected Pat. 'No, Mrs Tubridy! She'll be there next week. It's that bloody phlebitis. It's started to play up again.'

'Oh I declare to God!' exclaimed Mrs Tubridy. 'Why didn't you say so, Pat! Sure I have the liniment in my handbag! I'll go up this very second and give her a rub down! God love the poor craythur and her up there all on her own! I had it myself, you know! Look! Do you see these veins? Swollen up the size of that, Pat!'

Mrs Tubridy balled her fist, then continued:

'Only for Dr Horan's liniment, I was finished! Wait till you see! You won't know your mother tomorrow when you see her! Good luck now, Pat – I'm away off to administer my own private medicine to her!'

Pat's voice appeared to ring off a nearby milk churn, partly obscured in the ditch by some whitethorn bushes.

'No!' he cried, his hand curling about Mrs Tubridy's arm.

'Pat!' she declared, endeavouring to move backwards a little.

Pat, she noted, had turned quite pale.

'You can't do that!' he cried aloud. 'You can't go up there, Mrs Tubridy! Wasn't she asleep in the bed when I left and not so much as a peep out of her! You can't go ringing bells and waking her out of her sound sleep! Not now, Mrs Tubridy!'

Mrs Tubridy chucked her sleeve – quite firmly – extricating it from Pat's grasp.

'Jesus, Mary and Joseph!' she curtly responded. 'You didn't have to take the face off me! Amn't I only saying that I'll go up and show her the medicine, medicine she'll thank me for, you can be sure of—'

At an angle, Pat's voice recoiled off the polished metal of the obscured churn. There was a painted number on it. It was number 22.

'Can't you give it to her another time! Can't you give it to her some other day! Why can't you do that?'

'Of course I can, Pat,' went on Mrs Tubridy, lowering her head ever so slightly, 'sure I can give it to her any time you like. You don't have to act like the Antichrist to tell me that!'

Pat's response was as a dart thudding into the bark of a nearby sycamore tree.

'I have to go to Sullivan's!' he snapped.

The flesh above the bridge of Mrs Tubridy's nose gathered itself into the shape of a small arrowhead.

'I thought you said you weren't going to Sullivan's?' she enquired quizzically.

Pat coughed and said: 'I'm not!'

Mrs Tubridy's expression darkened and a whiteness appeared upon the knuckles of the fingers which clasped themselves about the handle of her bag.

'What goes on in the dim corners of that place you would be hard pressed to witness in the back alleys of hell!' she said.

Pat raised his voice and replied: 'I said – I'm not going to it, Mrs Tubridy!'

Mrs Tubridy shook her head.

'I know you're not, Pat,' she went on, 'for your mother has you better reared. She knows better than to let you go gallivanting about the streets of Gullytown. Myself and her know the likes of Timmy Sullivan and those people! Your mother told you all about him, didn't she, Pat? Sullivan, I mean?'

Now it was Pat's turn to lower his head.

'Yes, Mrs Tubridy,' he said.

'Alcoholics!' she cried suddenly. 'Alcoholics, whoremasters and fornicators! That's all you'll find about that place! And Timmy Sullivan raking it in hand over fist! Isn't that right, Pat?'

Pat frowned and, abstractedly picking at a corner of his front tooth, replied: 'Yes, Mrs Tubridy.'

Mrs Tubridy nodded. A new sense of equanimity emanated from her.

'A young fellow like yourself – you have far more sense. For your mother's made sure of it. I'll be on my way so, Pat. Tell your mother I'll be up to see her in a few days now, won't you?'

Pat nodded and said: 'I will, to be sure now, Mrs Tubridy! Good luck now!'

*

16

It was this conversation, or selected parts of it, which was now providing Pat with a source of great amusement as he sat at the counter of Sullivan's Select Bar some hours later with a bewildering array of coloured drinks floating before him like some delightful carnival jamboree of alcohol. As all the while he continued to repeat to himself: 'I will shurely, Misshish Tubridy! Haw haw! Gluck now!' with one eye closed, attracting the attention of Timmy the barman, as he added insistently: 'The big mishtake they made wash – they hadn't reckoned on Pat McNab, Timmy Shull!'

Timmy smiled and wiped the counter in front of his enthusiastic customer as he placed another bottle of Bols Advocaat – for Pat was not in the slightest particular as to the type or brand of alcohol which was consumed by him – directly in front of his customer, and went off whistling the tune to *The Dukes of Hazzard* before his eyes met those of another patron and he gave himself once more to pint-pouring.

*

The gravel of the laneway crunched beneath Mrs Tubridy's slippers. She was quite surprised to find the back door off the latch. But she wasn't complaining, as she crept onward into the maw of the gloom of the scullery.

*

It was well past twelve when Pat arrived home, humming away repeatedly to himself as he searched for his keys deep in the pocket of his long black coat which occasionally served as a duvet or bedspread, the words: 'Yeah! They shure hadn't, buddy, my friend!' gliding from his lips as he entered his house and prepared to help himself to 'a little drinkie', in this case a large measure of Cointreau in a pint glass.

It is quite difficult to determine exactly how long Pat had been sipping and smiling to himself while drumming his fingers on the side of his glass before he realized Mrs Tubridy was sitting in the chair but without a doubt it was quite a considerable amount of time. What was probably most embarrassing for Pat was that when he did, he was actually continuing in a rotating movement about the floor, intermittently exclaiming 'Ha ha!' and utilizing the liqueur-filled receptacle as some form of impromptu microphone. It came as a severe shock when at last the barely audible sentence: 'Dear God in heaven!' reached his ears. Even as it was uttered by him, he realized just how inappropriate and unsatisfactory his response was. 'Misshish Tubridy!' he ejaculated. Her rejoinder was tenebrous and uncompromising. 'Put that drink down!' she said. 'And get up them stairs. I'll talk to you in the morning.'

Pat smiled ever so slightly, a moist film of perspiration appearing on the side of the glass beneath his fingers. 'What?' he laughed, adding: 'Ha ha.'

Mrs Tubridy's eyes became hooded. 'You'd be as well to do what I say,' she hissed, 'after all the lies you've told me, Mister!'

Pat raised his right eyebrow and for no particular reason gazed into the aquamarine depths of his beverage. 'After all the lies I told you!' he replied curtly, a wave of courage sweeping through him from some unnamed place. 'Mrs Tubridy – who do you think you are? My mother? You can't tell me what to do! I can do what I like! Look!'

With bewildering alacrity, a considerable amount of the green-tinted drink went swooshing down his mouth, an array of wet beads forming on his lower lip. With renewed vigour, he cleared his throat and continued: 'Ha ha! Lies! Lies, is it, Mrs Tubridy? Sure I can tell you all the lies I like! No – I wasn't in Sullivan's! I was in Barney Nelly's, actually! Why as a matter of fact I wasn't – I was in Sullivan's!'

Pat shook his head and repaired to the sideboard to replenish his drink. For some reason he felt warm as toast.

'Misshish Tubridy,' he said, 'would you like a drink? Have a drink! Go on there, you girl you! You must want one! Ah sure what harm! I'll have one with you, won't I? Give us a song there, Mrs Tubridy, you auld housebreaker you! Do you know one? Och, you do surely! Yourself and meself, Mrs Tubridy!'

It might well have been the happiest day of Pat McNab's life as his hand in a wide arc cleaved the air and in a rich brown voice he launched himself into song. '*He sits on the corner of Beggar's Bush!*' he intoned beautifully,

'*Astride of an old packing case.*
And the dolls on the end of the plank go dancing
As he croons with a smile on his face
Oo-oo-oo-oo come day go day
Wishing my heart it was Sunday
Drinking buttermilk all the week
Whisky on a Sunday.'

Quite how he became entangled in the large velvet drapes which adorned the high windows of the room was not quite clear but was perhaps attributable to a combination of his preoccupation with accuracy in the delivery of the song's lyrics and his continued consumption of alcohol. There was something inevitable about his eventual collapse and the connection of his head with the side of the Victorian chaise longue which his father had purchased many years before in a London market in a bout of uncharacteristic largesse. The pain of the blow – albeit glancing – proved to be quite unbearable. His cries attained an almost shrill note as he remained prostrate upon the floor. 'Oh Jesus!' he groaned. 'Jesus, Mary and Joseph! I've hurt my head! Oh God, Mrs Tubridy – help me! Please help me!'

There was something quite unexpected about the figure of Mrs Tubridy as it made its way towards him through an undoubtedly bleary, fogged-up haze. For a moment Pat could not ascertain exactly what the nature of this 'unexpectedness' was but then – it came to him. His mother's friend was smiling in a most unusual fashion and undulating the lower portions

19

of her body. Pat was quite taken aback. 'Oh!' he groaned anew as he felt her soft fingers on his forehead and her gentle hands easing his head ever so slowly in the direction of her lap. It was some moments before the damp cloth began to soothe the pain about his temples. 'Mrs Tubridy! It's so sore!' cried Pat, precariously close to all-out weeping. As she spoke, Mrs Tubridy's voice seemed to have the very consistency of silk itself.

'Is that better, Pat?' she huskily soothed as Pat replied: 'Oh, Mrs Tubridy! I'm a disgrace. I've gone and made a complete fool of myself!'

Mrs Tubridy squeezed his temple gently between her thumb and forefinger.

'I told you not to go in there, Pat,' she said, 'I told you not to go there, didn't I?'

An almost imperceptible moistness appeared in the corner of Pat's left eye. 'It's that Timmy Sullivan, Mrs Tubridy!' he cried aloud. 'He never says no! He never says no Pat that's enough now! He keeps on giving you drink!'

Mrs Tubridy nodded and moved the cloth a little bit.

'Lift your head a little bit, Pat,' she said, adding: 'That's it. Is that better?'

Pat nodded and said: 'Yes, Mrs Tubridy. It is.'

He was heartened to see a smile appearing on Mrs Tubridy's face. Her eyes glittered as she said: 'Is that how your Mammy does it?'

For a fraction of a second, Pat was taken aback. There was a slight tautness to the rear of his throat as he said: 'What, Mrs Tubridy?'

Mrs Tubridy smiled again and said: 'Your Mammy – is that how she does it?'

Pat flushed ever so slightly – simply because he was a little confused.

'Mrs Tubridy – what?' he asked her.

'If you fell,' Mrs Tubridy explained. 'Is that how she'd do it – to ease your pain, I mean?'

There was something about Mrs Tubridy's voice that made Pat feel uneasy.

'Yes, Mrs Tubridy. Mrs Tubridy, I think you'd better go,' he said.

In the succeeding moments, the moon seemed exceptionally, unaccountably large. And there was a quality to the darkness he hadn't noticed before. It seemed a long time before Mrs Tubridy made any reply. And when she did, it was as follows: 'Go, Pat?' in a faintly aggressive, non-compliant tone.

The crimson shade of Pat's cheeks was now quite pronounced.

'Yes, Mrs Tubridy. In case the neighbours might be talking.'

Pat expected the pressure exerted by Mrs Tubridy's fingers to become somewhat relieved at this – but this did not happen. In fact, if anything, it could be said to have increased.

'Talking, Pat?' Mrs Tubridy replied. 'But sure, Pat – I'm an old woman.'

A flushed, discomfiting confusion began to gather within Pat's mind. Words appeared to elude him and it was only with supreme effort he succeeded in making the reply: 'I know that, Mrs Tubridy. But you know what they're like. They imagine things. They make things up.'

Pat felt the cloth being relocated to a spot directly above his eye.

'Does it hurt here?' Mrs Tubridy said softly. 'Will I rub it just a little more?'

What exactly happened in the intervening seconds is unclear. What is apparent is that somehow Pat broke free and found himself standing above the older woman, clearly in a state of tremulous anxiety now.

'Mrs Tubridy!' he cried, his voice quivering like a lost leaf in a countryside-denuding storm, 'I'm afraid you'll have to go!'

There followed a silence and then Mrs Tubridy lowered her head and said softly, yieldingly: 'Very well – I'll just go get my umbrella.'

A wave of remorse – infinitely larger than the one which had conveniently provided him with courage earlier on – crashed through Pat.

'Mrs Tubridy!' he groaned. 'It's just that—'

'Yes, Pat – I know,' came the reply.

As she was going past the hatstand in the hallway, Pat picked at his fingernail and said: 'Goodnight then, Mrs Tubridy.' The older woman adjusted her coat and said: 'Goodnight, Pat.'

It was only as she was opening the front door to venture out into the quiet night of the sleeping town and its surrounding countryside that she turned and said tenderly: 'You know, Pat – you know your mother's a very lucky woman. Drunk or no, you could be one of the nicest young fellows in the town. You always were. You know that, don't you, Pat?'

A twinge of uncertainty nagged at Pat as she spoke. But nonetheless he managed a reply.

'Yes, Mrs Tubridy.'

'She loved you, Pat,' continued Mrs Tubridy, 'I know – because she told me. "I love Pat," she said, "my son Pat."'

Pat found himself choking a little.

'Mrs Tubridy . . .' he began.

Mrs Tubridy's voice was soft as downy feathers now.

'"He's the nicest little fellow ever I carried in my stomach,"' she said, '"I don't care who makes a laugh of him."'

'Please, Mrs Tubridy . . .' said Pat, a trifle dizzy now.

It was some moments before he realized at all that Mrs Tubridy's fingers were in his hair, running through it ever so

22

gently. Her lips soft and warm close to his ear as she said: 'Why did you do it, Pat? Did you have an argument with her?'

An imaginary icy hand placed its hand flat on Pat's back.

'Do what, Mrs Tubridy?' he replied, endeavouring to be noncommittal.

Mrs Tubridy lowered her head as if disappointed.

'Oh, Pat, Pat,' she said, adding with disorienting swiftness, 'Was she upsetting you?'

A fully-formed tear shone in Pat's right eye as he replied: 'Yes, Mrs Tubridy. She was. She wouldn't leave me alone.'

The older woman moved exceptionally close to him and said: 'I wouldn't upset you, Pat. As long as you did what I said. As long as you were my nice little boy. Would you be that, Pat? Would you? And then I wouldn't have to tell them all the little things I know about you. I wouldn't have to tell them not to whisper a word about it. Not so much as a word about it all. Wouldn't that be lovely, Pat?'

Already some of the tear was drying on Pat's cheek. His right one.

'Yes, Mrs Tubridy,' he said.

'And you'd never touch that horrible old stuff again?'

'No, Mrs Tubridy.'

'Never go near Sullivan's as long as you live.'

'No, Mrs Tubridy.'

'Does your head hurt, Pat?'

Mrs Tubridy pressed a soft spot which was located directly above his left eye.

'Horrible ugly drink!' she said, and squeezed it again.

*

It was some days later and Pat was busier than ever cleaning out cupboards and trying to get everything done before dinner. Mrs Tubridy's voice came ringing clear and uncompromising from the scullery. 'And don't forget that other one! I see one hidden away in at the back there! Do you hear me, Pat McNab?'

'Yes, Mrs Tubridy,' replied Pat as his fingers closed around the last remaining whisky bottle located in the nether darkness at the rear of the cupboard. He added it to the contents of his wheelie bin and pushed the glittering container of redundant glass out into the backyard where it would be collected the following day by the council men. He remained resolutely silent as Mrs Tubridy stood over him ensuring that each receptacle was added to the mound of glass whose peak was now level with the top of the gate. When she was satisfied, she smiled contentedly and said: 'Well, Pat! That's the last we'll see of them!'

Pat nodded compliantly and rubbed his hands on his apron.

'Yes, Mrs Tubridy,' he said.

Mrs Tubridy smiled and placed her smooth, moistened hand on his cheek. She used Pond's cold cream.

'More than your mother was able to do, Pat, at the end of the day!'

Two things happened in between Mrs Tubridy making this statement and Pat making a reply. A small bird landed on a twig above Mrs Tubridy's head and a blue Fiat went by on the road. They had distracted Pat for a moment. Then he heard himself saying: 'What?' to be greeted with the short, not quite peremptory but certainly cursory response: 'Oh – and would you clear out the coalhouse too when you're finished, Pat – I meant to say that to you.'

The taste at the back of Pat's throat was sickly as he obsequiously slouched towards the flapping door of the coal-house.

*

It was the following day when he was doing the hoovering that he looked up to see Mrs Tubridy putting her head around the door. 'Pat? Are you there?' he heard her say.

'Yes I am, Mrs Tubridy,' he replied, scooping up some dust which had gathered in behind the armchair close to the leg of the sideboard.

'I have a surprise for you-oo!' he heard her trill.

Pat jerked ever so slightly as the older woman entered the room bearing a tray upon which stood triumphantly a bottle of Taylor Keith lemonade and two glasses.

'Now, Pat!' she said. 'Put that hoover down and come over here to me! Put it down now, Pat!'

Pat could hear various acids coursing about deep within his stomach as Mrs Tubridy raised one of the glasses in a toast and declared: 'For all your hard work!' Her eyes seemed to dance as she gazed towards him, eagerly eliciting a reply. Which, eventually, he supplied, to wit: 'Yes, Mrs Tubridy.'

At which point the older woman frowned.

'Pat – there something wrong?' she said. 'Aren't you pleased?'

'Yes, Mrs Tubridy. I'm pleased,' said Pat.

'You don't look pleased to me with that long face on you like a donkey. Is there something wrong with it? Is there something wrong with the lemonade I got specially below in Kinch's for you?'

Pat's eyelashes drooped.

'No, Mrs Tubridy. There's nothing wrong with it.'

'Well – drink it, then!' she insisted. 'Drink it like a Christian, can't you!'

Pat's lips advanced and began to apply themselves to a tentative sip of the sparkling liquid. But this apparently did not satisfy the older woman and to his horror Pat found the glass flying out of his grasp as her small pudgy hand hit it and her words bit into him.

'No!' she barked. 'It's not good enough for you when I do it but if it was her you'd be gurgling away there like a halfwit till it choked you, wouldn't you?'

'If it was who, Mrs Tubridy?' Pat replied, almost shamefully, although he had nothing to be ashamed about.

Her response was astonishing as she faced him with an expression blank as the mirror on the bedroom wall.

'If it was who! If it was who! I'll put a stop to your gallop yet and make no mistake, if you don't stop playing the fly boy with me! I suppose you think you're going to sneak bottles in behind my back – I suppose that's the little plan you have in mind!'

'No!' cried Pat. 'No, Mrs Tubridy – it's not true!'

But she was having none of it.

'Just like him and every one of them!' she snapped inexplicably. 'Pack of useless God's cursed crowd of wasters, ne'er do wells and gangsters! Stay away from the Tubridys, they have the hand out for everything they can get! I should have listened to my poor mother, God rest her! Rue the day! Rue the day you will, she said! God but how she was right! Beat me black and blue he did! I'll give it up, alanna, on my mother's grave I'll never touch another drop! Bruises the size of that on my back and on my legs! But you wait! You needn't think you'll get up to the same tricks, Mr Pat McNab, for you won't! Do you hear me, you treacherous little pup, you?'

Out of nowhere, her hands began to beat Pat about the head like small, out-of-control birds. He pleaded in vain. 'No, Mrs Tubridy! Stop, stop!' he cried.

'You'll not do what he did to me, nor any of your crowd!' she continued. 'For I won't give you the chance – I'll do what I should have done long ago! Do you hear me? Do you hear me, Pat McNab?'

Fearfully, Pat replied:

'Yes, Mrs Tubridy!'

'Now get up them stairs and do the bedrooms,' she insisted, 'do you hear me?'

His reply – predictable by now – was in the affirmative. The older woman composed herself.

'And when I come up – if I find so much as a speck of dirt! If I find so much as a speck of—'

Pat interrupted her.

'Yes, Mrs Tubridy,' he said.

'Now! Go on!' she icily instructed.

*

The moon shone on the window. Mrs Tubridy was asleep now. Or so Pat thought as he lay there in his striped pyjamas, consumed by a huge, ocean-sized sadness. Until he heard the whisper: 'Pat?'

His response was timid – fearful, even. But it need not have been.

'Yes?' he said.

'I'm sorry for what I said earlier,' said Mrs Tubridy, abstractedly adjusting a curler beneath her hairnet.

'It's all right, Mrs Tubridy,' said Pat.

She coughed – ever so politely. She could be so polite sometimes, Mrs Tubridy.

'I know you're not like him.'

'Yes, Mrs Tubridy.'

'But, Pat – you know something? He wasn't always like that either.'

Pat's eyes nervously followed the Ganges-like crack on the ceiling.

'Was he not, Mrs Tubridy?' he said.

'He used to come marching down the aisle after Communion with a lovely quiff in his hair and a black tie and there wasn't a woman in the town but didn't have her eye on him. Including—'

Mrs Tubridy broke off abruptly. The moon's light fell on the little carved feet of the wardrobe. The silence fed upon itself until Pat said: 'Hmm, Mrs Tubridy?'

'Including your own mother,' Mrs Tubridy said.

Pat's heart leaped.

'My own mother, Mrs Tubridy?'

Pat could feel Mrs Tubridy's body tensing up as she prepared herself to speak.

'She used to think she could get him. The way she thought she could get everybody. But she didn't get him. He never let on he seen her.'

Pat frowned and felt his mouth go dry.

'Never let on . . . ?'

'I used to go by with my arm in his – and the face of her!'

'The face of her, Mrs Tubridy?'

'Lepping, Pat! She used to be absolutely lepping! Couldn't bear to think of anyone wiping her eye! Must have thought she was Rita Hayworth or someone, the eejit! Sure he never even so much as let on he seen her!'

Pat construed his mouth being filled up with a substance not unlike glue or perhaps thick tasteless preserves.

'Yes, Mrs Tubridy,' he said, crestfallen.

'But you liked her, didn't you, Pat?' said Mrs Tubridy, adding more forcefully, 'Didn't you?'

'Yes, Mrs Tubridy,' Pat replied.

'Even though she didn't look after you right – you still liked her.'

A piece of wire seemed to tighten itself around the top of Pat's chest.

'No, Mrs Tubridy – she did look after me right.'

'No, Pat, she didn't. She'd give you soup and a potato when she should have been cooking you a dinner. A dinner with mash and gravy and a nice wee bit of meat. Instead of doing that she'd be up and down the town trying to get other women's men to look at her. Either that or tramping off to the bingo again.'

Pat's resolve appeared to momentarily stiffen.

'Mrs Tubridy – you go to the bingo yourself.'

Her tight fist placed itself behind his shoulder blades. A slight push dislodged him.

'What did you say? That I go to the bingo? But I don't have wains, do I, Pat McNab? I don't have a little boy whose future is my responsibility! I don't have a little boy to leave behind and see to it that he grows up quare on account of my neglect! I don't have him, you know!'

This was more than Pat could endure. He cried aloud in the moon-washed darkness: 'I'm not quare!'

Mrs Tubridy's reply was instant.

'No! You're not now! And thanks to me you won't be! You'll be one of the best-looking handsomest men in the town! I'll see to it you drive them all mad, you wait and see! By the time I'm finished with you, they'll all want to be Pat McNab! Instead of being a poor wee gom with the whole place laughing at you, the way she had you growing up!'

'It's not true, Mrs Tubridy!' cried Pat pitifully. 'She had not!'

'It's not true! It's not true!' sneered Mrs Tubridy. 'Sure didn't I see you going to school with my own two eyes, and a shirt on you like a girl and a wee wine tie with elastic on it. And them all falling about the place like Duffy's circus had come to town!'

Pat was aware that he was beginning to choke now as he said: 'It's not true! They were not!'

But Mrs Tubridy had not yet concluded.

'And the little ankle socks,' she continued, 'the little ankle socks she put on you! Is it any wonder they'd call you names and make a cod of you! Is it?'

'They didn't!' shrieked Pat. 'They didn't make a cod of me!'

'They did, Pat. They did, and you know it! Every day you walked that street, they had a new name for you. And that's why you were miserable. That's why sometimes you even wanted to die. Because of her.'

'No, Mrs Tubridy!' cried Pat, almost pleadingly. 'You've got it all wrong!'

There was something shocking now in Mrs Tubridy's equanimity.

'I haven't, Pat,' she said, 'and the other person in this room knows it.'

The light of the moon glittered for a long time in Pat's subsequent tears as his head forced its way towards her breast and she stroked his head as many times before.

'It's going to be all right, Pat,' her soothing voice continued. 'From now on, it's going to be all right. Just so long as you remember that from now on you're mine.'

She paused and inserted her little finger into his ear.

'You'll be just like my little Paudgeen. You understand, don't you, Pat?'

Pat nodded. This time he didn't say: 'Yes, Mrs Tubridy.'

He knew she understood.

'I don't blame you for doing what you did, Pat. Nobody would. She should have cared more. She just should have cared more.'

*

Throughout the following hours, the sobs of Pat McNab were pitiful as he found himself slipping away. As indeed did Mrs Tubridy, to the hospital of a dream which seemed at once so strange and yet bewilderingly familiar. What appeared to be a younger – and startlingly attractive – version of herself, sans headscarf, was sitting up in bed, clearly anxiously awaiting someone or something. It was only some moments before a grave young doctor arrived in his white coat.

'How is my baby?' the young Mrs Tubridy cried. 'How is my little baby?'

Tonelessly, the doctor replied:

'I'm sorry, Mrs Tubridy.'

The screams of that young woman, in a hospital of long ago – they just cannot be described. And go a long way towards explaining why exactly it was that within that dream

Mr Tubridy was to be found the following day surrounded by a seemingly endless array of bottles and completely enshrouded in cigarette smoke, as Timmy Sullivan did his best to attract his attention, repeatedly insisting: 'Mr Tubridy! There's a phone call for you! It's about your son!'

Which succeeded only in eliciting the gruff reply:

'What are you talking about? Give me another drink! What do I care about sons!'

As, far away at the other end of town, in a spotless but clinically spartan maternity ward, a heartbreak was borne alone.

*

Pat, approximately one week later, and in the middle of preparing the dinner – Brussels sprouts and fish – was shocked when he looked up to see Mrs Tubridy, fresh from town, bearing in her arms a large brown parcel and uttering the words: 'Wait till you see what I have for you!' Barely a few moments later, equally shocked, perhaps – although embarrassed is probably much more apt in the circumstances – to find himself attired from head to foot in a white shirt, black tie and spotless white lounge jacket, with Mrs Tubridy proud as punch extravagant with her compliments as she declaimed: 'Now! Who are you going to make a nice cup of tea for because she's good to you?'

Pat smiled at the request but there was something crushed and resentful about him as he inserted the plug of the electric kettle into the socket.

*

She always insisted on long, even strokes so Pat endeavoured to comply as he drew the brush through Mrs Tubridy's wavy salt and pepper hair as she continued talking where she was seated at the dressing table. 'Oh, it's not that I mind him having a drink!' she said, with a troubling bitterness. 'Sure

31

there's nothing wrong with drink in moderation! But when you see what it does to people! Setting fire to the kitchen, insulting the priest! But – after Paudgeen – I didn't care, you see! I didn't care after that! Do you know what I mean, Pat?'

Pat brought the brush back from the pale, occasionally liver-spotted neck and replied: 'Yes, Mrs Tubridy.'

'He could drink himself from here to Mullingar after that as far as I was concerned. Because Paudgeen wasn't going to grow up. Do you know what I mean, Pat?'

He nodded. There was a smell of perfume off the brush.

'He was never going to grow up. I was never going to be able to watch him grow. But if I had – if I had, Pat – do you know something?'

'What, Mrs Tubridy?'

'He would have been one of the most handsome little boys in the world, wouldn't he?'

'Yes, Mrs Tubridy.'

Mrs Tubridy coughed – politely again, Pat noticed – and he caught the reflection of her raised eyebrow in the looking glass.

'Pat,' she continued, 'would you mind if I called you something?'

'Called me what, Mrs Tubridy?'

He caught a long strand of her hair between his fingers and removed it from the teeth of the brush.

'Paudgeen, Pat. Would you mind if I called you that?'

Pat perceived the blood coursing decisively in the direction of his cheeks.

'Mrs Tubridy,' he said, 'I'd rather you didn't.'

Her expression in the mirror remained motionless.

'What?' she said and he jerked a little.

'It's just that,' he said, 'it's just that I'd rather you didn't. It's not my name!'

Mrs Tubridy's reaction shocked him.

'O it isn't your name is it not!' she snapped. 'Well – what

32

name would you rather have? Pat McNab? You'd rather have that than Tubridy that everyone would look up to! You'd rather have that, after what you've done!'

At this, Pat's left temple began to throb.

'After what I've done?' he ventured agitatedly.

'Yes! After what you've done!'

She eyed him with a stare of great significance, at that very moment lowering her voice as she said: 'You know what I mean.'

Pat felt his cheeks turn from red-hot to dough-pale as she smirked and placed her hand on his and said: 'You know what I mean – Paudgeen.'

Far off in the hallway, the grandfather clock ticked heavily.

'You do, don't you?' she repeated.

'Yes, Mrs Tubridy,' as he saw her smirk anew.

'No,' she said, 'don't call me that. Call me Mammy. Just for a laugh, will you call me that?'

A look of pain flashed across the countenance of Pat McNab.

'I can't,' he pleaded, 'please, Mrs Tubridy. I can't.'

There was nothing tender or considerate about the stare with which she fixed him, her voice cold as steel.

'Call me it!' she demanded.

Pat's head fell upon his chest as though he had somehow been transformed into a pathetic nodding dog.

'Yes, Mammy,' were the words that passed his lips.

*

It is difficult to determine, certainly with any degree of exactitude, the significant occurrences in the life of Pat McNab which eventually led to his becoming the person he was, but it is unlikely that it could be contested that that incident and what had passed between them during it ought to be considered as one of such; for, almost as soon as she left the room, it became clear that Mrs Tubridy had rendered Pat McNab into such a state of high dudgeon and perspiring, overwhelming confusion (indubitably a consequence of the self-hatred and malignant shame that were themselves the results of his pitiful inaction) that his entire surroundings began to assume a startling sharp-edged clarity, unsettlingly closer to the states of distorted hallucination familiar to habitual drug-users than any feasible notion of tangible, empirical reality. Which explains, no doubt, why, when later that – again moonwashed – night, whilst in Mrs Tubridy's bed (for her instructions now extended to include his sleeping arrangements), he awoke to find himself staring directly into what could not possibly have been – but to all intents and purposes, clearly now was – the face of his own mother!

An enormous wave of sorrow swept through him as he touched his cheek and felt the moonlight play upon it. His mother's smile too was sad.

'I know she did a lot of things, Tubridy. But this. This makes me sad, Pat.'

He repeated each word after her and every syllable that passed his lips was as a rusted fish-hook drawn painfully and indulgently from his throat.

'Sad, Mammy?' he said then.

'Her lying there. Telling you lies. Because that's what she's doing, Pat.'

His throat dried up hopelessly.

'Mammy?'

It was a struggle to utter the word.

'Telling lies. Once, you know, a half-crown went missing on me. I asked her did she see it. And do you know where I found it?'

Pat was close to the edge of hysteria now.

'Where, Mammy?'

'In her handbag. Hidden inside her handbag behind her prayerbook. What do you think of that, Pat?'

Pat found himself instinctively grinding his teeth.

'It's terrible!' he heard himself say.

'Not terrible compared to some of the other things she's done. Did you know she put her husband Mattie in the mental hospital?'

'Mental hospital?'

'Poor Mattie Tubridy that was one of the handsomest men ever walked the streets of the town. Couldn't let him be himself, you see. Why, if you didn't like him the way he was, you didn't have to marry him, I said to her. And she did not like it! Because it was the truth! What harm if Mattie took a drink, God rest him. The only reason he took it was to get away from her. Just because she couldn't have a wain, she didn't have to take it out on him!'

Pat swallowed and did his level best to formulate the words he feared would elude him.

'Couldn't have a wain?'

He felt – although it wasn't, or to a casual observer would not have appeared so – as though the skin on his face had been drawn unreasonably tightly across his bones.

'Barren as Rogey Rock,' his mother informed him, 'that's what the doctor said, although not in those words.'

Thoughts appeared as randomly intersecting lights in the murkier corners of Pat's mind.

'Mammy!' he said. 'But are you sure? Are you sure all this is true?'

There was no mistaking the pain on his mother's face.

'And now, worst of all – she's turned my own son against me. My own son that would not have doubted me in his life. She's turned him against me too!'

Something leaped inside Pat when he heard his mother say that, as certain as if a pebble or stone had been cast from a catapult. He clasped her right shoulder firmly with his hand.

'No, Mammy!' he cried aloud. 'She hasn't!'

It was hard for Pat to bear the sight of the salt tear that now gleamed in the corner of his mother's eye. But even harder to bear on opening his own to their optimum width and finding himself gazing no longer upon the mother who had carried him for nine months and cared and nurtured him for so long, but – *Mrs Tubridy!* Upon her lips the words: 'Paudgeen! What are you doing? It's five o'clock in the morning!'

Pat felt the back of his throat contract until it was the size of a small seed.

'My name's not Paudgeen!' he retorted angrily.

'Go back to sleep and no more lip out of you or it will be down to the station with me first thing in the morning. Do you hear me?'

Perhaps Mrs Tubridy felt it was crucial for her to assert her authority in a firm and unequivocal manner at that time and it is tempting to speculate as to what might have happened if she had adopted a more conciliatory approach. But she didn't and what was clear now was that in conjunction with what had taken place earlier – entirely unknown to Mrs Tubridy, of course – the otherwise – or what seemed to be otherwise – placid Pat McNab had, although to all intents and purposes unaware of it himself, been set upon a course, the outcome of which could now but spell disaster. Although it is unlikely that an independent observer, as Pat in the days that followed continued to proceed around the kitchen, pottering awkwardly and muttering abstractedly, 'Hello! My name is Paudgeen! Paudgeen Tubridy! Do you know me at all?' would necessarily have drawn such a drastic conclusion. Or surmised that, from sudden cries of: 'That's me! Afraid to go down to Sullivan's because my Mammy won't let me! She says if I do she'll get the guards on me! She has me so scared, you see! Why I'm so scared I think I need a drink!' a state of heartbroken, helpless anxiety might have inevitably ensued.

Far more likely is that the comments on such occasions (from independent observers, that is) would have been more along the lines of: 'Poor Pat!' or 'Isn't he a sad case?' But perhaps these rather casual commentators – putative, it is true – might not have been so eager to declare him a sad case if they had observed him some evenings later, brandishing a bottle of Cointreau, the contents of which he had practically consumed in their entirety, donning one of Mrs Tubridy's hats (a blue one with a white net) and curtseying in pantomime fashion as he flailed about the kitchen, crying: 'Howya, Mrs Tubridy! How's Paudgeen getting on? Like I mean – is he born yet? Ha ha! Only coddin'!' as, as before, into the neck of his impromptu bottle-microphone, he began to sing, rotating his arms all the while, his voice attaining the very peak of his register:

'*Come day, go day.*
Wish in me heart for Sunday
Drinking buttermilk all the week,
Whiskey on a Sunday. Yee-hoo!'

It is difficult, perhaps, to describe the suddenness with which Pat lapsed into silence, or to adequately indicate the impact the glowering scowl of Mrs Tubridy actually had as the door opened and revealed her standing there in the shadowy aperture. Suffice to say that Pat felt his lips had been turned to stone, as had most of the rest of his body.

*

How unpleasant it was for him to end up in the cellar is equally difficult to convey to the reader. What is certain is that a stratagem which had been pitilessly devised to serve the purpose of ultimate punishment, to effectively cripple Pat's spirit to the point where he would in future pursue his broom throughout the length and breadth of the house like a hapless ghost for the remainder of his mortal days, can be said to have failed utterly in its purpose. Had the independent observers referred to heretofore been calmly evaluating Pat at this point, however, this is the last thing they would have concluded from his general demeanour as he sat crouched in the dankest of corners. Their conclusion – if his wide, extended grin and happy, dancing eyes were to be considered any indication – could but be that here was a man very much at ease with his surroundings, and indeed – aside, perhaps, from the whitish skin drawn over his cheekbones which seemed about to snap at any time – deriving nothing less than great pleasure from them. And which, they would undoubtedly feel, explained the intermittent chuckles into the twins of his bunched fists and the occasional address to a visiting mouse who considered him insouciantly from a nearby air vent, along the lines of: 'Putting me in prison now, if you don't mind! Well, boys O boys! Have you any idea what next, mouse? For I'm afraid I don't!'

There may be a school of thought which subscribes to the theory that periods in confined darkness must inevitably result in the mind drawing on its infinite resources – even in hopelessly adverse circumstances – and ensuing in creating, imaginatively, of course, surroundings of a much more congenial nature: I cannot say for certain. What is certain, however, is that it was the course of action decided upon and most emphatically followed by Pat McNab, as became plainly evident when he woke up one morning to find himself, not burdened by damp and dark and the asphyxiation-inducing aroma of crumbling plaster, but bearing witness to one of the brightest of sunny days that it is possible for the mind to conceive, sitting within that very cellar with his mother – seeing them both beneath a spreading elm, chaining daisies. Such was his happiness at being with her once again that he was giddy as a young goat you would see prancing about any mountainside.

'But what I can't get over, Mammy,' he continued – they were discussing Mrs Tubridy – 'is the big hole in her chin!'

His mother shook her head.

'Aye! With the hair coming out of it, I declare to God, for

all the world like a coiled spring! God help poor Mattie Tubridy, Pat! Having to look at that every morning of his life!'

Pat nodded and wiped the tears from his eyes.

'Aye!' he said. 'But sure he's dead now, God rest him!'

Just then, his mother opened the lid of the picnic basket.

'Pat?' she smiled. 'Would you like a sup of lemonade?'

Pat beamed.

'Yes, Mammy,' he replied.

He was a little unsure as to whether he had noted a little twinkle in his mother's eye. But this was confirmed as she continued: 'Or maybe something a bit stronger?'

'Now you're talking, Mammy!' cried Pat, slapping his hands together as the bottle of Johnnie Walker gleamed golden in the afternoon summer sun.

He smiled as his mother ran her fingers through his hair.

'Now who's good to you!' she cried. 'It'd be a long time before that old haverel, that old haybag you-know-who'd let you have a little glugeen, Pat! Am I right?'

'Now you're talking, Mammy!' Pat cried, filling his mouth up with whisky.

'Just because you'd need a hose to get it down her auld tight gob!'

Pat nearly fell over when he heard his mother saying this. He certainly spilt whisky all down the front of his coat!

'Ha ha, Mammy!' he cried helplessly. 'A hose! Oh, God bless us!'

'Have another drop, son!' his mother encouraged him. 'Get it down you!'

Pat shook his head and rubbed whisky beads off his chin with his sleeve.

'Oh, Mammy, you're an awful case!' he cried.

Then his mother went and spilt some whisky.

'God bless us, I think I'm stocious myself! Get up out of that, Pat McNab, you boy you!'

'Wo-ho! Mrs McNab, fine girl you are! Cripes but you're powerful! C'mere out of that till I give you a dance!'

'Bejapers now make sure and mind me corns!' yelped his mother as she took his hand and rose to her feet.

The sunlight was like a shoal of arrows loosed by some invisible medieval army, showering through the interlocking boughs of the trees, and it was difficult for the birds not to display some twinges of jealousy as he and his mother sang together:

'Come day, go day.
Wish in me heart for Sunday
Drinking buttermilk all the week . . .'

Pat rounded off the verse with a sweep of his arm and a declamatory: 'Whiskey on a Sunday!'

*

It may be that if he had been forced to remain in his place of confinement for even one more single day it would have had the required effect on Pat McNab by Mrs Tubridy, but opening the door and revealing herself standing in a shaft of light in an almost apologetic manner was not perhaps, in retrospect, the wisest course of action for his self-appointed behaviour modifier. As indeed neither were any of her repeated insistences that it had been incumbent upon her to embark upon the course she had.

'I had to be cruel to be kind, Pat,' she said softly as Pat set down some hours later the piping hot meal she had requested he prepare for her.

'It's all right, Mrs Tubridy,' he replied, the combination of sadness and marble-cold stoniness in his voice tragically inaudible to her ear.

Mrs Tubridy sliced some meat and placed her fork at an angle to her cheek, looking upwards and smiling in the way she did before saying: 'You know – you're a very handsome boy, Paudgeen. I mean, Pat, of course!'

'Thank you, Mrs Tubridy.'

The smile slowly metamorphosed into a smirk as she laid down her fork and said: 'Come here.'

Very gently, Pat felt her fingers close about his upper arm. They reminded him of a pound of Castlebar sausages.

Mrs Tubridy coughed – politely, of course – and said: 'After you've cleaned out the yard, we can have biscakes and tea in the parlour. Just you and me. All right?'

'Yes, Mrs Tubridy,' Pat said, 'after I've hosed down the yard.'

'You're hosing it down, are you?' replied Mrs Tubridy. 'Well – after you've that done, we can sit in there together.'

*

Had Mrs Tubridy been possessed of telepathic powers, it is highly likely if not even more so that things would have worked out much differently. For she would have clearly seen that what Pat was thinking as he was discussing the hosing of the yard and the repairing to the parlour with her in reasonable, civilized tones was: 'Yes! And after we have those two things done, what you can do is drive me mad the same as you did your dead husband!'

And would have attached a logic, and, perhaps, a meaning, to the six words of his succeeding statement, which, as it stood, made absolutely no sense at all. The statement being: 'Except that you won't, Mrs Tubridy!'

Initially, its seeming eccentricity elicited a tiny flicker of amusement from Mrs Tubridy's cheek. As she nibbled her meat and said: 'What's that, Pat?' satisfactorily receiving the reply: 'I said except you won't be hosing the yard, Mrs Tubridy, because I'll be doing it all by myself!'

*

Would it have ended significantly differently if the aforementioned 'telepathic powers' or even the slightest approximation of them had been in evidence? Who can possibly say? All that must remain, for posterity, in the realm of pure conjecture.

What is not in the realm of conjecture, however, is that, as he was removing Mrs Tubridy's plate to ferry it in the direction of the pedal bin that evening, her eyes twinkled with an unusual abandon and gaiety as she said: 'You know what I was thinking, Pat? I was thinking that maybe – why one night, we could get ourselves a little brandy? Or whisky, maybe? Just the two of us!'

The sight of a post-menopausal if not indeed elderly lady inflating steadily – to the point of absurdity, in fact – to a degree where she is a palpable danger to others is not immediately what we would expect to be the direct consequence of what is essentially an unremarkable suggestion, or would be in other circumstances. But these were not other circumstances, as the glint in Pat McNab's eye as he hoarsely cried: 'Mrs McNab! I don't know what to say! How can I ever thank you, Mrs McNab!' ought to have indicated to the older woman, and most certainly would have had she been alert. Which she wasn't, perhaps due to the quantity of food she had consumed, but for whatever reason, a shortcoming which was now about to lead inevitably to what might be called 'The Fate of Dolly Tubridy', soon to be formerly of 36 Mounthelmet Gardens, Gullytown.

*

If anyone, a neighbour or anyone just casually passing by, had encountered Pat sitting on a rock in his garden puffing on a Major cigarette and smiling, what they most likely would have thought to themselves would have been: 'Now there's a fellow looking happy and contented with himself. I suppose that's what making a good job of hosing down the yard does for you!' Which would have been diverting and amusing but would have absolutely no connection with the actual reasons behind Pat's undeniably broad and sunnily engaging smile. Or indeed any of his thoughts at that particular smoke-puffing moment, which were more along the lines of 'What a time we had last night!' and 'I hope you're happy down there, Mrs Tubridy – or should I say Mrs Whale!'

*

What had happened was Pat had arrived in to find Mrs Tubridy dressed up to the nines, with a lovely little chiffon scarf knotted gaily around her neck and a definite whiff of quite-expensive perfume emanating from her person. Not to mention a little glasheen of whisky cradled mischievously in her hand! So it wasn't long before herself and her landlord – for what else was Pat, if not that! – were getting along like a house on fire as if to say to the bad times they had put behind them: 'Bad times? What might you be doing loitering about this vicinity? I think you had best be off about your business, don't you?'

'Oh, Pat!' was all you could hear Mrs Tubridy squeal after they'd had two or three drinks, 'Pat but you're an awful man!'

Quite what Mrs Tubridy must have thought when she woke up some hours later with her face wreathed in shadow and her wrists securely fastened to the head of what had once been Pat and Mrs McNab's bed, it is impossible to say for certain. One thing is for sure, it was shot through with a considerable measure of anxiety, for if it wasn't, why would she bother to shriek: 'Pat! Pat, what are you doing to me, for the love of God!' Which was of very little value for Pat did not even appear to hear this – he certainly made no effort to acknowledge it – as he busied himself attending to her ankles with some cord and repeating, with what must have been, to Mrs Tubridy, a devastating irreverence, 'Paudgeen! Sure call me Paudgeen, Mrs Tubridy! Paudgeen will do just fine!'

It could not have been pleasant for Mrs Tubridy to perceive Pat approaching her – a matter of moments later – bearing a tundish and insisting that she open her mouth, all the better for him to insert the rusted zinc implement correctly. 'Open up now! were his exact words. 'Open up now for Paudgeen like a good girl!'

Her resistance – what there was of it – was quite useless. In any case, her trepidation, when she witnessed the length of blue hose being uncoiled through the window from the yard, had effectively rendered her entire body weak and bereft of any form of physical strength or mental resolve. Her psychological reaction to Pat's 'After all – we can't have you taking whisky without water!' can only be imagined.

Initially, haste as regards the replenishment of the tundish's contents was not a major concern of Pat's, but this was not to last, and within a matter of mere minutes, the dazzling array of bottles – such a stupendous catalogue of disparate brands: Johnnie Walker, Glenfiddich, Grouse, Bell's, and Paddy of course! – were being utilized to form what was a veritable amber whirlpool which was subsumed with speed-of-light rapidity into the system of the prone and inert – however wide-eyed – Mrs Tubridy, to be followed by a liberal dispensation of the natural mineral H_2O – a very liberal dispensation indeed, it has to be admitted, the what might be termed 'The Irrigation of Dolly Tubridy' having already begun, not to mention continuing apace. As Pat – feeling it appropriate at this advanced stage – lightened the proceedings by quipping:

'Perhaps you'd like a drop of water, Mrs Tubridy? You would? Why certainly, Mrs Tubs! We have some right here!' The hose leaping into his hand as some well-trained, dutiful house-snake.

*

There were all sorts of rumours to be heard doing the rounds in Gullytown for the few weeks following – but then, there are always rumours. One even led to Smiler McAlpine, a council man who was working on the roads near the McNab house (pruning bushes, mostly), leaning over the hedge and observing through the curling horns of smoke that unwound from his pipe to Pat who was yet again enjoying a Major cigarette upon what might be considered his little rock-throne, 'I'm damned if I can make out what happened, Pat! It has me beat. A woman her age – disappearing like that! Is your mother inside by any chance? A lot of people have been saying they haven't seen her about lately. Maybe she could throw some light on the subject!'

'No. She's gone away to America. I mean England, for a week. She'll be back in a month.'

'I see,' replied the council man, his hand making a rasping sound against the bristles of his chin as he rubbed them reflectively.

'It's a mystery – that's all I can say!' replied Pat, an image of the persistently inflating Whale-woman appearing at the back of his mind, rising from his rock and stretching himself as the remains of his cigarette twisted and spun in the air, 'It's like these fellows who never took a drink in their lives, laying down the law for everyone else, and before you know it they're down in Sullivan's raising trouble and roaring and shouting and driving everybody half-daft with their stupid songs! What I mean is – you think you know somebody and then they go and do the opposite of what you expect. When all's said and done, life never really does tend to conform to expectations, does it, Smiler?'

Pat was pleased to hear himself saying this. He had read it in a book once.

'There's no knowing,' mused Smiler, shaking his pipe and assuming for a passing moment what he took to be the stance of a learned philosopher. 'It's just that you'd be afraid when you're used to seeing someone and then you don't – you'd be afraid they might have got themselves murdered or something.'

'I know what you mean, Smiler,' replied Pat, adding: 'With some of the things you read in the papers these days.'

'This is it,' was the council man's rueful reply.

'Still – who knows?' went on Pat as he turned to go back inside. 'Maybe one day she will show up. Till then, I suppose all we can do is hope.'

'I suppose you're right, Pat. I suppose so,' agreed Smiler, a trifle confused by Pat's unexpected sympathy and warm-hearted neighbourliness – for, after all, this was not the reaction which the 'rumours' would have led one to expect (what with there having been, at the very least, seven different reports of 'sightings' of Mrs Tubridy in the vicinity of the McNab household).

But finding it all the more heartening for that reason, which was why he found himself smiling (not that it took very much to elicit this response – hence his nickname), and why he ended up whispering a little prayer for the vanished woman's soul – 'Wherever she may be, God love her' – as he picked up his clippers and returned to work, a briskness entering his step as he set off down the road which led to the town, already over two hundred yards between him and the dim but well-kept kitchen where Pat McNab – now bent double, and with tears, not only of mirth but it has to be said of triumph also! coursing copiously down his cheeks – continuing to repeat to the recalcitrant cork of a Johnnie Walker bottle which fiercely resisted his best efforts: 'Come on, you effing effer! Come on, you boy you!' before at last its life-giving contents swooshed gaily down his throat, his upraised arms then seeming to embrace the entire sky as once more he serenaded the world with those precious words that had set him free:

'*Come day go day*
Wishing my heart it was Sunday
Drinking buttermilk all the week
Whisky on a Sunday!'

as outside, upon a carpet of leaves which had somehow arranged itself on the window sill, a chorus of small and beady-eyed birds paused to chirp in unison.

CHAPTER TWO

The Turfman From Ardee

The Turfman From Ardee

For sake of health I took a walk last week at early dawn
I met a jolly turfman as I slowly walked along
The greatest conversation passed between that man and me
And soon I got acquainted with the turfman from Ardee

We chatted very freely as we jogged along the road
He said my ass is tired and I'd like to see his load
For I got no refreshments since I left home you see
And I am wearied out with travelling, said the turfman from Ardee.

Your cart is wracked and worn, friend, your ass is very tired,
It must be twenty summers since that animal foaled
Yoked to a cart where I was born, September forty-three
And carried for the midwife, says the turfman from Ardee.

IT WAS AN ORDINARY DAY in the middle of September and Pat was busy in the kitchen doing the dishes. He was listening to the news but there wasn't much on. There was talk of Ireland getting a lot of money from the Common Market and a man had been blown into the sea in Bray, Co. Wicklow. Just then there was a knock at the door. 'Hmm,' pondered Pat to himself as he set down a dish on the draining board, 'I wonder who that could be now?' He untied his apron and went off to see who his visitor might be. He opened the door and discovered a shortish man in an old sports coat with hay coming out of its pockets standing on the step. His trousers were held up by a fraying halter and the top of his grey felt hat (which had once boasted a band) seemed quite bashed in.

'Hello,' Pat said, smiling, adding: 'And what might I do for you?'

'There you are now,' the man said. 'It's looking like it's not going to be such a bad day.'

Pat nodded and made as if to inspect the sun, which was positioned just above the chemist's.

'No – it certainly looks as if it's going to pick up,' he replied.

The man nodded and inhaled some mucus.

'I'm selling turf,' he replied.

Pat leaned over – for no apparent reason – and replied: 'Indeed. I see.'

'I have it here in a bag,' the man said.

He opened a plastic sack which was half-filled with turf.

It was the sort of sack which normally contained fertilizer or perhaps chicken feed.

'It's grand turf,' the man said, 'it comes all the way from Ardee.'

'Ardee?' mused Pat.

'Aye,' the man said, 'it's in County Louth. Did you ever hear tell of it, I wonder?'

Pat frowned and placed his index finger close to his lower lip.

'I think I might have heard a fellow talking about it one night in Sullivan's.'

The man made a sucking sound with his teeth and hoisted up his trousers.

'There's a man by the name of McNab lives in it,' he said. 'He's from this town. You would probably know him all right.'

Pat chewed the tip of his index finger.

'McNab?' he said, frowning.

'Aye!' the man replied perkily. 'He'd be a Tom McNab!'

Pat shook his head.

'No,' he said, 'I don't know any Tom now, I have to say.'

Now it was the visitor's turn to frown.

'Or maybe it could be Joe. I'm not sure,' he said.

'No,' asserted Pat, 'nor Joe either.'

The man tugged absentmindedly on a nostril-hair.

'Unless of course his name isn't McNab at all,' he said.

Pat nodded, unthinkingly.

'It might be somebody else, I suppose,' he said.

'Aye,' came the reply, 'it might be Grue, for example. Or Halliwell, maybe.'

Pat placed a hand on either hip.

'I wouldn't know him so,' he said.

'No. Sure he's gone out of this town this years, anyway!'

'Oh – is he?' replied Pat.

His caller nodded – with vigour.

'Aye!' he continued. 'He says it was a dump. He says all

there is in it is child-molesters and men whose idea of enjoyment is to batter their wives.'

Pat felt a little bit of tension manifesting itself just over his left eye.

'Batter their wives?' he said. 'Beat them?'

The man looked at his toes.

'Aye,' he said, 'with hammers.'

Pat swallowed.

'Hammers?' he gasped, incredulously.

The man knitted his brow.

'Sure didn't one fellow leave half his wife's head on the wall of the coalhouse,' he said.

Pat drew a deep breath.

'Half her head? No!' he weakly responded – half as a question.

The response was quite firm.

'No – not no! Took the hammer and hit her with it, I'm telling you! For nothing! It was like eggs. They say her brains was like eggs.'

Pat found himself swallowing again.

'Like eggs?' he said.

The man gazed directly at him.

'On the wall. For nothing.'

'Good God Almighty,' moaned Pat.

The man was continuing.

'There you are now,' he said, 'that's the type of people you're dealing with. Hitting women with hammers for doing damn all.'

He paused and hooked a weatherbeaten thumb into the waistband of his trousers. They were oatmeal-coloured.

'Well – not damn all, exactly.'

He sighed. Then he said:

'Women can be odd sometimes, you know.'

Pat tossed back his head and laughed.

'Oh now! Sure don't I know it only too well!' he cried.

The man brightened.

'Indeed and I'm sure I don't have to tell you that, sir!' he said. 'Sure don't you have eyes of your own! And I dare say there's any amount of women around this town would be glad to go odd if they were let!'

'Indeed and there sure is!' laughed Pat, now hitching up his own trousers.

At the far end of the town, a woman went by with her shopping. The turf-selling visitor hesitated and said to Pat:

'Sometimes you couldn't even be sure of your own sister,' he said.

'Sure?' asked Pat, so dry at the back of his throat he had to ask it again – 'Sure?'

'Aye,' came the reply, 'sure that they wouldn't go odd, I mean.'

'Oh, aye,' answered Pat, pretending to understand – although he really didn't.

'Or your mother aither!' he began again. 'Sure who's to say your own mother wouldn't do the same? And then what would you do? I say – what would you do then? Your own bloody mother that carried your around in her stomick?'

The toes of the man's boots moved closer to Pat, his tongue lodged firmly in his cheek as his gaze fixed intensely upon him.

'What?' was the word which attempted to leave Pat's throat – although, because of the man's somewhat overpowering proximity, it might have been more accurately described as a 'thin croak' which left it. The eyes now fastened to Pat were small as currants. Or studs. The studs his father used to put in his shirt on Sunday mornings.

'I mean – you couldn't be taking a hammer to your own mother,' he continued. 'I mean – Jesus, Mary and Joseph! You couldn't be at the like of that! You'd have to find some other way!'

'Some other way?' queried Pat. He was chewing on the ends of his fingers now.

'Aye! The way I see it – that wouldn't be right! Not with me, anyhow! Do you get my meaning, Mister?'

Pat could almost feel his hot breath on his neck. The stud-eyes bit deep into him.

'Unless of course – unless maybe you think it's OK,' he went on, 'unless maybe you think it's not so bad at all?'

Pat regretted the eagerness which insinuated itself – despite his best efforts – into his voice.

'No! No I don't!' he cried aloud.

The man sighed and drew the back of his hand across his peat-caked, furrowed brow.

'Thank God for that!' he gasped, and, with intense relief, shook his head.

There was a long pause. There were some rooks on the wires above them, staring down. They looked like notes you would see on the page of a music book. Eventually the halter-belted visitor said:

'Right. I'll just leave you the half-bag so.'

Pat stiffened.

'What?' he said.

'The half-bag,' he replied, 'the half-bag's all I'll leave.'

Pat scratched his right eyebrow and said:

'But I didn't ask you!'

He hesitated and then added:

'I don't want any, you see! I have enough turf! Anyway I use mostly coal!'

In that moment, or perhaps the direct aftermath of it, it was as if time appeared to stand still. When the reply to Pat's statement came, it was barely audible, and appeared to issue from the darkest, most impregnable depths of the fuel-salesman's soul.

'What?' he said.

Pat swallowed. His saliva had a pungent, acidic taste.

'Turf,' said Pat, 'I have enough of it, thanks.'

A broodiness, which seemed to come out of nowhere,

appeared to consume the man. He looked half at Pat, half at the rain barrel by the side of the house.

'Is it because I'm from Ardee? Is that it?' he said quietly.

'What?' Pat said, paling somewhat.

There was a distinct lack of emotion in the caller's voice now as he spoke.

'I knew, you know,' he began, 'from the minute I came through the gate, I knew.'

Now it was the turn of Pat's brow to knit.

'Knew?' he said, hoarsely. 'Knew what?'

The back of his throat felt like sandpaper.

The man's lips seemed to thin out before Pat's very eyes.

'Oh, you're the funny fellow all right!' he said then, 'Keep me talking! And all the time thinking: "Look at him! Look at him, auld Ardee!" It's a wonder you didn't keep me going till I sang my song for you! It's a wonder you didn't do that!'

'Song?' asked Pat, perplexed. 'What song?'

'Don't cod me! Every time I make a sale, I usually give them a bar of a song. But of course you don't know, do you, Mister? Mr I Know Everything! Mr I Can See Behind Your Eyes! Mr So You Like To Sing While You Sell, Do You? Yes! I like to sing! Damn bleddy right I do! And I won't be stopped by the likes of you! Do you hear me, do you? Eh? Well?'

Without wavering, the toe of his right-hand boot began to tap in six-eight time as – also taken by surprise – the rooks (there were three of them) altogether suddenly evacuated the electric wires in favour of the slated rooftops to the north-west of the town as the late summer air became filled with the sound of a familiar air. The gesticulations of the vocalist were unexpectedly debonair, tending indeed towards the operatic:

'*For sake of health I took a walk last week at early morn*
I met a jolly turfman as I slowly walked along
The greatest conversation passed between this man and me
And so I got acquainted with the Turfman from Ardee.'

The tranquil evening resounded with the dying echoes of

the sprightly ballad as Pat shrunk before the penetrating set of eyes.

'What do you think of that song?' he found himself asked.

Pat coughed politely.

'I think it's very good,' he said.

The turf-selling vocalist frowned.

'Good, eh? You think it's good, do you?'

'Yes! Yes!' enthused Pat. 'Excellent.'

The now quiet surroundings reverberated with the sound of teeth being sucked.

'I see,' the caller said softly. Then, after some time, with a hint of abjection, continued:

'Not like my turf.'

'No!' cried Pat. 'Your turf's good! It—'

'If I had said: "I'm from Carrick. I'm not the Turfman from Ardee – I'm the Turfman from Carrick" – would you have bought it then, maybe?'

'No!' cried Pat. 'Of course I wouldn't!'

The man hung his head and narrowed his eyes.

'No. No, of course you wouldn't. You wouldn't have said: "Two full bags," or "A bag and a half!" You'd have said: "No bags! No bags at all!" Isn't that right?'

'That's right,' agreed Pat.

'You know what's the worst thing in the world?' said the turfman.

'What?' he said.

'Never mind what! Say: "What is it? What is the worst thing in the world, turfman?"'

'What is the worst thing in the world, turfman?' repeated Pat as instructed.

There wasn't a sound for a second and then the peddler of kindling and peat said:

'The liar.'

'Liar?' choked Pat.

'More than the husband who puts his wife's brains in with

a hammer, steals another man's kidneys, poisons his own dog – the liar. Because he's the man looks into your eye and says: "I wouldn't do it. I'd buy no turf from a Carrick man." He's the man looks into your eye and says: "Up Ardee!" When all the time he's thinking. . . . .'

A tense pause followed. Then the turfman said:

'Say: "Up Ardee", Mister!'

'Huh?' said Pat.

'Up Ardee. Say it. Go on now!'

'Up Ardee,' complied Pat.

'Worse than the man who mutilates himself to become a woman. Worse than the man who lays down with beasts of the field. Worse than the vilest fornications the mind can ever dream of, worse than . . .'

Pat felt hot breath on his neck. Then, paradoxically, a wintry tremor went running through him as he heard the words:

'Worse even than the man who murders his own mother.'

Pat's smile was faint and sickly as he replied:

'Do you know what I was just thinking, Ardee, or whatever your name is. It said on the forecast we could be in for a rough spell come October. I think I'd be as well to take ten bags – if you happen to have them, that is!'

'Ten bags?'

Pat nodded.

'Aye,' he said, 'ten bags. Ah sure, to hell – make it a dozen. I'll take the dozen!'

'You'd make a nice warm fire with that. You wouldn't be long getting a nice roaring fire going with a dozen bags, eh?'

'What?' blurted Pat, forgetting himself for a second, then smiled and said: 'Oh now! Now you're talking!'

'Oh indeed and begod you would not!' continued the turfman. 'You wouldn't be long heating up if you had the dozen bags to be going on with!'

'That's right! Isn't it?' beamed Pat, becoming a trifle disorientated for no immediately identifiable reason.

'Do your cooking and the whole lot!' he affirmed. 'Your griddle bread, for example!'

'You could bake away – couldn't you?'

'Your griddle bread. Caraway cake. Not to mention boiling the water. All the water you need!'

'The water too! As much as you could use!'

'Like the fellow who threw the pan of water over his wife in Longford! It was turf he used to boil the water! I believe she was heard screaming for three days!'

'Three days?' gasped Pat.

'The doctors done all they could! But it was a waste of time! They said she was even worse when they finished with her! One of her eyes was blinded and there was a big red scorch mark the size of that all the way down her face. Then she started screaming in the night. Howling and howling! Howling: "You did it! You did it!"'

Pat coughed and looked around him.

'I think I hear someone at the back door!' he said. 'I have to go in.'

'Imagine that!' continued the turfman – oblivious of Pat's previous comments – 'Someone screaming – night after night, over and over again: "You did it! It was you did it!"'

'There it is again,' Pat said, inclining his head towards the back of the house.

'Shouting it without end! "You did it!" Never giving you a minute's peace! Every time you'd turn on a light, there she'd be at the window . . .'

The words hung in the air as if each letter was ringed with fire.

The turfman seemed to take half an hour to draw his breath. Then he lowered his head and said: 'I'm sorry. I'd best be on my way. I knew I made a mistake coming here. They never liked the Ardee people about this town.'

He lifted his bag of turf and placed it across his left shoulder.

'Well – goodbye, Mister. I'll go on down to the station so and be off about my business. I hope I didn't trouble you too much.'

Pat gulped.

'The station?' he whimpered.

The turfman contemplated his blackened thumbnail and nodded.

'Aye. I want to have a few words with the sergeant, you see. About doing a bit of digging.'

Pat's skin grew clammy all over as his eyes instinctively travelled – as two small cameras whose lenses came to rest upon a particular spot adjacent to a laurel bush.

'Digging?' he asked, hesitantly, and somewhat hoarse.

'Aye. There's a bog below in Ardee full of turf. But I need a permit, you see. Aye. Well – I'd best be off. I have my ass round here at the back where he's been standing all this time. Isn't he a patient soul? Good man, Neddy.'

Some moments later, he was gathering up the frayed rope which was tied around the ass's head and leading the sad-eyed donkey down the lane towards the main road. But before he reached the elm tree, Pat found himself crying out: 'No! Wait! Turfman – please!'

Both animal and hawker of peat hesitated.

'Eh?' he called back.

'Why don't youse stay the night?' cried Pat. 'I mean, like – it's a long way to Ardee from here!'

The turfman shook his head.

'Oh we couldn't do that, now. The sergeant is below waiting for me.'

'No! Please!' Pat pleaded. 'We can put on a big roaring fire and make caraway cake! Griddle bread! Toasted griddle bread – wouldn't that be nice?'

The turfman scratched his head and said:

'Now I don't mean to be a class of what you might call ungrateful – but you wouldn't be lying to me, would you? You wouldn't be trying to make a cod of the Ardee man, would you?'

Standing there in a shaft of evening sunlight, Pat thought: 'Oh no! Now why on earth would we do that when all they do is come about your own private place with stupid, droopy-eyed animals! Oh no, why Neddy, we'll have to get him a mouthful of hay too, after we've bought some of your shitty old bags of turf!!'

Words which he did not utter, of course, or give the slightest indication of ever having harboured. Instead, rubbing his hands and buoyantly crying: 'Absolutely not! Please! Please accept my invitation – both of you!'

*

Which, happily, they did, with the result that that very evening they found themselves as he had promised, devouring large slabs of hot, butter-soaked griddle bread and reclining beside a nice roaring fire, with Neddy giving all his attention to the hay that Pat had liberally forked for him into the plywood crate that had once housed Jaffa oranges. Pat smiled as he considered the industriously masticating jaws.

'He likes it, doesn't he, turfman?' said Pat. 'He sure does like that old hay!'

The turfman beamed.

'Oh indeed and he does! The Ardee asses like their dinner, sure enough! They'd ate you out of house and home if they were let, Pat!'

Pat handed the donkey another handful of hay.

'There you are, Neddy!' he said. 'Come on now – eat up! Eat up, you auld divil you!'

*

There can be no doubt but that there is something idyllic about the surroundings in which Pat McNab resides – the spacious and well-appointed, if somewhat cobwebbed rooms and fabulous whitewashed outhouses could not but be the envy of many in these property-coveting days, not to mention the stables. Especially the stables, indeed, which in days gone by housed all the trusty steeds which ferried gentlemen in their galloping pursuits of unfortunate foxes. In the month of September, there is something particularly peaceful and poignant about the house and its surroundings, and if a visiting tourist or even just casual stroller, perhaps, happened to be passing by, they would be hard-pressed not to produce a camera and take any number of photographs to record the scene for posterity. Thoughts which occupy the mind of Pat McNab as he stands by the window once more, peering out through the curtain now that some months have passed and all is quiet again and the telltale creak of the garden gate announces no more unwanted callers. 'By all means photograph my residence,' he muses, 'but do not call.' Although, he had to admit, that he might have to insist that any would-be recorder for posterity make an exception of the stables. 'For their sake more than anything,' – meaning the turfman and his 'animal' – he murmurs as he chortles a little into his hands. For the simple reason that he hasn't gotten around to cleaning up the unfortunate outhouses yet! Well, actually – that's not true. The truth is that he simply couldn't be bothered any more! 'Auld bucking ass,' he thinks, 'who cares about him and his auld guts!' Who, indeed, for the scene can hardly be described as a 'palatable' one. Reminiscent, perhaps, of one of these *Friday the Thirteenth* or *Chainsaw Massacre*-type films – indeed any horror vehicle specifically targeted at the youth market. It might well be argued that the outbuilding concerned is virtually unrecognizable as a stable. For daubed across the ceiling now are huge big sploshes of blood, and in great long streaks along the side and back walls are the very same. Nailed to the half door in the most casually dismissive fashion are two crimson-stained donkey's ears. A ghosthunting, infrared-type camera might reveal a photographic negative impression of Pat, cold yet crazed with his pitchfork, performing a crude and primitive blood-soaked cabaret interspersed with heart-rending brays and squeals. A torn halter providing a sad, heart-rending epitaph. Who owns the scarlet mask that leaps into the air and raises hands now gloved with blood? It may not be, it cannot be, but *is* – the face of none other than Pat McNab!

*

A long way from the smiling, benevolent visage which had once glowed in the firelight of a September evening as a contented visitor burped a little and placed his plate upon the table, with the grateful remark: 'Boys but that was a powerful dinner, Pat! I tell you, you wouldn't get better in Ardee!'

As a gracious host replied:

'Why, I'm honoured that you liked it – at least now you're beginning to understand that all of us are not hostile towards the town of your birth.'

'No! Indeed and youse are not, it's true, Pat!'

'And to prove it to you more, I've taken the liberty of supplying Neddy with a little surprise!'

'A surprise, Pat? No!'

'Oh but very much yes! Just so long as you will make a promise!'

'A promise?'

'You'll sing my favourite song of all!'

'Not—'

'The very one! You promise?'

'Well, what can I say? Begod and I do!'

'Hold on till I get my pitchfork! I have it here behind the door! And Neddy's already without?'

'He's in the stable, Pat.'

'Where you and me are going now! For we're not going to abandon old Ned when there's a bit of a come-all-ye in the offing! Would I be right?'

'Indeed, and I dare say you would,' the Ardee man replied, the tiniest bit flummoxed.

*

It is a quiet evening now. The birds are twittering brightly and clearly in the trees and the footsteps of Pat and his visitor echo around the rectangle of a manure-covered yard. 'Ah but that air would do your heart good,' he remarks, 'I'll bet it smells good all the way from here back to the station.'

'I'll bet it does,' his visitor replies, unguardedly.

Pat lifts the pitchfork across his shoulder and places his hand on the older man's shoulder.

'So – is the Ardee man going to sing?' he smiles as he sits himself down on a tightly packed haybale.

'Begod and he is! He is that! Try to stop the turfmen from singing!' the County Louth man laughs.

'I wouldn't dream of it!' laughs Pat as the mucus in his visitor's throat rolls loud and strong and musical.

'Good man!' claps Pat as a cow – visible over the half door – leans quizzically over a hedge. 'Away with you now!'

The turfman begins to tap his foot and sing, with unmatchable gusto:

'We chatted very freely as we walked along the road
He said my ass is tired and I'd like to see his load
For I got no refreshments since I left home you see
And I'm wearied out with travelling, said the turfman from Ardee.'

*

It is not true that the 'greatest' of conversations – as attested by the first verse of the song – passed between Pat McNab and his visitor, the Turfman from Ardee, at least not on that last evening in the half-light by the half door of the stables. In fact, the only words exchanged between them on that occasion, from the moment the song concluded (*'A fine rendition!'* Pat had trumpeted) until the entire quota of blood had been drained from the journeyman's face, were: 'What are you doing with that pitchfork, Pat?' And ones fated to receive in response nothing other than the succinct and unadorned sentence: 'Sending you back to Ardee once and for all, you interfering peddler of dirt!'

As for the animal, it too went to its doom in the same hopelessly insouciant manner which it had displayed all its life, regardless of world politics, trauma or incident. Even Pat's deranged cries (for how else can they be described?) along the lines of: 'Carry turf now! Go on, you bollocky bucking ass! Let's see you do it now!' failed to make any impression upon it, even as it buckled hopelessly to its knees, on its last, sad journey towards eternity's meadow.

*

It may be so that Pat's visitor upon that fateful evening one September long ago was well regarded and always had been so in the small County Louth town of Ardee, it somehow ordained that his absence not only be noted but for generations mourned with Niagaras of tears and wailing lamentations. It is indeed possible that he and his turf-bearing ass were as part of the landscape itself in their travels throughout the length and breadth of the county. But if such were the case, no evidence to suggest it ever came the way of Pat McNab who, occasionally, long after he had cleaned out the stables, and was satisfied that all trace of any event, terrible or other-wise, ever having taken place within those walls had well and truly been removed for ever, would pause for a moment from his polishing (inveterate cleaner, Pat McNab!) and, satisfied once again that the sound which had distracted him had not, in fact, been the strange and lonely braying of a restless ass from some unmapped, timeless phantom zone, but the simple, insignificant whine of a broken fencepost buffeted by the wind, give himself once more to his work and the soft humming, contented and protracted, of a certain popular tune from the oft-unfeted County of Louth, which in its own special and unspoken way was destined to be his for evermore.

CHAPTER THREE

Old Flames

Old Flames

Downtown tonight I saw an old friend
Someone who I used to take comfort from
Long before I met you
I caught a spark from her eyes of forgotten desire
With a word or a touch, Lord,
I could have rekindled that fire

Chorus
But old flames can't hold a candle to you
No one can light up the night like you do
Flickering embers of love I've known one or two
But old flames can't hold a candle to you.

Sometimes at night I think of all the lovers I've known
And I remember how holding them made me feel not so alone
Then I feel you beside me even their memories are gone
Like stars in the night lost in the sweet light of dawn.

ONE EVENING in or around five past six, Pat was coming along past Brennan's Gap (Billy Brennan was a farmer who concerned himself mostly with milch cows) when who should he meet only Mrs Ellen McCrumley. Now Pat was in a little bit of a giddy mood (perhaps because of the grand stretch in the evenings – for he had only had two bottles of Guinness!) and was on the verge of saying to her: 'Oh hello there, Mrs McCrumley! And how might *you* happen to be getting on this evening in this wonderful Town of Liars?' Which, as he turned the corner past Ned McGahey's welding shed, he was glad he didn't, for he knew only too well the answer he could expect. A croaky old scrake of a whine to the effect that Mrs Ellen McCrumley 'really wouldn't know' or didn't 'quite hear him', perhaps. And why? Why, because she herself was a citizen of the esteemed place to which he referred. The place thenceforth to be known as Town of Liars! But which it always had been, of course, as Pat well knew. Along with everyone else in Gullytown, but of course they would never admit it. Why? Simply because they couldn't as every time they opened their mouths all that appeared to come out was lies. 'Oh yes!' Pat turned suddenly and cried, pointing his finger at Mrs Mc-Crumley who was now making her way up the hill with her shopping bags: 'Oh but yes, Mrs Mac! Oh but yes, you see!'

Pat had already strode onwards when Mrs McCrumley eventually lost her balance and collapsed over a stone which had been positioned directly in front of her.

*

The large hand lurched towards the hour. 8 p.m. 'Ah, time for a cigarette,' thought Pat. He was relaxing in the sitting room, tapping his thumbs together and thinking things over. As he puffed on his smoke, he fancied himself explaining his thoughts to a psychiatrist of some sophistication who had been dispatched for the very purpose of conversing at length with the sole occupant of McNab Mansions. 'Hmm,' continued Pat through a cloud of smoke, 'you ask me how come I live in Town of Liars, Hektor?' (for that would be his name). 'Well, for a start – I was born here.'

The psychiatrist's subject examined his nails.

'My mother – Mrs Maimie McNab, husband of Victor (how alike your names are!) carried me in her stomach, you understand – and before I knew it, here I was! Surrounded by people who wouldn't know what the truth was if it came up to them and sat in their lap, shouting: "Hello! Truth calling!" Or perhaps you didn't know that, Hektor? What – I've told you before, have I? Hektor – I do apologize. But it annoys me, you see! It really does annoy me, you see!'

Without realizing it, Pat was leaving deep indentations around the rim of his cigarette with his teeth. There were two or three tiny beads of sweat which had just appeared over his right eyebrow as he drew a deep breath and said: 'And as for Mammy – my own mother – you can imagine what it must have done to her!'

There was about one half-inch of actual cigarette remaining as Pat rubbed his forehead and Hektor proceeded to meticulously inscribe notes in his lined spiral-bound notebook. Pat sighed as he saw his mother (in his mind's eye, of course!) approaching the telephone in her slippers once again, deep anxieties etched all over her face as she tentatively removed the receiver from its Bakelite cradle.

'Hello?' she said, with an unmistakable catch in her voice, simultaneously tapping her chest with her hand as if mimicking the flapping of a trapped bird's wing, before seeming to fold like a piece of crumpled paper tissue, saying chokingly: 'Oh dear God no!' then adding hopefully, but without conviction, 'But maybe it wasn't him, Sergeant!'

His mother stood trembling in the middle of the floor as she saw it before her clear as day, the small, dome-shaped haystack erupting, the flames as flickering fingers reflected in a pair of wild and dancing eyes. Eyes which were set, unmistakably, in the scorch-streaked face of her son, Pat McNab!

The howls which continued throughout the beating which Pat received as a consequence of that particular incident may only be described as pitiful. 'Mammy!' he screeched, 'I didn't do it! I swear! They're all against me because they don't like me!'

His mother raised the strap anew (it was the belt from one of her husband's army uniforms).

'Don't lie to me!' she snapped harshly. 'Don't lie to me, you rapscallion you, lie to your own mother! I'll tan you within an inch of your life!'

The tears hurtled from Pat's eyes and smacked against the floor like pieces of broken glass.

'It's not me!' he pleaded, but in vain, adding, 'It's them, Ma! It's them that's lying! It's all they ever do!'

As he sat there now finishing his cigarette, the sound of his bedroom door closing and the key being turned that evening was as an open hand laid firmly across his already burning cheek.

*

It was 9.30 p.m. Pat rose from his chair and repaired to the drinks cabinet. 'You see, Hektor,' he continued, as he liberally poured himself a measure of Bols Advocaat, 'what makes me laugh is that according to them, I was out every night of the week! Well, excuse me but just how much do you think paraffin costs?' Pat shook his head as he sipped his drink. 'Tsk! Tsk!' he sighed, adding: 'Dear oh dear!'

Coincidentally, the record he selected to place on the turntable of the radiogram was entitled 'Old Flames'. It brought a wry smile to his face as he stood there in the middle of the parlour, its lilting words melting into the gloom:

Downtown tonight I saw an old friend
Someone I used to take comfort from
Long before I met you
I caught a spark from her eyes of forgotten desire
With a word or a touch, Lord,
I could have rekindled that fire.

Pat's eyes twinkled as he tilted the yellow meniscus and discerned within the shimmering depths of that viscous liquid a myriad of swirling memories. 'Why yes,' he mused quietly, 'according to them, I didn't seem to have spent a single night at home in over three years! First, it was the Widow McGinn's mattresses! Oh yes – Pat McNab did it! Pat McNab, certainly – who else!'

It was so absurd Pat almost flung his drink – glass and all! – at the wall. It had even made the local papers – a photograph of the Widow staring whitefaced in her nightdress trying to explain how she had left some mattresses outside in the yard for airing and was awakened in the middle of the night by the sound of their crackling and burning. Swearing, to boot, that she had caught sight of a 'small blackfaced figure' making good its escape into the night.

Pat sighed as he refilled his glass. Eschewing the Bols Advocaat this time for some fine Glenfiddich whisky. His eyes twinkled as the amber liquid made its warm journey through the sinuous tunnel of his oesophagus. 'Then there was the doctor's car!' he chortled softly. 'The famous doctor's precious car! And it only a wreck!'

Which wasn't exactly how it was perceived in those very same famous local papers, of course. 'Oh no!' laughed Pat. 'Why, it was a $40,000 BMW! Of course it was!'

It was time for him to sit down again, thought Pat. He

placed his glass on the arm of his chair and laced his fingers. 'Yes – I did that, Hektor!' he said, with a smile. 'Of course I did! I mean – I wasn't at home doing my homework! How could I be? I was out setting fire to the doctor's fine upholstery and beautiful bodywork! Just like I was supposed to have burnt McGlinchey's cat!'

The discovery of the smoking corpse had caused an uproar. McGlinchey's cat was well known and loved in the area.

'Which is what you are accused of if you happen to be unlucky enough to live in Town of Liars, Hektor!' explained Pat. 'Because, you see, if you live in a normal town, people have more to do with their time. They have more to do than go around blaming the wrong people. Not that they don't have their reasons! Why, of course they do! O if they don't like you – if the inhabitants of Town of Liars don't happen to like you – why, they'll make up the most atrocious lies about you, won't they?'

Something which they learned early on, thought Pat, as he sipped his Glenfiddich (very tasty!) – at their mother's knee, in fact. In an instant, he found himself transported back to a small schoolroom round about the year 1965. There was an ink cupboard and a giant wooden compass and, of course, the turnip-shaped figure of Master Butty Halpin with his feet up on the desk. Pat's young eyes burned with resentment as the boy beside him stood poker-stiff and made his brazen declaration.

'Sir – it was Pat McNab burnt Mrs McGinn's mattresses. He told me, so he did. And I think it might have been him set fire to Artie McCrann's haystack!'

It was more than the nine-year-old Pat could bear.

'Sir!' he cried aloud, his hand shooting sharply into the air. 'Sir, he's making that up! He's making it up because he hates me!'

The schoolmaster's response was unyielding in its brevity.

'McNab! Out!'

It would be hard for Pat McNab ever to forget the punishment inflicted on him in the moments which followed. Or the fist-obfuscated sniggers of his 'classmates'. 'McNab!' the teacher had barked. 'Get out into that yard and cut a good big switch. Then trot back in here till we see what we can do with it!' As he passed the playground alone, what he seemed to possess at the end of his arms (sunk into the pockets of his short trousers in a pitiful attempt at pain-amelioration) were not hands but two pounds of raw bloody steak. There was no mistaking, muted as they might have been, the words which passed Pat's lips as he leaned against the wall of the dog-dirt-spotted handball alley, observing his laughing, cavorting class-mates. 'One day they'll pay. And so will Halpin. Most of all, Halpin! I'll burn him, so I will!'

It was some nights later Butty Halpin was in his study preparing some work for Irish grammar and some mental arithmetic problems when he heard his wife's voice cry out into the night (she had gone to the back door to throw out some tea leaves): 'Butty! Butty! Come quick! The chickens are on fire!'

The sight which met his eyes as he appeared in his own back yard pulling on his dressing gown – of hopping, squawk-ing – literally, balls of living flame – does not bear describing.

*

Pat stared at his reflection in the glass of Glenfiddich. 'Oops!' he remarked. 'I seem a little woozy.' He tilted the glass to see how far he could permit it to go without spilling it. Then he sniggered a little bit. 'He – Butty Halpin – tried to make me say I did it – but I wouldn't!'

Pat lit a cigarette and puffed out some smoke. 'No! I wouldn't. Not in a million years!' he said. 'No matter how many times he battered me!'

And batter him Butty Halpin certainly did. Shaking him, indeed, to within an inch of his life, and, on one occasion, actually slamming his head directly against the blackboard, crying: 'Can't you admit it, can't you! We all know you did it! Do you hear me?'

No conclusion was reached on that occasion, with the master eventually collapsing from exhaustion, still pleading: 'Why can't you admit you burned the chickens, McNab?' and Pat's eyes for all the world like stones inside in his head.

*

The record had long since finished. Pat rose from his chair and replaced the stylus at the beginning of his 'favourite song'. He smiled as its waltzing melody consumed the night once more. Angling his elbow, he leaned against the mantelpiece and said: 'Yes, Hektor, that is the way it is, unfortunately. You believe the people of Liar Town and soon you are convinced that Pat McNab had nothing to do with his time only be out every night burning things. Burning things, Hektor! Burning, burning, burning!'

A thought struck Pat: 'You know – I think I wouldn't mind some ice!' He repaired to the kitchen and popped a pair of ice cubes into his glass – which he then replenished – except this time with some fine old Hennessy brandy (VSOP brand). As he sipped anew, he continued: 'Although I did burn some things. I'm not about to deny that. But only things that deserved to be burnt.'

He paused for a moment as the life-enhancing liquid settled itself deep within him.

'But,' he continued then as he puffed on his Major cigarette, 'all the things they said I did? Why, Hektor, there would have been a million Pat McNabs running around the town if even a quarter of the things were to have taken place! But then I guess – that's what liars do, in the place called Town of Liars!'

A thin serpent of smoke wound its way out of Pat's left nostril as he continued:

'What I find most amusing about liars, of course, is that

they're so busy lying they get all the other things wrong! Like poor old Bat McGaw! Dear oh dear! What a dreary old idiot!'

*

It was late now so Pat turned on his tilley lamp, which sent out its big large shadows across the room like people of the night. It was time for a glass of wine, Pat thought, as he opened his book and donned his reading glasses. A nice Bulgarian, perhaps, he thought. *The Towering Inferno*, announced the book's title in letters of fire. Beneath a flaming building, tiny figures, including ant-sized firemen clutching a hose that seemed alive, recoiled in terror. Pat sipped his wine and, as if addressing Hektor over the top of his novel, remarked: 'What's funny, of course, is that poor old McGaw wasn't actually *from* Town of Liars! If perhaps he had been, there might have been a chance he'd have had more sense!'

It now appeared as if Pat was addressing the small mound of ash piling up in the centre of the ashtray.

'Isn't that right? Isn't that right, Bat? Oh indeed and it is surely!'

He tapped the book's glossy cover and continued:

'Oh, Bat, you silly old canoodle you! If only you'd had more sense than coming about the place!'

*

The wine in Pat's glass seemed so clear and fresh it furnished the illusion of that very first day with Bat McGaw coming to revisit him right there in that very room between the chairs and the table and the mantelpiece. How best to describe Bat McGaw? An agrarian soul of distressing amplitude, perhaps, perennially attired in turned-down wellingtons (gumboots) and an inordinately cigarette-holed waistcoat.

'Oh, there you are, Pat!' had been his opening greeting to Pat. 'I was just looking for you! You don't know me – I'm Bat McGaw! My brother has the family place above on the hill!'

'Oh, aye – Ernie McGaw!' replied Pat.

'Aye, Ernie, that'd be the brother – God rest him. Well, you see, I've just moved into the area and I don't know whether Ernie was telling you or not but we were thinking of going into sheep.'

'Going into sheep?' replied Pat.

'Aye,' Bat nodded, 'we were thinking of going into sheep so you see we'd be needing this bit of land round about here where the house is.'

Pat frowned and folded his arms.

'Round about where the house is?' he queried, tentatively.

Bat nodded and spat, narrowly missing the toe of his wellington.

'Aye,' he said.

Pat scratched the back of his head.

'What house?' he asked.

Bat McGaw's features displayed puzzlement.

'What house?' he replied, somewhat incredulously. 'Ah, come on now, Pat. There's only one house – that house there looking at you!'

Pat – still with his arms folded – turned to gaze upon the large Victorian building directly behind him.

'But that's my house!' he said. 'That's Mammy's house!'

Bat McGaw stripped his teeth in a grin.

'Mammy's house! Do you hear you, Pat! And you a grown man! But don't worry – I'd be giving you a fair price! The McGaws were never known for anything only giving a man a fair shake!'

Pat looked away and gave his attention to the horizon.

'I'm sorry, Mr McGaw. It's not for sale.'

Bat McGaw frowned. Pat perceived him moving a little closer to him.

'How's that, Pat?' he said, lowering his voice.

'I'm sorry, Mr McGaw,' repeated Pat, impassively, 'it's not for sale. The house – it's not for sale, I'm afraid.'

Now it was Bat McGaw's turn to lower his head and scratch the back of it.

'I'm sorry, Pat, but you don't seem to understand,' he continued, grinning. 'You see – I own the rights to this land. And your mother – she doesn't own the house at all!'

'What?' Pat heard himself say. His saliva thickened.

'C'mere!' Bat McGaw continued. 'Come over here till I show you.'

Seemingly oblivious of the manure and mud stains which were a prominent feature of his paraffin-coloured dungarees, Bat McGaw produced from his back pocket an expansive Ordnance Survey map which he proceeded to unfold on the ground before him. He might have been a professor illuminating the labyrinthine intricacies of biochemistry or advanced physics.

'You see,' he began, 'all this here is McGaws' land. And, back in 1942 – during the war, Pat, when your father was away – or so they tell me – not that I'd know for I'm not from about here – your mother sold my brother this bit and this bit and this bit here. She was strapped for cash, you follow. And he allowed her to keep the house – to hold on to it until such time as—?'

Bat McGaw broke off and Pat felt a cold patch forming somewhere in the region of the base of his spine.

'Such time as . . . ?' he said, hesitantly.

'Such time as we wanted to go intill the sheep or whatever. Do you follow?'

Pat's brow knitted and he began to pick the sleeve of his jumper with the fingers of his right hand.

'No. I don't follow,' he said, without emotion.

Bat McGaw fixed him with a piercing gaze.

'You what, Pat?' he said.

A nerve jerked – imperceptibly – in Pat's right cheek. He smiled caustically.

'It's a pretty good lie, Bat,' he said, 'even if you're not from the Town of Liars, I have to grant you – it's still a pretty good lie.'

Bat hitched up his trousers and sighed.

'I suppose it would be, Pat,' he said, 'I suppose it would be – if it was. Which it isn't. So what do you say to ten big ones?'

Pat was taken by surprise.

'What?' was his reply.

'Ten big ones,' continued Bat, 'in the paw. Right here and now. On account of you being out by Saturday.'

Pat smiled and looked down. From the tan water of the puddle hole, his smiling reflection stared back at him.

'Out by Saturday?' he said. 'But you don't understand. I can't leave here! This is Mammy's house! All my memories are here!'

There was a pause. Then Bat said:

'All your what?'

His grin broadened and he placed his large left hand on Pat's shoulder.

'Pat – you're a gas, man!' he went on. 'I heard a few yarns regarding your good self. I heard them say – I heard plenty! – but you've caught me up short with that, I have to say! Bucking memories, he says!'

Pat flushed – ever so slightly.

'Do you not have memories?' he said to Bat McGaw.

Bat shook his head – as if he could not for the life of him credit the words he was hearing.

'The only memories I have is of the last eejit I put one over on, Pat! That's the only memories worth having in this world!'

Pat's response was slow and grave and measured.

'Get out of my garden!' he said, his eyes locking with those of Bat McGaw.

Now it was the turn of Bat's cheek to jerk a little.

'How's that, Pat?' he said.

Pat's tone was now, however cautiously, a touch more strident in nature.

'Get out of my garden!' he snapped, placing his hand on the garden fence railings as if to emphasize ownership. But his proprietorial stance was simply lost on Bat McGaw, who did little more than smile and rake thick fingers through accordion-pleated hair.

'Ah come on now, Pat,' he said, 'I've been here long enough. Come on and we'll close the deal and we're right, we can set the wheels in motion. What do you say to that?'

Pat's unambiguous, considered words issued from lips so taut they seemed barely visible at all. It was as though he possessed a length of carpet for a mouth.

'Get out of my garden or I'll stick this in you!'

The garden fork appeared to jump into his hands. Bat McGaw glared darkly at the unremarkable tool.

'So that's it!' he sneered sourly. 'That's the way of it, is it? Well, by cripes I heard plenty about you, McNab, but I never thought you were this stupid! Would you go away out of that, you lug you, and put that thing down! I'm going! But one thing I'll say to you – lug! – one thing I'll say to you is: "You've had it!"'

*

There can be little doubt but that it was a happy, if not indeed triumphant Pat McNab who closed the door of Sullivan's behind him later that same night, declaiming 'When The Swallows Come Back To Capistrano' to the bushes and brambles that lined the road upon which he made his way towards home. '*When the swallows come back to Capistrano*,' he sang aloud, his cheeks aglow with pride. As indeed why wouldn't they be? Had he not shown Mr Bat McGaw where to get off? He certainly had! He sure had shown him that you can't come about a person's home calling them 'lugs' and expecting to get away with it! No sir! The very sentiments he was exchanging with the enormous silhouette of a sycamore tree not one hundred yards from his house when, suddenly, he was surprised to hear his name being unexpectedly called from somewhere out of the darkness. 'Hey, McNab!' the voice cried, followed by yet another, just as Pat was acclimatizing himself to the first. Lower in tone, but less attenuated. 'Yeah! You big lug you!' it continued confrontationally. Pat swallowed and was about to make a response. But it was already too late. A large stick thudded against his head and he fell to his knees, raising his forearms to protect himself as best he could from the savage blows which had begun to rain down upon him. He fancied he perceived something bursting – a vein, perhaps.

'Maybe that will put a bit of manners on you! Maybe now you'll see sense!' he heard in the distance.

As Pat swooned towards the arms of unconsciousness, paradoxically he found himself wordlessly proclaiming his gratitude that his torment was at an end. But it was not to be. Another blow fell across his right eyebrow and he cried out in agony. 'You'd do good to remember what he said, McNab!' were the final words which reached his ears before the redemptive twins of Ladies Numbness and Despair came at last to bear him away.

*

Norman Kidwell, of Kidwell and McCart, Solicitors, tapped his thumbs and considered the heavily bandaged client who was seated directly across from him. 'I see,' he continued, inexplicably moving a pink blotter pad in front of him, 'so you want to sell everything to Mr McGaw, then? Everything? Lock, stock and barrel?'

Pat flicked the tip of his tongue against the back of his front teeth.

'Yes, Mr Kidwell,' he replied.

Norman Kidwell took a pen from his pocket and steadied it for a moment between two index fingers, closing one eye and examining it as if endeavouring to determine once and for all its precise nature. Then, he cradled his chin in his hand and leaned across the desk.

'Are you sure this is a good idea now, Pat? Do you think you've thought it over enough?'

Pat placed his open palms flat on his thighs and nodded.

'Yes, Mr Kidwell,' he replied, 'I've been thinking long and hard this past few weeks. I've been thinking – it's not good me being up there in that house on my own now that Mammy's gone. There are too many memories.'

It was as though the solicitor was satisfied at last as regards the writing instrument's 'pen-ness'. He replaced the biro on the desk beside the blotter pad. 'I know, Pat,' he said, 'I know what you mean.' He paused and checked a piece of nail on the top of his index finger, continuing: 'By the way – where is she? Your mother?'

The sound of Pat's swallowing seemed unnaturally loud to him. The solicitor, however, gave no indication whatever of noticing it.

'What?' Pat responded, with an urgency that was quite unnecessary. 'Oh – she's gone to America. She says the hot weather'll be good for her veins.'

'I see,' the solicitor replied and went to the window to stand there staring out with his hands behind his back. 'Ah yes,' he went on, contemplating the irregular-shaped roofs of the town, 'memories. They can be a heavy burden sometimes.'

There was an unmistakable hint of melancholy in Pat's eyes. He found himself suddenly declaring:

'Sometimes, Mr Kidwell, I think of us going out the road – down the lane from the house and off out the road to gather pussy foots.'

The solicitor turned from the window. His countenance bore a look of puzzlement as he stroked his chin.

'Gather what, Pat?' he said.

'Pussy foots,' his client replied, 'that's what she used to call them.'

A smile of recognition began to manifest itself on the young solicitor's face.

'Ah yes!' he declared. 'The catkins! The catkins of spring! Didn't I used to collect the little buggers myself!'

Pat lowered his head as though in disappointment.

'Don't call them that, Mr Kidwell,' Pat pleaded softly, 'I'd rather you didn't call them that.'

Mr Kidwell knitted his brow.

'Call them what, Pat?' he asked earnestly. 'I didn't mean to –'

'Little buggers,' Pat replied. 'It's just that it sounds – well, disrespectful, quite frankly.'

The solicitor's cheek jerked.

'What?' he gasped, then modified his tone to say: 'Ha ha. Yes. Why, of course it does! I'm sorry, Pat.'

He rested his hand on his client's shoulder.

'I shouldn't have,' he murmured apologetically.

'It's all right, Mr Kidwell,' Pat said, 'I suppose it doesn't matter now anyway. Now that the memories are gone. And the house.'

The solicitor was seated once more.

'No matter, Pat!' he said, donning his spectacles. 'I'm sure you'll be able to start a new life for yourself. Start all over again with the money you get from Mr McGaw. Who's going to be pleased, don't you think? Now that everything's worked out so well. Don't you think he'll be pleased, Pat?'

It was as though Pat's face had been mysteriously trans-mogrified into a blank sheet of canvas. As, without a single, identifiable trace of emotion, he responded: 'Yes. I'm quite sure he'll be delighted, Mr Kidwell.'

There can be no doubt but that the chill wind which appeared to disturb the shutters of the solicitor's office window found its source in the arctic stillness that formed the 'inscape' of the gaze of Pat McNab.

*

At three o'clock exactly the following day, the telephone rang in the McNab residence and Pat removed the receiver from its cradle to hear a familiar voice uttering the following words in clearly delighted tones: 'Absolutely over the moon, Pat! Sure the likes of you and me shouldn't be fighting! Didn't your mother know my mother! Jasus, Pat, this is great news! And do you know what – just for being so dacent, I'm prepared to throw in another fifty pound! What do you think of that, eh? Another fifty pound – free gratis and for nothing! What do you say, Pat? And I'll bring it over this very evening – along with a bottle of the best phwishkey! What do you say to that, eh?'

In an unconscious gesture, Pat pressed his closed fist to his lips and coughed in a polite, almost feminine manner. 'Bring the sheep too,' he said into the receiver.

There was a pause.

'What was that, Pat?' was Bat McGaw's reply.

'Bring the sheep too, will you, Mr McGaw?' continued Pat softly. 'You might as well move in now as later. Sure, aren't the sheds lying there idle? Especially the big haybarn.'

For a fraction of a second, Bat stammered a little.

'What's that, Pat?' he said. 'Are you sure? God, but that's very decent of you! And it just so happens I had two dozen come in this morning on the lorry! Thanks, Pat, I will! I'll bring them over and the pair of us will drink till cockcrow! Just like old pals! Like frigging old pals, you and me, Pat! Yes sir!'

Not a flicker of emotion registered itself on the face of Pat McNab as into the receiver he piped: 'Like old pals, Mr McGaw! Old frigging pals!'

'Gluck now! You're a good one!' cried Bat chirpily as he hung up and the phone went dead.

'Gluck now,' repeated Pat to himself, impassively, his eyes fixed on the small hills outside the window, 'gluck now, indeed! Gluck gluck gluck!'

*

There was a considerable amount of shovelling and cleaning up to be done in the haybarn but, paradoxically, rather than putting Pat in bad humour and causing him to mutter: 'Ah to hell with this!' or 'Will I ever be bloody well finished here!' it had the effect of actually putting him in quite good humour. Indeed he was smiling as he swept up all the dirt and dust and manure, wiping his brow and saying: 'Have to make sure we have the place nice and tidy for them, don't we? After all, there was nobody liked sheep better than me and Mammy. We used to look in at them every day when we'd be coming home from gathering the pussy foots!'

As he swept vigorously, every so often he would pause and lean his elbow on the top of the brush, staring out the window as if it were a small television, upon which was displayed the image of Pat's younger self in his green knitted v-neck pullover and long short trousers, standing holding his Mammy's hand as they stared in through the wire fence at the sheep masticating quietly in the afternoon sunshine.

'Look, Ma!' Pat heard his younger self say. 'Aren't they lovely? And the way they look at you!'

He shivered a little as he saw his mother smile.

'Yes, Pat,' she said, squeezing his fingers a little, 'they are.'

She squeezed his fingers again and crinkled up her nose a little.

'Little fluffies!' she said.

Pat giggled and placed his hand over his mouth.

'Little fluffies!' he repeated. 'Ha ha!'

*

At about half-past three, all the work was done and Pat set about preparing himself inside the house, polishing drinking glasses, plumping armchair cushions and what have you. When he had everything completed to his satisfaction, he decided to treat himself to a little nip of Bols Advocaat and sat beneath the window puffing on a cigarette and reflecting on recent developments. On the third puff of his cigarette, he was disconcerted by a small wave of melancholy which, unexpectedly, swept past within him, and he found himself thinking: 'It's a pity all the same that it had to be spoiled. That he had to go and spoil it. Because that seems to be what has happened really, isn't it? O, you can say: "No. No, it isn't" – and the pain you have in your stomach all the time now doesn't come from everything being spoiled, it comes from something else. You can say it and keep on saying it but that's only because you want it to be true. Simply because that's the way you want it to be.'

A wisp of smoke grew from each of Pat's nostrils as he contemplated the glowing tip of his cigarette and said, softly: 'But it isn't true. And deep down, you know it. You know it more than anything in the world.'

*

The sun was still coming through the branches of the trees like small shoals of arrows as Bat McGaw flapped along the road in his wellingtons, guiding his flock of sheep with a straight and narrow switch and, tucked under his arm, a brown paper bag containing his ten-ounce bottle of 'phwishkey'. As he came past the creamery, Bat had never been in better form. 'Haw haw!' he chortled to himself. 'What a laugh! God, but there's some suckers about this town! Hup back! Ho! Whoa, boy! Get out of there, you effing bockedy melt of a God's own hoor, you!'

The chastened blackface ewe withdrew from the culvert and complied.

Bat was chuffed to find Pat awaiting him at the back gate leading into his garden.

'Ah, there you are, Bat,' he said, extending his hand. 'Isn't it great to see such a stretch in the evenings?'

Bat had not expected such a display of friendliness and was somewhat flattered.

'It is indeed, Pat,' he replied brightly. 'It's always glad I am to see the back of that winter.'

'Oh now, don't be talking!' replied Pat, taking his hands out of his pockets and rubbing them together. 'Anyhow – let's get these little fellows into the pens over here in the haybarn so yourself and myself can sit down and have a right old natter!'

'Right you be, Pat!' answered Bat, now rubbing *his* hands together.

It took only twenty-five minutes before the rump of the last of the sheep disappeared through the door and into the haybarn. Bat wiped some perspiration from his forehead with the back of his hand and said:

'There we are now! Last leg of mutton all present and correct! Now you and me can have ourselfs a dacent drink – dealing man to dealing man! What do you say, Pat?'

Pat grinned from ear to ear.

'A drop of drink for the dealing man!'

Bat shook his head and a merry light danced inside his eyes.

'Now you're talking, Pat!' he said, as he started walking. 'Now you're fecking well talking!'

*

It was now 3 a.m. and Bat was still talking. Pat stared at his own reflection floating across the surface of the brandy and felt a cold shudder ripple through him. He sighed. And what the cause of that sigh was, he knew. Because somehow deep inside, he had been hoping that – irrationally, perhaps – Bat McGaw would defy expectations and turn out not to be like himself at all. That he and Pat would indeed enjoy a 'dacent drink' and that, somehow – inexplicably – thereby would be revealed a side of him so kind and sweet that Pat would no longer have to contemplate proceeding with the course of action he had decided upon. And that, against all the odds, he and his new neighbour would be – triumphantly! – confirmed friends for life.

'But it was not to be,' murmured Pat to himself as he raised his glass to his lips. 'Sadly.'

'Eh?' roared Bat McGaw, reaching for another bottle of Macardles Ale and elevating a corduroy-clad buttock to expel some wind. 'Phwat did ye say, Pat?'

*

It was well past five o'clock in the morning when a smiling, bleary-eyed Bat McGaw announced that it was his intention to leave and make for home. Or: 'Hit the high road!' as he termed it. 'You're the besht man in the town!' he declared, as he made his way towards the hallway. 'I really enjoyed the ayvenin'!'

A flicker of a smile passed across Pat's face.

'Yes, Bat,' he replied, 'so did I.'

The visitor raised his hand in the air as he negotiated his way past a basket of turf adjacent to the door.

'I'll see you soon again then, Pat!' he cried.

The figure standing in the centre of the kitchen staring after him might have been a statue carved from the most ungiving stone. A figure thinking: 'But it isn't going to happen like that, is it, Bat? That's not the way it's going to happen. You've gone and made sure of that, haven't you?'

*

There was no mistaking the distaste etched on the countenance of Pat McNab as he recalled some snippets from the earlier part of the night's conversation. He considered momentarily that Bat McGaw might benefit from a rechristening. That it might be apposite for his mother to bear him along to the nearest baptismal font and have the clergyman announce: 'I now rechristen you: The Living Mouth.'

'For that's what the experience of the past six hours has

been like,' reflected Pat, 'trapped in a kitchen with a mouth that cannot close. The biggest mouth in human history.'

An acidic taste came into Pat's own mouth then as he saw Bat McGaw join his hands behind his head and continue – as no doubt he would have even if the room had been entirely empty – 'You see the ting is – the ting is, Pat! Bat McGaw had to pull himself up by his bootstraps, you see! You know what we used to have to ate, Pat? Gristle! That's what the Mam used to give us! Gristle sandwiches! What do you think of that? Sure I'll bet you even your mad mother didn't give you the like of that! Oops, sorry, Pat! But no, seriously – I'll bet she didn't! Even the worst raving old witch would have more respect for her children than to give them that! But that's what we got! Gristle sandwiches – and glad to get them! Pat – is there any more drink?'

Which there had been, Pat reflected, and plenty of it. He had seen to that. Crates and crates of it, Mr McGaw, he had said. As much Macardles Ale as you can drink.

'I suppose you'll be sorry to go all the same! To layve the house, I mane!' Pat's visitor had observed somewhere in the vicinity of 4 a.m. 'Them auld memories you were talking about, eh?'

'That's right,' Pat had smiled thinly, 'me and my memories, Bat!'

'Oh now – memories! Don't be talking!'

Bat shook his head and wiped his strawberry-like nose with his forearm.

'They'd break your heart, wouldn't they?' replied Pat, with the sick feeling coming into his stomach again.

Bat McGaw slapped the arm of the chair with his open palm.

'Oh indeed and they would surely! They would surely, Pat!'

'Every time I think of her singing,' said Pat. With a wistful tone in his voice.

'A good singer, was she, Pat?' asked Bat McGaw. 'Was she a good singer?'

Pat nodded.

'The best in the town, Bat. No matter what lies they tell. Sing till she'd drop, my mother.'

Bat McGaw winked appreciatively and took a slug of his ale.

'God love her, Pat. And what did she sing?'

'She sang this,' Pat replied as he made his way to the radiogram, 'she sang this, so she did.'

A melody that was the colour of liquid amber filled the room and Bat McGaw closed his eyes as he digested the words:

'Old flames can't hold a candle to you
No one can light up the night like you do
Flickering embers of love I've known one or two
But old flames can't hold a candle to you.'

'Boys oh dear,' said Bat, 'man but that's a good one. Memories! Don't be talking to me! I mind the time me and the brother were above in Mullingar—!'

It was as though the words which followed were carried across some vast cowboy-style canyon or valley.

What disappointed Pat most was that McGaw was incapable of seeing that he was trying to tell him something. Hoping against hope that he might understand him, even the tiniest little bit, so that he might be spared the inevitable. For, in truth, Pat had no real appetite for what it was he knew he had to do, and would have dearly welcomed a way out. But McGaw ensured that it became impossible. Eventually, making it hopelessly, irrevocably impossible. By uttering the following words:

'Ah would you shut up out of that, Pat, you and your effing memories! You'd put a body astray in the head! Have ye any more drink there, have ye?'

With this statement – the veracity of which was, in its

directness, a blessed relief – the die was cast. It was as though, as Pat sat there in those last few dwindling hours before dawn, he was staring across the room at what was nothing other than a suppurating pile of human mud.

*

There can be little denying that the bleats of the poor unfortunate animals were anything but pitiful. They were cries for assistance which would have melted the hardest of hearts. And, in truth, Pat's heart as he stood there with his hands in his pockets observing the enormous sweeping sheet of orange flame that wound its way upwards from the haybarn and into the pale clear light of dawn, can only be accurately described by the use of the following word – broken. Or, as Bat McGaw might have said – 'bruk!' Bruk in any number of places, with the only sentence audible to his ears now that which repeated: 'If only somehow it could have been different. If only it could have been some other way!'

The blackened corpse of Bat McGaw lay prone and silent now as the last roof beam fell to earth. Had he been alive, his choking words might have been, as he leaned over to inspect a hay-filled crate, 'There's no fecking drink here! Pat, you said there was drink here – and there's not! There's not a drop! Just what is going on – *aaaaagh!*'

But that would have been all, for the cascade of Esso Blue paraffin which descended upon him within some seconds after that ended all further rumination, as did the flaring ball of heat that enveloped him.

*

Some days later, Pat was reclining in the chimney corner, sipping a 'phwishkey' and thinking over the events of recent times. There actually was a fire inside the grate this time, some turf briquettes surrounded by interlocking twists of the *Irish Independent* and the *Irish Press*. He sipped his Bols Advocaat and smiled as he thought of what his mother had said about the fire in the old days: 'If you stare into it for long enough, Pat, you can see all sorts of things.' One night she had cried out, stabbing the air with her index finger: 'Look, Pat! A ship! There's a ship gone by just now!' Pat chuckled a little. Chuckled because he remembered nearly having wet himself when she had said it, it took him by surprise so much! But, as always, she had been right. Why, you could see things in there you had never dreamed of, or even begun to dream of! Sometimes it could seem for all the world like a tiny dancing carnival! One night, long after 'the end', as Pat had come to think of it, he could have sworn he saw a tiny shrunken Bat McGaw large (well, not quite) as life and waving out from the flames as if to say: 'Hey, Pat! It's me! No hard feelings! I understand your predicament!' And did that make Pat Mc-Nab happy! It was as if Bat was now making a supreme effort to ensure that relations between them could be as they ought to have been all along! A Bat transformed who would sit in the armchair swirling his ale in his glass and with big eyes say, warm as toast: 'There was no one like her, you know – your mother. The yarns she used to tell. There was no one in town could touch her when it came to telling the stories. Isn't that right, Pat?'

'I have great memories of her, Bat,' Pat heard himself say – smiling all over his face – 'I have to say it.'

And what beautiful memories he and Bat would have had between them, if it could ever have been possible! The pair of them sitting below in Sullivan's, Timmy leaning across the counter and placing his hand under his chin, beaming: 'Well, guv! What's it gonna be tonight?' as Pat and Bat fought wildly over who was going to pay for the drink.

*

Except that it hadn't transpired that way. 'Has it?' sighed Pat softly as he rose. And it hadn't. For Bat McGaw was gone, as a consequence of his actions nothing more now than some piece of forgotten, smoking charcoal.

*

Early morning was spreading its gossamer cloak across the countryside. The field was startlingly empty as Pat leaned over the five-barred gate. There was some dew on the ground and thistles, he noted. Far off a truck drove away. 'Probably to Belfast or somewhere like that,' Pat sighed. He was relieved now that it was all over. Of course, he knew what they'd say. That it was all his fault, entirely and unequivocally the fault of Pat McNab. That Bat McGaw had never harmed a soul in his life and that only by coming into contact with Pat could anything have . . .

*

Which was exactly the intimation which came his way that very night while he was sitting enjoying a quiet glass of Guinness at the counter in Sullivan's. A large dairy farmer by the name of O'Coyle, Pat remembered, had edged his way close to him along the stools and eventually intoned darkly behind his newspaper (the *Evening Herald*): 'Take care some night would something happen to you, as happened to poor Bat McGaw.'

It had been pure coincidence that the packet of Maguire and Patterson Friendly matches was placed directly in front of Pat. But fortunate, for within seconds O'Coyle's entire *Evening Herald* was engulfed in flames.

'Jesus! Jesus Christ Almighty!' cried O'Coyle, haplessly endeavouring to extinguish the fire with his sports coat. 'Jesus, Mary and Joseph, did you see that! Did youse see what he did?'

*

But Pat was already gone, the comments either way on the incident of as much concern to him as the cowpat some days later which was directly beside his foot as he hummed softly to himself, industriously snipping the catkins directly above him and neatly arranging them in a plastic basin which he had brought along for that specific purpose. Yes, the comments were indeed of little consequence to him, he thought, as he bundled the snipped furry sticks in his arms. And why might that be? Why, because he lived in Town of Liars, of course! Town where behind every curtain sits someone waiting to make up lies about you, certainly, but most of all about your mother!

*

Pat stood back and cleaned his hands with a cloth. The catkins looked nice in the vase on the mantelpiece, he thought. He knew his mother would have liked that. He felt proud.

Which indeed he was. And as he sat watching the 'ballerinas of flame' perform so beautifully for him in the grate that night, Pat could not help but think, as his eyes moved even closer to the heart of the fire, that one of those tender creatures bore the face of his own mother, pale and wan and serene, smiling out at him – waving, indeed! – as she parted her lips and whispered: 'Memories, Pat love. Remember the memories!' and as her kiss a little butterfly became, in that instant he saw them both, together in the open field, now waltzing hand in hand, high in the trees the birds ecstatic in the catkins, as she ruffled his hair and tweaked his cheek, her eyes all moist but twinkling as she cried: 'Pat, alanna! Pat, our little tune!' and the countryside rang out – like a living thing! – as to the horizon now they danced, two exultant tiny figures singing:

'Old flames can't hold a candle to you
No one can light up the night like you do
Flickering embers of love I've known one or two
But old flames can't hold a candle to you.'

CHAPTER FOUR

South of the Border

South of the Border

South of the border down Mexico way
That's where I fell in love when stars above came out to play
And now as I wander, my thoughts ever stray
South of the border down Mexico way.

Chorus
Then she sighed as she whispered 'Mañana'
Never dreamed that we were parting
And I lied as I whispered 'Mañana'
For our tomorrow never came.

South of the border I rode back one day
There in a veil of white by candlelight she knelt to pray
The mission bells told me that I couldn't stay
South of the border down Mexico way.

Ay! Ay! Ay! – – – Ay! Ay! Ay! Ay!

THERE ARE A LOT OF PEOPLE who would claim in mitigation where Pat's case is concerned, whether perhaps out of a sense of responsibility towards him, or because of their long-term acquaintanceship with his family (some of them would have been, without doubt, witnesses to Captain McNab's departure on that fateful day in 1964 when he slung his kitbag across his shoulder and snapped back at his dumbstruck wife: 'I'm off now, you old shitebag, and don't think that I'll be back, for I won't — you can rest assured of that!'), that he had, in the circumstances, demonstrated remarkable degrees of resource-fulness. Indeed, there might even be among them some pre-pared to advance even more extraordinary claims, along the lines of Pat's 'being an example to all of us' what with his being so good as he actually was, considering all he had been through. 'He could, for example,' they might be likely to assert, 'have ended up taking drugs, for example. The least we can allow him is that much credit.' Their desire to do well by Pat and extend towards him some measure of empathy and affection, however small, is of course, wholly creditable. For Pat, unquestionably, had many good sides to him, and was not like some of the foul miscreants who clog up our courts and prisons today and merit punishments far greater than are ever likely to be administered. But neither was he — and I am not about to suggest any such thing — a saint, by any manner of means. He was more than capable — quite apart from what we might term his 'under the laurel bush' and 'digging' episodes — of transgressing in many other ways. Transgressions which, sadly – and this is not intended as any slight upon the magnanimous people to whom I have earlier referred (i.e. Pat's would-be benefactors) – included the consumption of drugs. Nevertheless, it is true, albeit coming about quite by accident, and at the insistence of others who ought to have had more sense.

The 'chain of events' saw its beginning one heady summer's afternoon when Pat found himself standing by the roadside clutching under his arm a very large book which had as its subject philosophy, perception and the modulating nature of reality. It was upon such matters he was ruminating, vigorously stroking his chin, when he looked up to descry two figures emerging from the shimmering wall of heat haze that had established itself between Maguire's Gap and the creamery wall close to the dip in the road. It did not take him very long to realize that he was being approached by some colleagues he had not laid eyes upon since primary school and who were already gesticulating in his direction.

'Hey look! There's Pat McNab!' cried Pasty McGookin, with the sun's light lancing off the golden buckle of his tattered Wrangler denim trousers.

'Hey!' cried his companion Honky McCool, breaking into a trot which was hampered slightly by the flapping of his knitted Mexican poncho and the awkwardness of his flip-flop sandals.

But nonetheless, within seconds they were standing by Pat's side.

'That's not a bad day now, lads,' Pat said cheerily. 'There's a power of heat in that sun yonder.'

'There is!' agreed Pasty. 'Do you mind if we sit beside you, Pat? We're frigged with the walking, aren't we, Honky?'

Honky nodded and gave a small, somewhat distracted wave.

'Be my guest,' Pat said, moving over a little. 'It's a free country.'

'Aye!' chirped Pasty, leaping up onto the fence. 'For who'd buy it?'

'What's that, Pasty?' said Pat, taken a little aback by Pasty's forthrightness. For it has to be remembered that he had not seen him in quite a long time. Since they had both been in fourth class under the tutelage of Master Halpin, in fact.

Pasty shook his head and continued.

'Look, Pat – all I'm saying is it's doing my head in! Every morning – up the town, round by Pick and Choose, past McCormack's and then into Sullivan's. I just can't take any more of it, man!'

'Any more of what, Pasty?' replied Pat, a trifle awkwardly.

A rolled-up cigarette mysteriously appeared in the bowl of Pasty's hand and almost magically transferred itself to the aperture between his lips as he continued.

'I'm getting out of this town, Pat! I'm blowing it! And to hell with them! You talk to Honky here about it! You talk to the Man, Pat! He'll tell you some stories! He'll put some pictures in your head!'

'Pictures in my head?' Pat replied – almost squeaked, in fact.

Pasty nodded with some passion.

'You talk to him! He'll show you some things! Take you places you never even dreamt of going to. Right, Honky?'

It was just then Pat noticed how exhausted Honky's eyes seemed, and how long it actually appeared to take for him to make a response of any kind to what might be construed as the simplest of questions. But he thought nothing of it and nodded as Pasty continued:

'Fact is, Pat – we only got one chance. You got one chance – don't blow it, man! Right, Honky?'

Honky nodded and, surprisingly, Pat reflected, replied in an accent that was not contiguous with the locality. It seemed quite Spanish, in fact.

'There ees no choice. Ees up to you, my frien'.'

'You see! I told you!' cried Pasty, slapping Pat firmly on the back. 'Honky's the main man! It'll only cost you ten pound!'

Pat frowned.

'What will?' he asked. 'What'll cost me ten pound?'

Pasty contemplated the toes of his brown, once-polished cowboy boots with the faded engravings.

'Ah, Pat – come on now!' he went on. 'Honky didn't come all the way from Mexico for you to start that.'

Pat stared at the small hill of his index-finger knuckle.

'Mexico?' he said.

Pasty's eyes lit up.

'Aye!' he cried. 'Wasn't he out there this past ten years? Where the hell do you think he got it? Ah, come on now, Pat!'

'Got it? Got what?' asked Pat, puzzled.

Without warning, Pasty leaped down from his position on the fence, taking his companion by the arm.

'Ah, to hell with this!' he said. 'Come on, Honky! We're wasting our time here!'

He jabbed a contemptuous finger at Pat's philosophy book and looked askance at its owner.

'And you supposed to be the big-time philosopher!'

Honky fixed him with a sleepy stare through the tiny vents that were his eyes.

'The doors enclose the darkness, my frien',' he remarked, with a touch of sadness.

'Come on – let us go,' said Pasty, taking a step forward.

'No! Don't go!' cried Pat suddenly.

Pasty's reply was firm and instantaneous.

'Well, you needn't think you're getting it for nothing!' he said.

Pat remained puzzled by this.

'But getting what, Pasty?' he wished to know.

'Show him, Honky,' was the denim-clad youth's response.

There was something weighted, epochal, about Honky's movements as his knitted poncho moved slowly back and out from under it appeared his bronzed hand, within it located a small, glistening ball of silver paper.

'The Sacred Root of the Samalayuca tribe,' he intoned gravely. 'Ees peyote. The key to ze truth so many aeons past. You want or no?'

Pat hesitated.

'Well, I . . .' he began.

Pasty tugged impatiently at a tassel on his poncho.

'Come on, Honky!' he barked. 'We've work to do! We might as well be pegging stones in bogholes as talking to McNab!'

'No!' cried Pat.

'Ten pound, then!' snapped Pasty. 'And no more of this acting the tube!'

His stare was unequivocal. Behind him, two giant legs of sunlight pirouetted in main street.

'Come on in here behind this tree,' said Pasty.

*

Quite what transpired in those few short moments afterwards, Pat was never to be quite certain. All he knew was that, as the peyote was passed around – with a pronounced sense of devotion, he observed – a curious quality entered the pupils of both Pasty's and Honky's eyes – and, Pat presumed, his own. Its nature could be described, perhaps, as possessing a 'zinging' aspect. Whatever the terminology employed to encapsulate its character and texture, what was undeniable was the effect it had, particularly upon Honky, who had now begun to flail his arms and dart directionlessly about the undergrowth, crying: 'We got to get out of here! Ees the crimson-headed devil with horns which gorge your eyes! El Conjeito Verde! El Conjeito Verde! Hasta luego! Hasta luego!'

His companion responded instantly, if a little anxiously.

'Stop it, Honky!' he cried. 'Don't go starting that crack again!'

'He devours our insides with the tongue of a lizard!' replied Honky. '*Y Diablos!*'

Pasty squeezed the flesh of his colleague's arm fiercely.

'Stop it – do you hear me?' he insisted, turning to Pat and saying: 'He started this before, you know!'

Pat responded with a smile. He thought of it as 'shot through' with the sun's translucent light.

'The sky,' he reflected, 'it's peachy pink.'

But Pasty did not hear Pat's remark, for his irritation with his companion had deepened, and he was now, despite himself, shouting at him.

'Stop it!' he cried. 'Stop it or I'll burst you! Do you hear me, Honky?'

Suddenly the red and cream nose of a travelling vehicle declared itself, making its way out of the thick-slabbed fence of heat. Taking himself totally by surprise, Pat found himself crying, in tones of near-childlike stridency: 'Here comes the bus!'

'Thanks be to Jesus!' cried Honky, a mysterious calm descending upon him.

*

'That'll be ninety pee, lads,' said the driver, whistling a small, abstracted tune.

Some seconds elapsed before Pat succeeded in locating the words for which he had been striving. 'Where are you going?' he said.

His smile – in its sheer breadth – seemed to indicate that it was the happiest, sunniest day of his life. But it was not enough to distract him from the unmistakable alteration in the driver's tone and the shadowy shrinkage of his expression beneath the polished slopes of his eye-covering peak.

'We're crossing the border in half an hour,' he said.

Pat gasped.

'Half an hour?' he said.

He could barely release the words.

'Next stop Ballingad!' called the driver as the doors flapped closed and Pat took his seat, followed by Honky, who continued to kiss the driver's hand and repeat: 'Thanks be to Jesus! Drive me pliss through doorways of dreams, thees place I wann' go! You, my friend, I shall treasure for ever, beautiful driver of buses!'

'Isn't he an awful man,' chirped Pasty to a woman who was staring at them, simultaneously endeavouring to determine beyond doubt the presence of his hand in the pocket of his denim jacket, 'him and the auld chat of him!'

*

The woman had a furry collar on her coat and two bags (plastic) full of shopping on the floor beside her. There was a smell of musty perfume off her as she turned (it seemed to take her an age) and said:

'Where are you headed, boys?'

Pat noted with interest the dimensions of her lips. They appeared to suit themselves in this regard, expanding and retracting at will, at once exhibiting a tubrous quality and rendering themselves insignificant and threadlike almost to the point of invisibility.

Pasty split a match and inserted it beneath a nicotine-stained fingernail.

'We're headed south,' he said, in a sonorous voice that seemed to disappear beneath the floor of the bus and re-emerge from its grease-caked interior.

The woman nodded and gripped the top of the seat.

'Are youse going to see friends or are youse just going for the drive?'

'Oh, just for the—' began Pasty as Honky's stabbing arm shot up in front of him and he cried:

'Pasty! You got to help me, please! The demon has horns of gleaming jade! Help me, my brother! You got to! No! No, please! He eats my soul for breakfast!'

Pasty slapped him firmly on the back of the head and silence descended once again. Pasty smiled and said:

'It must be the hot weather. Ha ha,' he explained to the woman.

She shrugged good-naturedly.

'Sure, pass no remarks! My Paddy is far worse!' she said, referring, presumably, to her life-partner of thirty-five years.

*

Pat did not expect to encounter trees that possessed a greenness so intense that you would almost require Polaroid sunglasses to look upon them. But this was exactly what happened as they found themselves disembarking. Neither did he consider that a bird of multicoloured plumage would address him in perfect English – albeit with an accent – from the irregular topography of a nearby elm bough, but this too is what transpired. As for the sounds all about him – why, it was as though sound itself had become colour and was sparkling, melting in the manner of a child's crayon subjected to the intense heat of a flaring match. Pat nodded as far away the driver's voice rang out: 'There now, boys! Youse are on your own now!'

Within seconds the vehicle was but as an infinitesimal cream and red speck swallowed up by an engulfing cloud of dust. Somewhere close by there was the sound of a whistling wind. 'Strange,' thought Pat, 'as up until this moment, it has been quite a sunny, pleasant day.'

Pat noted that each of his companions was moving as if each had been somehow inexplicably fitted with standard issue deep-sea diving boots, the movements of their other limbs slow and languid also, but not, it could be deemed, without a lyricism that was both strange and beautiful.

'I been here before, you know. Ees true. Everyzink I see, I know. I been here before. You got to believe me. La Canara Prohibida!'

There was a taste in Pat's mouth now which he had not noticed before. Something about it reminded him of aniseed balls but that was not quite right either. 'No – it's more like—' he began, as he perceived his smile extending across the expanse of his face, reminding him of the taut elastic of his catapult as a boy. 'But no,' he reflected, 'in fact I think it reminds me more of—'

But he never finished the sentence for just then the dust cleared and he found himself being curiously contemplated by three gravel-pecking chickens (of the Rhode Island Red breed) against the blocky unblemished whiteness of two adobe haciendas where a sweaty mustang bided its time. As a bitter cry echoed out across the muggy, bell-ringing afternoon.

'I don't like it,' remarked Pasty, taking a hesitant step backwards, 'I don't like it at all. I think maybe we got off at the wrong stop.'

But it was too late. Already a door had been flung open and a girl with hair black as a raven's wing was stumbling forward, shoeless, into the space between the mustang and the dry-snouted glumness of the village pump. 'Come back here!' reverberated a snarl, and to their horror they looked up to see a grimacing, shirtless soldier, making for the wasteground with the gold buttons of his red tunic gleaming in the sun, hurling himself forward to expertly bring down the unfortunate female in a rugby tackle (or whatever the Mexican equivalent was – for he was surely Mexican) and skidding along with her until they came to a clamorous halt at the foot of the pump which instantaneously released a parasol-spume of water, the clarity of which Pat had never, he reflected, in his whole life, encountered before. The moustachioed generalissimo rose stoutly to his feet.

'Now you geef me what I ask for, you beesh, you expect

me to eat food wheesh you geef to peegs? I cut off both your legs and eat *zem*!'

The sound of him chastising her was heartbreaking in the silence. But when he shoved her head – brutally, for there was no other word for it – beneath the cascading waters, Pat could no longer contain himself.

'Hey, you! You!' he cried. 'Leave her alone!'

'No! No, Pat!' cautioned Pasty, but it was already too late.

The teeth of the generalissimo introduced themselves one by one to the visitors, as if to declare themselves proud of their time-ravaged blackness and crumbling tombstone aspect. A string of saliva swung vinelike from his lips before being snapped and flung disdainfully into the high vermilion of the afternoon.

'Hey! Hey!' the generalissimo sneered. 'Eet is no good, my friend, ze gringo! Hey hey – you very stupid man!'

Pat stabbed the air with his finger as if it were a gun.

'I said – leave her alone!' he demanded anew.

'No, Pat!' cried Pasty, alarmed.

'Back off!' called Pat to the stricken, dust-coated girl. 'Stay well back, Missus! You hear?'

The generalissimo wiped his chops and, abstractedly buttoning his dust-mapped jacket, began to advance upon Pat. The chickens continued to poke unconcerned at the spot where the large round shadow of his head fell.

'You know, my frien', you make a very beeg mistake! Liver of yours – ees my dinner!'

His bloated lips parted to reveal the ramshackle military formations of his devastated molars as he said: 'You theenk he make a beeg mistake, your frien'? Me – I theenk so. This type of mistake – make you sad, ever you make it. You know?'

How it could have been, Pat did not know but it definitely did seem as though time had stopped at that precise moment in the village square. And the generalissimo seemed as unconcerned about it as the fly which now made its way across the dunes of his cheeks in the direction of the swing bridge of his expansive nose.

'One time,' he continued at last, 'one time a gringo he get off ze bus. O yes – he know all ze answers. Ze generalissimo, he try to reason weeth heem. Say: "My frien' – maybe you get back on ze bus, hey? We forget all zees and everyone ees happy." But he don't do that – and now he is at ze bottom of ze well.'

It was the first time Pat had noticed the well. Despite the fact that it was bluntly situated directly in the middle of the village. It also seemed that it was the first time Honky's eyes had fallen upon it. As was the case with Pasty's. And the generalissimo's. Everyone was looking at the well.

'Hey! You wan' look at ze well, huh?' growled the generalissimo, simultaneously reaching in his boot and producing with a tiny flash a squat object which, it became clear, was in fact a derringer pistol. But he hadn't reckoned on Pat, who had already flung himself to the ground and was rolling at a furious speed towards the Winchester rifle which lay at an angle to the water bucket lying on its side in the sand.

'No!' cried Pasty instinctively as the lethally levelled Winchester spat fire.

By the time Pat had stopped firing there were three holes in the military man's body, one above his heart, one directly in the centre of his abdomen and one right between his eyes. The sound of feet was that of Pasty and Honky running up.

'Oh no! Oh, Jesus! Pat! Now look what you've gone and done!' cried Pasty almost hysterically.

He knelt down and felt the generalissimo's pulse. There was no doubt about it – there was none. He was dead.

'He shot the fuzz! Man, you did it! You shot the fuzz!' repeated Honky, turning around in circles. 'I can't believe my eyes what you done!'

There was an edge to Pasty's voice as he faced Pat and said gravely: 'You've done it now! You've really gone and done it now, McNab!'

Pat was about to explain himself but before he could, a raven-haired beauty had taken hold of his arm and was rendering any such explications redundant by her fury.

'He was a pig!' she snapped. 'A thousand deaths for a man like him who is a pig! Beside him, a pig is as a king!'

Then, to Pat:

'For ever I will love you for what you do for me and my village!'

She kissed him eight times on the face and said her name was Rosa.

'I work in the cantina,' she said. 'Come with me.'

Pat found himself taking her hand and stumbling forwards as he called back to his companions: 'Come on, boys!'

Reluctantly – in desperation, perhaps – they meekly complied.

*

As they approached Rosa's house, Pat considered for a split second the resemblance the elderly, silver-haired man standing by the window bore – his sallow skin aside – to Hoss McGinnity who often sang in Sullivan's on Saturdays. Considered for a moment, indeed, the likelihood of them being actually one and the same man. But he knew this to be impossible, and was simply a consequence of the melody oft favoured by the rotund Hoss which was now, quite coincidentally, pouring with equal fervour from a complete stranger's throat, lighting up the tranquil Mexican sky with its beautifully painted word pictures of a love harboured for a beautiful woman:

'*South of the border down Mexico way.*
That's where I fell in love when stars above came out to play
And now as I wander, my thoughts ever stray
South of the border down Mexico way!'

'Papa!' cried Rosa as they all came crashing in the door. The tenderness displayed on the face of the old, linen-clad (linen that had seen better days, indeed, particularly the torn, knee-length pantalette-type things that hung melancholically about his knees) man was wonderful to behold.

'Rosa!' he cried, and ran to his daughter. They embraced.

'How can I ever thank you?' he said to his visitors when Rosa explained all that had happened.

*

Some hours later, as they shared stories around a table in the cantina, Rosa smiling (particularly at Pat) whilst she ferried tin plates of blackened beans back and forth, not to mention endless carafes of red wine, Papa – anxiously – fixed them with a darkening stare as he said: 'So now you see the generalissimo's brother will be looking everywhere for you. He is a crazy man! One hundred children he kill! To him it is as nothing! But first – Rosa, my darling!'

Without warning, the old man clicked his fingers and his daughter was in his arms as they spun wildly about the floor. Then, in each of their hands, a castanet – where had they come from? What wonderful people they were! Pat reflected as once more the song it echoed in the Mexican night now hot as peppers:

'She was a picture in old Spanish lace
Just for a tender while I kissed the smile upon her face
For it was "Fiesta" and we were so gay
South of the border down Mexico way.'

Pat flushed ever so slightly as suddenly he looked down and Rosa was in his lap, the entropic tendrils of her hair seeming to reach to every corner of the room. The old man smiled and said: 'She is a good girl, my Rosa, no? The generalissimo – he want her for himself! And his brother! And the whole village! But you, gringo, my friend! You can have her – if you can rid us of this curse!'

The pain in Rosa's eyes was almost heartbreaking as she stroked Pat's face and said: 'Can you do that? Can you do that for us, please?'

Inexplicably, Pasty and Honky beamed with pride although they hadn't been addressed at all.

*

As expected, a large crowd had gathered outside the small mission hall where the funeral of the generalissimo was to take place. It was now the afternoon of the following day and the sun was burning even hotter like a rotating ball making a hole in the middle of the sky. A low harmonium played, its sombre note causing the generalissimo's brother to hopelessly break down over the coffin. The padre's condolences were all to no avail, as he was rebuffed by a stray blow to the side of the head. In time, the howls became unbearable for all present. As did the risk of being beaten to a pulp by some crazed soldier – such as the one now punching and kicking wildly all about him as he roared, in a cascade of spit-beads: 'Who has done this to my brother I love more than my mother? I will feed his miserable heart to the vultures! Agh! Agh!'

Quite how many people were assaulted, jostled or forced to endure temporary chokings at the hands of this man it is impossible to say. There could be no question but that it reached double figures before at last he fell to his knees, all the while kissing the padre's ring as he vowed unspeakable vengeance.

*

All this was witnessed by the triumvirate which comprised Pat McNab, Pasty McGookin and Honky McCool, as regards whose reactions it could be said that they possessed a certain homogeneity. Best described by Pasty's words which were: 'That's it! That's enough! We're getting out of here! Tomorrow! Right, Pat?'

Reluctantly, Pat lowered his head and assented.

'We don't have any choice,' he said.

Honky's voice was almost a high-pitched squeal.

'Freakzoids! Freakzoids! This is not Mehico! This is some crazy place! *La Canara Prohibida!*'

'We'll leave first thing in the morning,' Pat said.

Even the evanescent image of a weeping Rosa which fleetingly passed across his mind was not enough to weaken the resolve of Pat McNab.

*

They spent the night in a disused adobe not far from the cantina and outside the relentless tramp of marching feet persisted in the suffocating, eye-darting darkness. Beneath the window where they lay crouched upon the floor, Honky cried: 'I can't stand this! Why did we have to come here?'

This was more than Pasty could bear.

'What are you talking about?' he snapped. 'Who was it was always going on about Mexico – how great it was!'

Honky blanched to the roots.

'What are you talking about? This isn't Mexico! This is a filthy mad world of crazy men and she-devils!'

'Well, it's your fault we came here! It was you brought us! You did it, so stop complaining!'

'I did it?' rasped Honky. 'Did what? I was only supposed to get the bus to Dundalk! That was all I was supposed to do!'

'Aye, well why didn't you get it then instead of coming round with all your big talk about Mexico!'

'All my big talk about Mexico! It was you started that, with your "Tell me about Mexico! Tell me about Mexico, Honky! I'd love to go!" You wouldn't shut up about Mexico!'

Something broke within Pat.

'Lads!' he demanded. 'Will you shut up!'

Pasty scowled and hid his eyes behind the eave of his right hand.

'Shut up! Who's talking to you!'

'Ah, I can't stand this! I'm fed up with it! I can't – do you hear me? I'm getting out of here!' Honky snarled.

He leaped to his feet and stomped across the floor as Pat cried after him: 'No, Honky! Wait!'

But he was already gone, the sad, badly assembled door swinging forlornly behind him.

*

Rosa looked even more beautiful than ever, thought Pat (he had come to say goodbye to her), as Luis – a friend of her father's with a coal-black *mucca* – strummed a guitar in the corner of the small, cramped but once – before all this had happened – so happy house. Luis, drawing his thumb down along the strings, released a melody so lonesome it almost brought tears to her father's eyes as he sat by the window, his lips miming:

> *Then she smiled as she whispered 'Mañana'*
> *Never dreaming that we were parting*
> *Then I lied as I whispered 'Mañana'*
> *For our tomorrow never came.*

The closing words were 'South of the border – I rode back one day' but they were never uttered for just at the moment when they were about to be delivered, the door splintered open and Ramon (a serving boy who often assisted Rosa in the cantina) fell in crying: 'Papa! Papa! Ees the gringo! Captured, he . . . !'

'Honky!' gasped Pat, leaping to his feet.

Pasty slapped his forehead with a despairing palm.

*

The pale light of dawn was beginning to enfold the sleeping town, the depth of Honky's plight dawning on Pat and Pasty as through the broken slats of the stables they observed the tragedy of his fate being played out before their very eyes. The metal toecaps of his boots barely touched the straw on the floor as the generalissimo's brother (Manchita) slowly tightened the noose of the rope about his neck. General Manchita (for he too was a general) suddenly turned and slammed open the stable door, crying out to the chicken-peppered silence: 'You out there? You listen to me! Or perhaps you don' have ears! You have until zis time tomorrow to give yourselfs up! If you don't – zen you die weeth heem!'

The door shot closed as he returned to the wan (clearly broken) Honky and placed the handle of his curled bullwhip close to his Adam's apple.

'So, my frien'? You comfortable? Ha ha!' he sneered.

His indulgent whinnies, thought Pat as his affronted knuckles paled, might have been the braying of an ass, hopelessly oblivious, as many of its compatriots, of the nature and depth of its self-deluding foolishness.

*

Some hours later, Pat was in an awful state as he paced the floor of the cantina crying: 'This is our fault, Pasty! Ours! It'll be all our fault if he dies!'

'Why did he have to bring us here in the first place!' was Pasty's response. 'If he hadn't done that! Pat, I don't care! I'm getting out of here first thing tomorrow!'

'But he'll be dead by then! Stop it, Pasty! You hear me? Stop that talk and stop it now, I tell you!'

'The first bus that comes along I'm climbing on it! I'm getting on it, Pat, and I'm going!'

Nobody was more shocked than Pat McNab to hear the sharp, uncompromising crack his palm made across the vivid red cheek of Pasty McGookin's face.

'Stop it now, Pasty! Stop it, I said!'

The effect on Pasty was quite remarkable. Clearly he had been suffering from hysteria. He calmed down almost instantaneously.

'I'm sorry, Pat,' he said placidly, adding: 'But what are we going to do? Honky's going to die!'

*

The sharp hammer-clips pounding in the nails of the makeshift scaffold which was at that moment being constructed in the village square copper-fastened Pasty's anguished appraisal. Perhaps it was merciful that this was the only intimation of Honky's worsening situation that was to be visited upon them that night; for anything approaching the true facts might well have proved unbearable.

*

The leather thong binding Honky's wrists as he writhed upon the badly constructed kitchen chair formed red fleshy bangles that seemed to be on fire. His tormentors had not seen fit to permit him so much as a glass of water in over twelve hours. All they granted him were two cigarettes which were inserted in each nostril and various lung-choking taunts of 'Ha ha ha! What seems to be ze problem? You don' smoke?' which they delivered raucously whilst wiping their eyes and supporting each other physically lest they should fall to the ground in a state of incapacitation from sheer mirth.

Their laughter as Honky passed out yet again was as a coil of wire barbed and rusted that sprang from their crusted lips and leaped through a hole in the roof to cruelly encircle the entire town.

*

The chimes which emanated from the burnished gold timepiece were oddly haunting as Pat, despondent now in a way he'd never been before in his life, contemplated the faded oval watercolour portrait within. He felt Rosa's bronzed hand touching his shoulder tenderly. 'Who is it, Pat?' she softly enquired. He put his hand on hers. 'It's Mammy,' he said and slowly clasped it shut. Rosa nodded. She understood. Then, smoothing her skirt behind her, she lowered her head then raised it and stared with glittering eyes in the direction of the heat-hung horizon. 'He was a beautiful man, your friend Honky,' she said. 'Ees hard to believe that in the morning he will be little more than a corpse!'

The distorted image of Pat's face in the back of the engraved timepiece seemed to mirror the inner state of his soul. In the instant she spoke, he saw himself and Pasty entirely attired in black, hands crossed over their stomachs where they held their silk top hats, as the coffin waited by the open grave and deep male voices rang out, singing:

Let's all gather at the river
The beautiful the beautiful river
Let's all gather at the river
That flows from the throne of The Lord.'

Pat gripped the timepiece, his fingers entirely closed around it, and sprang suddenly to his feet.

'No!' he cried out. 'We can't allow it to happen! We can't allow it, you hear me?'

Rosa's eyes shone with both helplessness and the promise of promise. She spread her nut-brown hands.

'But what can we do, Señor Pat?' she pleaded heartbreakingly. 'What can we do?'

*

It was night. The moon shone. It looked like a sickly eye. The military had occupied the cantina and inside what could be said to be chaos reigned. Bare-chested soldiers waved carafes of wine and flung their unpolished boots on the tables. Aloft upon a decrepit podium, as he had been instructed, a

trembling guitarist frantically sought the minor chords that
would save his life, to accompany the words:

'Out in the west Texas town of El Paso
I fell in love with a Mexican girl
Night-time would find me in Rosa's cantina
Music would play and Felina would whirl!

A tawny scarf of jettisoned wine curvaceously wound itself
around his neck as the air was rent with cries of: 'H'ho! Good
man! The man from Dundalk every time! Sing up, you boy
you!'

The musician complied.

'Blacker than night were the eyes of Felina
Wicked and evil while casting her spell.'

Sadly his efforts were not to satisfy everybody and a
number of bullets embedded themselves in the wall behind
him, one or two of them extracting troubling music from a
bronze gourd suspended upon the wall, another skimming off
the gleaming face of a frying pan. But such discordant notes
were heard no longer when a vision emerged out of the all-
encompassing cloud of dust and transformed the foul-smelling
cantina, the belching, recumbent military men finding themselves in the presence of what were surely two of the most
beautiful girls in all Mexico. It was only a matter of moments
– they had barely time to get to the bar – before Pat (for it
was indeed he – clad from head to toe in Rosa's finest
cheesecloth and linen) found himself the focus of attention
which perhaps only females well versed in certain skills might
accept as a matter of course. Initially – not without some
justification, surely – Pat was intimidated – not to say mortally
embarrassed – by his pigtails – but gradually, with the assistance of some wine, and the flawless tutelage of Rosa – who
seemed to be having a whale of a time! – he found himself
slowly graduating towards a sense of ease. 'Heh heh heh!'
snarled the soldier as he gripped Pat by the thigh and rolled

his eyes. 'Now now!' chirped Pat, tapping him playfully on the nose with his index finger.

'*My love was deep for this Mexican maiden*
I was in love but in vain I could tell.'

The faint echoes of the song drifted out through the open door of the cantina into the clammy cicada-chirping night to the scaffold where Honky awaited his fate, the remnants of one of his cigarettes still clogging up his nose. Deep within his nostril, a tiny speck of tobacco taunted him to within an inch of his sanity, vibrating, teasing—

Had the fly not arrived he might have found it within him to withstand such torment. But this was too much.

'Get away!' he cried (his wrists were handcuffed). 'Get away, you bastard! Get away!'

He prayed for whatever strength remained within him not to desert him, but it was all to no avail. His head fell upon his chest as though it had been increased to five times its normal weight.

Then – inexplicably! – the insect's tentative perambulations ceased! Just as it reached the corner of his left eyelid. A sensation close to euphoria took hold of Honky. But then the little bastard began walking all over again.

*

The soldier lying prostrate on the bed was feeling very pleased with himself. Rarely did señoritas such as this find their way into the barracks, he reflected. And even more rarely still did they see fit to apply themselves with such fervour to the tickling of – not to mention the cooing into – ears of underling soldiers such as he whose station was fated never to rise above the rank of mere custodian.

'You señoritas!' he cried with the near-whoop of a young boy who has captured a bee in a jar. 'You want to be my friends? You want to be my friends? Eh – heh – heh – heh!'

115

Rosa fluttered her black eyelashes.

'You are the nicest man in the whole Mexican army!' she said.

'Hey, señorita – you know zomezing?' he said. 'I like you! You like some more wine?'

The pigmentation of the soldier's cheeks attained an even more incredulously incandescent crimson. His plump hand huzza'ed uncertainly.

'Come! More wine, señorita!' he gurgled.

And Pat – skipping with tiny little steps – obliged.

*

Some thirty-five minutes later, the atmosphere in the room had metamorphosed utterly, as Rosa, holding up her skirt, spat viciously into the face of the snoring soldier. 'You son of a pig!' she hissed as Pat nodded. 'You son of a pig of the mother of a thousand pigs! Raper of virgins! Thiever of sacred objects! Passer of counterfeit money! Armed robber of banks, citizens and post offices! Bigamist! Kidnapper! Receiver of stolen goods! Murderer! Enciter of prostitution! Perjurer!'

'Come, Rosa! We must not waste our time!' said Pat, turning towards the window and flinging his pigtails and skirt onto the bed.

*

The cellar was cold and musty and you could have sliced the darkness with a knife, peeled off large chunks of it. The beads of sweat shone on Pat's face as, breathlessly, he shifted a large wooden packing case marked upon which the word DYNA-MITE was stencilled in black.

'How are you getting on, Rosa?' he whispered.

Rosa nodded as, with all her strength, she placed all the weight of her body behind the Gatling gun and heaved with all her might.

'I am doing fine, Señor Pat,' she replied.

'Soon it will be all over,' was the answer she received from Pat McNab.

*

In the village square, all was quiet. Even the chickens had turned in, and were lying on their sides dead to the world. It seemed like the quietest town in all of Mexico. Until a huge explosion set the sky aflame and the air was filled with the sound of rearing horses. Back in the barracks, the duped soldier leaped awake and reached, furiously for his pistol, crying: '*Caramba!*' and pulling on his boots.

What followed was not chaos but something beyond that state for which perhaps there is no word which can truly encapsulate the wild and random – not to say terrifying – nature of what was to subsequently transpire. As, within seconds, the entire village had been transformed from a quiet sleeping town of seeming tranquillity to a living, pulsing sheet of flame which might well have served as a depiction of hell itself. And through which the boots of disorientated military now thundered as officers hoarsely cried: 'No! Not that way! This way, you fools!'

Until the heart-stopping words: 'Look out! Ees a trap!' reached their ears.

'You beesh!' cried the generalissimo's brother, breaking ranks and attempting what can only be described as a valiant attack, circumscribing huge arcs all about him with a sword, only to be almost riven entirely from head to foot by the hail of bullets which Rosa – to Pat's delight (for he was jumping up and down, clapping his hands along with Pasty – as though his protracted wearing of pigtails had finally taken their giddy toll) – had ebulliently released from the Gatling gun expertly positioned by her on the hill overlooking the square. In what seemed hardly the wink of an eye, the dusty main street was piled high with lead-perforated bodies. But just then the church bell pealed and Rosa looked at Pat and Pat looked at

117

Rosa and frantically it dawned on them what they had completely forgotten in their obsessive thirst for retribution.

'Honky!' barked Pat, as he flung a rifle at Pasty and gestured towards Rosa. 'Let's go!' he snapped.

*

It was heartbreaking to see Honky, a broken man now, being led like the meekest of lambs to the scaffold and the white bag being placed over his head. The gulp he emitted as the rope's knot was tightened against his throat seemed to carry for miles across the landscape. The padre stepped back and began to read. Each word seemed black as molasses. Until at last the clergyman cut a cross into the air and said: 'May the Lord have mercy on your immortal soul.' Even now, the ungiving sentry who had mercilessly taunted him throughout his incarceration in the stable could not see fit to let the moment pass. 'Perhaps you like one last request before you die – a cigarette, no? But zen I forgot – you don' smoke! Eh – heh – heh!' he sneered through stripped, tobacco-stained teeth.

With all the strength he could muster, from behind the flapping bag (it tickled his nostrils), Honky croaked: 'Someday I'll get even with you, you dying-looking son of a hoor!'

It was to be sooner than Honky could have dreamed as a single shot rang out and instantly severed the rope in two. Who can say whether it was the sudden sense of elation which consumed Honky that was responsible for what happened next or whether its occurrence was inevitable? Regardless, within a matter of seconds, the acerbic sentry was lying on his back and the bag-less Honky was squatting astride him administering a liberal number of headbutts to the face, raising his head to apply yet another, to his further delight deciphering the familiar figures of his old friends Pat and Pasty (and now Rosa) coming tearing down the road in a buckboard. Hard and fast close by the raised platform of the scaffold, Pat cried: 'Jump, Honky!' An instruction with which he more than competently complied to the delight of all, and to which their unrestrained applause amply testified.

*

Rarely had such a feeling of wellbeing enfolded the village as a moist-eyed Papa quieted the throng and exultantly declared: 'Now you see what happens when you get off your knees, my peoples!'

In that instant, a community once clad only in cotton and ragged linen trousers considered themselves now tailored after the manner of kings. In each set of eyes shone two tiny, triumphant suns.

'Never again must we tolerate such evil in our midst!' said Papa.

A thousand cheers rose up and myriad trouser legs fluttered as, without the need of further instruction, the what had once been considered 'rabble' united as one and charged off in the direction of the military barracks, Papa shaking his head as he took his daughter's hand, clearing his throat as he began his famous song anew: 'South of the border, down Mexico way—'

*

The farewell was scheduled to take place in the cantina and once more almost the entire village had deigned to attend. Obviously, because of the size of the building, many had to have admission refused and were heartbroken as a consequence, falling to their knees and weeping in the village square, some even hurling themselves to certain death in the penumbral, engulfing blackness of the well. Pat, Pasty and Honky smiled warmly as the time came for Papa to rise to his feet. They were stuffed to the gills and had eaten so many portions of blackened beans and enchiladas they felt certain they would burst.

'And now – a toast to our three friends from – where ees?'
'Gullytown,' said Pasty. 'It's only fifty mile!'

Papa smiled and held his glass aloft.

'To all in Gullytown!' he smiled and placed his hand across his chest, beginning to sing:

'*The mission bell told me that I couldn't stay*
South of the border down Mexico way!'

As all – with one voice – rapturously affirmed:

'*Aye – yi yi yi! Aye – yi yi yi!*'

*

Behind Rosa, a small insect did its best to climb up the intense, if precarious, green slope of a palm tree frond. She lowered her head and gave her nails full attention. How beautiful they were, Pat thought . . .

'Will you ever come back to me, Pat?' she whispered, a glimmering moistness in her eyes.

'You know I will, Rosa,' Pat replied.

The insect was almost halfway there. His valour could almost have served as a metaphor for –

'Perhaps one day,' Pat added. 'One day – who knows?'

Rosa moved closer to him and touched his upper arm tenderly. Her kiss on his cheek was something that he would remember for a long, long time.

'Goodbye, Pat,' she said.

He took her in his arms and looked into her eyes.

'Adios, my Rosa,' he said, 'I'll never forget you.'

Just then, a familiar sound reached his ears and they looked up to see Papa, standing by the open window, inside the adobe hacienda, his declamatory gestures accompanying a now-familiar melody:

'*South of the border down Mexico way!*
That's where I fell in love when stars above came out to play . . .'

Rosa reddened a little then leaned in to Pat's chest as a burst of affectionate chuckling took hold of her.

*

There wasn't a sound as Pat McNab, Honky McCool and Pasty McGookin stood by the side of the road. In actual fact, there is only some measure of truth in that statement, for there was one, in fact, albeit of a very low, almost inaudible nature. And possessing an eerie, whistling quality. Pat shivered and ran his hands along his arms in a stroking, reassuring motion. Across from them, beside the stiff, if abbreviated sentinel of the village pump, three chickens poked industriously in the dust. Above the door of a dilapidated roadside house, a sign which had once borne the name (its letters long since faded) The Border Bar creaked yearningly with each occasional gust of wind that happened to come floating by. Honky looked at Pat from beneath hooded eyes and gave an involuntary shiver. As if to emphasize his discomfort, the faint peal of a mission bell tinkled skeletally behind the clouds.

'This is some weird place, man,' he said.

As if to answer him, out of the heat haze, over the cusp of the road, what appeared as the bright red distorted grin of some indeterminate medieval creature approached but seemed to take an age, as though in one spot inexplicably restrained by wavering lines of heat, only to suddenly and without warning leap forward, its metal jaws springing open to reveal the shadowy occupants within.

'It's the bus!' gasped Pat incredulously. 'At last!'

Honky drew his bead-sewn arm across his forehead as Pasty steadied himself against the fence.

'Thank God for that!' he said.

*

There was a broad smile on Pat McNab's face as he fingered out the coins to the bluff and genial driver. But one which faded as a small hand of ice slipped its fingers with a gentle firmness about the base of his spine as he – replacing his change in his pocket – turned to gaze upon the swarthy form of an oily figure some way down the aisle seats, adorned with a two-pronged, satin-black moustache. His heart leaped. '*The generalissimo!*' he gasped.

'Not a bad day now!' called the swarthy individual, returning to his *Irish Independent*. 'Great to see it!'

A similar experience was – although Pat was entirely unaware of it – being undergone by Honky who, having taken his seat, found himself positioned directly behind the despised sentry! Who, flipping the packet open, had then turned to him, chirping shamelessly as he brandished the cigarettes beneath Honky's nose, 'A smoke, perhaps?'

*

There have been many arguments down through the years as to the nature of being and the benefits or otherwise of such substances as might substantially alter what we commonly refer to as empirical, tangible 'reality'.

Quite what Pasty and Honky's views on such subjects were, Pat was never to truly ascertain for they never discussed them or indeed 'that day' again. All that can be said is that had anyone been walking past on the road that day as the driver released the brake and called out: 'Ballingad next stop!' and had they investigated what they took to be the flap of a passing bird or a stray deposited dropping from that same creature, they would have found that the source of the dull, unexpected sound was nothing other than the glancing blow made by a small twisted root of peyote plant which the horrified Honky had cast from him (in a fit of anxiety occasioned by his recognition of 'the sentry') into the abyss of the dying summer evening through the open window of the bus.

*

But somehow, in its own special way, it was an experience never to be absolutely entirely forgotten by Pat McNab and there were nights when he would find himself sitting alone in Sullivan's Select Bar poring over a drab pint of Guinness, listening to Hoss McGinnity as he gesticulated wildly – yet again! – making his way through his rendition of 'South of the Border', when, once more, he would see himself proudly attired in a crimson cummerbund, Rosa smiling by his side as she inclined her head ever so slightly just a little to avoid the confetti, Papa shedding a tear and shaking his head, as off they drove (in a battered truck – who cared! – past the hitching post, the gospel hall, the well – and the chickens, of course!) into the dust and the shimmering heat, between them now a love to which none could compare, one which he knew was destined to be his for ever, as bright and clear and infinite as the waters of the Rio Grande itself.

CHAPTER FIVE

Courting in the Kitchen

Courting in the Kitchen

Come single belle and beau to me now pay attention
Don't ever fall in love, 'tis the divil's own invention
For once I fell in love, with a maiden so bewitching
Miss Henrietta Bell, down in Captain Kelly's kitchen.

Chorus
Tooraloora loo, a tooraloora laddy
Tooraloora loo, a tooraloora laddy.

At the age of seventeen I was 'prenticed to a grocer
Not far from Stephen's Green where Miss Henry used to go, sir
Her manners were sublime, she set my heart a-twitching
And she invited me to a hooley in the kitchen.

Chorus

Next Sunday being the day we were to have the flare-up
I dressed myself quite gay and I frizzed and oiled my hair up
The Captain had no wife, faith, he had gone out fishing
So we kicked up high life down below stairs in the kitchen.

Chorus

Pat was lost in contemplation, staring in the window of the greengrocer's, wondering what he was going to have for his dinner when he heard a shout coming from the far side of the street. It was Bullock McCoy, already halfway across the road on his way over to Pat. How best to describe Bullock? A cattle-dealer-type man, perhaps, with exorbitantly large brown boots and a flat cap (extremely shiny) tilted on what was casually referred to locally as 'the Kildare side'. 'There you are, McNab!' exclaimed Bullock, landing as if with a thump beside Pat. 'I was just looking at the spuds, Bullock,' replied Pat, 'one pound fifty per stone. Isn't that very dear for spuds?'

'Never mind spuds,' said Bullock, 'where's your auntie? She was supposed to ring me.'

Pat stared at Bullock.

'Ring you?' he said. 'Is that what she said?'

Bullock nodded.

'Aye. Tuesday, she said. She said she'd ring Tuesday.'

Pat stroked his chin quizzically.

'And she never did?'

'No,' replied Bullock glumly, 'I waited the whole night.'

'That's a pity,' said Pat.

Bullock stared at a flattened sweet paper on the pavement for a moment, then raised his head.

'We were going to go to the hotel,' he said.

'Were you?' asked Pat.

'Aye. I was going to have a mate stew and she was going to have chicken curry. Did you ever hear of that?'

Pat nodded.

'Yes. She made it for me. They make it in America the whole time.'

A flicker of melancholy passed across Bullock's eyes.

'It was all planned,' he said. 'And then she never phoned.'

He broke off, then resumed.

'Maybe she hurt herself?'

Adding hopefully:

'Maybe she fell and hurt her leg?'

Pat shook his head.

'No,' he replied impassively, 'her leg's fine.'

'Is it?' Bullock asked eagerly. 'Then maybe you'll tell her to ring me?'

Pat pushed out his lower lip, thought for a moment and then said:

'No – I can't!'

There was a short pause and then he continued:

'She's gone, you see.'

The sound of Bullock swallowing was deadly audible in the early afternoon.

'Gone?' he said.

'Yes,' was Pat's reply. 'Gone back to America.'

The skin on Bullock's forehead tightened. He moved in closer to Pat.

'But that can't be!' he cried shrilly. 'I bought her a ring!'

Pat frowned and coughed a little.

'Bought her a ring?' he said.

'Aye!' cried Bullock. 'It cost me fifty pound!'

Pat considered for a moment or two and said:

'I could send it to her if you like . . .'

Bullock's face flushed a little and his voice acquired an almost falsetto quality.

'Send it to her?' he cried. 'You don't send rings! Who ever heard tell of sending rings? We were supposed to be engaged, for the love of Jasus! Pat – are you trying to cod me?'

128

Pat shook his head vigorously.

'No, Bullock,' he assured the larger man, 'she went yesterday, you see. She left a note. As a matter of fact, I think I might have it with me!'

Pat searched for some moments in the depths of his long black coat before eventually producing, among other things, a bottlecap bearing the inscription Time Ale, a chewing gum card of Ricky Nelson, a crushed packet of cigarettes, some pebbles and then eventually a piece of rolled-up paper. 'Look! Here it is!' he cried, as he unfolded the beautifully written note. The handwriting could only be described as copperplate.

Dear Pat; I am afraid I have to go home, it said.

The colour drained from Bullock's face as he devoured its contents anew. There was a weariness in his voice (as though he had, all along, feared the worst). 'Dear God!' he groaned mournfully. 'And the crack we had!'

Pat's smile spread right across his face as he placed his open palm on Bullock's shoulder and remarked wistfully: 'Oh indeed and I'm sure it was good now! I'll bet not many had crack like youse, Bullock! For she's a great girl! A great girl and no mistake!'

Bullock lowered his head sadly and took a last look at the crumpled piece of paper he held in his hand.

*

Pat's first experience of this 'crack', as Bullock termed it, was arriving home with the messages to find his Auntie Babbie (the 'living image of his mother', they said in the town), who had just the very day before arrived home from America, now dancing in and out of an arrangement of chairs as Bullock McCoy stood in the corner clutching at the lapel of his Sunday blazer and winking – a tad excessively – as though afflicted with a severe nervous tic. When it was remarked that Babbie was the 'living image' of Mrs McNab (i.e. Maimie, her sister) this was to ignore the large peroxide beehive hairstyle which

129

she possessed and the staggeringly vivid lime-green trouser (or 'pant') suit which appeared to be the most favoured item in her wardrobe. 'For she never seems to take it off,' thought Pat as he peered through the crack in the doorway – the dancers (for Bullock had now given himself wholeheartedly to the spirited manoeuvres) throughout remaining entirely oblivious of his presence. As they proceeded now to whirl about the perimeter of the kitchen with even greater abandon, Babbie, in that curiously hybrid speech which appears common to all those who have resided for any appreciable length of time in both Brooklyn and Gullytown, cried breathlessly: 'Phwee – oo! Ya wanna go round again, Bullock?' as her companion – his cheeks truly incandescent with excitement – replied: 'Hell! Why not!' in what, it has to be acknowledged, was a somewhat unconvincing echo of big city 'chutzpah'. Something which was not lost on Pat's Auntie Babbie at all as she tweaked his cheek and teased him about it, squealing (for how else could you describe it?), 'Listen to you!' before mimicking tiny mincing steps (her rear was enormous, Pat reflected, perhaps even four times the size of his mother's) and, skipping across the room to the hi-fi, upon which she placed a long-playing record so that the entire house rang out with the shrill song she piped and encouraged her partner to emulate:

'*Come single belle and beau, to me now pay attention*
Don't ever fall in love, 'tis the divil's own invention
For once I fell in love, with a maiden so bewitching
Miss Henrietta Bell, down in Captain Kelly's kitchen.
Tooraloora loo, ri – tooraloora laddy!
Toooraloora a laddy!'

The last thing Pat could remember was the sound of his aunt's high-pitched laughter as what appeared to be a four-legged technicoloured animal lost its balance and disappeared behind the settee.

*

There are some things which perhaps can never be adequately explained and surely this applies more than anything to certain aspects of human behaviour. Why the mere echo of laughter ought to have elicited from Pat the reaction which it did that day – and there can be no denying that it was one which can be best described as being of an edgy, tremulous and resentful nature – manifested most tangibly by the violence which he exacted upon the bagful of what were locally known as 'messages' (in effect, unremarkable foodstuffs), raining blow after blow down upon the unfortunate cloth receptacle until all that remained was a shapeless and broken mess of eggs, citrus fruits and sundry comestibles, from which coursed a variety of winding, intersecting rivers of thick liquid dribbling their way across the back door step. Aligned to this also was his disappearance to his room for a total of three days on end, throughout which he partook of no solids whatsoever, covering his ears with his hands and repeating, in the manner of an Eastern mystic applying himself to the incantation of a mantra, '*I don't hear anything! I don't hear anything!*' Something which he might well have continued to indulge himself in for a further quota of days had his aunt (in that intuitive manner Pat was to come to know extremely well in the weeks that followed – those glorious times before the 'stab in the back' as he came to privately think of it) not lowered her voice and whispered in a deliciously lusty timbre: 'If you come out, you might get a little surprise, Pat. You really might, you know! Oh yes!'

*

That Pat McNab should have found himself having the time of his life simply as a reward for vacating his room on request would probably come as a surprise to most people, considering he was at an age when most mature men would be busying themselves in their work and ensuring a good future for their children. Indeed, the very idea of a grown man lying back in the arms of a considerably ample woman who also happened to be his aunt would, in all likelihood, prove anathema to most people. But such was not the case with Pat McNab, and as he stared up into the big blue eyes of his mother's sister (they were so like hers), it was hard for him not to utter every second when she smiled the words: 'I love you, Aunt Babbie. I'm sorry I went bad for a while there.' As he knew he had, and felt thoroughly ashamed when she sniffled into her hankie: 'I was only having a little bit of fun with him, Pat, that's all. We used to play together in the square when we were kids, you see.'

From the moment his aunt made that declaration, Pat privately took a solemn vow that he would never again upset her, and afterwards rarely a day went by but she would wake up to find her favourite nephew standing at the bottom of the bed clad in his apron and removing the silver dome from a steamy plate of delicious food which he had prepared for her – a truly sumptuous repast of yummy breakfast, or 'brekkie' as she and Pat came to call it later. Except not only brekkie – but brekkie *American style*! Yes, any amount of maple-syrup-covered pancakes stacked as high as they would go and alongside them crispy rashers and eggs over easy and just about as many hash browns as you could get into your mouth. 'Do you like that, Auntie?' Pat would say as he sat there admiring her from the side of the bed. As inevitably she replied: 'I sure do, Patty!'

Which she sometimes called him. Patty! And oh boy did he like that! Especially when she put on her favourite record and gave him that special look, the look that said: 'Wouldja like a little dance, Patty?' and off they'd go spinning around the kitchen to the sound of the very same tune that had Bullock McCoy almost tumbling the wildcat with desire on that very first day.

*

There are undoubtedly those who would be of the opinion that the relationship in which Pat and his aunt found themselves increasingly involved was ill-fated from the start and that, regardless of the complications which the involvement of Bullock McCoy were to eventually present, it would have been difficult, to say the least, to envisage any situation which might have ensured any alternate conclusion. Certainly, this would appear to be true from the moment Babbie – lightheartedly, it has to be said, for that was (tragically, as it transpired) how she perceived their relationship – permitted Pat to join her beneath the covers of her bed – not only that, but cradle his head on her shoulder and coo: 'Go sleepies, my little fellow. Sleepies for Auntie Babs now!' Attaboy! If the clock were indeed to be turned back and perhaps some action of an interventionist nature be taken, to avoid the inexorable, subsequent catastrophe, then this clearly would have been the precise moment.

*

There is something particularly tragic about the fissure which eventually opened up between Pat and his aunt – for there can be little doubt that he adored the woman. Loved her, like Othello, beyond any reasonable expectation, a tendency which led him to place her upon a pedestal and, consequently, set in motion a train of events which would spell – for both of them, without doubt (and, in a peripheral sense, for Bullock McCoy) – tragedy destined to plunge them both into a pitch-black abyss of incalculable depth.

For what was unknown to Pat McNab was that his aunt, while outwardly an ordinary lime-green-suited mature lady returned from America, was secretly – and had been for a long time – a considerable amount more than that. It seems uncanny – almost absurd – that Pat did not note with some anxiety his aunt's peculiar attitude to the absence of his mother (perhaps he did, but feared to admit it to himself).

Professing herself, as she did, contented with his explanation of 'She's gone to England on business,' seeming relieved – gratified, even – when, after repeated questioning sessions, for the duration of which she would grip him by the shoulders and breathlessly insist: 'Where is she?' and 'Are you sure?' and 'Whereabouts?' she would eventually profess herself 'disappointed' but disposed towards 'endurance' when informed that her sister had been compelled to depart for England 'to tidy up a few bits and pieces and that'.

A journey which, to all who knew her – particularly her own blood kin, surely – must have defied logic, as Pat's mother had never been to England in her life, much less involved herself in commercial transactions within its shores. What is undoubtedly tragic – duplicitous though it might seem (but what of it, if it succeeded in precluding heartache!) – is Pat's failure to uncover earlier what might be described as '*Auntie Babbie's secret holdall*'. An item which only came to light after his aunt 'went away' and which contained within its remarkable interior what is best called '*The Truth About Auntie Babbie*'. As he clutched the videotapes in his hands, on that lachrymose day so long after all had turned to dust (they seemed to him as condensed blocks of sheer black badness) tears of regret and 'What might have been' coursed down the cheeks of Pat McNab. For deep within him, he still loved his auntie and would have done anything to turn back the accursed tide of history that had made her what she was.

*

And not what she had been on that beautiful spring day in 1945 when she had first arrived in Ellis Island, clad in a light blue frock and swinging her cardboard suitcase as she strode along Madison Avenue, thinking to herself: 'I'm Babbie Hawness! I sure am a long way from Gullytown now, guys!' already putting on an American accent to impress everyone. But Babbie Hawness was soon to discover just how difficult it could be impressing anyone in the City of New York in those dark, lacking-in-opportunity years of the forties. 'Hurry up and clear those tables! Your phony Noo Yoik accent don't impress me, Irish!'

was the caustic type of response she found she could expect for her efforts. That and 'Get yore ass in here and pull some beers!'

It should hardly come as any surprise that late into those New York nights she might sob herself to sleep and curse the day she ever saw fit to leave her beautiful, if impoverished, Gullytown. Where everyone looked out for you and where each evening all the neighbours gathered in the kitchen, shifted the dresser and cheered wildly as the local fiddlers and musicians played wheeling, skirt-lifting music to the sound of:

Next Sunday being the day we were to have the flare-up
I dressed myself quite gay and I frizzed and oiled my hair up
The Captain had no wife, faith, he had gone out fishing
So we kicked up high life down below stairs in the kitchen.
Tooralooraloo tooraloora laddy
Tooralooraloo tooraloora laddy!

Memories of which – although it was arguable if any such incidents had ever *actually* occurred, for the Hawnesses had never owned a dresser – drilled into Babbie's heart with the efficiency of a red-hot needle each and every night she left her miserable job in Sam's Grill on 1st and 1st (or 'Foist an Foist' as the perspiring oaf of a proprietor habitually referred to it). Added to that were the constant letters she received from her sister Maimie (How she hated her! But even more than ever now!) informing her of how she was 'walking out' with a beautiful Army Captain who had promised to marry her soon and install her in a big old Victorian house on the edge of Gullytown where they were to make a lovely home for themselves and tentatively take the first steps towards rearing a family. How Babbie Hawness loathed those letters! How many times she had scrunched them up and spat all over them there are not enough numbers in any mathematical system to quantify! On occasion, her animosity reached such extremes that she would shove open the window of the damp and dreary hostel and call out to the cacophonous, honking parade below: 'The bitch! She gets everything and I get nothing!'

Something which it would be very difficult to deny, for the sad facts are that right from the day she was born, Dodie Hawness (Pat's maternal grandmother) had hated Babbie with a passion. 'Little Miss Barbara,' she would often sneer, 'with her knickers around her ankles again. Well, you needn't think I'm pulling them up! Do it yourself, her ladyship with the snout!' Every attempt the small child that was Barbara Hawness made to elicit affection for herself would be met with a harsh rebuff. Her psychological body was bruised as if by repeated assaults of a resin-plastered boxing glove. Which may well be why eventually – inevitably, perhaps – a certain iron began to enter the soul of Babbie Hawness. It may be that, to employ the terminology current in this era of high technology and telecommunications, such data having been downloaded at an early age, there was a gloomy predictability about its appearance at a later stage. Or, as the Americans themselves might have it, reappearance *and then some*!

*

It all happened quite unexpectedly, on a grand Sunday morning in 1948, with events proceeding as per usual in the cafeteria, Sam taking absolutely no notice of people's feelings as he flapped his white cotton cloth and barked: 'You do dis!' and 'You do dat!' – absolutely astonished – for there is no other word for it – when the girl whom he had taken to be the meekest in the diner – the most cowed, certainly – turned on her heel, suddenly rasping at him with a tongue that protruded serpentlike from her lips: 'Why don't you go and do it yourself for a change, you big fat meaty-jawed Greek bastard!'

Suffice to say that there was no employment available to her at that particular establishment thenceforward. But, in the days that followed, what dignity and sense of purpose Babbie Hawness might have expected as a dividend came close to being almost totally eroded by the hardship she was forced to endure as a consequence of her actions. There were many times when thoughts of self-destruction surfaced ominously, looming ever so logical and sweetly inviting. When, sitting on her suitcase, staring at the mass of rigging and webbed steel that swept out across the Hudson, she would bury her wet face in her fists and cry: 'Oh God! How I wish I was dead!'

Which was, coincidentally, the very same sentiment she had just uttered in a small 42nd Street cafe ('Dino's') precisely at the moment she found herself being joined by a man with the softest and most soothing voice she had ever heard. He too, it transpired, had some relatives in Ireland, a McGurty from Dublin and some other acquaintances in Mayo. He was a film-maker, he informed her, and that was how it all began, with the touch of his olive, signet-ringed hand and the words: 'Would you like another milkshake, honey?'

*

The first time – long after it had all ended – Pat at last located within him the courage to insert one of the 'blocks of black sin' (which was not how they had appeared to Pat's eyes initially, of course, the salacious titles underneath cleverly obliterated by strategically placed stickers trumpeting the delights of *Babbie's Annual Vacation, National Geographic* and *Natural Wonders of the World!*) into the machine – expressly rented for the purpose – he appeared to take leave of his senses entirely. There can be little doubt but that he expected to encounter something which might distress him a little, but he had been thinking along the lines of animated holiday snaps with a former lover, perhaps, or footage, even, of her performing a little dance on a beach in a coloured swimsuit. But such apprehensions were as nothing, nothing to what met his eyes on that first, dark, curtain-drawn day of 1982. There was a certain innocence about how it all unfolded, with a simple cardboard title card displaying the words *Double D Productions Presents: Bun Crazy starring Babbie Bazoom*. But before three minutes had elapsed, the library in which Pat McNab had settled himself to 'investigate' or 'discover' something about the woman he had – even now, despite himself! – loved so much, had come to resemble the aftermath of Hiroshima. There were lampstands in the corner which had been snapped in two, cushions out of which the filling was now spilling like innards, as well as walls with jam and assorted dairy products smeared all over them. And, somewhere amid the devastation, the finger of a bent-over Pat McNab, sobbing his heart out in a way he remembered only from the earliest, most vulnerable years of his life. 'Why?' he cried helplessly, 'Why?' as he beat his fists against the arm of the rocking chair.

The sad fact is that up until that moment – effectively until the second in which he flicked the television button to 'on' – Pat McNab had been in a state of what the psychologists call 'delusionary incapacitation', and had succeeded in firmly convincing himself that there was a very strong possibility that he was about to witness educational documentaries regarding deserts, natural rock formations and wildebeests, as well as uplifting travelogues with humorous commentary from the early years of Babbie Hawness's sojourn in one of the world's most wondrous cities. It is no wonder, then, after *Bun Crazy* – a lighthearted piece of anodyne froth, really, to all intents and purposes, with little to offer, perhaps, apart from a sequence involving revolving silver tassels (which appeared to delight his aunt no end) – that *Domesto Sexo* (in which she indulged herself, willingly, with a superfluity of hirsute, leather-clad Hell's Angels, piling, in absurd numbers, through the various windows of what seemed – in comparison to that of the McNab household – an ultramodern kitchen, complete with every available mod con) should sock him brutally in the solar plexus with the solid persistence of a large demolition hammer.

*

The following morning, a large bonfire appeared at the back of Mrs McNab's house, delivering up a plume of smoke which could be observed from quite a distance. Smoke which had as its source, not the 'pile of old papers' which Pat had decided upon as his intended explanation should some inquisitive neighbours come dropping by, but a small holdall full of black plastic rectangles whose casings and titles bent and curled as melted toffee in the flames. Titles including *Martin and Olga*, *Depravos* and *Love Camp 11*. All of them, at various stages of her life, featuring the woman Pat had known as Babbie.

Babbie Hawness, aunt and lover.

Who, he now reflected, raking over the remains of the ashes, would now no longer be either, because she was gone. There seemed a parched, arid quality to his voice as he paused by the laurel bush on his return to the house and remarked to the carpet of leaves beneath his feet: 'Gone. And it breaks my heart.'

*

Which it did, and never a day went past afterwards when Pat would not sit by the window and look out thinking he could see her again as large as life, disembarking from the bus in her lime-green pantsuit, waving excitedly towards him and shouting: 'Pat! Is that you! I'm home!', upon her face not the slightest trace of the duplicity destined to pollute all that was good and wholesome and true. Except that he would be wrong about that too, wouldn't he? For it would be there all right. Invisible to his credulous eye, perhaps, but nonetheless present – a thick grey web of lies surreptitiously and cunningly concealed behind her skin. As it had been all along. 'Oh, hi Pat!' ought to have been the words she spoke that day. 'Hi Pat, honey! I'm home to cheat you out of house and home! Because I know your mother's gone!'

Or perhaps: 'I'm home to show you how to make a movie, Pat! Yeah! To show you all my Goddamned Hollywood tricks!'

'Yes, that would be a good one! Indeed, why don't you show me that one!' thought Pat as he sat there with a certain wilfulness in his eyes, '*How to make a darn good movie!* by Babbie Hawness!'

Just like the one herself and McCoy had made the time they thought he had remained overnight in Dublin. He had telephoned to say that he would be delayed because of an unexpected bus strike but had been fortunate enough to secure a lift home – quite unexpectedly! – in Tommy Caffrey's coal lorry. It would have been better had it never happened, however. For the music which reached his ears as he closed the door behind him, having prepared him for a scene of romantic farmhouse jollity – she often liked to dance alone, as herself and his mother had done when young girls long ago – might just as soon have reached in and removed his innards, the open door admitting the rollicking banjo and jaunty, jigging fiddle as two pistons – which later revealed themselves to be legs – scythed the air and large drops of perspiration smacked the kitchen table as Bullock McCoy (his voice *in excelsis* a high-pitched shriek) gave himself fully to the scratch-pocked tune:

'*Come single belle and beau, to me now pay attention*
Don't ever fall in love, 'tis the divil's own invention –'

before collapsing, with mammalian indecorum, upon the floor. As Pat's aunt, now turning pink, now deathly pale, faced the door and, raising herself upon one elbow, gasped when she saw him, chokingly declaring, in falsetto alarm: 'Pat!'

*

There is a dream which sometimes comes in the quiet gloom of what can only be the McNab house, in which a soft green light in the distance glows, revealing itself as a beautiful, high-cheeked woman who turns with open arms and calls a name. A name which belongs to a young boy who moves across that hayfield, eyes as bright as the sun that shines, before being swept at last into the welcoming arms of Babbie Hawness. But mostly there is another vision, one which is forever blurred and indistinct, with the infuriatingly low definition of poor-quality fifth-generation video, lost somewhere in the grey snow a single waving figure of familiar, peroxided amplitude pleading ceaselessly, but hopelessly, for mitigation.

And there is the final one, in which a lone figure in a long black coat stands by a dying fire watching a black rectangle of plastic burn until at last it melts away, and with it a browning, peeling sticker which names a song once beautiful.

*

Standing now with Pat outside the window of the green-grocer's, Bullock McCoy stared one last time at the piece of paper he held in his hand. There was no mistaking the words – for the message was clear and unequivocal. But it still made no sense. He clearly remembered Babbie saying she would telephone him on Tuesday so they would go to the hotel for a meal. 'I was to have mate,' he said to himself, 'and she was to have chicken curry.' He scratched his head and tried to understand it – to no avail. He turned and called after Pat: 'Maybe you could tell her to drop down to Sullivan's tonight – say around nine o'clock? I'll be in there having a few pints! She could have a Manhattan! She likes Manhattans, Pat!'

But Pat was already gone, Bullock's entreaties aching and orphaned. Lost in the smoky light of an evening which now too was dying, as though to emulate the performance of a perfumed creature so adored, beneath a laurel bush now finally at rest, eyes once full of hope freeze-framed beneath the stars.

CHAPTER SIX

Three Lovely Lassies
in Bannion

Three Lovely Lassies in Bannion

There are three lovely lassies in Bannion
Bannion, Bannion, Bannion
There are three lovely lassies in Bannion
And I am the best of them all
And I am the best of them all

For my father has forty white shillings
Shillings, shillings, shillings,
For my father has forty white shillings
And the grass of a goat and a cow
And the grass of a goat and a cow.

And my mother she says I can marry
Marry, marry, marry
And my mother she says I can marry
And she'll leave me her bed when she dies
And she'll leave me her bed when she dies.

And on next Sunday morning I'll meet him
Meet him, meet him, meet him
And on next Sunday morning I'll meet him
And I shall be dressed like a queen
And I shall be dressed like a queen.

THERE WERE, INDISPUTABLY, those in Gullytown who, as regards Pat's 'eccentric' behaviour, continued to vociferously express about it, generally along the lines of: 'Ah sure what would you expect?' and 'You're not going to tell me that you're surprised? Sure the whole effing tribe of them is mad!!' But such callous estimations must surely be unfair, for, if anything, Pat's valiant efforts to remain on what might be termed 'terra firma' were worthy only of praise. That forces outside his control conspired to make this impossible ought to be considered no fault of his. For how many times had he attempted to restrain himself in the face of yet another verbal barrage from his mother, with such words as 'Look at the cut of it! Small wonder the whole town's laughing at you!' or 'Go on to the dance, then, for all the luck you'll have at it, you dying-looking scarecrow on legs!' wearing down his resistance until, at last, his endurance came to an end? One single blow of the aluminium saucepan felled her, rendering her prone and silent at his feet, as some stuffed large, life-sized doll. No, there may indeed be many cases in the history of the world's criminology where the bard's chilling observation from the pages of *Macbeth* – '*I am in blood stepp'd in so far that, should I wade no more, returning were as tedious as go o'er*' – are more than applicable, but it should have been impossible to consider 'the McNab Affair' as one of them. For the plain truth is, readers, that Pat was simply one of life's unfortunates. And was such right from the very first day when he laid his dear beloved – and make no mistake about it, he did love her! – in the earth beneath the laurel bush

145

(even, on occasions, going so far as to disinter her and ferry her – again – into the 'warmth' so that it would be 'just like old times'), events moving with a rapidity that pitched a perfectly innocent young man into the very heart of a black and swirling cosmos, the inevitable outcome of which could only be – the inclusion of Pat McNab among the sinister pages of a tome entitled, perhaps, *Great Murderers and Sociopaths of History*.

But what great murderer wants simply to don RayBan shades, sing songs and imbibe a few social glasses of Macardles Ale in his local hostelry? What sociopath? None – for such a description of Pat McNab is surely as inaccurate as asserting that the town of Ballynahinch is situated in the middle of O'Connell Street. No, Pat was no sociopath and in the fullness of time the truth will emerge and the enormity of Pat's heart and generous nature be finally revealed to the world. As it might long ago have been but for the occurrence of what he himself liked to term 'saucepan day', and one or two other unfortunate 'days' which might be considered a direct consequence of it. Readers, who would have dreamt that the insignificant actions of some innocent young girls in a 'caring institution' literally miles from Gullytown would prove to have such a devastating effect on Pat's mental condition, eventually being almost single-handedly responsible for propelling him towards that state which would make the deaths of his old schoolmaster Butty Halpin and the officer of the law Sergeant Foley hopelessly inevitable? No one, but such did indeed prove to be the case. Ironically, upon a day when Pat found himself waking, stretching and observing to himself, in tones of buoyant optimism which he felt had been lost to him for ever: 'Today, Pat old bean, is the day when everything is going to be different. I just know it! I can feel it inside in my very bones!'

Such were the thoughts that continued to inhabit Pat's head as he pottered about downstairs, searching for tea bags and doing a hundred and one different things at once, humming to himself in the manner of one who has just scooped the jackpot in the Lotto. As, right at that very moment, in the St Teresa of Lisieux dormitory of a nurses' home over seventy-five miles away, a young girl whose complexion was soft as fresh flowers shot suddenly up in her apple-festooned nightie and cried aloud: 'It's today!'

'Today!' cried her friend Ann, also shooting up in bed.

'Today!' squealed Jo, already up and standing by the wardrobe with a toothbrush.

'Today! Today! Today's a holiday!' yelped Mary (the nightie-girl), clapping her hands together.

'Hooray!' the three friends cried in unison as the second bell began to ring.

How best to describe the three – 'friends for life!' as they classified themselves – now cleaning their teeth with bewilderingly synchronized precision? 'What a fabulous triumvirate of life-loving fluffies they make!' is a phrase which might come to mind, perhaps.

'Oh, I can't wait!' cried Mary.

'I've been waiting for this day all term!' gasped Jo.

'Me too!' nodded Ann.

'Why, the three of us are going to go absolutely mad!' they shrilly chirped in unison, as though a single person replete with three heads.

Some hours later, they found themselves sitting excitedly and expectantly at the back of the bus which was already nosing down the driveway as it negotiated its way towards the open road, in the mirror the driver rolling his eyes as he contemplated the riot of flared skirts and shoulder-draped lambswool cardigans, a sense of 'sisterhood' and 'house spirit', he could tell, being ostentatiously displayed before himself and the sad-eyed sheep and cows who bewilderingly contemplated the world outside.

'Come on, girls!' squealed Mary, tugging her cardy and conducting with a flourish, as her companions cleared their throats and began:

'*There are three lovely lassies in Bannion*
Bannion, Bannion, Bannion,
There are three lovely lassies in Bannion
And I am the best of them all!'

They had just drawn breath and were about to sally forth with zest into the second verse when, suddenly, Mary's extended hand froze in midair as she cried: 'Stop!'

'Huh?' replied Jo and Ann as with one voice.

The stark grey limestone structure rose up out of the trees, its crudely painted sign McNAB'S B&B (a recent innovation of the cash-strapped Pat's) visible from the road. A wry, mischievous smile began to play about Mary's lips. The mischievous Jo gave her a naughty push.

'You can't be serious!' she chuckled.

'Serious – you can't be!' chimed Ann.

'Stop the bus!' called Mary, cupping her hands for the purposes of amplification. The driver cast his eyes towards heaven as he chucked the handbrake.

'We want to make a stop here, drivey-pips!' cooed Mary as she undulated along the aisle, presently drawing a little line with her fingernail across the driver's forehead.

'You can't!' he protested. 'It's more than my job's worth!'

'If you don't,' countered Jo, 'we'll say you – did certain . . . bad things!'

'We'll say you . . .'

The colour drained from the busman's face.

'Whatever you say, Miss,' he agreed, shamefacedly.

'Tee hee!' laughed Jo as she tipped his cap down over his eyes and they began to disembark, cacophonous as a flock of starlings liberated from a cage.

Their laughter rippled out across the countryside now as they weaved their way through lines of cowpats, combating untamed foliage, the greater proportion of which seemed as clusters of living rhododendrons.

'Never mind her,' yelled Jo, 'she's mad!'

'Come on, O'Boyle!' yelped Mary. 'You silly cow!'

Some distance away, the driver's head rested wearily on the steering wheel, as, on the verge of virtual collapse, he murmured: 'It's the parents I feel sorry for,' before, inexplicably, rallying and crying: 'Get back, you bitches! I don't have to take this from you! Get back here, I say!'

But his cargo had all but vanished as had, within seconds, the bus, furiously speeding on down the road, piloted by a purplish-faced fifty-year-old who, in his own phrase, was no longer intending to 'effing well take it any more!'

Jo giggled, Ann giggled and Mary giggled as they went past a big hedge linking arms and singing:

'*For my father has forty white shillings*
Shillings, shillings, shillings,
For my father has forty white shillings
And the grass of a goat and a cow
And the grass of a goat and a cow.'

'Tee hee!' chirped Jo.

'Tee hee!' laughed Mary.

'Tee hee hee!' added Ann.

They stood – not a little curious – beneath the large red wooden B&B sign. It swung a little in the light wind. They considered the crudely painted inscription (it dribbled in quite a few places) beneath the towering twin letters.

'It says what?' said Mary.

'What?' said Jo.

'It says what?' said Mary.

'No girls,' laughed Ann, as they all squealed mirthfully together. 'It says – *No Girls!*'

'Oo!' chirped Mary.

'Ha ha!' laughed Jo.

'Ha ha!' squealed Mary as slowly the door opened and they

looked up to witness Pat McNab standing directly before them on the step. His hair was uncombed and he was attired in his long black coat. He found his cheeks flushing a deep crimson as he was formally addressed.

'We're on holiday, you see,' went on Jo in what were reasonably convincing 'adult' tones, 'we're on holiday—'

'And we thought—' interjected Jo.

'We thought we'd go on a little mystery tour—' said Ann.

'Hop on the bus,' said Mary.

'Hop off the bus,' smiled Jo.

'Hop hop hop,' laughed Ann.

'And go where we like!'

'Go anywhere we like!' said Mary.

'Just get on the bus and go!' chirped Ann.

'Whee!' laughed Jo.

'Who cares where it takes you?' Mary said.

'Not me!'

'Nor me!'

'Nor me!'

'*For we're three lovely lassies from Bannion!*' erupted Jo at the top of her voice, making little wriggly waves in the air with her fingers.

'Ssh!' chided Ann.

'I'm sorry, but like it says above on the sign – there's "no girls", you see,' stammered Pat, staring at the step, his face an even deeper shade of red than before.

There was a pause. During it, birds sang unremarkable melodies.

'Is that your final word, then?' asked Mary.

'I'm afraid it is,' said Pat, regretfully.

'Very well, then,' said Mary.

'McKenna! What are you on about?' hissed Jo behind her back, giving her a little push.

There was another pause. The birds were still singing. Mary cleared her throat. She smiled as she turned to Ann and

Jo and said: 'Look! Goodness gracious me! There's a button come loose on your coat!'

Pat swallowed, the saliva seeming to take an age to get past his tonsils.

'Loose?' he replied, pinpricks of sweat pushing through the flesh of his palms. He experienced the sensation of wearing gloves fashioned from barbed wire.

'Yes, loose!' continued Mary. 'It looks like it's about to fall off! Look, girls!'

Her two friends moved in closer as they inclined their heads the better to inspect said garment and its faulty accessory. Mary's fingers curled about the button as she began, ever so slowly, to rotate it clockwise in what might be considered a 'suggestive' fashion.

'Gosh! You're right, Mary!' exclaimed Jo in husky tones.

'It's about to fall off!' said Ann.

'Imagine what we could have done with it if we had known about it in time,' said Mary.

'We could have sewn it right back on!' said Ann.

'Right back on like it had never been off,' said Jo.

Mary fluttered her eyelashes and said to Pat:

'Because that's what we do, you know!'

Pat sneezed and a little silver drop of mucus appeared below his right nostril. Considerately, Mary turned away and said:

'We look after people!'

'We look after people!' said Jo.

'Take them under our wing!' said Ann.

'And look after them, right, girls?' said Mary.

'Like nobody else!' they cried in unison.

Mary coughed, placing the back of her hand delicately against her lips.

'If you have a cold—'

'Or heartburn,' said Ann.

'Or if your appendix burst,' said Jo.

'Or if you had cancer,' advised Mary.

'We'd look after you,' three voices said together.

'Just like we'd sew on a button,' Mary's soft voice told him.

'Or blacklead a range,' said Jo.

'Or iron your jammies,' said Mary.

'We'd do it,' said Ann.

'Because we're—' said Mary.

'Because we're—' said Jo.

'Because we're—' said Ann.

'*Three lovely lassies from*—' said Jo.

'Now, girlies – *ssh*!' chided Ann.

Mary's tongue touched the tip of her teeth as she said: 'So – where's your thread?'

A large bead of sweat splintered over Pat's left eyebrow.

'Where's your thread?' asked Jo.

'Where's your thread?' asked Ann.

Pat's lip trembled as three voices – husky, beguiling – seemed to call to him from far away.

'Where's your thread?' one said.

'Where's your thread?' another said.

'Where's your thread?' another said.

'Where's your thread?' another said.

As the final one, with a rapid flutter of eyelashes, shrilly remarked:

'Well then! We'll simply have to find it for him, won't we?'

*

Pat was sitting in his chair by the fire fingering his newly sewn button, feeling as though he were a pile of old clothes abandoned in this sparkling, recently feminized environment, redolent of air freshener and pot-pourri, as at his table three 'visitors' sipped from china teacups and nibbled on snack fingers, annihilating colleagues with great gusto.

'The cow, the cow – I never liked the cow!' hissed Ann, crinkling up her nose.

'Do you know she took my Pond's face cream and never gave it back!'

'Your Pond's?'

'Yes – my Pond's! And you know how much it costs!'

'For all the good it'll do her!'

'The cow!' they chimed as one.

'And the face!' snapped Mary, nibbling. 'Like a hen's hole upturned in rain! Oops! Sorry, Pat!'

'Don't mind her, Pat!' squealed Ann. 'Don't you know you can't bring her anywhere!'

'Ha ha,' squealed Jo.

'Ha ha!' yelped Mary.

'Ha ha,' laughed Pat, nervous and ill at ease, still twirling his button.

'Bring her nowhere!' cried Ann, pouring some more tea. 'I don't know why we took her with us at all!'

'No!' cried Mary. 'We should have left the trollop in St Ita's!'

'In St Ita's!'

'St Ita's!'

'Ah ha ha ha ha!'

'Long live St Ita's! Stupid Nurses' Home! More tea, Mary?'

But Mary wasn't listening, for between her intermittent ejaculations and the delicious taste of her snack fingers, she had become momentarily distracted by Pat's persistent pre-occupation with his button. She coughed politely and, brushing some crumbs off the sleeve of her pink lambswool cardigan, said: 'Pat – do you mind me asking you – why are you doing that?'

Pat shifted abruptly in his chair, quite startled.

'Doing? I'm doing nothing!' was his smart rejoinder.

Mary touched her upper lip with the tip of her tongue and smoothed her skirt over her knees, saying:

'Don't you know if you do that, Pat, I'm only going to have to go and sew it on all over again!'

'Sew it?' replied Pat, a trifle hoarsely. 'Well, in that case, I'll leave it alone, then!'

Mary smiled tenderly, as at an infant child, perhaps.

'Arra – I don't mind!' she went on. 'But—'

'I'll leave it alone,' Pat replied, unconsciously tugging even harder on the button, becoming quite flushed and agitated as he, unknown to himself, cried out in a very loud voice: *'Then I'll leave it, I said! I said – I'll leave it alone! Did you not hear me?'*

There ensued an extremely long pause. If the birds were still singing out in the trees or far away or anywhere, their tunes went unremarked upon. The sole audible sound as the shocked girls stared at each other was the sound of the grandfather clock ticking in the hallway. The sole sound, that is, before the air was rent asunder by a triply hysterical effusion, accompanied by an almost primitive percussive rhythm of table-slapping abandon. Pat's grey and hangdog silence seemed shameful by comparison. In his ears the noise of his swallowing was as the rush of rain-swelled rapids. His fear for a moment was that they could hear it too, but in this he was mistaken, for they couldn't – they were too busy laughing themselves sick to hear anything.

*

A dainty white nylon blouse with frilled front, high neck buttoned at the back, and full sleeves with lace cuffs might be described as 'very feminine'. So too might a bottle of Chanel No. 19 perfume, but a combination of both would not even present a close approximation of femininity when compared to the interior of the bedroom which had been appropriated by Pat's 'visitors', scattered as it was with any amount of filmy pyjamas and powder clouds of talc, a furious amount of hairbrushing proceeding and false fingernails littering dressing tables like confetti. Why, it appeared as if the slumber party to end all slumber parties was taking place right there in the McNab house!

'But he's not bad-looking!' continued Mary, as she drew the hairbrush through her coiffure with deft but delicate strokes. 'I mean I wouldn't say he's bad-looking!'

'Perhaps not, Mary – if you took a hose to him, at any rate!' squealed Jo.

'Or a blowlamp, maybe!' interjected Ann.

'Shut up, you cows!' snapped Mary, slapping Jo on the shoulder. 'He's shy, that's all!'

'Oo! Do you hear her!' mocked Jo. 'Do you hear her, Ann Magee!'

'He's shy, that's all!' mimicked Ann wickedly.

Jo raised her eyebrows and put on a baby voice.

'I think she fancies him!' she said cheekily.

'Fancies him!' squealed Ann.

'Do you, Mary?' asked Jo. 'Fancy him, I mean?'

'Oo! Fancies him! Fancies him!'

Ann's shoulders heaved.

'Pat! Yoo hoo! Hello there, Pat!'

Jo mimicked Mary's voice.

'Mary wants to talk to you!'

Mary shrugged and hissed disapprovingly, but not without displaying a twinkle in her eye.

'Shut up, you wagons!' she demanded, waving the hairbrush at them. At once she found herself attacked and pummelled with pillows.

'Look, Mary!' yelped Jo. 'This pillow here is Pat! Give it a kiss! Go on! Give it a kiss!'

At first, Mary's hesitancy appeared to indicate that she was hurt by the rumours. But then, suddenly, she gripped the pillow with both arms, giddily hugging it and making a large 'smacking' noise on the bulky cloth with her lips.

'Look! I told you!' yelled Jo.

'Ha ha!' laughed Ann. 'If only Matron was here now!'

'We'd get Pat to give her a great big coort!' laughed Ann.

As though a wickedly impish, mysterious force had been

unleashed, they began to squeal anew and set about each other with a variety of fluffy toys. By the time they were finished, their fit, red-cheeked young bodies were exhausted.

*

The following day the three friends were as living, flapping aprons, cooking smells wafting out the door and along the hallway, up the stairs and into every nook and cranny of the house. In the corner, Pat sat fiddling with his fingers.

'You won't regret this, Pat,' Mary said. 'A few more days and we'll have this place looking spick and span!'

'It will be the nicest house in the country,' affirmed Jo.

'The nicest B&B!' contradicted Ann. 'The nicest B&B, you mean!'

'Oh, all right, then, you cow!' hissed Jo, adding: 'Pshaw! Stickler for detail!'

'Now now! Stop bickering, girls!' insisted Mary. 'You know what Sister Boniface would say!'

Jo screwed up her face and in a cracked voice, mocked:

'If you ask me, youse gird-ills is mad – mad!'

'Mad after anything in trousers anyway, Sister Boney-face!' echoed Ann.

Mary's hands shot to her face.

'Oh no!' she cried. 'I've no eggs!'

'No eggs?' cried Jo.

'No eggs?' cried Ann.

'How can I make an omelette to go with potatoes and peas if I've no eggs?' moaned Mary.

'I'll go get them! I'll get the eggs!' volunteered Jo.

'And I'll go with you!' offered Ann. 'The pair of us will go and get them!'

'Oh, would you?' cried Mary. 'That would be just peachy!'

'Don't worry!' chirped Jo.

'After all,' said Ann, as they spontaneously sang, extremely tunefully, '*We are three lovely lassies from Bannion* – are we not?'

before locking together their lithe young bodies in an embrace which gave the illusion of one single elegant, sweet-smelling person, albeit, as has been noted earlier, one in possession upon its shoulders of a trinity of gay and agile wavy heads.

*

Not long after her friends had departed for the town, Pat was busy sweeping up when he heard Mary say:

'Pat – it doesn't matter if you miss a bit, you know. I won't mind.'

He knew she had been observing him for some time.

'What?' he gulped, without raising his head.

'I was just saying,' continued his visitor, 'it doesn't matter if you miss a bit of the floor by accident. I'll do it later.'

Pat reddened, barely audible as he replied:

'No. It's OK. I'll do it.'

Mary approached, extending her hand.

'No, I'll do it,' she went on, 'honestly. It's woman's work, anyway. We do it all the time in the Nurses' Home. We're used to it, Pat – really.'

'Used to it?' replied Pat, unaware, however, of exactly which words had at that moment passed his lips. They might equally have been: 'You like marmalade?' or 'Horses eat oats.'

'Yes,' continued Mary. 'Cooking. Cleaning. Sweeping up the floor. We don't mind doing it. Girls don't mind. After all – men work in the fields, don't they? And on the farm too. Lifting all that hay. Digging. Thinning turnips, for example!'

She paused. A thin, tiny sigh escaped her breast.

'Yes, digging. And getting clay all over their hands. Clay and mud all over their hands.'

She paused anew, then said:

'Here – let me.'

Pat withdrew, a little startled.

'No. It's all right, Mary,' he repeated.

157

Her eyes met his.

'Mary,' she said softly, 'you called me Mary.'

'I'm sorry!' cried Pat suddenly.

'No! It's all right,' she reassured him, continuing: 'Here! Please let me!'

Slowly Pat handed her the brush, meekly averting his eyes as she gazed out at him from beneath the beautifully clipped awnings of her lashes.

'You have enough to do, Pat,' she said as she manoeuvred the brush deftly with short, effective strokes, 'digging – and working out in the fields. Anyway – I like doing it for you. Sometimes, you know – sometimes you get fed up with girls being around you all the time. Girls, girls, girls – do you know what I mean, Pat? Girls everywhere you go. It's sickening!'

Pat swallowed and bent his thumb back, staring at it for no reason he could elucidate.

'Huh?' he said.

'If there was a competition, Pat,' went on Mary, 'if someone was to say to you: "Of all the three girls – " just saying there was a competition – "which one, if you were asked, would you say is the best looking? Which one would you pick?" I mean – it's only a joke now!'

Pat stared at the floor and raised his head.

'Which one?' he said.

'Yeah! Which one!' said Mary excitedly. 'Jo or Ann or—'

Pat looked away, once again experiencing the encroach-ment of deep colour in the environs of his cheeks.

'I don't know,' he replied uncertainly, 'I'm not sure.'

Mary nodded, with understanding.

'I know you're not,' she said, 'but supposing you *had* to say. Suppose you simply had to say and there was no way out of it. Which one then would it be then?'

Saliva, thick as custard, tried to push its way past Pat's Adam's apple.

'The best looking?' he asked.

'Yes!' Mary nodded. 'The best hair, best eyes, best lips – and best legs! No, I'm only joking! Not the best legs! Just the best looking overall!'

'I—'

Pat nibbled on the inside of his cheek.

'Yes?' Mary enquired eagerly.

'I don't—'

'Like – if you had to pick one to marry – which one would it be?'

'I think,' began Pat, 'I think it would be—'

Mary strained to hear Pat's low voice.

'I think it would be—'

To Mary's annoyance, just then the kitchen swung open and her two friends fell in singing:

'*There are three lovely lassies in Bannion, Bannion, Bannion,*
There are three lovely lassies in Bannion
And I am the best of them all!'

'Phew! I'm bushed!' cried Jo, flopping down on the sofa with her shopping bags.

'Well! Here's the eggs!' chirped Ann, extending the grey ridged box.

'Get frying, Mary McKeogh, you great big ugly wagon you!'

'Ha ha!' laughed Ann.

'Just joking, Mary!' Jo assured her friend, or attempted to, for there was clearly something tenebrous and unappreciative in the manner Mary accepted the container of eggs. Which was not lost on Jo who, the moment Mary turned her back, exchanged looks with Ann, glances which unmistakably were meant to articulate feelings of a most emphatic nature, something along the lines of 'Hmmph! Well mercy me! I wonder who stole her bun?'

*

Ann was seated at her dressing table some hours later, drawing an emery board across her fingernails, Jo absorbed in a

159

magazine (*Modern Screen*) as she lay with one leg crossed upon the bed, chewing some gum and picturing herself chatting animatedly to assorted Top Twenty stars when Mary entered in her pink quilted dressing gown. Both girls noted that she looked none too pleased. She stood in the centre of the floor with her arms folded and said, crossly:

'Did anyone see my Ponds?'

'Hmmph?' Jo responded without looking up from her reading.

Mary's lips tightened.

'I said – did anyone see my Ponds? Are you deaf or something?'

Ann coughed and inspected her right eye closely in the looking glass.

'No, I didn't,' she said, flicking at her eyelash with her index finger and adding, 'I don't use Ponds anyway.'

Mary made a clicking sound with her tongue but remained quite firm, if not obdurate indeed.

'Well, it's gone,' she said, 'I can't find it anywhere and I want it. I have to do my face.'

'Hey – listen to this!' Jo cried abruptly. 'In California a woman married to a man for thirty years discovered that he had been a woman all along! Mrs Ellen Mankiewicz, of 22 Sycamore, Berkeley, was shocked to discover that her husband, Errol, had all of their married life been harbouring a sinister secret . . .'

Mary stamped her satin-encased foot.

'Am I talking to myself here or what?' she demanded to know. 'Where is my Ponds, I said!'

Ann swung in her chair and blurted:

'We don't know anything about your Ponds! Listen, Mary – do you mind! I am trying to listen to what Jo is saying!'

Jo continued:

'Ha ha! Listen to this, Ann! "*And then, to her amazement,*

discovered that the person whose bed she had shared for so long, was in fact a—'' '

There was a new iciness in Mary's voice as she barked: 'And what, may I ask, do you call this?'

In her hand, like a small white Indian temple, sat a jar of cold cream labelled: *Ponds.*

The moment seemed to shudder between them until, at last, Jo snapped: 'Oh, why don't you leave us alone, Mary, you and your stupid old cold cream! Fat lot of good it'll do you, anyway! Ha ha!'

Her mocking, needling laughter was boisterously augmented by Ann.

'Ha ha!' they cried in unison. 'Ha ha!'

Mary sucked in her cheeks and drew her quilted arms more tightly about her.

'And just what is that supposed to mean?' she frostily enquired, continuing: 'Are you listening to me? I said – just what is that supposed to mean?'

Jo looked at Ann. Ann looked at Jo. Jo was the first to speak.

'Nothing, Mary,' she said, with a hint of irritation, 'it was just a joke. Wasn't it, Ann?'

Ann nodded.

'Yeah,' she said, 'Jo – read out some more, will you? Is there more? What does it say about his—'

But before she could finish, Mary had stormed out of the room, slamming the door loudly behind her.

*

It was after midnight when Jo turned over on her side and whispered to Ann in the bed beside her: 'Ann?'

'Mm,' Ann responded sleepily.

'Do you think it's strange?'

'What, Jo?' Ann responded.

'Mrs Mankiewicz,' continued Jo, 'being married to someone all that time and not knowing. Not knowing – you know . . .'

Ann touched her lips with her tongue and replied drowsily: 'Yes – it is strange, isn't it?'

Jo pulled the bedcovers tighter to her breast and frowned.

'I don't understand it,' she said. Outside the moon was fat and full in a corner of the window. Suddenly a thought struck Ann and she said: 'Jo – do you think it could ever happen to one of us?'

'What?' replied her companion.

'Marry a man – and then discover he's a woman!'

In her imagination, an arrowhead of fear went speeding past Jo's eyes.

'Oh God! I couldn't bear it!' she said.

Far off across the town, a dog barked (Towser McGarry, in fact) and Ann, now troublingly awake, said: 'Sometimes I worry, Jo. Because, I mean – we don't know that much about it, do we? When all you see are girls, you don't really know what men are like, do you? What it might be like to—'

'Ann?' Jo said.

'Hmmph?' came the reply.

'I don't like to be talking but – you know Mary?'

'Yes?' Ann whispered anxiously.

'You remember the time her tights went missing? Around last November?'

'Yes,' Ann nodded, 'I remember that.'

'Do you know what she said to me?'

'What? What did she say?'

There was a pause, then Jo said – with some reluctance:

'She said that you took them. Ann took them, she said.'

You could hear the dry clacks of Ann's tongue against the roof of her mouth. Large shadows moved across the ceiling of the room.

'She said *I* took them?' gasped Ann.

'Yes. You stole them from her room, she said.'

Suddenly Ann hissed:

'The liar! I did not!'

'And that's not all she said,' continued Jo. 'She said the reason you did it was that you couldn't afford to buy your own.'

Ann clenched her fists.

'I'll kill her!' she snapped.

'Couldn't afford them because your father was just an old farmer,' continued Jo, 'that him and his tinker's trousers were the talk of Bannion!'

Ann was close to tears as she hissed:

'Oh, the bitch! I'll kill her! I swear I will!'

Jo coughed politely and said:

'I wouldn't have mentioned it only she came in here tonight narking about Pond's.'

'I'll give her Ponds, the heifer!' snarled Ann. 'Blaming me!'

Jo coughed softly again and said:

'Do you know what I think, Ann?'

'What?' Ann croaked happily.

'I think she's jealous of us!'

There was no mistaking the thin line that Ann's lips had become as she lay there bathed in the milky moonlight, or the resentment within her that had stiffened every muscle and drawn both, as friends, so tightly together.

*

It was morning and Mary was as busy as a bee in her gingham apron. Pat and Jo and Ann were seated at the table with the delft and cutlery neatly laid out before them as Mary turned and, smiling, said to Pat: 'Pat – would you like another rasher?', without hesitation adding: 'Of course you will!'

Pat smiled bashfully and looked at his hands cradled in his lap as she forked the crispy rasher onto his plate. Mary was already on her way back to the cooker when Pat, to his horror, found Ann's hand resting upon his, gently prising his fingers apart and lacing them with her own. The net result of which was that he almost choked on his bacon.

'Are you all right, Pat?' enquired Mary, deftly flicking the fish slice.

'Yes, he's fine!' replied Ann chirpily, nibbling on a piece of toast and exchanging glances with Jo, without releasing her grip on Pat's (clammy) hand.

*

They had all been watching *The Riordans* on television and now it was over. It was approximately ten o'clock. Pat was sitting by the fire sipping a mug of tea, Jo had her legs tucked underneath her bottom, reading a magazine, and Ann was sewing, her lips pursed as she intermittently cast her eyes about the shadow-flickering room (they had built a big fire).

'Is there enough sugar in it, Pat?' Mary said then as she smiled over at him.

Jo coughed and, adjusting her legs, said:

'Were you down the town today, Mary?'

'Yes, I was,' replied Mary, momentarily distracted, 'I was in Mullaney's. I bought a new petticoat.'

The very mention of the word was enough to result in Pat covering himself in a cascade of hot tea. If she noticed, Jo gave no indication of it.

'Oh – did you?' she went on. 'What colour was it?'

'Green,' replied Mary.

It was impossible to decipher Ann's remark, her intonation being so muted. It was, however: 'Green! Like her teeth!' And, at which, Jo erupted into a bout of laughter which she attempted to stifle with her hand. Pat's cheeks were afire.

'They say there's going to be rain,' he unexpectedly declared. In the ensuing silence, he continued to feel tiny hot hammers beating with a dead insistence as though deep within some blast furnace of flesh.

*

Later that night – the hands of the clock showed 2 a.m. – Pat was adrift in the borderlands of sleep when there came a knock to his door. He felt very warm and his throat was dry again. An uncomfortable, rasping dryness, as that of a fever.

'Come in,' he said, having to repeat the phrase, as it was inaudible. 'Come in!'

A shaft of moonlight illuminated Mary in the doorway, her green petticoat flaring lacily out from her waist, making the tiniest of soft whispering sounds. Her small feet made no noise at all as she moved across the bedroom floor. Soon she was seated on the edge of Pat's bed, her manicured hands as mating doves in the verdant hammock of her lap.

'Pat?' she murmured softly. 'Can I come in?'

'Mary – of course you can,' replied Pat, adding rather incongruously, 'You already are in.'

'Pat,' continued his visitor hesitantly, 'you know when we came here first we were real cheeky and you didn't want us to stay. And the way we acted like we owned the place—'

'Yes,' Pat answered, anxiety invading his eyes.

'Pat – I want you to know something. It isn't like that now. I want you to know that I'm ashamed of all that. It's just that we didn't know how to behave with men around and we got giddy, sort of – Pat, did something ever happen to you that you couldn't understand?'

Pat's Adam's apple felt as though it had enlarged to the size of a large golf or tennis ball.

'Something you couldn't understand? Like what, for example?' he asked, doing his best to squeeze the words out.

Mary laced her fingers and looked down at them, as though not entirely convinced she would find them there.

'Pat – did anyone ever tell you have beautiful eyes?'

'Mammy used to,' choked Pat, 'she used to say it all the time.'

Mary's eyelids dropped then rose again.

'Pat,' she went on, 'did you ever think what it would be like – if we had this place – this house – all to ourselves? Just you and me.'

'Just you and me?' gulped Pat, looking up in amazement to find her full, sensuous lips adjacent to his.

'Yes,' she said, 'like man and wife. Like the happiest man and wife who ever lived.'

A swooshing sensation overcame Pat – as if he were being airlifted out over the roofs and houses and steeples of Gullytown and piloted into the very heart of the vast and limitless cosmos itself.

*

It was 3 p.m. two days later. Jo and Ann were furious in the hallway with their suitcases. Mary in her apron stood behind Pat. Jo was the first to speak or, perhaps more accurately, seethe. 'Oh – we know all!' she snapped at Mary. 'Mrs Green Petticoat with her Pond's cream!' Then, to Pat, 'But you'll soon learn, Mister! Wait till she gets her claws into you! You'll know all about it then! Everybody in the hospital hates her! We only pal around with her because we took pity on her!'

'Bockedy Arse!' interjected Jo. 'Here she comes now – Bockedy Arse! That's what everybody says!'

'I'm sorry, girls,' Pat protested weakly, 'I—'

'Oh, you needn't be sorry, Mister!' snapped Ann. 'For you'll be sorry soon enough, don't you worry!'

Her parting shot was a repeat of her admonition: 'You'll be sorry soon enough,' ringing in Pat's ears as she pulled the door behind her.

The silence which followed the departure of Jo and Ann might accurately be described as 'cavernous'. But this was, however, only for a short time, as Pat and Mary became acclimatized to their new situation. And by the time they sat down to dinner that evening, it had almost entirely dissipated. As Mary raised her glass of wine to her lips, she fluttered her eyelashes slightly and said to her host: 'I never thought this would happen to me, Pat.'

Pat broke a piece of garlic bread as a smile jerked elastically to one side of his mouth.

'Me neither,' he croaked.

'Would you like some more Pavlova?' asked Mary.

'Yes, please,' replied Pat as she spooned it onto his plate, noticing that a small blob of hollandaise sauce had lodged itself on his sleeve. The spoon fell resonantly to the floor.

'Pat!' she cried unexpectedly. 'Look at you! God, sometimes you can be so clumsy! Get out there and clean that off!'

Her index finger was horizontal and stiff as it indicated the kitchen.

'What? I'm sorry,' stammered Pat, confused.

Mary bent her knees and retrieved the spoon.

'It doesn't matter,' she said curtly as Pat left the table, knocking over some knives as he did so.

*

The following afternoon, Pat was in his working clothes busying himself in the yard with his graip (a three-pronged farming implement). Mary appeared at the back door with her handbag and said: 'I should be back around twelve. Make sure you have all that dung cleaned up when I get back. God, how you could bear to live in these conditions! See you then, pet!'

As Mary's heels clacked off down the lane in the direction of the main road, little did she know that close by, behind a hedge, two sets of eyes were fixed as rivets upon her back.

'There she goes!' hissed Jo.

'Ssh!' replied Ann.

Not long afterwards, Pat was inside sitting at the table

167

availing himself of a 'cigarette break' when he looked up and there, to his astonishment, beheld both Jo and Ann staring down at him, both also smoking cigarettes. The curling smoke seemed to take an age to make its journey to the ceiling as did their extending smiles before they could be called complete. It was the painful endurance of this leadenly passing time that inexplicably preoccupied Pat and caused him to jump when, together, they burst into song!

'*There are two lovely lassies in Bannion!*' they sang as one.

'*Bannion!*' cried Ann.

'*Ah, Bannion!*' responded Jo.

'*There are two lovely lassies in Bannion*
And we are the best of them all!
Ah, we are the best of them all!'

Pat trembled as Jo slid onto his knee and flung her arms around his neck.

'Come on now, Pat!' she yelped. 'Give us a song, you wee divil you!' as Ann crinkled up her nose and raked her long, slender fingers through his hair, squealing (or pretending to squeal), 'Let's have a look at you, you bold little rascal you!'

*

A very short time later, Pat found himself in the bedroom staring in mute amazement as Jo amused herself blowing smoke rings as she lay back upon the bed, attired in a green petticoat, mimicking cruelly, 'Oh! I'm going to be a staff nurse! Oh, I'm going to be this! Oh, I'm going to be that! Why, of course I am! Because my name's Mary! My name's Mary and I'm the best of the lot! Oh, but where is my face cream? Where oh where is my precious Ponds, I wonder?'

Pat edged tentatively towards the door, his mind hot and confused and a maze of interlocking contradictions, his hand curling about the handle as Ann cried, viciously, stabbing the air with her finger: 'Get back on that bed you, this instant, till I tear the trunks off you!'

The sound of their squeals was now becoming unbearable. Pat found himself trapped beneath their bodies (they had literally *fallen* upon him!) as they set about putting their 'plan' into action when downstairs, a familiar voice rang out: 'Yoo hoo! Pat! I'm home!'

The spectacle that was Pat McNab as those words echoed throughout the vast old house was a sorry one indeed, the apposite epithet perhaps being 'burlesque' as he stumbled, jester-like, across the floor, the twin legs of the nylon tights which his powdered assailants had applied to his head swinging preposterously as he spluttered through the lopsided slash of lipstick, his countenance that of a pantomime-style spectre with its liberal coating of Ponds cold cream.

'Oh look!' cried Ann. 'What a lovely lassie! I do declare!'

'*There is one lovely lassie in Bannion,*' chirped Jo.

'*Bannion!*' answered Ann.

'*Ah, Bannion!*' chuckled Jo, exuberantly.

'*There is one lovely lassie in Bannion,*' they sang together, squealing, '*and Pat is the best of them all!*'

Through his Lycra and net cage, all Pat could hear was the taunting valediction:

'Totty-bye then, honeybun!' as the curtains fluttered, the door swinging open at that precise moment and Mary's horrified scream swooping out into the shocked soft twilight that now touched the roofs of Gullytown.

*

As might be expected, nothing was ever quite the same after that. The days went by, the passing of each marked with the leaden sullenness of deep-sea divers' boots, as Mary sewed in the corner, intermittently snapping: 'And when you've that sweeping done, you can do the washing! Do you hear me? Leave the digging to me, for the like of that washing's all you're good for!'

A quavering melancholy subsequently took hold of Pat, its

origins not simply in the fact that she refused to understand, but also in her unwillingness to desist from her taunts. Had she been capable of that, even an approximation thereof, he would reflect in quiet moments (when she left him alone, which was rarely enough), events might have taken a different turn.

'What I can't understand,' she hissed one day as he hung out the washing, 'what I can't understand is your letting them do it to you! Two girls! How can you bear to look at yourself in the mirror, Pat McNab?'

'Perhaps if she had left Mammy out of it,' Pat murmured to himself that evening when she had at last gone to town, 'maybe there might have been hope. But no – she had to do it. She couldn't leave her out of it, could she? Someone who had nothing to do with it. Nothing in the wide world.'

The entire house seemed to shrink before his eyes to the size of a handful of dust, a thimbleful of unbearable sadness.

Later that night, sitting in the chair by the fire, Pat felt her long sharp fingers moving through his hair, stroking it slowly and softly and tenderly. There was a strange quality in her voice, he thought, as she said, as though she'd been thinking about it: 'It was her made you like that, wasn't it, Pat – your Mammy? Never mind those two trollops. It was her really, wasn't it? She did it to you. Mm, Pat?'

A wave of shame engulfed Pat as he lowered his head and replied: 'Yes, Mary.'

He could feel her nodding above him as she said, her fingers tickling the back of his neck. 'I know,' he heard her say, 'well, Pat – you needn't worry for much longer. I'll be leaving you soon. And you can forget all about us. It'll be like we were never here. Me – or those two other turncoats! Myself and those two other – bitches! Isn't that right, Pat?'

'Yes, Mary,' Pat replied, chokingly.

He felt Mary tapping him briskly on the shoulder.

'Now – go and make my bed for me like a good girl.'

'Yes, Mary,' Pat replied, hopelessly, slouching towards the door.

*

It was very late that night, the kitchen in silent semi-darkness when the queerest of smells materialized. At first Pat thought he was imagining it. It seemed that of freshest flowers, the fragrant breath of the voice he heard now, softly issuing from the chimney corner. Pat started.

'Mammy!' he gasped. There was no mistaking the familiar crossover pinny, the distinctive zippered boots.

There was little emotion in his mother's voice as she spoke.

'She had to blame me, didn't she? She couldn't leave me out of it! Like them all, Pat!'

It was hard for Pat to withhold the tears when he heard those words.

'Yes, Mammy,' he said, 'they're always blaming you.'

His mother took a step forward, towards him.

'Pat?' she said softly.

'Yes, Mammy,' Pat replied.

'Come here, son,' she said, 'I want you to do something for me.'

Pat nodded as she took his hand in hers and, curving her other one around his neck, gently cradled his head on her shoulder.

*

It was quite late, close to 12.30 a.m., in fact, as Pat busied himself in his overalls, shovelling manure with his graip, beads of perspiration glittering on his forehead. He heard some footsteps and looked up to see Mary in her nightgown standing by the gable end of the house.

'I was looking for you,' she said, frostily, with her arms folded. 'I thought I told you to do the cooker?'

Pat did not immediately reply but continued in fact with his work.

'No – I prefer doing this,' he said then.

Mary pursed her lips.

'Prefer doing that, do you? How about you give me the fork and let a real woman do the job!'

Pat slowly raised his head. His words were measured and steady and considered.

'You want it, do you? Is that what you want – the fork?'

Mary stiffened, her reply attaining a new level of ungenerous acidity.

'Why, yes – I believe I do!' she sneered.

'Well then – here it is!' was Pat's reply as he plunged the three prongs directly into the centre of her abdomen. The moonlight swamped her face – liberally daubed with Ponds cold cream – as she lay astride the cold unsteaming dungheap.

*

There were those – as we have seen – who derided Pat as a 'complete and utter oddity', if not a 'lunatic of the highest order'. But those making such comments – whether in Sullivan's Select Bar or anywhere else – knew nothing of the personality of Pat McNab. They would never know of the emotional turmoil and deep, impenetrable hurt which had led him to commit what were, incontrovertibly, by 'normal society' classified as 'unspeakable acts'. Never know of the tenderness he was capable of displaying as he tended the anonymous resting places here and there arrayed throughout his garden. They were not to know of the thoughts that went through his mind as he moved some leaves with his foot and silently – chokingly – murmured the words: 'What's saddening is that it could have been so beautiful, Mary. We didn't even have to be married. We could have all lived here, because I liked you, all three of you. Maybe in time even Mammy would have understood.'

It was ironic that Jo and Ann should have ended up so close to their so-called 'mortal enemy', Mary (which she wasn't really!), having come upon the scene only moments after Mary's nocturnal altercation with Pat. But then, it was sad the way everything happened, wasn't it, thought Pat McNab, as he forsook his laurel patch (a triumvirate of shrubs now fresh and tender!) and turned to go back inside, in his mind the sound of three gorgeous young girls singing, fragrant and flower-tender in their crisp print frocks, their tuneful melody of 'Three Lovely Lassies In Bannion' as a posy of perfect pink cast out across the shining blue of a heart-lifting, shimmering summer's day.

CHAPTER SEVEN

The Little Drummer Boy

The Little Drummer Boy

Come, they told me, pa rup pup pum pum
A new-born king to see pa rup pup pum pum
Our finest gifts to bring pa rup pup pum pum
To lay before the king, pa rup pup pum pum
Rup pup pum pum, rup pup pum pum
So to honour him pa rup pup pum pum
When we come.

Baby Jesus, pa rup pup pum pum
I'm a poor boy too pa rup pup pum pum
I have no gifts to bring pa rup pup pum pum
That's fit to give our king pa rup pum pum pum
Shall I play for you pa rup pum pum pum
On my drum?

THERE CAN BE very little doubt, even on a December morning so hard and glassy, starched and invigorating, that there are very few people indeed who would be capable of evincing with any measure of accuracy the breathtakingly optimistic inner contentment which is evident at this moment on the face of Mr Pat McNab as he breezes (whizzes, indeed, might be a more apposite verb!) about his kitchen – tastefully decorated, in honour of the Yuletide season, in hues of dazzling primary. The heretofore unremarkable room is, in fact, now a veritable riot of colour. As Pat – beads of sweat a-glinting on that old forehead which bears also a speck or two of dusty flour – flits hither and thither and roundabout, with 'a hundred and one things to do', as he gasps to himself, and no time in which to do them. Is it any wonder that he'd pause and sigh, run a flour-gloved paw through his excited hair and go: 'Phew! Is there ever any end to it – that's what I'd like to know!' Then smile and reflect as he shook his head, and like many another across the world, remark with affection: 'Ah, but it's for the kids really!'

Which is why, with renewed zest sometime later, a party hat appears, in radiant crimson crepe. ('The very exact same as Captain Pugwash's, I do declare!' Pat is to be heard observing in the quiet sitting room as onto his head it is placed.) Quite how many sponge cakes were completed in the space of three or four hours, it is impossible to say. Somewhere in the region of fifty-seven. Very close to the amount of confections which were consumed (illicitly!) by the preoccupied party-maker! Is it possible for a grown person to consume Cadbury's Lucky Numbers in such quantities? It most certainly and definitely is! As it is for them to happily uncap and devour the contents of seventeen sparkling bottles of pop! Which the proud monarch of the McNab household sucked and gulped with impressive dedication through the funnel of a striped and seriously overworked straw!

Then of course, there was the turkey! Bird of celebration, seasonal feathered friend who euphoniously spat and roasted in the oven's depths! Now with its wing in one fell swoop removed as – *snap!* – Pat, crunching indulgently on its mouth-watering crispiness, does loudly proclaim: 'Yes! And down it goes, crackling wing of he who once had feathers, eminent acquaintance of His Dukeship Turkey Turks!'

And boy is he tasty! Rivalled only by old Pat, in fact! But not the one we know as Pat McNab! Which Pat, then? Why, old Pat Plum Pud, of course! Small currant-studded foothill of fruit! Without whom Christmas could not be complete!

'Do you like him?' Pat enquired of the teapot's spout, for no particular reason. 'For *I* certainly do!'

And, in order to add further emphasis, gave himself to directly addressing the regal, raisin-packed dome.

'Do you hear that, pud?' he cried. 'I like you! Pat likes you – O but yes he does! As a matter of fact, he loves you! Why, if you don't believe me, I'll prove it! Yes, prove it indeed I shall!'

What a surprise that innocent little kitchen confection must have received when Pat's entire hand came dunking down, with not the slightest hint of compromise, rotating right into the still-warm depth of its centre as might into the bowels of the earth some out-of-control oil pump! After which Pat could – no difficulty whatsoever! – have changed his name and become thenceforward not Pat McNab at all but – the Redoubtable Mr Currant Face! A sobriquet with which he is clearly now at ease, shrilly declaring: 'Now do you believe me! Believe me now, Mr Pud? I'll bet you do! Because it's true!

Old Pat here loves you more than you'll ever know! Just thought you were a pile of ingredients topped with a sprig of holly? O but you see that's where you're wrong, my sweet plum-pudding friend!'

There is something poignant about the inevitable impregnability of a plum pudding's silence, accepting as it must such bountiful compliments. A strange mute glumness which may suggest as Pat further extends his magnanimity that it might be a tad excessive? Nay, for is it not the Xmas season of goodwill and cheeriness? And why it is *more* than acceptable at this time to heap one's arms brimful of Christmas crackers and leap upon the kitchen table as to the world you do declare: 'Yes, pud, I love you all right, mute and glum or no! As I do each and every one of these, my tried and trusted friends! What about this fellow, for example? Little Mr Blue! Couldn't forget him, could we? All right, Mr Blue? Of course you are! And then, of course, we have old Red! Hello, old Red! Doing well, are we? Excellent! So why not all of us start cracking, then? Yes indeed, all you Christmas crackers! Let's hear you crack! Crack crack crack crack crackity crack!'

What a flurry of paper fragments there appears, in slow motion twirling lino-ward. For all the world like coloured snow! As Pat leaps into the wastes of outer space, crying: 'Ho ho! Merry Xmas everybody!' but unfortunately landing with a bang on the north face of the table and loudly smacking his head off the side of the fridge. What a dazed man he now is as he realizes just what has transpired. 'Oops!' he exclaims. 'I don't think I effected a very professional landing there, did I?' It is quite some time before he succeeds in relocating his bearings! But, as he remarks himself, clutching tightly on to the table's side, 'Who cares – it's Christmas!'

A sentiment which not so very long afterwards he had no hesitation whatever in sharing with his neighbours and all who had found themselves in the vicinity of Gullytown and its hinterland for the season's celebrations. His cry triple-echoing across the starched and frozen fields as he cupped his hands over his mouth and repeated: 'Do you hear me, you bastards! It's Christmas! Happy Yuletide and a merry New Year, you stupid silent neighbours! Do you hear me? I'm wishing you lots of fun and good cheer!' It was to be over fifteen minutes before exasperation set in and he violently set about a zinc bucket, kicking it forcefully and sending it with a musical ring across the other side of the yard. Smoothing his hair back with his hands (it was liberally lathered in hair oil) and remarking, to himself and no one else in particular at all: 'Oh very well then! Be like that! I don't care! Why – I'll make my own fun! Yes! That's what I'll do! Make my own entertainment! How do you like that, you long-faced moaning bastards!'

*

Some hours later, Pat was halfway through building his snow-man in the field directly beyond the yard of the house. He was having the time of his life as he pulled his black coat around him and cried: 'Yes! If all else fails, make your own fun! Be jolly by yourself! Make yourself a little friend! A snowman! After all – who cares in the end if no friends call around to wish you a merry Xmas? You can still have jingo japes, by golly you can! All you have to do – yessir! – is build yourself a little snowman, rustle up a nice turkey dinner and in the evening have yourself a nice plate of hot mince pies and a nice warm glass of rum punch! And then what's the word? The word is – hurray for Christmas! Do you hear that everyone? Hurray for Christmas!'

It was just when he was about to issue forth another cry of appreciation for the season of goodwill that something hap-pened. Time appeared to stand still as he felt the colour draining from his face and, paradoxically, espied beneath him on the pale white snow a small scarlet map which was already extending its boundaries in a mass of irregularly shaped elongated tendrils. As the pain began to manifest itself deep in the tip of his index finger, Pat McNab fancied he heard the faint echo of a military tattoo resounding in the distance. It was then he saw the sudden sharp gleam of silver spring before his eyes like the trajectory of the tiniest star. 'No! It can't be!' he gasped, as he plunged his finger into the moist warm comforting depths of his mouth. 'It simply cannot be!'

His eagerness in clearing away the packed snow beneath him can only be described as frenzied. With the result that it was only a matter of a few short minutes before he had uncovered what he knew – instinctively – had been lodged there, a little tin soldier complete with decorated drum and upraised bayonet – now crimson-tipped, of course, having pricked his thumb, drawing a tiny bead of blood – and scarlet military tunic. The long-forgotten – but so familiar! – favourite toy of his childhood dreams! A wave of euphoria swept through Pat McNab as he exultantly clasped the small metal effigy with both hands and called out: 'God has done this! God has done this – to remind me of those Christmases and those years long ago when Mammy was alive and everyone was so happy!'

Intuitively, he shot to his feet and cried once more to all the world, or all within it prepared to hear: 'So happy you'll never know, all those Christmases ago! With him – my little friend!' He elevated the miniature musician aloft in defiance: 'My one and only best old pal!'

The tiny crumbs of clay fell from the little soldier's face now as Pat tenderly brushed them away. He thought of all those long years he had lain buried in the earth, but aware that one day the darkness would be banished and he would find himself once more safe in the company of the boy he had known for the duration of his short life. Lying close beside him, perhaps, assured that this was the way it was destined to remain for ever.

It was hard to be certain whether it was just a trickle of melting snow falling from the soldier's eye as Pat removed the final crumb, or whether it was a real tear, his owner hugging him one last time and tucking him snugly beneath his coat as he crunched homeward across the tufty field into the snug and waiting welcome of the toast-warm house.

*

Pat put two more sods of turf on the roaring fire and smiled over at the short soldier reclining in the comfortable vastness of the library chesterfield. He thought – as the flames flickered and made interesting, irregular shadow shapes on the ceiling – that perhaps he had never been as happy before in his life. He was wearing his smoking jacket.

'Little soldier,' he said, 'do you think there's a destiny that shapes our ends? I do! To think that all these years my heart was broken and you turn up in the snow to mend it again! It's wonderful! So wonderful it almost erases the memory of that saddest day when I went and lost you, as I thought, for ever!'

As Pat gave his full attention to the fire, those days now seemed to live all over again, deep within its heart so orange and wayward-flickering.

*

It was 1962. Pat was seven years old. His mother was at her wits' end, endeavouring to placate him as she feared asphyxiation, but effectively shaking the life out of him.

'Do you hear me!' she snapped again. 'Listen to me! What is wrong with you! What is wrong with you!'

Pat made a trojan effort but again the words proved recalcitrant. He extended his index finger weakly in an aimless gesture.

'He's g-g-g-gone! My fr-fr-fr-friend! He's gone!'

His mother was perplexed. She shook him again.

'Who? Paul? Liam? Who are you talking about? Petey Lynam?'

'No!' choked Pat. 'They're not my friends! I hate them! It is my only real friend in the wide world who's gone!'

His mother was exhausted. She ground her moist gums and tweaked his raw cheek.

'Pat! Come on now!' she cried. 'Do you hear me now? Stop this nonsense!'

It was some moments after that statement had left her lips that the shadow fell. It was a shadow bearing the outline of a captain's cap and a thick bushy moustache. An impassive expression hard as granite dramatically revealed itself. The voice that emerged from between the moving lips possessed the hostile timbre of a bass drum struck. It was black and full of foreboding as the interior of the darkest of cellars.

'What's going on here?' it said.

Pat became aware that his mother had begun to stammer.

'Nothing,' she said, 'I was just going to make Pat his tea. I'll just go and make it now—'

She rose to her feet and began to make her way towards the doorway. A trunklike, hairy arm inside a military jacket uncompromisingly barred her way.

'I said – what's going on here? You – do you hear me? Look at me when I'm talking to you!'

A clammy finger of fear traced a line all the way down the middle of Pat's back as he realized his father was now addressing him. He too stammered fiercely.

'I've lost – I've lost—' he choked.

'What have you lost?' boomed his father's voice. 'Have you lost your dolly? Lost your little dolly, have you?'

Suddenly his mother's voice rang out.

'Don't say that to him, Victor!'

Within seconds she had been levelled with a solid blow. The sound of her falling tore at Pat's heart and he cried aloud: 'No!'

But it was to no avail. His father towered over him.

'Do you hear me, you fool, you?' he barked. 'I said – what have you lost?'

At last the words came to Pat and he found himself crying out:

'I've lost the only thing I loved in the world!'

His father's mouth contorted into a snarl.

'What did you say?' his father began again. 'What did you say to your father, you dirty little bottle of perfume! Did I hear you say what I thought you said? Don't talk like that! Don't talk like that in front of your father! Talk like that and I'll leave you so you can't speak! That's the way a woman talks! Do you understand that? Do you understand that?'

Pat lowered his head shamefully.

'Yes, Daddy,' he replied compliantly.

His father sucked his teeth, the rasping sound filling the room.

'Why, I don't believe you do!' he continued. 'I don't believe you do at all! I believe you're only saying it! I said – do you understand that – what I just said?'

'Yes, Daddy,' croaked Pat.

His father's eyes burned into him.

'You do, eh? What do you understand?'

'That it's the way a woman talks.'

'Correct. The way a woman talks. And how do you expect to get into the army if you talk the way a woman does? How do you expect to do that if you talk like a woman?'

Pat locked his thumbs together.

'I don't, Daddy,' he said, lowering his head.

His father coughed.

'You don't what?'

'I don't expect to get into the army.'

His father nodded.

'That's right. Expect nothing for it's what you're going to

184

get. O, sewing shirts or mending flies – but shouldering a weapon or bashing a square? No! Do you hear me? No! What did I say?'

'No!'

'That's right! Now get out there and stand in that snow for three hours until I call you in!'

His mother rallied from beneath the dresser and tried to raise herself to her feet as she pleaded: 'Ah, Victor! For the love of God don't do that to him!'

But it was to no avail for he felled her with another blow.

'Ah, shut up, you!' he growled. 'It's you has him the way he is!'

*

Pat cut a sad shivering figure in the falling snow, an invisible sliver of ice forming in his heart as he endeavoured, without success, to think of anything but his little comrade of whom he was now entirely bereft. Beyond him the snow-capped garden stretched like some heartbreaking Siberia. In that long three hours, it became clear to him that the truth about the world was that it was as a well-scrubbed void, a white emptiness that continued for ever and in the end counted for absolutely nothing. He would never understand how the thing you loved could be taken from you, its place usurped by a pain so unimaginable that no words at your disposal would ever make it known to someone else. 'Where is he? Where is my friend?' he croaked anew. A phrase which kept ringing, piercing like a persistent drill inside his mind as the tips of his fingers slowly turned to stone. Just then he heard his father's footsteps coming grinding towards him across the snow.

'Can I look for him?' pleaded Pat. 'Please, Da!'

His father's left eye narrowed suspiciously.

'Look for what?' he hissed. 'What are you talking about?'

185

as he spat some phlegm onto the hard, icy ground. 'Get in there till I teach you about war!'

*

The fire flickered in the library grate as Pat's father chomped on the stem of his briar and moved the small black cannon a little further to the east. The battlefield was arrayed with lines of Napoleonic infantrymen in perfectly formed military formations. Through a cloud of smoke, Victor McNab informed his son: 'I had to execute two men once. Oh, yes.'

In his heart, Pat McNab longed to reply: 'That must have been so hard for you, dearest Father. Unskilled as you are in the art of casual brutality, I mean.' But, sadly, at that moment, he did not possess such courage, and simply found himself biting his knuckle and replying: 'Oh, really?'

'Yes,' his father continued, 'barely older than yourself I was, actually. But I knew it had to be done. It was a matter of regimental discipline, you see.'

Pat felt a shadow falling. Not his father's this time, however, but one deep inside his own soul.

'So what did you do?' he heard a whisper echo. 'Bash his head in with your gun butt? Make him eat dynamite? Is that what you did, Daddy? Please tell me!'

His father lowered his pipe and observed his son quizzically.

'Did you say something?' he said then. 'I could have sworn I heard you saying something—'

'I said,' smiled Pat, 'I said – hard as it might be, it has to be done. Everyone expects it, don't they?'

'That's right, son,' his father replied. He seemed pleased now. He lit his pipe, which had just gone out.

'And they are well aware that it takes a courageous man to do it,' he assured his son.

'So what did you do, Daddy?' asked Pat, swinging his legs

186

and crinkling up his eyes, a little more confident in his father's company now.

'I shot him three times in the mouth,' replied Captain Victor McNab.

A field marshal was deftly moved west as a cloud of blue smoke went skyward.

*

Later that same night, a pall of gloom settled on Pat McNab as his mother tucked him into his bed. She stroked his cheek tenderly and said: 'Don't worry your head, son. It's just stories. Your father and these wars – he's imagining things. You understand that, don't you?'

Pat hesitated. He knew his eyes were red. He could feel them. Like small pieces of meat stuck onto his face.

'Yes, Mammy,' he said, 'I think so.'

His mother smiled maternally.

'That's a good boy.'

But the truth was that Pat didn't understand. And as the door closed softly behind his mother, he knew that he didn't. But was still not expecting it when later that night he awoke with the moon's light pouring onto his face and the perspiration breaking on his skin, the young soldier who had been so heartlessly dispatched to eternity by his father appearing before him white as a corpse and saying: 'He killed me. Why did he do it? Why did your father kill me?'

He had not meant to scream. It was the last thing Pat had wanted to do that night. But it was already too late. The door of the bedroom burst open and the light from the landing filled the room. Before Pat stood his father with a heavy leather belt (of standard military issue) wrapped around his knuckles.

'What in the hell do you think you're doing?' he barked. 'Do you want to wake the whole house? Is that it?'

The words had left Pat's lips before he realized it.

'You killed him! You killed the young soldier!'

His mother pulled her candlewick dressing gown about her as she appeared in the doorway of the bedroom.

'What's wrong, son?' she cried, then, turning to her husband. 'Did you hit him?'

'No!' snarled Victor McNab. 'But by the living God I will now!'

'No, Victor! Please, no!' begged Mrs McNab.

'Get out of my way!' he cried, as she stumbled backwards across a Hoover. 'It's you has him the way he is!'

The noise of the whuppiting leather belt rang loud and long into the night.

It seemed defeat had finally come to the fore behind the eyes of Pat McNab.

*

Some days later, his father decided that it was time to teach Pat how to shoot a gun. They went together into the field directly across from the house and his father placed a revolver in Pat's hand.

'You've got to make sure and hold it steady,' he instructed. 'Grip it good and hard and hold it nice and steady! Now!'

The bullet lodged itself in a tree stump some hundred yards wide of the target.

'Jesus!' cried his father. 'You'd be court-martialled for that!'

He grabbed the revolver.

'Still – at least you're trying,' he remarked, in a voice bearing an infinitesimal ingredient of warmth.

*

The tailor-made military tunic arrived a week or so later and Pat marched rigidly up and down the library floor with his wooden rifle angled on his shoulder. His father reclined imperiously in the chesterfield, calling:

'Left right! Left right! Private McNab! About turn!'

'Sah!' replied Pat, with impressive bearing.

'Private McNab! Fall out!' commanded his father, as Pat two-stepped off out the library door.

*

The transformation in Pat seemed remarkable, but for his obsessive interest in the military history book he kept hidden in his bedroom. Which contained innumerable pictures and photos savagely obliterated in what must have been some kind of maddened frenzy, the extremities of flight lieutenants and, indeed, four-star generals, reduced to a state of disfigurement by what can only be described as unmercifully applied streaks of the heaviest of lead pencil. Apart from this, however, all seemed well.

It seems fanciful to suggest now that each night as Pat McNab repaired to bed he was secretly looking forward to the dreams he was about to savour, many of which concerned his father experiencing his demise in military manoeuvres which would go horribly wrong. But it was true, nevertheless. And provided an explanation – simple and uncomplicated – for the smile which played regularly upon Pat's face as he chuckled into his hands and repeated: 'Go on, Germans! That's it! Blow him up with sticky bombs and grenades!'

*

His most exciting dream of all it was his habit to reserve for the weekend, the Friday night upon which Pat McNab – *hero!* – would at last find within himself the courage to perform the deed himself.

'Go on! Go on then, Miss Pat! Little Miss Patty!' he would hear his father sneer at him. 'Do it! Shoot your own father! You great big dangerous girl, you! Oo! I'm so scared!'

Except that it was never to happen. Not even in the landscape of the imagination could some small glimmer of hope be sanctioned, Pat now falling to his knees as his father pushed him aside, striding past disdainfully as mucus and tears mingled inextricably, making their way in pathetic rivers towards the churning mud into which his son now sank.

Sometimes, too, the most beautiful dream of all it would come, and there would be Pat sitting sadly by the fire with his little drummer boy soldier cradled in his lap and his father ('Da!' he would call him then! Like a real boy!) being brought home from the war with a bandaged hand. Pat and his mother would hear him outside and run to the door to help him in to sit down by the fire, crying: 'It's all right, Da! We'll look after you!'

*

Why, it would be the most wonderful world of all to have lived in, if only even a tiny portion of it had happened!

'Look at him sleeping by the fire,' Pat would hear himself say, 'bandaged Da – our closest living friend, Ma,' as his mother smiled and darned a sock.

'What do you think they did to him over there, Ma?' Pat would enquire innocently then, the way any son might.

'Blew him up, son,' his mother would reply.

And Pat would nod.

'It affected his nerves, didn't it, Ma?' he'd say.

'Yes, son. That's why he beats you up with the belt and calls you names. Like saying you're a girl.'

And then everything would make sense. It would have all made sense and he wouldn't feel so badly about it at all.

'It's hard being in the army – isn't it, Ma?'

'Yes, son. We've no idea, you and me. We shouldn't judge your father too harshly.'

'No, Ma. We shouldn't,' he'd say – and feel all warm and understanding.

Something which he would relate to his little tin soldier

friend later on in the library, repeating as he stroked his red and blue drum: 'Little tin soldier. Even if it breaks our hearts, the truth is we shouldn't judge him.' And there would be a glittering moistness in his right eye as he contemplated his pal's painted, impassive face and added: 'Not even if he were to break our hearts on what is supposed to be the most beautiful day of the year!'

*

Which is, sadly, what he did, of course. What happened was, Pat had been moping about in the snow (having foolishly been horseplaying and gone and lost his little friend!) which had begun to fall that Xmas morning when suddenly his heart gave a leap – he could see the tip of the little rifle bayonet protruding from behind a pile of boxes covered in the lightest blanket of snow. He was so excited that by the time he reached it he had already fallen over three times! Simply because he could not believe it had happened – he had once more found the best friend he had ever had in the whole world! On the happiest morning of the whole year! It was fantastic! It was by sheer good fortune that he did not take another tumble as he hurtled towards the back door calling out: 'Ma! Ma! Guess what! You'll never believe it! Oh boy! What news!'

But it was news his mother was not destined to receive – not at that particular time, at any rate – for Pat found himself hesitating, to say the least, clutching his scarlet-coated companion close to his heart as his words seemed to ice over deep within his mouth when he perceived the sight which now confronted him. His mother was kneeling on one knee on the kitchen floor with both arms raised in the manner of two irregular boughs of a tree sprouting from a formidable trunk in what was clearly an effort to protect herself. His father's eyes, as he towered above her, burned with a by now familiar fire.

'I distinctly said medium!' he shouted. 'Did I not say medium, woman?'

'Yes! Yes, you did, Victor, but—' pleaded Mrs McNab.

'Yes, you did Victor, but! Yes you did Victor but! If you were in the army they'd strip you of whatever Godforsaken miserable rank you possessed and make you run the gauntlet! And these – you call these Brussels sprouts? Well – do you?'

'Yes, Victor! No, Victor!' was Pat's mother's hapless reply.

'No, Victor! Well no Victor is exactly the right answer! For you know what I call them? Mush! What's that I said, woman?'

'Mush, Victor!'

'Correct. And as for the rest of this muck masquerading as Christmas dinner, why you wouldn't feed it to a barrack house rat! To a what, madam?'

'To a barrack house rat, Victor!'

'Clever girl. Now take it away and cook it again!'

*

It may be that the relentless stress – for what else can you call it – of this particular period in Pat's life could not have possibly have concluded but in the manner which it did. Or it may be that it was Pat's proximity to his mother's side on that particular evening as the tears (tears the size of plums, he reflected) rolled down her cheeks and onto the paisley patterned material of her dress which tipped him 'over the edge', for want of a better expression. Either way, the shift within Pat McNab's soul which occurred in the kitchen that night, while to others imperceptible, can for him be described as nothing short of seismic. As he trudged, his feet gradually acquiring, it seemed, the consistency of molten lead, his earlier anodyne reassurances to his mother (he had insisted that everything would be 'all right') now draped themselves about his body like chains. Thus it was a nine-year-old boy who seemed to weigh close on fourteen stone who climbed in beneath the covers of his bed on that eventful Xmas night. One which, almost within seconds of Pat's head touching the pillow, was about to prove even more so. Eventful, indeed, beyond one's wildest dreams, perhaps – the tiny crimson glow which slowly became apparent, expanding until it illuminated the entire room with a phosphorescence best described as immense! It was as if the diminutive percussionist had been consumed by a conflagration ignited from within yet utterly disproportionate to his size! Pat could barely conceal his excitement as he clutched the covers and leaped up in bed. For his best friend of all time was actually speaking now – addressing him! With little lips that moved up and down, and small, perfectly formed wooden teeth through which emerged the words: 'You know what we're going to have to do, Pat, don't you?'

Initially, the toy's appointed custodian was so taken aback that his reply was little more than a dry, inaudible husk of sound anonymously lodged at the back of his throat. But soon, through a supreme effort on his part, this formed itself into the word: 'What?' a tingling beginning at the base of his spine as soon as the completed sentence – phlegmatically delivered by the miniature military man – '*We're going to have to kill him*' reached his ears.

Pat's heart began to beat with great rapidity. Counterpane tassels were attacked with some fierceness.

'But how, little tin soldier? You're just a peaceful little drummer boy! Surely it would be impossible for you to kill someone!' he pleaded.

The little drummer boy nodded.

'Yes it is, Pat,' he said. 'But I've seen it done so often I really think I could be of some help in that area!'

Pat's eyes brightened as the moon's light glanced off them.

'You could?' he said.

The military man/toy nodded again, with a renewed enthusiasm that was unmistakable.

'Yes! I could keep watch and if you got frightened I could encourage you to keep going, saying: "Do it now, Pat! Do it!" and so on.'

Pat clutched the coverlets close to his chest.

'Oh, little tin soldier! Little drummer boy! No!'

'And play the drum so you'd keep going until the deed was done!'

'Tin soldier! It's impossible! I can't! I simply can't!'

The little voice was low and tender.

'I saw your mother crying today,' he said, adding ominously, 'Again.'

Pat plunged his head into the pillow.

'I hate him!' he wept bitterly. 'I hate my father!'

'He punched her in the stomach. I saw him!'

'Why! Why does he do such things?' howled Pat.

'I saw him make her crawl around on all fours with a potato in her mouth. It was terrible!'

'No! Please tell me it's not true!'

'He made her call him general. "Call me general!" he said. 'General, Pat!'

'He's not a general!' squealed Pat, leaping up in the bed. 'He's only a stupid old captain!'

It was but moments later that a familiar, booming voice rang out across the landing.

'What the hell's going on, waking up the whole house on a Christmas night!'

The door of the bedroom shot open and Pat found himself confronted by a slavering hulk in a dressing gown. Stabbing its index finger fiercely in the direction of the small, brightly coloured figure now clutched tightly to Pat's chest.

'Give me that thing!' snapped Pat's father.

The painted metal figure spun in the air, smacking against the wall and making a heart-rending *ping* noise as it did so.

*

Quite a mistake, Pat found himself reflecting now, all these years later, as he stared, glassy-eyed, into the heart of the library fire. And not without the hint of a smile, either! What he had not realized, of course, and possibly was incapable of doing, was that following the perpetration of such a heinous act, the effect on his son could not but be inevitable. And so it was to prove, for now Pat – why he simply didn't care what happened! 'As a matter of fact,' he recollected now, 'it was as if my father couldn't have done me a better favour! Bestowed on me at last my own personal and private Christmas! Belonging to me and the only person who mattered to me in the entire universe – the Little Drummer Boy!'

*

Which indeed did appear to be the case, for subsequent to that incident, Pat and his six-inch-high companion appeared to be having the time of their lives! Rarely a night went by now but they'd discuss it and with a grin so wicked coming to that shining little enamel face you would think that everything they were saying was every bit as real as if it were happening. A small grey hand tugged Pat's sleeve and, with that strange expression clouding his features again, the gay-coloured percussionist said: 'And then what I'll do is – I'll creep into his room after you, OK?' as Pat tapped his closed fists together and enthused, wild-eyed: 'Yeah, Little Drummer Boy!!'

There was a delicious feeling in his stomach, the like of which he had never known before, as Pat – as though observing himself – moved slowly across the floor of his father's – or as he was now known, 'The Hog's' – bedroom. His snoring for all the world as two large sheets of corrugated cardboard torn in two.

'Now Pat! Now!' whispered his friend and confidant – and, now, conscience – his sharpened bayonet-tip gleaming in the moon's pale spectral light.

195

Pat could feel every muscle in his body begin to tighten. He was ramrod-stiff as he stood by the wardrobe.

'Captain Victor McNab!' he declared. 'You have been found guilty by this court and sentence of death has been pronounced upon you. How do you plead?

The solitary beat on the small red and blue drum seemed to enfold the entire room.

'I said – how do you plead?' repeated Pat in tones which were unyielding.

The first faint echoes of a fragile, lonely melody began to issue from between two rows of wooden teeth.

'*Ta ra ra ra ra ra ra – bump a bum bum*
Me and my drum!'

*

Pat knew in his heart that it could not possibly be but it seemed to him that with the first two notes of that piercing, haunting melody, all those sad, hurt souls whose lives Captain Slaughter (one of their increasingly more colourful names for his father) had ruined (a euphemism, surely, considering most of them had been cruelly dispatched to their eternal reward) were right there with him in the library. High walls of shadows surrounded him.

'I said – how do you plead?' he had demanded to know that fateful night so many years before.

The racking cries of pain and strangled gurgling that issued from his father's throat as he shot up in bed clutching his ears and throat were, despite Pat's protracted psychological preparation for it, close to – it is pointless to deny it – unbearable.

*

'That was all so, so long ago now, of course,' murmured Pat to himself as he leaned on the gatepost the following morning, looking down the garden. He ran his finger along the top of the stone pillar which was covered entirely in the most beautifully delicate lacework of snow. 'Sad thing is,' he said, his breath condensing in the hard, still air, 'you always hope there's a way out and if Mammy hadn't gone to Dublin that day, he might still be alive. But another way of looking at it is that that's the way it's meant to be.'

His eyes shone as he held up the small companion in his right hand and stared fondly at the little beads of melted snow on his rose-red cheeks. The paint of his drum had long since flaked and faded.

'There is no other way it could have been,' his old pal seemed to say. 'No other way, friend. He made it inevitable.'

*

It seemed as yesterday now, when the inevitable had begun in earnest. Pat had been doing his homework at the kitchen table when his mother arrived back from Dublin. She put her head around the door and said: 'Look at that! Well, who's a busy fellow now!' as she tiptoed up behind him and cried: 'Guess what I've got for you!'

Pat nearly fainted when he saw her open the package.

The uniform was almost exactly like his pal's, right down to the last detail – the knee britches sparkling white and a beautiful, swallow-tailed scarlet coat with brass buttons. Pat could not believe his eyes as he stared at himself in the bedroom mirror. He gasped.

'Mammy! It's exactly like him!'

He kissed his small toy – instinctively – and slipped it into the pocket of his military tunic. His mother hugged him.

'We'll have a good Christmas yet, you and me – and to hell with – him! Won't we, love?'

Pat had nodded so fiercely he feared his head would come rolling off.

*

What fun they had some days later – his father was in Carrickmacross: Mammy marching up and down the field with her arms swinging and Pat directly behind her beating a tattoo.

'*Ta ra ra ra ra boys oh boys!*' sang his mother proudly.

'More, Mammy! More!' cried Pat.

'*Rup pup pup pum pum me and my drum!*' went on his mother.

'Oh, Mammy! This is the best day of my life!' cried Pat McNab as his mother enveloped him in her large arms, crying: 'Pat McNab, my little drummer boy!' smothering his forehead in kisses.

*

That his visit to Carrickmacross should have been cut short was fortunate for the Captain but of course would prove ultimately tragic for Mrs McNab and her son. Although that was not how it seemed as they fell in the door of the house that evening, laughing together until the tears flowed down their faces. Anyone observing them would have assumed them without question to be hopelessly intoxicated, mother and son or not.

'Oh, Pat,' cried his mother – out of sheer exultation – 'you're an awful man! The drumming out of you!'

'And then, Mammy – ' squealed Pat, almost catching his tailcoat in the door – 'you nearly tripping over the thistle!'

It was not to be very long before they sensed a particular presence within the room and found themselves confronting a tense, familiar shape blackly enthroned in a wingbacked chair.

'Victor!' cried Mrs McNab – haplessly. 'We were just up the town getting the messages!'

As she spoke these words, despite the pristine excellence of his expertly tailored regalia, Pat McNab had fancied himself covered entirely from head to toe in slime.

His father's snarling cough filled the kitchen with ease.

'Messages,' he intoned gravely.

'Yes,' replied Mrs McNab.

It was plain that her voice was filled with pure terror.

'Of course,' replied her husband. 'And I see you bought something.'

He paused.

'For your son,' he added, acidly.

'Sure it was only a little present, Victor. A little something before he goes back to school.'

His father's words were cold as tombstones.

'And that's what you'd like him to be, is it? A son of mine a little nancy drummer boy, stomping about the place with little sticks to humiliate his father! Is it? Is it!'

'No, Victor!' squealed Mrs McNab.

'No, Victor! Well by God it'll be no Victor by the time this Christmas is out! C'mere, you!'

Within seconds, each brass button had been gruffly torn from the coat and the coat itself ripped from Pat's back. As a consequence of which the little drummer boy fell from his pocket, clanging musically onto the tiles of the floor. Instantaneously, his father picked him up and began to cuff his mother violently with him before flinging him out of the open window, once more to be swallowed up by the horizonless steppes of the McNab garden.

Words cannot describe what ensued that day. 'The horror' delineated by Conrad in his tale of Congolese insanity would be but an approximation.

*

It was to be a defeated and badly injured Pat McNab who whiled away his holiday hours, racked by hopeless sobs as he poked the snow-dusted hogweeds and battered dock leaves that dotted the arctic wastes which had taken his friend for ever with a piece of broken stick. He was heartbroken that he could be so close and yet so far away! Hoping in vain for the play of sunlight upon a bayonet-tip that would reveal for him

199

the location of his cold and lonely grave, the hard-crusted pit
into which his shortish metal pal had been so callously cast.
But it was not to be that evening – indeed, fourteen such
finger-numbing garden-combing searches were to take place
before his companion's eventual discovery – and the cry that
erupted from the depths of Pat's being to cleave the cosmos
was truly heart-rending.

*

'So many years past,' thought Pat McNab as he finished raking
the fire and went to the window to contemplate the once more
still and tranquil countryside. He smiled. 'So many years and
now at last, thank God, a kind of peace has come over the earth.'

As it had over her, his mother Maimie, eventually, that
Christmas so long ago. He smiled as he thought of her falling
through the bedroom door that fateful night after 'the incident', clutching her throat with the vomit pouring out of her
mouth in a dun-coloured stream. A feeling of great calm
encompassed him as he stroked the head of his pint-sized
companion and gazed upon his glazed eyes and time-worn
face. (There was a piece of grass in his ear and beneath his
right eye there was a tiny scratch of paint which gave for all
the world the impression of a tear.) Pat stroked him and said:
'I know some people say little tin soldiers have no feelings.
That it's all in your imagination. And maybe it is. Maybe it is,
little tin soldier, friend of mine and thus to be for all time.'

Pat kissed the top of the small head and replaced the figure
in his pocket before going upstairs, repeating as he did so:
'Maybe it *was* all our imagination.' A consideration to which
he had given much thought many months later, searching
that very same pocket which had become the toy's home,
to discover – yet again – what can only be described as the
vastest of holes and the hugest of absences.

*

But that was not how it seemed that Christmas night as the bedroom door creaked slowly open and a moonlit shadow fell upon a pillow where Captain McNab now lay asleep, the peace which he had for so long denied to others plainly etched upon his face.

*

At first, Mrs McNab proved inconsolable, sobbing hopelessly by the kitchen window. Pat did his best to comfort her.

'It's going to be all right, Ma,' he said, 'I promise you. He'll never bother us again.'

'But I loved him, son,' she protested. 'You don't understand. You shouldn't have done it!'

Pat winced and, despite himself, found himself being quite caustic with her. He clamped his fingers about her shoulder.

'You'll have to stop saying that, Ma!' he cried. 'It's not fair! He ruined our Christmas! He ruined everything!'

His mother took his hand in hers and dabbed her eyes with a Kleenex tissue. She nodded.

'I know, son, I know. It's just that I wasn't expecting—'

The sight of her dead husband prone on the pillow with a snapped drumstick protruding from each ear and the shiny spike of a bayonet smeared with blood inserted in his throat came shooting into her mind anew and it was all she could do not to begin sobbing once more.

Pat smiled and his eyes twinkled. He squeezed her shoulder.

'I promise you, Ma,' he said. 'Everything will be all right from now on. You'll see.'

*

It was dusk and the last flakes of snow were falling as Pat sat at the kitchen table. In the centre of it stood his friend – angled drumsticks at the ready – a little bruised, perhaps but who cared, after what had seemed an absence of centuries! How magnificent life, Pat thought, could sometimes be, against all the odds, to deliver up one's memories as pure and unblemished and pristine as they had been even in one's dreams! He shook his head. For a tiny second, he fancied his little friend's right eye winked, as if to say: '*Correct, Pat!*'

Sadly it was not so. But what *was* so was that they were together once more, and as he fingered the last few remaining currants of the Christmas pudding into his mouth, Pat McNab thought to himself how beautiful it was that, despite it all, the Christmas that would see both him and all the children of the world who had ever lived being happy in a way they could never heretofore have dreamed, had, against all the odds, been delivered unto them. As a tear at last came to his cheek and he nodded to a little old soldier whose seasonal tattoo rang out now in the closing hours of the day as Pat took up the tune and proudly sang with him a song that would be theirs for ever, the light from the Yuletide logs flickering upon his raw and glittering cheeks, ringing the words *pa ra ra rup pup pum pum* out with a lonesome majesty in the dying light of evening.

CHAPTER EIGHT

Fly Me To The Moon

Fly Me To The Moon

Poets often use many words to say
A simple thing
It takes tho' and time and rhyme to make
A poem sing
With music and words I've been playing
For you I have written a song
To be sure that you'll know what I'm saying
I'll translate as I go along:

Fly me to the moon
And let me play among the stars
Let me see what spring is like
On Jupiter and Mars.
In other words darling kiss me!

Fill my life with song
And let me sing for evermore
You are all I hope for
All I worship and adore
In other words please be true
In other words I love you

THERE ARE THOSE who are quite emphatic that the genesis of what might be termed Pat's 'fevered imaginings' or the 'loosing of his reason unto the terrain of untramelled delusions' was determined solely by a single encounter to which we have earlier referred and which took place upon an otherwise insignificant summer afternoon when Honky McCool, his associate, saw fit to ply him with Mexican hallucinogenics. But, in all truth, it would be fallacious to assume that this alone could have been responsible for the extraordinary deliriums and general technicolour phantasmagoria which became an inextricable part of Pat McNab's life around this time. To put it succinctly, these can only be properly understood when the night he received the solid blow to the head is taken into account. Which resulted in him pottering uncertainly about his immediate environment, gingerly touching the backs of chairs and repeating: '*Ouch!*' as he recalled the hurtful events of that dark and troubling night.

'It's the Pope I blame!' he murmured to himself as he stirred some sugar into his tea, wincing as the sharp pain stabbed him directly – yet again! – over his left eyebrow. 'He shouldn't have said it. Even if he did think it was true – he still shouldn't have said it.'

What Pat was referring to was the statement which had been made by the Supreme Pontiff in an Italian newspaper called *L'Osservatore Romano* – reported in the *Irish Press* – to the effect that 'If there were human beings on the moon, they would probably be like Adam and Eve in Paradise.' Pat cupped his hands around his blue-striped mug, his brow furrowing as he considered: 'If he hadn't said that, I would never have started thinking about it. About it being a beautiful place and everything. Up until then – would I ever have thought about that? No. Because the truth is, I didn't care about the moon at all. I paid no mind to it in the wide world. The very last thing I was likely to start thinking was: "I wish I was up there on that beautiful orb of silver. Maybe then I'd be happy."'

Pat touched the large turbanlike bandage tentatively and felt a wave of sadness consume him. In a corner of the window, the fat lunar sphere rested impassively – untauntingly, it has to be said – observing him like a single blue eyeball.

*

It seemed no time ago at all since Pat had been sitting at the bar in Sullivan's, about three-quarters of the way through his third bottle of Macardles Ale, when he looked up from his newspaper, frowned and remarked to Timmy Sullivan: 'Timmy – do you think the Pope's right?'

Timmy flicked his lower lip against the back of his front teeth making a 'plupp' sound as he narrowed his brow and said: 'Right about which now, Pat?'

Pat stared into the bubbles which had assembled on the surface of his beverage. Such was the level of activity in there that new lifeforms might be being born before his very eyes. A medium-sized sparkling dome of liquid went 'Pop!' as Pat replied: 'About people on the moon, I mean, Timmy,' he continued, 'about them being like Adam and Eve in Paradise and so on.'

Timmy Sullivan's reply was instantaneous and unequivocal.

'Ha ha!' he cried aloud, flicking his teacloth across his shoulder and appealing to the other customers. 'Do you hear that, lads! Sure there's no people on the moon, Pat! Weren't we only talking about it last night!'

Pat sighed, a little disappointed by what he considered Timmy's excessive and unnecessary vehemence.

'I know that, Timmy,' he nodded, 'I know there mightn't be. But I read it in the paper that the Pope said *if* there was – *if* there was – they'd have to be like Adam and Eve were. They'd have to be like them.'

Pat was taken aback to find the barman's face looming as if out of nowhere before him, to the extent that one's iris might have been the mirror image of the other.

'Where did you read that, Pat?' he heard Timmy cry, slapping his open palm onto the marble-topped counter. 'Tell me now – where did you hear all this? Go on – tell me!'

Despite himself, Pat felt a lump forming in his throat as he searched for the words which would explain his case.

'I read it here – in the *Irish Press*!' he began. 'He said it in an Italian paper. He said . . . it said . . .'

Timmy Sullivan slapped the counter anew and thundered:

'Pat! *He* said! *It* said! Pat – are you going to start believing all you read in the papers? Look here, Pat! I have nothing against the *Irish Press*, and paper-men have to do their job like everybody else. But I'll tell you this, Pat – when it comes to the moon, do you know what that man knows? Do you know what His Holiness knows about that piece of rock above yonder? Do you, Pat?'

Pat lowered his head and replied softly: 'No, Timmy.'

The barman's gaze was fierce and penetrating as he wound the teacloth about his knuckles in a gesture which might befit a prizefighter.

'As much as this backside knows about snipe-shooting,' he declared, 'and do you know why that is? Do you know why that might be, Pat?'

Pat swallowed and noted with some anxiety the imprint of his fingers on the side of his glass.

'No, Timmy,' he replied, 'why?'

The barman's closed fist hit the counter with a dull 'thupping' sound.

'Because they can't, Pat!' he barked – quite shrilly. 'Because they can't! And do you know why that is, Pat? Do you know why?'

Pat shook his head. The barman leaned in close, intimate and conspiratorial. Every word seemed careful and considered.

'Because they never went! They never went near the moon!'

Pat stared at the frozen yet animated countenance directly in front of him. He felt as if he were suspended somewhere in outer space.

'Never went near it?' he croaked.

'No!' snapped the barman. 'Cooked the whole thing up above in Washington! And done it all like a film in the Nevada desert! Sure you knew that, Pat! Don't tell me you're going to sit there and say you didn't know it! Weren't we only talking about it in here last night!'

The barman swung on his heel, the stained teacloth as some sad epaulette wilting upon his shoulder.

'I say, Josie!' he cried. 'Wait till you hear this! Pat believes—'

The words leaped from Pat's mouth as he tugged at the barman's sleeve.

'No! I don't!' he cried.

Every muscle in Timmy Sullivan's body seemed to relax as he brightened and, smiling, said: 'Indeed and don't I know well you don't! What do you take me for, Pat, huh? Do they think the people's eejits? Do they think the people's eejits?'

'The people's no eejits!' shouted Josie (Jones) at exactly that moment, discarding his high stool with disdain. 'The people has as much brains as any of them!'

The barman closed one eye and nodded gratefully.

'That's right. Now you're talking, Josie. The people has brains surely, and they'll not be codded by the likes of these NASA boys above. Am I right? Any boy in this bar, you ask him about your iron cores, magnetic fields or even your lunar phase. Do you think he won't know? He'll know all right, for he's forgotten more about lithospheres and molten zones than Mr Cape Canaveral Press-The-Button will ever know. Have I it right there, Josie, would you say?'

'You have it in the shell of a nut,' replied Josie, clearly pleased.

Timmy Sullivan's eyes twinkled as he turned to Pat and said: 'Now, Pat! Do you hear that!'

Pat smiled and weakly ordered another glass of Macardles accompanied by a treble Johnnie Walker whisky chaser. 'Oh now but it's a good one, boys, but it's a good one!' smiled Timmy Sullivan as he acknowledged the signal of a dedicated customer down at the far end of the bar.

*

Towards the end of the evening, there were quite an amount of empty glasses on the counter in front of Pat, to the extent that he was almost invisible to Timmy Sullivan who was darting about his premises flicking his teacloth vigorously as he called: 'Time now! Come on! Time now, please!' Much of the frenetic activity which was proceeding around Pat was invisible to him as he, for no discernible reason, smiled vacantly to himself and searched for his cigarettes before overhearing, somewhere close by: 'There he is! Say it now, why don't you!'

Pat paused for a moment. His head seemed inordinately heavy to him. He was taken aback to see a scarlet-tinted countenance glaring lividly at him as his response – which was: 'Huh?' – at last found itself.

'Go on, I tault ye! Say it now! Make a laugh of the Pope now!' he heard again.

Pat's saliva felt quite thick and sickly. 'What?' he said.

'Don't what me!' snapped the voice, harsh as rusted steel. 'Don't what me, you Protestant ye! You can drink none!'

Pat was relieved to hear the comforting, steady voice of

Timmy Sullivan as his teacloth swept into view like a flag of peace. 'Ah come on, lads! It's way past time!' he shouted, adding with a smile: 'Youse leave Pat alone there now! It's time he was off up the wooden hill! Right, Pat?'

Pat's smile in reply was somewhat faint and sickly.

*

A strange placidity descended on Pat as he made his way home some time moments later, already having almost forgotten the unpleasant interlude, preoccupied as he was with the bluish rays of the light which were emanating from the distended orb directly above his head.

'Like some magic and mysterious light,' thought Pat to himself as he searched once more for his cigarettes. For the tiniest of seconds he could have sworn he heard voices close by. 'Pah!' he murmured dismissively, inserting the Major between two fingers. But the push he felt against his shoulder soon banished the possibility of further '*Pahs!*' or similar exclamations of disregard.

'Say the "Our Father"!' growled the voice of a familiar figure from Sullivan's Bar.

'Aye!' exhorted its companion – a rotund figure encased in ravelled cardigan and muffler – 'And quick too!'

Pat did not know either man. They were not from the district. He thought, in the circumstances, that he had better comply.

'*Our father who hash in handbook!*' he began, somewhat clumsily, the words heavy as overripe plums in his mouth.

A smile of deep satisfaction began to creep across the visage of his interlocutor.

'You see?' he said, giving Pat another push. 'Didn't I tell you?'

'You sure did,' came the reply. 'You sure did! And to think I wasn't going t'balayve ya!'

The first blow caught Pat in the solar plexus and doubled

him up helplessly. The beating which he then began to receive can only be described as merciless. A piece of stick which they found to hand – completely by accident – was employed with savage efficiency. Blow after blow rained down on the head of Pat McNab as he lay face down in the gravel.

'Now! See how you like that, you atheist!' heard Pat in the distance, the sound of the discarded stick falling on the gravel, followed by the gallops of retreating feet and cries of: 'Come on!'

It is not inaccurate to say that – inexplicably, perhaps, and clearly inappropriately – Pat now felt a strange sense of peacefulness descending upon him, as though that pale and fragile planet – the last thing he saw before his heaving lids at long last closed – had cast about him yellow nets of light and comfort, as though to draw him towards her and the man within her who forever seemed to smile.

Initially, Pat felt quite odd, and indubitably, there was a nagging sense of unease which despite himself he simply could not seem to elude. Understandable, surely, for one does not – indeed, why should one – expect the sartorial splendour emblematic of one's dreams to be within one's grasp in what was, in effect, but the infinitesimal fraction of a second. And yet – there he was, Pat McNab, impeccably attired in a suit of velvet plum, complete with dicky bow and cuffs of crafted lace. Equally unexpected – and with comparable alacrity – was the sight of literally hundreds of what in former generations might have been described as 'teenyboppers', screaming with such vigour that their voices had reached an almost unbearable, unearthly pitch, hurtling as in a single wave in one direction. Ecstatic cries of: 'Pat! Please! Sign my autograph book!' leaping from their lips as they wept: 'Oh! If only we were old enough to get into your show at the Copacabana!', their tender young bodies collapsing into states of unconsciousness, cheeks streaking with tears. Had Bud O'Kane not appeared only seconds later, Pat would most certainly not have known what course of action to pursue. Such a quandary as he found himself in now, he had no precedent for and neither the firmness of purpose or language which might assist him in the negotiation of it.

Bud's large hand almost covered half of Pat's back as he slapped it firmly.

'Hey, Pat!' he grinned. 'There you are! Look – I got some people you oughta meet. How about you drop by the Copa for a beer? That OK with you?'

At once, Pat McNab appeared to relocate his misplaced bearings. He felt comfortable with Bud O'Kane. From the breast pocket of his jacket, he produced his RayBan spectacles, reflecting a diminutive Bud O'Kane in each lens.

'Yup?' quizzed Bud hopefully.

'Why sure, Bud!' replied Pat brightly – almost incandescently, indeed! – 'I don't mind if I do!'

*

There were few patrons in the Copacabana Lounge at that hour but Pat didn't mind for right at that moment, as he twirled the angled umbrella in his turquoise-coloured cocktail, he was just about the happiest guy in town. He smiled to himself as he thought: 'Well, I don't know if I'm in Paradise or not but one thing is – it's as close as I've ever come to it! And you'd better believe it!'

What Pat was specifically referring to was the luxurious spectacle of loveliness which had just strolled – strolled? – no, floated! – across the dance floor to stand directly before him. Bearing – he reflected for a second – the oddest resemblance to a woman who had once been known as Bridie Cunningham. With her copper-coloured hair and freckle-splashed dimples, a creature who'd stepped from a dream.

'Pat!' grinned Bud, placing his large hand on Pat's shoulder. 'I'd like you to meet Lee. She's a big fan!'

Pat McNab watched his hand as it seemed to take for ever

to extend, as though in the slowest motion possible. The only words which would come into his mind were: 'If every bit of her doesn't look like Eve, the very first woman born, well all I can say is that whatever bit is missing ain't worth a whole lotta hollering about!'

The words at the back of Pat's throat seemed to form themselves slowly and individually like the smallest and tiniest of seeds.

'You're a very beautiful lady, Lee –' his voice seemed lighter than he had intended it to be – 'has anyone ever told you that?'

The slightest touch of pink that came into Lee's cheeks as she lowered her head had the effect of turning Pat's legs to strings of spaghetti. A fact which ought to have troubled him. Why then did he feel more exhilarated than he ever had in his whole life?

*

'*Fly me to the moon*
And let me play among the stars
Let me see what spring is like
On Jupiter and Mars!'

Pat clicked his fingers as his reflection moved about the vast glass dome that overlooked the packed nightclub. Outside, the temperature was 150 degrees. Beyond the glass, planets and stars gleamed and glowed like so many thousand million marbles.

'I'd like to dedicate this one to the woman who's gonna be my wife,' clicked Pat, 'Miss Lee Stravoni!'

Miss Lee Stravoni looked away shyly as the strings of the orchestra swept away the inevitable cries of heartbreak and hopelessly youthful envy. 'And they say we got no atmosphere? Come on, guys!' clicked Pat as he caressed the microphone like a child long loved.

*

The careers of pop and cabaret musicians are littered with the burnt-out ash of bad decisions, mistaken choices and the consequences of hubris. But such was not going to happen to Pat McNab, who three weeks later married the most beautiful woman he had ever in his life encountered. And who now, in her forget-me-not patterned nightdress, lay back in his arms and gazed into his eyes. Barely a month together, he thought, and already it seemed like they'd come a million miles.

'A million light-years,' he repeated, fingering her long copper tresses as he reflected just how right the Pope had been.

'He was right all along,' he whispered to his wife, 'he was number one dude all along, babe.'

Lee nodded and snuggled in towards his shoulder.

*

There had never been a crowd like it in the Paradise Bar. Outside, hordes of disappointed punters wept uncontrollably. Bud O'Kane took the mike.

'Ladies and gentlemen! Here comes the moment you've all been waiting for! I know how many of you have travelled a long way to be here tonight – so without further ado, let me introduce to you, ladies and gentlemen – Mr Pat McNab!'

There can be no word employed here to adequately describe the performance delivered by Pat that night in his sequinned leisure suit and gold medallion. The encore of 'Fly Me To The Moon' was not deemed sufficient by the distraught, emotional crowd.

*

There has been a lot written about time and space and alternative universes and the notion of perception vis-à-vis the incalculable vastness of the cosmos, but little of it was of any interest to Pat. All he knew now was that he woke up each and every morning to see the world in a way which he had never done before. The way, perhaps it could be argued, most people had, since time began, perceived it to be. But not Pat McNab. And when he cast his eyes across it now, all that he wished to do was stride uncompromisingly in the direction of his telephone and place a call to the Vatican, directly to the head of the one true Church himself. He smiled as he thought of the words he would use. 'Pope,' he would say, 'you were right. All the time, you were right. They *are* like Adam and Eve. She is the palest, purest creature ever created from a mere handful of clay. Thank you. Thank you so much, Pope.'

*

Pat's space-age house was second to none; the video screen which you pulled down like a calendar on the south-facing wall would take the sight from your eyes. The cube-shaped chairs, fashioned from a rare alloy found only on Mars, had the effect of rendering visitors utterly slack-jawed. The 'Living Delft', which rearranged itself randomly to supply whatever dish might be required at any particular time, rendered the dreariest of domestic routines as a glorious carnival. The family pet – Argo, the lizard-dog – was a constant heart-warming companion. Pat and Lee's children, Anco and Zok, loved him. Happiness itself almost seemed to take human form within their silver-domed abode, located close by the Sea of Tranquillity.

'Pat,' Lee said one day, playing with one of the hairs on her jumper (it was one thousand years old), 'you know what I sometimes think?'

Pat left down his hand-held news console and smiled. 'What's that, honey?' he said.

His wife came and sat on his knee, raking her long, slender fingers through his hair. There was no mistaking the transparent, guileless generosity in those eyes. 'I think we're in

Paradise,' she said. Argo gurgle-barked and the children chuckled shyly. Outside, Saturn basked, necklaced with gaseous rings. Pat squeezed his wife's hand.

*

Thus the days went by, with Pat in his shirtsleeves at the white and shiny grand piano (there were crotchets and quavers all over it), frowning and scratching his head as he chewed on his pencil and made corrections on his music sheets.

'Come on, honey!' Lee would cry as she appeared in the doorway with an appetizing tray of nibbles. 'Give yourself a break! You deserve it!'

And indeed, that was something Pat could not deny as each night he flopped down exhausted beside the woman he adored, constellations of ill-matched notes swirling before his tired eyes, the faces of his adoring fans melding into an adulatory blur. But who could deny that it was worth it, all of it, as each day upon the hour, the video screen shimmered with dry-mouthed newscasters who excitedly spoke of the 'singing sensation Pat McNab' whose success 'continued apace', and was astounding even the most experienced hands in the music industry as his sellout concerts persisted in 'wowing' the universe. As one 'talking head' eagerly put it, 'Pat's rendition of "Fly Me To The Moon" is hotly tipped to scoop the much-coveted top award at this season's Sea of Joy Bash in September!'

*

Clearly Bud O'Kane was delighted most of all! Indeed, his career – after a series of scandals involving his previous protégé, Ned 'Mr Moog' McGeery – had been on the verge of virtual collapse until the fortuitous appearance. 'Pat,' Bud said brightly, placing his hand on the arm of the universally acclaimed songsmith, 'you are one motherfreaking star – and I mean it!'

Their mutual good fortune showed no signs of abating.

Hordes of weeping teenage girls continued to congregate at airports, talk-show hosts tossed back their heads and marvelled at Pat's off-the-cuff witticisms; middle-aged women flung themselves prostrate in front of the stage as he, Pat, stroked his microphone and crooned: '*Let me know what spring is like on Jupiter and Mars!*' The Day-Glo nomenclature upon a thousand video screens proclaimed ecstatically: '*McNab no. 1 again!*'

The home front too, was as some magnetic field of good fortune. His children had been described by the teacher as 'the brightest planets in the firmament' and it was hard for Pat to hold back a tear of pride when his ten-year-old daughter presented him with a report card which read: 'Ist in Class'. Was it any wonder that late at night he might find himself reflecting that he had been almost blessed with too much happiness, more being bestowed upon him than a man could be feasibly expected to bear? Consequently experiencing the slightest frisson of fear and trepidation that it might all be taken away from him?

But Pat need not have worried. For, just as he was considering the incipient disappearance of his myriad good fortunes and almost unbearable happinesses, the forces ranged about him were preparing to confer further honours upon him.

Or so it seemed.

*

Pat was drying himself off with his monogrammed towel after another fabulous encore when a knock came to his dressing-room door. Humming, Pat turned the doorknob to reveal Bud, standing beaming in the doorway in his rectangular-patterned sportscoat and yellow tie. 'Hi buddy, my old pal!' chirped his manager. 'Someone here to see you, I do believe! Permission to send 'em up, sir?'

Pat smiled and nodded his head. 'Of course, Bud!' he replied as he continued drying himself and went back inside, whistling. It was quite a few moments later that he heard the door opening and looked up to see the reflection of his mother in the mirror. At first, the truth is, that it didn't seem like her at all, and out of his mouth the ejaculation: 'Ha! That's not Mammy! No way! Sure what would she be doing here?' would not have seemed inappropriate in the slightest. Admittedly, it was perhaps a more sophisticated, urbane version of the woman who had borne him, but there could be no denying – it *was* the woman who had borne him, all right. As soon as Pat had accepted this admission, however invisibly, the effect was instantaneous. His lower lip began to tremble and he burst into copious tears. The woman in the doorway seemed to glide soundlessly across the floor, stroking her son's hair gently and cradling his head upon her shoulder. There can be no adequate description of Pat's sobs now other than 'huge' and his entire body, from head to toe, shuddered violently.

'It's just that I didn't expect to see you!' he stammered. 'I didn't expect to see you, Mammy!'

His mother's voice seemed to him a mixture of velvet and honey.

'It's all right, Pat,' she said, 'it's all right. I'm here now. Mammy's here.'

In the days and weeks that followed, Pat was well aware that there would be people who would say: 'Well well! How do you like that! Auld McNab turning up out of the blue like that! Letting on she wanted to look after her grandkiddies! Her that couldn't hold on to her husband or rear her only son without putting him mad in the head!'

Pat knew that this was what would be said and – even as he thought it – *was*! He could hear the voices plain as day as if they were speaking directly to him, right there in his living room. But he also knew what rubbish it was! Complete, total, utterly unadulterated rubbish that should be put out that very night for the refuse men! For not only was his mother willing and able to look after the grandkiddies – she was a genius at it, for heaven's sake!

'Do it again, Gran!' the children would yelp as she bounced them on her knee, a little tear forming in her eye because she had been reunited with her son, something she had been dreaming of for so long.

'Give us a little gooser!' she would exhort, exultantly rejoicing as their moist lips smacked against her cheek.

*

It was a very happy grandmother (and mother!), consequently, who lay in bed in the small hours of the night now as the door opened softly and a thin shaft of light slanted inwards at a perfect forty-five-degree angle.

'Mammy?' Pat whispered, fingering the cord of his pyjamas. 'Psst! Mammy?'

'Pat?' he heard her reply. 'Is that you?'

'Yes, Mammy,' he answered, continuing, 'Can I come in and talk to you?'

'Of course, son,' he heard her say, 'but of course. Of course, love.'

Outside, the whole universe seemed asleep. As he sat on the bed, Pat twined his fingers and affirmed, shyly: 'I just wanted to say I'm sorry, Mammy. I just wanted to say I'm sorry.'

He felt her fingers curling around a lock of his hair as she said:

'Pat?'

'Mm?' he said, choked.

'Pat, love? Can I say something to you?'

'What, Ma?' was Pat's reply.

'So am I, son. So am I.'

With those words, it was as though the synthetic curtains became somehow swept apart and a ludicrously orange sunburst filled the entire room with its light. As though a cymbal had crashed and Pat had, mysteriously – magically! – magnificently! – donned his suit of velvet plum with the dashing waistcoat as he triumphantly pulverized the air, his sophisticated yet ample and comforting parent clapping her hands and crying: 'You haven't changed! You haven't changed a bit, our Pat!'

To which her red-cheeked son replied, with a delight that almost approached falsetto, 'And neither have you, Mammy! Neither have you!'

As, employing the suspension of the bedsprings to the full, the woman who had carried him for nine months sailed buoyantly through the air, crying: 'Give me that wee hand of yours this very minute, you little divil you!'

What can one say of what seems two tiny figures such as might be glimpsed on a wedding cake as they waltz in time, framed against the sloping black velvet backdrop that is infinite space? That they seem the very essence of tranquillity – a veritable ocean of it, indeed – as galactically they tumble, ringed around by stars and planets. Together for ever, singing:

'Fly me to the moon
And let me play among the stars
Let me see what spring is like
On Jupiter and Mars!
In other words, hold my hand
In other words, darling kiss me!'

As Pat lowered his head and murmured:

'I love you, Mammy!'

To which his elated mother replied:

'And I love you too, wee Pat McSkilly McNab! Sure we don't need her, that Lee one! She's not even from Gullytown!'

Pat's muffled laughter into his hands was as a spear through the heart of Lee Stravoni as alone she lay in the master bedroom, for her the beam of the moon's 'benevolent' light as a javelin bisecting her ventricles.

*

How far can such a *danse célèbre* be from the prone figure of Pat McNab as he lies bruised and battered in his long black tattered coat by the briars and whinbushes of the Gullytown district? Any number of light-years and, at that, a very conservative estimate indeed. And growing ever the further distant as, at last, his left leg begins to stir and his hand begins its first tentative journey towards the environs of his right eye above which a pain which can be adequately described as 'intense' is adding to his general sense of dislocation and lack of equanimity. From nowhere, a tidal wave of melancholy seems to sweep over him and the empurpled bruises upon his forearm make themselves startlingly, uncompromisingly clear. The memory of the 'assault stick' with which he was brutalized is so vivid it is as if he is at that moment enduring a re-enactment. But, as he raises himself up to find himself bathed from head to toe in a familiar milky light, realizing that this is not the case, shaking his head at the idiocy of the thought – for his assailants have long since fled – and now crying: 'Of course they're gone! They're hardly going to attack the universally acclaimed Pat McNab! Ha ha!' An assertion which he is about to repeat before being loudly interrupted by a series of what in Shakespeare are often referred to as 'alarums and excursions' some degrees south of the large sycamore tree near Brennan's field. To wit, cries of: 'There he is! We've found him at last!' Dazed though he might be, Pat at once recognized Timmy Sullivan's voice. Within seconds, they were upon him and Pat could see that the barman's companion was none other than Sergeant Foley, who laid a comforting hand on his shoulder and said, sympathetically: 'Jesus, Mary and Joseph! So this is what they did to you, Pat? Did you know them, Timmy? Did you get a good look at their faces?'

Timmy shook his head wistfully.

'No, Sergeant,' he explained, adding regretfully, 'I think they're from the north.'

'I've got to get to the Copacabana Club,' continued Pat in a strange, almost toneless voice, 'I'm playing in the Copacabana tonight, you see! Yes!'

Timmy Sullivan took him by the arm – he regarded Pat as an extremely valued patron – and said: 'Of course you are, Pat. Come on home now like a good lad.'

The whole of Pat McNab's body – his being, indeed – seemed washed in a sad, ineffable blue light.

*

It was some weeks later as Pat was sitting at the counter in Sullivan's listening to what could fairly be described as the worst band in the world – a Casio organ and drum-machine combination – surging towards the chorus of a rapturously received number, oblivious of the fact that they were, along with Timmy Sullivan the proprietor, responsible for the almost lapidary greyness that seemed now to film itself across the eyes of Pat McNab as he contemplated his perspiration-saturated and heavily fingerprinted glass of Macardles Ale.

'Oh, aye!' continued Timmy Sullivan, flicking his teacloth across his shoulder, obliquely, with arched eyebrow, observing Pat as he whispered: 'Gave him a right bloody going-over too! Hasn't been the same since it at all. Couple of nights back, couldn't shut him up! Literally, couldn't shut him up! Him and the moon! Wanted to talk all bloody night about it! And now, if you mention it, he just looks at you.'

Timmy Sullivan wiped a glass and stared (futilely) once more at his lone, silent patron. 'Doesn't want to talk about it at all!' he asserted. 'Funny the way people are, isn't it? What do you say, Josie?'

Josie Jones considered for a moment or two but in the end made no reply, simply turned the slim tube of his cigarette in his fingers and raised it to his lips. The band – The Two Lads – were about to conclude but the resurgence of enthusiasm for their efforts persuaded them otherwise, the dinner-jacketed lead vocalist gathering a handful of air and sending his microphone skyward as from the depths of his throat unfurled each word, a sputnik coursing spaceward:

'Fill my heart with song
And let me sing for evermore
You are all I long for,
All I worship and adore!'

as Pat McNab made no move, in his eyes reflected the tepid bubbles of a Macardles Ale which, to all intents and purposes, might have been three hundred and eighty thousand kilometres away.

CHAPTER NINE

Waka Waka

Waka Waka

Waka waka waka waka waka
Waka waka waka
Waka waka waka waka waka
Waka waka waka
Waka waka waka waka waka
Waka waka waka
Waka waka waka waka waka
Waka waka waka
Waka waka waka waka waka
Waka waka waka

THERE ARE SO MANY THEORIES with regard to 'perception' and the relationship one might contrive with the 'ineluctable modality of the visible', that if we were to go into it here in terms of attempting to understand Pat and how it affected his life around this time, it is likely that we would be expostulating until the proverbial *'kingdom come'*. Suffice to state, perhaps, that the 'bending' of reality or the realignment of the world around him in a peculiarly familiar yet unfamiliar way came about as a result of the recurrent, almost tropical weather conditions which had been prevailing in the area, the heat at times so thick you could almost slice it into large gungy slabs, and his consequent fondness for alcohol. Not to mention the residue of slightly dislocated, pleasurable yet uneasy feelings which remained in his 'psyche' some months now after his 'Mexican adventure' with the redoubtable Pasty McGookin and his associate Honky McCool. Which may go some way towards explaining why Pat was smiling to himself – a jerky, elastic smile, it has to be said – as he came past O'Hare's Bush one ordinary unspectacular evening in June. Muttering to himself glumly – for that was how he felt, regardless of any expressive, seemingly optimistic gesture – 'Ho ho. Welcome to Gullytown. The famous metropolis where things can get so exciting you have to be careful in case your heart might stop on the spot!' He shook his head and laughed at nothing in particular. For the tiniest of seconds he fancied he espied a small bird sporting startlingly technicolour plumage singing in the heart of the oak tree up ahead but when he looked again there was nothing to be seen. 'No! Nothing at all!' he continued. 'After all, what do you expect? I mean, we *are* talking about Gullytown here!' Such conversations – effectively with no one, or thin air, perhaps – might seem pointless but they had the effect of cheering Pat up slightly, and he was on the verge of extending and expanding upon the subject – virulent denunciations of his native heath – when suddenly he found himself distracted by the sharp squeal of brakes and to his amazement out of a cloud of dust not a hundred yards from where he stood (close by Hudie Madden's barn) descried a large American car (a polished black sedan in fact) shooting towards him. He could not be quite sure whether someone had shouted 'Look out!' or 'Move, buddy!' or whether it had been his own reflexes which alerted him in the nick of time, but as he composed himself and climbed – twig-specked and not a little muddied – out of the ditch into which he had been thrown, he instinctively crossed himself, realizing just how lucky he had been, composing himself as best he could to assimilate the bizarre tableau which had now begun to assemble in front of his eyes. For a split second, a wave of feverish, almost exasperated lassitude comparable to that which had become a frequent visitor of late in the hot, troubling nights threatened to overcome him once more with its oily, insistent whispers: 'You're at it again, Pat – imagining things.' As did the fleeting, phantom figures who now passed across his subconscious – Pasty and Honky McCool – nestled in each of their palms a deadly, pulsating root. No less significant in this regard the shocking screech of the sedan's brakes as they slammed into the base of the oak which only minutes before Pat had passed!! It soon became clear that this was no tenebrous shadow play upon the stage of a wounded, ultra-sensitive psyche. As Pat reflected, in literally a nanosecond from his vantage point, close by the ditch: 'Anybody who thinks that it is is going to wind up dead! History!' A huge plume of steam was rising now from the crushed bonnet of the car – it had folded like paper – and leaping from the interior and rolling over before landing expertly on two feet was a large man in black glasses clutching a revolver in a frantic, two-handed grip. Within the vehicle, the remaining passengers, including the driver who was clutching a black briefcase firmly (also frantically) to his chest, were as spectral masks pressed to the window.

'Step out of the car!' the gunman cried (yelled). 'Step out of the car!'

Another man – smaller, attired in a silk suit and a pork-pie hat which became dislodged and subsequently rolled into a cowpat – fell from the car and shouted: 'Take him, Jacy! Splatter his brains all over the tree!'

'Shut the fuppag! You hear me? Get the fupp over here!'

The door swung open and the driver appeared still clutching the briefcase to his chest. Behind the hedge, Pat's face was drained of all colour.

'Now hold it, Jacy! There ain't no need for this. You don't think we can work something out? Why, sure we can!'

Two sharp reports from the unmoving revolver ended both the sentence and his life. Pat could not believe the amount of blood that gushed from his mouth in a great big crimson arc. It was the most crimson blood Pat had ever seen. The other man ran to the corpse as it fell to the ground.

'Jesus, Jacy!' he cried. 'You've killed him! What's Bobbie-Ann going to say?'

Jacy slid his gun inside his pocket and spat:

'Fug the shut up!' (Pat wondered, initially, was he hearing it right, but then became satisfied that these indeed were the words uttered.) Jacy continued: 'You listenin' to me? Since we left Mary's, that's all you been sayin'! You got nothin' else to say? You know what I think of Bobbie-Ann? You know what I think of that fuccamackin' cockamacka? This is what I think!'

Pat winced as two more shots found their way into the chest of the already dead man. Jacy fell to his knees and, flicking open the catches on the briefcase, began to marvel at its contents – numerous stacked wads of pristine dollar bills – crying ecstatically: 'Ha ha! See how you like this, Bobbie-Ann! See who's Jackass Fughpig No-Dick now! Ha ha!'

In his excitement, Jacy had forgotten about the sole remaining occupant of the car, whose hand was now slowly moving inside his coat as he edged his way across the upholstery. 'You slimy fuggerball!' he cried as he rolled out onto the road. The metal of the gun barrel gleamed sprightly in the sun.

'No! Don't, you fool!' cried Jacy and his henchmen instantaneously.

More metal shone.

'Don't!' shouted Jacy.

But it was too late. Three whistling reports left three bodies lying in the sun. A slight wind flapped the crisp banknotes in the glittering shaft of a dead afternoon sun.

It seemed to Pat that in that moment the beat of his heart had slowed down to about one-third of its normal pace. It was as if the whole world behind the hedge had become a giant, vibrating heart going bump bump over and over. He felt his forehead tingle with sweat. Tiny needles. He gasped. All around him everything had changed. It was as if the entire world had been given a new coat of paint. But a paint that could blind you. His heart beat again and there was a strange taste in his mouth. He knew he was faced with a stark choice. Briskly, he began his walk towards the open briefcase.

*

The figure bursting through the underground in Mackie's Wood a mile from the town might have been some hunted, feral creature. Resonant in its ears the sound of pounding feet, the relentless staccato of fuzzbox guitars. There could be no denying now the sweat which rolled down Pat McNab's face. Tiny needles no longer. In large, coursing rivers it wound its way, until his entire mouth seemed filled with perspiration.

Upon his face, great streaks of mud, his hair aloft as like some vigilant regiment of twigs. 'No!' he cried as he raised his forearms, to protect himself, as he thought. But there was no one to be seen. Pat's heart beat again. 'What have I done?' he repeated as he fell behind a tree (a large, spreading tree, fortunately, affording him much cover). 'In God's name what have I done?'

For Pat to avail himself of some 'mushies', as Pasty and Honky McCool had been known to refer to them, a neatly ordered assembly of which conveniently presented themselves to him as he rested himself beneath the spreading boughs, would have been foolhardy in the extreme, for surely he needed all his wits about him. But this is, in fact, what he did – and in what might be considered reasonable quantities, to boot. His subsequent rationalization of his actions involved such thoughts as: 'Sure I need to eat something' and 'It can't get any worse as the little conical-capped fellows went tumbling down his throat.'

This perhaps explains why, despite the gravity of recent events – he had after all witnessed a fatal shootout which had left a normally tranquil country road literally stuffed with corpses, not to mention absconding with a briefcase filled with money which did not belong to him – he now willingly gave himself to hopeless chortling which, it would seem, to the independent observer at least, to possess a sort of wilful abandonment, which might have been expected from a three- or perhaps four-year-old.

*

However, as Pat was amusing himself deep in the sanctuary of Mackie's Wood beneath the cool shade of that expansive elm, what he did not know was that some considerable few miles away, in an establishment called Mary's, a certain gentleman whose name was, in fact, Mary, had just received some information which was not having the effect of making him feel that all was well with the world in any respect whatsoever.

As the person on the other end of the telephone had known for quite some time now. Mary was a large man of about eighteen stone in weight. He wore an orange shirt festooned with bending purple palm trees. His head was fat and inside it, his eyes were stony and dead.

'This is a very good joke,' he said, 'this is so good a joke I've wet my pants. Will I hold the phone down to my pants so you can see how wet they are? Hey, how are you, Ben? How the hell in the futhermugging sugar-shaking world are you fugging doing, huh?'

Suddenly Mary hit the table a kick.

'What?' he snapped. 'Now, Ben, I don't like you doing this! I don't like it when you do this to me! What did you say?'

He lifted a pink pool ball from the green baize surface where it rested placidly. It thudded against the padded leather of the secret door set into the wall.

'Well, then get the futhermugger! You hear me? Get the mothershakin' thing! Get it!'

Mary waved an index finger – very tremulously indeed, and drew his breath.

'Because if you don't,' he continued, 'if you don't—'

He broke off.

'Ben,' he barked down the receiver, 'take off your socks.'

There followed a pause, in which Mary appeared to lose his mind.

'I said – take off your socks!' he roared.

A static-filled reply satisfied him.

'That's better.'

Mary coughed politely. He seemed to be considering the reflection of his hair parting in the burnished, stainless steel of a paper knife.

'Now,' he went on, 'how many toes do you see?'

The reply was indistinct. But seemingly satisfactory.

'That's right,' said Mary, soothingly, 'and you know what it is about them toes? You already owe me one.'

The sound of the receiver being slammed down was shattering in the silence. Not unlike a large bear in a cave, Mary paced the office for some moments, considering various objects, assaulting others before eventually deciding upon a course of action and squeezing the reception buzzer with his thumb.

'Hi, Mary!'

'Tell Celia Mary wants him!' he barked.

'Sure thing, Mary! You got it,' came the receptionist's reply.

A thin employee in a silk suit inadvertently caught his employer's gaze then looked sharply away. A pool ball thudded dully into the wall behind him, narrowly missing his ear.

'What in the hellin's name you lookin' at? You hear me? Get outa here!'

It was some hours later when the studded leather secret door swung open and through it entered a pair of snakeskin winklepicker boots. Followed by some pink trousers and a leopardskin shirt which belonged to Celia, a six-foot black man now grinning from ear to ear beneath his wide-brimmed floppy hat. He liked jewellery, Celia. Gold, especially. He had lots of rings on either hand. '*As black as the riding boots of the Earl of Hell*' might have been an apposite way of describing him. Mary smiled as he turned from the window. His eyes met Celia's.

'I think we got a problem,' were the words he uttered.

*

The family pet had been introduced as Pongo. Celia smiled as he considered anew the tiny shivering terrier. Its fur was literally standing on end as it cowered in a corner behind the washing machine. Florrie Connolly was a quiet woman who had done nothing in her life except collect the pension and mind her own business. Now, inexplicably, she found herself being slammed up against the wall and shouted at for something she hadn't done, something she couldn't have done and knew nothing in the world about. But that wasn't good enough for Celia. He put his muscular arm around her slim neck once more and said: 'Now let's run through this one more time, lady. And this time you'd better get it right because you are puttin' red pepper on my ass and if you don't, I am gonna shove what's left of you down that fuggamutha's barking throat, you hear?'

Pongo shivered behind a jumper as Florrie Connolly, sweetshop owner (and one of the most popular figures in Gullytown), nodded. Her suede ankle boots hovered two inches from the floor.

'Please! Whatever you do, don't hurt him!'

'Then tell me what you know – and be quick about it!'

While he was waiting, Celia produced from his pocket a small rectangular cellophane packet which contained white powder, some of which he proceeded to remove and lick from the ends of his fingers.

As she hobbled away, Florrie Connolly thanked God that her mother wasn't alive.

'Please, Mister,' she pleaded shakily, 'all I know is that that was the man I saw through the window. And there was some kind of argument. I don't know what it was about – I think it was over money. They were—'

'Go on!' snapped Celia, interjecting and sniffing some 'snow'.

'No! Don't hurt me! They were arguing and shouting. And then – one of them pulled a gun!'

'And – ?'

'Then all I remember – I heard shooting. And when I looked again – they were all dead. That was when the other man appeared.'

'Other man?' shouted Celia, a small cloud of white dust ghostily ascending between them. 'What in the hell are you talking about? What did he look like? Who was he with? What

234

was he wearing? What did he say? How long did he stay? What was his name?'

Florrie Connolly covered her eyes with the back of her hand and sniffled.

'As God is my judge, Mister, I don't know,' she pleaded, 'I'm only telling you what I know. That I saw the man and he took the money and ran away with it.'

Celia smashed his fist into the wall.

'What did he look like? How did he speak? What did he wear?'

Florrie Connolly's cry was a heart-rending plea from the pit.

'I don't know, God help me! All I know is – he was wearing a big long coat!'

'Coat? What colour was it?'

'Black. Like yourself,' replied Florrie.

Celia released her and retreated slightly. The kitchen seemed full of his breathing.

'You'd better be right, pussyface,' he said, 'because if you're not—'

He kissed the butt of his Walther PPK. Florrie Connolly recoiled in horror, the eyes of her trusted pet seeming to transmit coded signals which sheepishly declared: 'If only I was bigger and could help.'

The small cottage rocked to its foundations as the door slammed behind the cold-blooded, ring-wearing Gun For Hire.

*

The following day was the wettest for months. There was no indication of any let-up. 'Torrential rainstorms are expected for the next three weeks,' the radio had said. Parked in a layby, Celia watched as his windscreen wipers swept back and forth in a sickening watery dance of tedium. To top it all, the only tape in the car was *Sergio Mendes – Brasil 66, Greatest Hits Compilation*.

'How the muggafuggin' fug did that get here?' he growled, tossing it out into the driving rain. He tapped the walnut-panelled dash with his amethyst ring. How he wished he was back in Detroit. With a long cool drink in front of him and Quincy Jones on the hi-fi. 'Damn!' he repeated. 'Fuggamuthin' damn!'

*

The old man with the umbrella and the tan raincoat shook his head emphatically.

'No!' he repeated irksomely. 'You're way off! You'll have to go back the way you came!'

Celia swore as he spun the steering wheel and negotiated the coupé backwards along the erratic necklace of potholes and puddles.

'You're not on Route 66 now! I suppose that's what you're thinkin'!' called the pensioner after him. 'Aye! Well, you're not!'

His thin, ungenerous face confused Celia. How he would have loved to reach in his pocket and – but no. He wasn't worth it, the piece of—

A huge swoosh of dirty brown water engulfed the pensioner as the coupé swept by.

'You effing bastard!' he shouted, umbrella-stabbing the air wildly. 'Look at me, you big black miserable string of misery! Come back here and I'll run Route 66 right up your hole!'

*

It was clear there was going to be some fun in Sullivan's whenever Pat would arrive in for his nightly drink. As he did now, dressed up to the nines in his swanky paisley shirt and matching tie, not to mention a beige safari jacket absolutely guaranteed to stop the street in its tracks. Timmy was the first to speak, spreading his hands on the marble counter and marvelling: 'Well, Pat! You're the man that's looking well tonight! I suppose you're for the dance, eh?'

Pat smiled as he settled himself on the high stool.

'Maybe, Timmy. Just maybe,' he replied, rubbing his hands as he surveyed the multicoloured xylophone of upended bottles before him.

'Right so, Pat,' continued Timmy. 'Now what'll it be? A pint, I suppose, as usual?'

Pat pursed his lips and considered thoughtfully. He stroked his chin and said:

'No, Timmy. Something tells me I'm going to have a Martini tonight.'

Timmy drummed his fingers on the surface of the counter and said: 'God bless us I don't know what's come over you this past while at all, Pat. Still, I suppose you could do worse.'

The barman smiled and began to sing softly, and very tunefully, the familiar melody:

'*It's the right one, it's the bright one –*'

As Pat, with a sunny grin, joined in enthusiastically:

'*That's Martini!*'

'It is indeed,' laughed Timmy Sullivan, 'it is indeed, Pat. And it's coming right up!'

Pat smiled happily to himself as his drink arrived, complete with a large cherry on a stick. He found its many-hued colours reassuring.

'You know, Timmy,' he said, 'you know, I think I might just have an old Cuban cigar to keep me company with this!'

Timmy inserted his little finger into his ear and rotated it abstractedly for a moment.

'Cripes, Pat,' he said good-naturedly, 'you know, sometimes I think it's worse you're getting.'

'Cheers,' laughed Pat as he raised his terrifically decorated drink to his lips.

*

It was some hours later and there were approximately eleven empty Martini glasses arranged before Pat on the marble-topped counter. Although his large-knotted tie could be considered a little askew, Pat was still reasonably well preserved, and thought himself so as he closed one eye and gazed at his reflection in the mirror opposite (his line of vision somewhat obscured by the now slightly irregular array of inverted receptacles) smiling as directly behind him, he perceived the satin-clad hourglass figure of Winnie McAdam, doused from head to toe in a sweet-smelling perfume, smoothing back her Farrah Fawcett-Major style hair as she elegantly draped herself across the high stool directly beside his and scratched her right eyelid (daubed in bright green eyeshadow) with her little fingernail as she exclaimed: 'Hiya, Pat! Are you going to the disco tonight, I wonder?'

Pat raised his right eyebrow and (without realizing it) adjusted his tie as he said: 'Begod now and do you know what – that mightn't be such a bad idea at all!'

Winnie smiled and looked down at her handbag. It was a small clutch one with a gold clasp. 'Pat,' she said then, touching him ever so lightly on the sleeve of his safari jacket, 'did you have a little bit of luck with the Lotto recently or what?'

This took Pat a little by surprise and he looked at her and said: 'What? What makes you say that, Winnie?'

Winnie's lips met and she paused for a moment. Then she pointed and said: 'Well – your clothes, for a start. And Timmy tells me you're drinking Martini!'

Pat nodded enthusiastically and slipped ever so slightly off the stool as he said: 'I am, Winnie! And I'll drink a lot more of it before the night's out!'

The large Havana seemed to appear from within his inside pocket as if by magic. 'Have a cigar,' he cried, grinning broadly.

Winnie chuckled and squeezed the clasp on her clutch bag.

'Pat! You're mad, do you know that!' she laughed. 'Girls don't smoke cigars!'

'That's right!' said Pat – and now *he* was chuckling. 'And they don't light them with pound notes either!'

Within seconds, Pat held a flaming banknote in his hand, and puffed away merrily as the tip of his cigar began to glow warmly, enveloping its owner in clouds of sweet-smelling blue smoke.

'Come on now, folks, ladies and gents – please!' called Timmy, snapping his cloth. 'Come on now, folks, it's long past time!' as Winnie put her two hands up to her mouth, mirthfully watching Pat – Pat McNab the famous smoker, that is!

When it was time to go, Winnie assisted Pat with his overcoat, stroking him gently on the back as she said: 'Still the same old topcoat anyway, Pat! No sign of that changing!'

Pat tossed his head back nonchalantly. 'Oh now!' he laughed, knocking his leg accidentally against the door. 'It'd take a lot of money to part me from that, Winnie!'

Winnie slanted her fingers and ran them slowly along Pat's right lapel.

'Pat,' she said (although 'cooed' might be more exact), 'were you ever in Barbados at all?'

For a moment, Pat's eyes seemed to move very close together as Winnie continued: 'What's it like, do you think?'

*

There was nothing spectacular happening in Harry Carney's Drapery the following day when the wheel of a car spun momentarily in the gravel making a crunching sound and subsequently grinding to a halt. This was no longer true, however, some moments later when a tall negro with seemingly polished skin entered the premises and dragged the surprised owner across the counter by his tie, shouting into his face: 'I got no time for pussy-footing around! I need a face! I need a name! I wanna know who comes in here! Who buys this shit!'

239

With bewildering speed, a long line of coats was swept to the floor (and some jackets) as Celia swept his forearm in a wide, uncompromising arc.

Harry Carney paled. He was a seemingly meek, mild-mannered man in his forties.

'Now you've done it. You've really done it now, Mister!'

There was an impressive firmness in his voice. Which went unnoticed by Celia, whose only response was to say: 'Ha ha!' Incredibly, the hired assassin was still laughing as Harry raised the baseball bat above his head and stood beside him. The short fat draper's composure was unique.

'What do you think?' he said to Celia, smiling. 'You think perhaps you're dealing with some jick jack mother-shaggin' puke-gutting albino whiteass pant girl who's just gonna let you take his place apart? Apart his place to take, come right in like some flat-assed mouse-man show he runs, well that is where you are wrong Mister! For this assmother – Harry Carney! – was shakin' shook in Brooklyn when you was knee-high to a culpepper coolshank! You hear?'

Before Celia had a chance to respond, the wooden implement caught him behind the left ear and Harry Carney continued to rain down blows upon the large negro as he crumpled to the floor like a Kleenex tissue, his oddly flat – almost monotonous – monologue continuing as he did. 'Honky hinny big-bobbed babe comes into my shop shaking the coat shit down, no sir! That is where you are wrong, very wrong, you big hat-wearing sugar sandwich beat up my ass you gangster pop why somehow I don't think so perhaps you got views, Mr Mother-shootin' Coat-wreckin' Ass! Huh! Take that!'

It was only by sheer force of will and the momentary distraction afforded by a pedestrian passing on the street that Celia succeeded in raising himself to his feet, struggling to find his 'piece'. Which he eventually did, stumbling backwards over a mound of coats and – absurdly! – a wedding dress, as he levelled it at the short fat, baseball-bat-wielding draper.

'Back off,' he growled, 'back off, you crazy mother! You hear me now?'

Harry Carney smiled, with an acidic wryness.

'Sure I do,' he said coolly, 'sure I do, big beat em up boy! But you shoulda done some shiggy shunky before you came into my shop! Open up, you great big popcorn kernel!'

'Stay back!' warned Celia, levelling the pistol.

But it was already too late and the rotund salesman was already hurtling towards him, rudimentary weapon aloft once more.

'I told you to stay—' cried Celia.

Before he had finished the sentence, his piece spat fire and Harry Carney lay dying beside a tattered windcheater. Despite himself, the ring-clad mercenary (for was that not what he was?) fell to one knee beside the gasping tradesman.

'Jesus! Jesus I'm sorry!' he apologized.

*

There was a strange, almost contented light in Harry Carney's eyes as he died now. He seemed about to say something as he touched the negro's arm but the approaching sound of police sirens effectively ended the sentence before it had the chance to begin.

'I'm sorry, man,' cried Celia, 'I swear to God I'm sorry!'

The negro grabbed a green anorak and made a pillow for the dying man's head. The sound of the draper's gurgling filled the entire shop as Celia leapt in behind the counter stuffing any bills or receipts he could find into the large, deep pockets of his maxi-length ermine coat. He froze as he felt the clutches of the dying man's hand on his right leg.

'Shit, man!' he cried, in a voice that was surprisingly almost falsetto. 'Let me go! It's the fuzz!'

'They're gonna put you away for a long time, you shick shack fur-tootin' man!'

There was nothing for it – although a part of him regretted it – but to kick the expiring shopkeeper in the face. There was something poignant about the flapping glass door and the squeaky sound it made as the wheels of the large blue coupé spun and it roared off into the distance.

*

Winnie crinkled up her nose and picked a tiny piece of dust off the left lens of Pat's wraparound glasses, plucked another grape from her large bunch and pressed it to her lips. She drew a long, deep breath and continued: 'But just saying we *were* there – in Barbados – what would we do? Pat – what would we do?' Pat laced his fingers and made a cradle of his hands as he lay back on the 'chaise longue' sofa. A long low whistle glided across the room as he clacked his tongue against his upper teeth and said: 'Sit by the pool, I guess. Have ourselves a long cool drink, maybe. And in the evening – take a helicopter out to the mountains.'

Winnie touched his chest with the flat of her hand as her eyes widened.

'Pat!' she gasped. 'A helicopter? You're crazy!'

Pat removed his RayBan spectacles and looked at her.

'Maybe I am, baby,' he said, 'maybe I am.'

Winnie found herself dumbstruck as he removed a handful of green notes from his top pocket and inserted them down the front of her blouse. His grin was so large it was almost the size of the room.

*

Mary was not grinning. He hit the chair a kick and sent it skidding across the carpet. 'What in the hell are you talking about?' he barked into the receiver. 'No, I don't want to hear any of your shaggy shakin' jumpin' jackshit-jimmy! Just find him! Find him – you hear me? Or your ass is on the line, you pink-face waka-waka candy-suckin' no-time loser, you got that?' The receiver was slammed into its cradle and in that instant the entire building seemed about to explode.

*

Time was running out for Celia and he knew it. The coupé tore down the country road with a startling squeal of tyres. There were indentations on the walnut dashboard where Celia had been repeatedly hitting it. 'Mother-hopper!' he repeated and it was just then he saw it. To the casual observer, there was nothing remarkably significant or spectacular in the sight of a fifty-three-year-old farmer scooping pig nuts from a bucket and scattering them into a trough for his hungry animals. But, as he clambered breathlessly from his coupé, Celia was any-thing but casual. Tan water skitted against his satin leopardskin hipsters as he made his way breathlessly in the direction of the field.

'I don't know what you're talking about!' stammered the countryman as Celia held him up against the wall of the dairy, a piece of paper fluttering in front of his face. It was a coat receipt from Harry Carney's. 'I've never had this coat cleaned in my life!' he croaked.

'Mother-yummy, fuggin' hen-ball!' snapped Celia and flung the hapless pig-breeder to the ground. The polished dashboard received another uncompromising blow as the vehicle took off towards the horizon.

*

It was the Ajax Dry Cleaner's counter assistant's worst night-mare. The day had started off quite unremarkably, as usual, with him sorting out the various items to be sent to the steampress room and now his head was down the toilet, being remorselessly pulled up again by Celia's polished black hand as he bellowed: 'Don't nowhere me, you country bush! I'm

243

through with mealy mouth and this and that and no I wasn't there, you dig?'

'I'm telling you the truth,' the assistant moaned, 'I gave it away years ago! It's the God's honest truth!'

The horrible sound of hissing and gurgling filled the counter assistant's ears.

*

The scarecrow stood dark and rigid in the centre of the field, exuding, despite its turnip head, a certain kind of nobility. Which the single blast from a Winchester pump-action shotgun ended in a fraction of a second, pieces of the vegetable scattered for miles, a scorch hole burnt right through the lapel of its long black coat.

'Hopping comedown! Blast in heaven!' shouted Celia, now turning his attention to the car's new tyres, upon which he rained unremitting kicks. His frustration was such that he might have cried out to the open sky.

*

The discotheque was in full swing as Celia sat slumped at the bar. The deejay was playing one of his favourite tunes, 'Oops Upside Your Head', but he didn't care. The barman wiped the counter in front of him. 'Don't you think you've had enough, Mister?'

There was a vulnerability in Celia's eyes now.

'You don't know what Mary's like,' he explained, 'he—'

Before he could finish, the barman tossed back his head and snorted:

'Not half I don't! My own Cissie is the very same! If I was you, I'd go home, Mister! I'll tell you this – that's one hell of a fine fur coat!'

'Huh?'

Celia was momentarily distracted but he reflected on the

barman's words of advice. He climbed down off his stool and said: 'Yeah. I guess you're right.'

It was just when Celia was approaching the exit and the deejay was introducing his new disc, which was 'The Bump' by Kenny, that he saw what he saw and felt the blood drain from his face to such an extent that he feared he must be turning white, such was the effect that the sight had upon him. He was forced to steady himself against one of the corner banquettes. For just at that moment, Pat McNab, resplendent in his wraparound shades and long black coat, had entered the building with Winnie McAdam on his arm, displaying the demeanour of someone who might be under the impression that he is some sort of 'visiting dignitary'.

The barman could not believe the transformation in his formerly remorseful, if not fragile, customer as he found himself sliding across his own counter on the end of his tie.

'Honky in the shades!' snapped Celia into his face. 'Who is he? I said – who is he?'

The barman gulped. He was genuinely frightened.

'P-P-P-P-Pat McNab!' he stammered. 'C-C-C-Can't you see you're choking me?'

'Tell me about him! Talk! Fast!'

'I don't know nothing about him only that his mother is mad and lately he seems to have come into a pile of money.'

'What did you say?' rasped Celia.

'His mother. She's nuts. And he's not much better, I hear.'

'No! About the money!'

'He won it, maybe. I don't know! I swear to God! All I know is he spends it like there's no tomorrow!'

'Spends it, huh?'

'Aye! Firing it round him like a millionaire this past while!'

A broad grin began to spread across Celia's face, the mirrorball reflected in his golden tooth.

'Well, is that a fact?' he said slowly and contentedly as he discarded the barman and bunched his fist inside his leopard-skin pocket, moving towards the dance floor as Quincy Jones belted out a '*waka-waka*' style song from the stacked speakers.

*

The dance performed by Pat in the centre of the floor could be described as a perfect example of what is known in America as the 'white man's overbite' or perhaps more locally as the 'social worker shuffle'. There appeared, it seemed, to be no pattern or coordination whatsoever to the manner in which he was wildly flailing both his arms and legs, mouthing words along with the tune which was in fact an instrumental hit. But he didn't mind – nor, indeed, did Winnie. They were having the time of their lives. At least until a large black hand settled on Pat's right shoulder.

'Mary wants to talk,' boomed Celia, ominously narrowing his eyes.

It seems incredible that Pat McNab should display such presence of mind as he did on this occasion. That within the space of a nanosecond he would succeed in evaluating the situation perfectly and, having instinctively determined the gravity of it, not waste a moment in translating his analysis into affirmative action. Celia reeled backwards as Pat's first blow caught him full square in the abdomen.

'Go, Winnie! Go!' cried Pat.

Winnie – shocked, perhaps – stared stupidly at him.

'Go where, Pat?'

'Don't ask questions!' he cried. 'Just go! I'll follow you!'

Another blow felled Celia and Pat followed his partner as they raced out into the night.

*

The hissing cymbals and staccato *wah-wah* of the guitars persisted inside the discotheque as Pat McNab and Winnie considered their limited options. All along the deserted street there were no Zodiacs or Zephyrs or any other high-powered vehicles which might have provided them with a triumphant, effortless getaway. The sole available vehicle, indeed, presented as a red and white Massey Ferguson tractor double-parked outside Donie Halligan's shoe shop. Pat pushed Winnie in the back and cried: 'Go!'

The tractor roared around the corner on two wheels. Winnie's hair was flying in the breeze. 'Pat,' she begged shakily, 'will you please tell me what's going on?'

'There's no time for that now, Winnie!' explained Pat, just as—

'Jesus!' he cried, whitefaced.

The tractor had stuttered to an emphatic halt. For a second, the entire town, road and trees seemed blurred. But Pat rapidly steadied himself. 'Get out, Winnie!' he yelled. 'Don't even think about it!'

There were two figures in the wide-open landscape that was Larry O'Halloran's field. Two frightened, hunted figures holding hands beneath a sky that to them was filled with helicopters searching for them. Two people alone but for each other, and their names were Pat McNab and Winnie McAdam.

*

Pat sat on the algae-mottled trough, his head slumped in his hands. Winnie touched him gently on the shoulder.

'But why didn't you tell me, Pat?' she said, compassionately, understandingly. 'Why didn't you say?'

Pat looked into her eyes. Such pain she had never before seen. 'What have I got you into, Winnie?' he said. 'What are we going to do?'

Winnie squeezed his shoulder.

'It's going to be OK, Pat. We've just got to think,' she said.

Pat nodded vigorously.

'You're right,' he said, 'think!'

He frowned.

'Think!' he repeated.

*

The pink ball glided silently across the flat expanse of green baize and was gratefully swallowed by the top left-hand pocket. Mary grinned and chalked his cue as he said: 'So the big fluffpops found his zig zag no-show man, huh? Well, ain't he a lucky hoo hoo, huh? Ain't he the jim jam go go!'

The hoodlum by the secret, leather-panelled door shifted nervously from foot to foot, fearful that any inappropriate gesture would result in many of his teeth being lost as a result of contact with a propelled pool ball.

*

It had all seemed so simple when Pat sat by the window working it out. Winnie standing by the poolside as he lay across a lounger in his costume, the burning sun reflected in his wraparounds. 'Would you like some Martini, dear?' she had said.

'No, hon,' he had replied, 'matter of fact I think I'll take me another swim!'

The blue of the swimming pool had been so real he could almost feel it right there all around him. 'I guess that was my problem,' he would often reflect years later, 'I didn't see that it was all too easy.'

*

They had arranged that they would check in separately, in different queues. As she approached the desk, Winnie gave him a distant, affectionate wave. Pat instinctively looked away. She looked beautiful, he thought. More beautiful than ever. Especially now that she was wearing Polaroids. A warm feeling swept over Pat. A warm feeling that said that in six hours he would be free. Free for ever and together. He smiled as he heard her say again: 'Would you like some Martini?'

'Good morning, sir,' said the attractive desk assistant as she opened Pat's ticket wallet.

'It is indeed,' Pat heard himself reply as he drummed his fingers on the desk, 'it is indeed.'

*

But that was but fantasy, the Paradise-on-earth that was Barbados was some distance away yet, the '*waka waka*' sound still ringing in Pat's ears as his eyes darted all about the field from his vantage point behind the bush. The moon was fat and full in the sky. 'Go!' cried Winnie, giving *him* an encouraging little push in the small of his back. 'Go now, Pat!' In a split second he was gone, a silhouette shooting across the night-time fields. What is tragic is that neither of them heard the screech of wheels or the crunch of gravel in a laneway not two fields away.

*

'*Open up! Open, damn you!*' gasped Pat breathlessly as he tore at the back door bolt which continued to resist him fiercely. He might have had twenty-five fingers. At last the heavy oaken door swung open before him. The portrait of his mother smiled at him as he removed it and revealed the safe. Now it was as though he had acquired ten more fingers! '*Open! Damn you, open!*' he cried shakily. 'Can't you open for me!' The safe door complied and at last the black briefcase was in his hands. Feverishly, he began to stuff the green notes into his coat – no pocket being left unfilled. How long Celia had been standing there – with his arms folded – *grinning!* – it is impossible to say. At first Pat thought it was his imagination again. 'The mushies, maybe. Making me hear things! Like the way I could feel the blue of the swimming pool! So real!' he thought.

But it had nothing to do with mushies, or swimming pools, as he soon realized when Celia took one step forward and, stroking his chin in a mischievous but all-powerful fashion, said: 'Why, mano hooch, if it ain't the perfumed smell of green!'

A cascade of notes snowstormed all around Pat.

'No! I can explain!' cried Pat.

'It's nothing personal, puppy,' explained Celia as he shot Pat dead.

*

It was many days later when Mary and Celia – closer friends now than they'd ever been in their lives – were sharing a bottle of bourbon and laughing and joshing over some 'spook' down in Washington, DC. Celia was puffing on a Cuban cigar and tossing back his head grinning over the finer details of this particular heist and so taken aback all of a sudden that the cigar remained steady on his lip with no visible means of support. 'Yeah? And then?' barked Mary. 'Don't stop! You struck dumb or what?'

In the ensuing seconds, there was no sound to be heard emanating from Celia's throat. The only sound in the room was that of Pat McNab's voice saying: 'Well, hello, fluffy bunnies! It's checking-in time!'

It was a pale Pat McNab, his face bearing the grim grey featurelessness of a concrete slab. But him nonetheless.

'What the—' snapped Mary, reaching for the drawer.

'Waka waka, micky moko!' barked Pat as the Winchester pump-action out of nowhere appeared in his hands and Celia went flying through the window in a carnival of shattered glass.

'Wait, please,' begged Mary pitifully, 'you don't under-stand!'

'I want my money!' Pat stonily intoned.

'But – you're dead!'

'I want my money. I said I want my—'

'Your money? Sure! Here – take all of it! It's your green! We want you to have it!'

He pushed the briefcase across the desk, momentarily deflecting Pat's attention in order to grab a pool ball to propel rapidly towards him. Within seconds his hand was on the door buzzer.

'Don't open it!' warned Pat, the pool ball having narrowly missed him. But it was already too late, the secret door having swivelled halfway open.

'Ha ha!' cried Mary, triumphant until two shotgun blasts caught him in the stomach. Within seconds, Pat McNab had hoods and goons and lackeys on top of him like other people got dandruff. Which was why, a minute later, Mary's famous 'back room' was akin to what an independent observer might have described as 'a slaughterhouse'. Pat shook his head – not now without a tinge of sadness – breaking his pump-action as a last pink ball rolled poignantly into a pocket.

*

There was something magical about the couple who stood together, brandishing their tickets and – in the same queue! – holding hands and gazing into one another's eyes. As there was about the bronzed, black-sunglassed figure in the pink floppy (Celia's) hat draped elegantly across the lounger by the pool, eyes twinkling as he sipped a pina colada. Which spilt all over his chest as the blood drained from his face, spasming as he felt the cold steel of a revolver pressed against the back of his neck.

'*Waka waka!*' he heard Winnie chuckle as she leaped up and down.

'Jesus, Mary and Joseph, fluffpops! You put the heart crossways in me!'

*

It is a most beautiful scene, perhaps as beautiful as a scene could ever be. The sky so blue you can almost feel it, touch it. And a long, long way from a cold grey house, a house of stone where breathes not a single soul, the only sound that of a broken shutter rattling, and the footsteps of the flies as they take their first tentative steps across the corpse of Pat McNab. Where now he lies, a single talon of blood congealed on his cheek, blue fingers stiffly fanning out as he dreams of vengeance. Which, departed from this earth as now he is, like his love for Winnie, is fated never to be.

CHAPTER TEN

Love Story

(Where do I begin) Love Story

Where do I begin to tell the story of a love as brave as life can be
The sweet love story that is older than the sea
The secret truth about the love she gave to me
Where do I start?

With the first hello, she gave a meaning
To this empty world of mine
There'll never be another love like the time
She came into my life and made the living fine.

She fills my heart, she fills my heart with very special things
With angel songs, with wild imaginings
She fills my soul with so much love
That everywhere I go I'm never lonely
With her around who could be lonely?

WHAT CAN YOU SAY ABOUT a twenty-five-year-old girl who died? That she was beautiful and brilliant? Loved Mozart and Bach. And the Kilfenora Ceilidh Band? That she should never have married Patsy Traynor?

That she should never have gone near the effing bastard, for that's all he was. Such were the thoughts running through Pat McNab's mind as he sat in the front pew of St Bartholomew's Church trying to hold back the tears as the lid was screwed down on the pine coffin within which reclined the body of the girl he had loved for almost the entirety of his adult life. She was attired in a knitted woollen cap, a tartan kilt and black tights and her complexion had that alabaster quality he always remembered her for. It was difficult to look as the six-foot box began its interminable journey towards the coal-black curtains. And even more difficult for him when they began to part. In his hands his hat was crushed to an almost unrecognizable mass of twisted felt.

Outside, as might have been expected, the rain had begun to fall. Pat felt a large, spadelike hand resting upon his shoulder. 'Poor Bridie,' said Big Jim Thompson, with eyes downcast, 'may God have mercy on her lovely young soul.'

*

There wasn't much of a crowd in Sullivan's Select Bar, apart from a few bank girls venomously discussing their superior, as Pat sat morosely on the counter thinking over the events of the day and sipping at the contents of his sixth pint. 'Ah well, Pat,' remarked Timmy Sullivan brusquely, as he ran a cloth across the wet marble top of the counter, 'that's Bridie gone anyhow.'

The reaction from Pat was instantaneous as he slapped his flat open palm down on the counter, splashing some beer onto the floor. 'Leave me alone!' he cried. 'Why can't you all leave me alone!'

Timmy Sullivan felt his jaw drop.

'Jesus, Pat!' he cried. 'There's no need to start a carry-on the like of that now!'

But Pat was already gone.

*

Sitting, in fact, by the dead fire back in his house surrounded by shadows and thinking about Patsy Traynor. And of how he had always had to get the upper hand, no matter what the cost to anyone else. If you had something he wanted, then he had to have it. Anything at all, if Patsy Traynor wanted it then Patsy Traynor had to have it. Those were the rules abiding in 'Patsy Land', as it might have been called. And always had been. Right from their very first days together in St Cashie's School.

Pat shivered as he thought of those days, all seeming now so long ago. He poked at a dead ember with his toe and shuddered slightly, but not without a wry smile, as in his mind's eye he saw himself once again coming strolling down the street, happily humming to himself a tune that had been popular in the charts at the time – 'Do Wah Diddy Diddy Diddy Dum Diddy Do!' by Manfred Mann and his band. Until suddenly, would hear a voice calling: 'Oi! McNab! Get over here!'

Reluctantly, Pat would make his way over to McGurk's Corner where Patsy Traynor loitered with a few of his associates. He saw it again now plain as day.

'Well, McGush!' sneered Traynor. 'What do you think of this fellow, then?'

Henry McGush rubbed his hands together ('paws' might have been a more accurate description) and tossed back his head.

'Oh now, he's some baby!' replied McGush. 'He's some baby now, Patsy! That's all you can say about him!'

Patsy nodded, his eyes twinkling delightedly.

'Do you see the wee tie he has on him?' he continued. 'I say – she has the tie on you again today, Pat. What has she?'

His meaty hand became a sort of crude trumpet as he placed it over his right ear, patiently awaiting Pat's reply.

Pat lowered his head.

'She has the tie on me again today,' he shamefully replied.

Now it was Patsy Traynor's turn to rub his hands together.

'She has the tie on me again today,' he repeated. He fixed Pat with a fierce gaze.

'She has the tie on me again today – Your Majesty!' he emphasized.

The crude trumpet was once more brought to bear on the situation. As an eyebrow was promptly arched.

'She has the tie on me again today, Your Majesty.'

Patsy nodded with satisfaction.

'That's better!' he declared. 'All must be heard to address King Patsy as His Majesty. Isn't that right, McGush?'

'Oh, indeed it is surely, Your Majesty! Haw haw!' replied Henry McGush, as though his colleague had only just shared with him the most hysterical joke in the history of the world.

Patsy coughed with counterfeit politeness.

'And now, young Pat – would you please be so kind as to step forward in order that we might have our rightful twang?' He paused. 'Mr McGush,' he intoned, 'what is it we require?'

'Our rightful twang of tie!' came the reply, with a seemingly instinctive, almost military, clicking of heels.

'Step forward, please!' snapped Traynor.

The waves of shame, beneath which Pat, within subsequent minutes, found himself sinking, can only be described as truly incalculable. His cheeks appeared to burn with generations of humiliation. As to the sound of shrill cries of delight, hands thunderclapped once again.

'Well, my my! What a twanging there is on here today, McGush! This is the best twanging day yet!'

Patsy shook his head.

'You have to hand it to her!' he said. 'I say – you have to hand it to yon haybag McNab! She never lets us down, McGush!'

Henry McGush nodded appreciatively.

'Never lets us down, he says!'

'Mad and all as she might be!' cried Patsy Traynor, plum-sized eyes craving affirmation. Readily supplied by Henry McGush who, in a high pitch, croaked:

'Mad and all as she fecking is! Haw haw! Ho ho!'

Patsy chortled and drew a small circle in the gravel with the toe of his boot.

'Haw haw ho ho is right!' he said. 'And I'll bet she's given this little gosson a few bright shillings for his lunch – would you say that'd be the case now, McGush?'

Henry McGush knitted his brow and stroked his chin slowly and contemplatively.

'I'd say she's looked after him well in that department, Patsy, now that's what I'd say!'

'Mm,' said Patsy, 'and which he is now about to hand over to help the Patsy Traynor/Henry McGush Fund. Isn't that right, young Pat McNab? Would I be right in saying that?'

Pat's cheeks were florid as those of a fever victim.

'It's all I have,' he answered in plaintive, fragile tones.

'And c'mere – how much do you think we want?' countered Patsy, lowering his voice in a significant manner. 'Sure what you have is all we want! McGush – he thinks we want more! What does he think we are – greedy guts?'

Henry McGush feigned astonishment.

'Ah now, Pat,' he said, 'don't be like that! Don't be thinking bad things about us!'

'Come on now, Pat,' went on Patsy Traynor, 'fork it out there like a good lad!'

Pat inserted his right hand into the pocket of his grey serge trousers and from it removed it the coins therein. Two silver shillings gleamed in his palm. Patsy Traynor's eyes lit up like matches flaring inside his sockets.

'Ah the blessings of God and his Holy Mother on you, Pat, from your old friends Patsy and young McGush! Money for the boys for drink! And plenty of it!'

'Plenty of money for Double Diamond, Smithwick's Ale and—'

'Phoenix, the best of all!'

'Phoenix – the bright beer!'

'The best available in the world of beer for Patsy and his old pal Henry McGush! Well – good luck now, Pat McNab. We've to be off now about our business! Say goodbye to us now till we quench our thirst, now there's a lad!'

Pat's mouth was dry as a well long forgotten in the vastest, most arid of deserts.

'Goodbye,' he choked, his voice only just audible.

An eyebrow was slowly elevated as Patsy smiled wryly and in tones of feigned hopefulness, enquired:

'And maybe, do you think – one last wee twang?'

Pat swallowed and fancied his face as a bush aflame.

'Please,' he pleaded.

'Ah go on,' said Patsy, 'don't be such an auld spoilsport, Pat! Here, McGush! Give it a twang there!'

It was as though Pat's entire body was being modulated towards a state of almost total elasticity, Henry McGush moving backwards and forwards on his heels, his face contorted with wickedness, the moments before he released the thin, knotted piece of cotton material which he clutched in his right hand seeming to Pat as though infinity itself.

'*Pitchaow!*' cried McGush aloud as he released his grip and, in a blur, the wine-coloured knot thudded against Pat's Adam's apple like a small missile careering through space. In that instant, he experienced a sense of total disorientation, a sickening, almost unbearable galactic solitude. He leaned backwards against the frontage of Linencare Dry Cleaners, their departing voices as smudges, tiny specks revolving beneath him.

'Well, Pat! Must be off now! See you then!' called back the loathed Traynor.

'Double Diamond works wonders! Works wonders! Double Diamond works wonders! Works wonders it does!' chuckled Henry McGush.

'Ha ha ha!' laughed Patsy Traynor.

There was something undeniably, perhaps hopelessly, abject about Pat's efforts to adjust his tie as his two adversaries were swallowed up by the thick warm darkness of Sullivan's Select Bar, which was situated directly across the street. It was as though someone else had succeeded in inhabiting his body as he lightheadedly began to negotiate his way homeward, knowing full well the reception which would be awaiting him when he arrived. 'But why did you let them do it?' his mother would say. 'Are you going to stand there all your life and let the likes of Traynor walk all over you? Well, you won't, for I'll go down this very minute and let him and the whole cheeky tribe of them know what I think of them! Traynors! Tramps and tinkers and twopence-halfpenny chancers!'

His pleas, he knew so well, would be in vain.

'No – please, Mammy! I beg you – don't!' he would cry, but she would already be pulling on her coat.

'Oh yes! I'll talk turkey to them for what they've done to my son! Not that it's any wonder, mind you! With that father of his lying on top of the melodeon outside Sullivan's every night God sends! As for the mother, if you could call her that!

Up every Sunday with the hat on her and the nose stuck in the air. When the whole country knows Jemmy McQuaid had her fixed before she was married. I wonder what they'll have to say when they hear a few home truths like that, them and their thieving sons!'

'Please, Mammy!' Pat would beg anew as she shook the life out of him in front of the fireplace, insisting that a repeat performance was never to be permitted.

'Pat McNab,' she'd cry, shivering, 'you'll have to learn to stand up for yourself! For if he's taking shillings off you now, what will it be later on? For God's sake, ask yourself! What will it be later on?'

*

His mother's trembling lip returned to Pat now as he sat facing the fire's dying embers, in his hands the gilt frame which contained the oval photo of the only girl he had ever loved. The inscription beneath read: *Bridie Cunningham, March 1972.* He swallowed painfully as he traced a line from the top of her head to the point of her chin and thought just how right his mother had been: 'Just as she always was,' he reflected. For Traynor indeed didn't call a halt after he'd extorted a few shillings. He had never had any intention of doing so.

Pat stared at Bridie in her knitted woollen cap and black polo neck. Sometimes she wore a gold chain with it. He got up and stood staring out the window, thinking of those times (dead now) when he would wait across the street from the convent until she and her colleagues emerged through the gates in an explosion of navy blue serge. He smiled. In some strange way, he knew that it had all been inevitable. For, once Patsy Traynor realized the intensity of his love for her, it had soon become clear that it was only a matter of time before he would endeavour with all his might to attend to that little matter too, not ceasing until he had succeeded in taking away from him the only woman – apart from his mother, of course – that Pat McNab had ever had the good fortune to love.

*

It was the autumn of 1971 and Bridie was going past the vegetable shop in her day clothes – a bright orange and red tank top with jeans covered in newspaper headlines.

'Hello, Pat,' she said.

'Hello, Bridie,' was Pat's reply.

'That's a nice day, Pat,' Bridie elaborated.

'Bridie,' Pat began in a dry, sort of choking voice, 'I was wondering if you were going to the dance on Friday?'

'You bet I am, Pat!' cried Bridie excitedly. 'I wouldn't miss it for the world! They're my favourite band!'

'Are they?' cried Pat excitedly. 'They're mine too! Who are they?'

'What, Pat? Why, the Square Pennies! Ha ha!'

'I might see you there, then!'

'Yes! I'll look forward to that!'

'Goodbye, Bridie!'

'Goodbye, Pat!'

*

1971 – Oct. 16, 12.35 a.m. Now that the dance was over, with the musicians packing all the gear into the van (The Square Pennies! Ireland's Newest Sensation!) and people streaming out into the humming, lit-up car park, as Pat stood with Bridie out among the cars he began to realize that what he was experiencing could possibly be the most beautiful and exciting night of his entire life. He found himself once more staring at Bridie's hands. He couldn't get over them. They were the smallest hands he had ever seen! His excitement overwhelmed him to the extent that he feared he would fall directly into the puddle in front of him.

'Look at how small your hands are!' he cried aloud. A man and his girlfriend turned from an Audi 1100 to look at him.

'What, Pat?' said Bridie.

'Nothing, Bridie,' Pat replied, 'I'm sorry.'

Bridie reddened a little and took Pat's hands in hers, her smaller ones.

'There's nothing to be sorry about,' she assured him.

Pat coughed and said:

'Bridie – would you like to come to the dance with me again next week?'

Bridie nodded and squeezed one of his fingers a little.

'Yes, I will!' she said, adding, 'Pat – do you know that I'm going to Dublin in a wee while?'

The startled reply leaped unbidden from Pat's parted lips.

'What?' he cried.

Bridie lowered her eyes.

'Yes. I've been accepted into college. I'm going to be a teacher, you see.'

Pat's head reeled.

'Teacher? What? Sums and all—?' he cried, a tension – as though steel wire had been abruptly strung all about it – manifesting itself in his chest.

'Yes. I'm going to be a primary teacher. I've always wanted to be one ever since I was a little girl. Oh! I can hardly wait!'

Pat trembled involuntarily. He could barely contain his excitement. Now he was squeezing her hands!

'Why! That's wonderful!' he cried. 'You'll be the best teacher ever, Bridie! I know you will!'

Bridie moved in closer to him and put her little cold hand behind his neck. There was a lovely smell of cream off it.

'Oh, Pat,' she said, 'you're so nice.'

It was all Pat could do not to take off into space when he found her lips touching him ever so softly on the cheek.

*

263

It may have been that the months which followed constituted the most beautiful summer ever enjoyed by a young couple in their teenage years. It also may not be the case, for such things must surely be difficult to quantify and notoriously open to dispute. But there can be no denying that the days enjoyed by Bridie Cunningham and her boyfriend Pat McNab were among the most enjoyable ever experienced by two human beings. For never a day went by now but they kept their assignations in the Lido Grill, staring into one another's eyes and selecting innumerable popular hits on the jukebox. Bridie placed her tiny hand – for all the world a bird of intricately carved china – on the formica as she said: 'Pat – do you like that one?'

Pat's reply – he remained ever eager to please her – continued to be hopelessly equivocal.

'I don't know. Do you?'

'Yes! I love it! I hope it goes to No. 1, in fact!'

'So do I! I think it's fantastic!'

Sometimes they walked over to the old water mill where Bridie would sit on the stone and hug her knees to her chest, lost in thoughts and the future's innumerable possibilities. Whenever he could pick up the courage, Pat would say: 'I'll miss you when you're in Dublin, Bridie – do you know that?'

As Bridie chewed on a grass stem, saying:

'I do, Pat. I'll miss you too.'

'What'll it be like, do you think? Dublin, I mean?'

'I don't know. I hope it's exciting!'

'They say there's something to do there every night.'

'Yeah! I'll bet there'll be some great bands!'

'I bet there will! You'll probably forget all about me.'

There would be a sad twinkle in Pat's eyes whenever those words left his lips.

'Pat – don't ever say that,' Bridie would sharply reply, 'you know I couldn't. As a matter of fact, I'll write to you every day.'

It was a sentence Pat was never to forget.

'Every day?' he said.

He could not believe his ears.

'Every day,' Bridie said, 'I promise with all my heart.'

*

Standing by the window now, Pat remembered those letters. He smiled as he thought of himself reading them. 'Dear Pat,' he recalled, 'The lectures are very good but I find French a bit hard. The food is – *yuk!* I miss you so much! Pat did you ever hear tell of a film called Love Story? Me and the girls were at it last night. I'll tell you about it when I get home! See you, Pat. Love you, Bridie.'

Letters which continued to arrive with heart-inflating regularity until that magnificent day she returned home on the bus and Pat was the most delirious youth in the whole town! His very legs going weak at the knees when he perceived the vision that presented itself to him. For a vision is what the woman he loved was as she stood there before him on the steps of the bus in her striped scarf, knitted woollen cap, tartan kilt and black tights. He could barely release the sound of her name from the pit of his throat.

'Bridie!'

'Pat!'

In slow motion, Pat McNab found himself crossing the square and melting into the arms of Bridie Cunningham.

*

Those Christmas holidays glittered in his memory. Bridie chewing a pencil and poring over her folder. Behind her a blazing fire burning in the grate. And, from the speaker of the Reynolds three-in-one which her father had purchased ('Prezzie for you, Bridie!') in Dundalk, the first few tinkling treble notes falling like milky rain, announcing the sound-track of the film which she most adored in the entire world

265

of celluloid. Memories such as these for him simply had no peer.

'I have to have this essay in in two weeks or they'll kill me!' his girlfriend would say then.

'Kill you, will they, Bridie?' Pat would reply hesitantly (for the groves of academe, in truth, were a source of almost impenetrable mystery, if not intimidation, indeed, to him). 'What is it about?'

'It's about Mallarmé and the French symbolist poets,' Bridie explained, with the tiniest hint of impatience.

'Oh,' Pat replied, as though he understood completely. He didn't, however. He looked away and felt his saliva thicken up inside his mouth, just as the door opened and Bridie's mother put her head around it (it was beautifully permed – her head) and said softly: 'Now. Would you two young people like a little cup of tea, perhaps?'

Even while they were happening to him, Pat knew that they were days and nights which would never in his life be repeated. How could they?

'Would you like some sugar, Pat?' he heard Bridie's soft voice enquire.

It was hard to believe that someone like Pat McNab had ever used the words employed by him some seconds later. But he had. He had said 'darling', all right, and 'sweetheart'. And she had not laughed. It was like winning the greatest prize of all time.

*

They had been sitting on the seesaws in the park for over an hour when the first few tentative flakes of snow began to come down.

'Bridie,' Pat said, 'if you were married to someone – would you have a child with them, maybe?'

Bridie's reply came without hesitation.

'Oh yes, Preppie,' she said, 'I'd have lots and lots.'

Pat was somewhat taken aback.

'What did you call me?' he said.

'Preppie,' responded Bridie brightly, 'Preppie McNab! Suits you, don't you think?'

Pat didn't know what to say. He stared at her with her legs swinging and her eyes twinkling and tiny beads of melted snow all over her polo neck and said: 'I don't know, Bridie.'

She crinkled up her nose in that way she did.

'Of course you do, silly!' she chided mischievously, before leaping off the seesaw and beginning to pelt him cheekily with snowballs. To which Pat duly responded in kind and within minutes they were both squealing and shouting: 'Stop!' and 'That's enough!' and 'Ow!' before falling across the expansive white carpet (making the 'Snow Angel') and onto their back-sides in one another's arms.

*

It was a happy Pat McNab who made his way home from Bridie's house that evening, his head liberally sprinkled with snow and his hands sunk deep into the pockets of his long black overcoat, a wide smile spreading across his features as he realized he was already contemplating both their lives together as man and wife. At least until he turned the key in the lock of the front door and while closing it directly behind him, perceived (he knew instinctively that it was not his imagination) a scaly anxiety enfolding his entire person and extending (like a living thing!) down the hallway right across the lino and as far as the stairs. To where his mother, clad in grey from head to toe (even her nightcap was grey) stood, her mouth like the slenderest of incisions in her face. It seemed each blink of her eyelids was the shutter of a camera, recording images which would indubitably serve as damning evidence at some point in the future. She drew a long breath before she uttered her first words. Which were: 'Well now! Lord, but aren't you the great fellow?'

It was as though Pat had swallowed a not insignificant portion of an oil slick.

'What, Ma?' he succeeded, with great effort, in replying.

'Making snowmen, I suppose,' his mother said.

The words were hard and uncompromising as the guillotine's steel.

'Making snowmen, Ma?'

'Making snowmen and her away off to tell Traynor all about your great adventures!'

Pat felt the skin between his eyebrows contracting.

'Traynor, Mammy? Telling T . . . ?'

The answer this time was curt, arrowhead-fast.

'Aye, Traynor! You'll find he doesn't bother with snowmen! Making cow's eyes at him every chance she gets! Sure any eejit would be fit to see that, if she hadn't him wrapped around her little finger, and the wee trollop hardly out of ankle socks! Lord save us above, what have I reared! Sweet Jesus and His Blessed Mother, what have I gone and reared!'

*

There can be no denying the fact that that night Pat McNab wept bitterly. Adrift in a paper sea of Bridie's letters (many of which he had read thirteen or fourteen times) copious amounts of tears were to be observed rolling down his cheeks. But in the end he knew – regardless of what people might surmise – that his mother had been only trying to help him. What was to eventually prove tragic was that all she succeeded in helping him to do was make what was perhaps the biggest mistake of his life so far on this earth.

Bridie stood back against the plate-glass window of Linen-care Dry Cleaners. Her face was as pale as the snow with which they had been 'making angels' only days before and she was clearly having difficulty in getting the words past her lips.

'What are you talking about? Please, Pat – will you please give me some idea what you are talking about!'

There could be no doubt about it now – her voice was trembling.

Pat spun and turned his back on her. 'Love means never having to say you're sorry' – he found himself recalling her words, and it was as though his mouth were filling up with recriminatory bile. He snapped:

'Nothing! I'm talking about nothing!'

A moistness glittered in Bridie Cunningham's eyes.

'You know what your problem is, Pat?' she ventured shakily. 'You put up a big glass wall to prevent you from getting hurt. But it also prevents you from getting touched!'

Resentment burned in the eyes of Pat McNab. Without turning, he said:

'So it means never having to say you're sorry, huh? That's a laugh!'

Bridie tore at the knitted woollen cap she held in both hands.

'How can I say I'm sorry for something I didn't do? For God's sake, please tell me – how can I?'

Pat covered his eyes with his right hand as he said:

'Just tell me one thing – do you like Patsy Traynor or not? Do you?'

Bridie was surprised to find herself staring glassily into space. The zigzag pattern on the black knitted cap began to animate wildly before her eyes.

'Well . . . I like him,' she began. 'I mean, he's nice and everything but . . . oh Pat! Pat, what is happening to you?'

Pat looked down at the ground. There were some pebbles there. And a large patch of oil.

'I just keep getting the feeling that something has died inside, that's all.'

What was emitted from Bridie's mouth could only be categorized as a howl.

'Pat! Pat! Oh God!' she cried.

The tears came then. Pat remained, as though ossified, with

his back to her, staring blankly at irregular arrangements of pebbles and crushed, discarded cigarette packets frozen into a variety of beer trails which found their source directly beneath the doorway of Sullivan's Select Bar.

*

It was later the same evening, and Pat sat blankly at the table. It was as though he had been imprisoned in a sarcophagus chiselled out of purest blackness. His mother's slippers flapped as she put his dinner in front of him and said: 'You'll get sense yet, my lad! The likes of her is out for only one thing – all they can get!'

It was more than her son could bear. He slammed his fork down on the table and cried: 'What do you know! All you can say about her is bad things! You can never leave her alone! You haybag! For that's all you are!'

A shadow the shape of Australia passed across his mother's face. It was of no significance, having simply been cast by a passing bird outside. But it chilled Pat.

'Don't you talk like that to me,' he heard then, each word as a slender serpent poking its head out of the tiny aperture that was his mother's mouth.

*

In the days that followed, the Lido Grill became as a world painted battleship-grey by some unseen misanthropic hand. Pat's eyes were glazed with sorrow as he sat across from the woman he loved and thought: 'You try to say something. You can hear the words. But what comes out bears no resemblance to them. What comes out are words so far away they might as well belong to a stranger.'

'Bridie?' Pat began.

Distorted in the prongs of a fork, Pat could see how raw-red his eyes now were. They appeared more as wounds than eyes. And he could see already what was written behind those

270

eyes, wounds, call them what you will. Words which, he knew, would haunt him till the day he died. Words which said: 'It's dead, Pat. It's dead for ever. And both of you know who killed it.'

*

Employing the word 'abject' to describe the state Pat found himself in at ten o'clock that evening as he lay upon his pillow – saturated with perspiration – issuing from deep within him cries of pain and grief the like of which he had never known would be essentially inadequate. The language does not exist which can encapsulate such sorrow. Which leads a man to cry: 'You murdered it! My love! You murdered it! You murdered it, you hear?' to his own mother.

All, in the end, to no avail. For Mrs McNab, patiently waiting until exhaustion did its work, made no secret of her feelings towards what she considered, although she did not overtly state as much, a meretricious display of the crudest emotion. 'Oh, would you shut your mouth and stop making an eejit of yourself! Shut your trap if you know what's good for you!' she snapped eventually.

The sound of the bedroom door slamming obliterated the renewed cries which issued from a torn and bereft soul, further rendered anonymous by the clattering and banging of plates and dishes downstairs.

*

It was to be some weeks before the folly of his response on that occasion became wholly clear to Pat. Because, of course, it had not been his mother who was to blame at all! And all that he had been witnessing was yet another example of his blaming her for absolutely everything! 'How could I have been so stupid?' he chided himself remorselessly. He shook his head. 'Phee-oow!' he said and looked out the window of his bedroom. It was like the sun was coming up. A lovely, hard,

271

glittering and shiningly optimistic sun. For one split second, he felt like doing a kick in the air. Now that, at last, everything had become clear to him, as it had once and for all the previous day.

He had been coming down from chapel (it was his aspiration that religion might provide him with some succour) when the street rang out with the sound of a familiar voice.

'Oi! McNab! Get over here!'

Instinctively – despite the fact that he was now nineteen years of age – he complied.

'Well, McGush!' barked Patsy Traynor. 'What do you think of this fellow?'

'Oho!' snorted Henry McGush. 'I've been hearing queer stories about this boy! Oh, indeed and I have! Oho, he's been some baby lately, the way I hear it!'

Patsy Traynor winked and elbowed his colleague in an exaggeratedly conspiratorial fashion.

'And me as well, McGush! Bad tales too, I tell you! What have you been up to, McNab, you rascal you!'

'Twanging a certain lassie, I hear!'

'Twanging her, eh? Twanging her now he has the tie off!'

'Is that what you're at, McNab? Giving her the twang? Oo, be cripes I'd say she likes it. I'd say she's fond of it, Pat, would you?'

'Yelping for the twang is what I'd say! That's what I'd say now, Henry!' grinned Patsy Traynor.

'Yelping for it, cripes I'd say she is!'

'Yelping for it! There's no two ways!' cheered Henry McGush.

'Yelping for it, begaw I'd say!'

'And McNab's the man to twang it!'

'Except for one thing,' said Patsy Traynor.

It was the moment before the lethal thumb hovers above the button. And then – the cataclysm.

'Except I got there early! The bould Patsy twanged her first!'

Twin faces exploding into crimson laughter rendered Pat dumbstruck.

'And the bucking eejit never knew it!'

*

How many letters (pink and many of them doused in perfume) Pat was surrounded by as he sat cross-legged upon his bed it is impossible to say. A 'clatter' or 'an avalanche' might go some way towards approximating the number. Perhaps it may not be even relevant. What certainly is relevant is the single thought which pulsated relentlessly now inside his mind – had he been wrong all along? Had he (no, it couldn't be true!) perhaps, even dreamed all those times they'd had together? The candyfloss, the snow, the laughter by the river, her cries as he pushed the swing ever higher – had, all along, he imagined the most precious, impervious, glistening stone when what he held in his hand was but a dead ember such as he could randomly pluck from the fireplace and disdainfully crush beneath his heel? It seemed a bony hand had taken hold of his stomach bag and squeezed, perhaps with an acidic bitterness, certainly without pity.

*

There is a man in a long coat standing by a graveside. The day seems fashioned for the purpose, expressly made for such a solitary vigil, with veils of rain sweeping up the hillside and getting lost in the maw of grey light that settles on the evening countryside. It might be expected that this man would weep but such is not the case for he is someone long since past sorrow and all its kin. Indeed, somewhere within him still burns a glow of what can only be described as hope. For, as he gazes upon the elegant calligraphy upon grey limestone

273

expertly hewn, *Bridie Traynor – Decd. 1980*, he permits a smile to come to his lips as he considers that somehow it might have come to pass that his worst fears had not proven true. That, all along, she had been his and his alone. And that maybe, had things been otherwise, he might somehow have made her happy.

'Happier than he ever did,' thinks Pat McNab as his eyes light upon her name once more and at last he turns to leave. Acknowledging the greeting of a fellow mourner, he sinks his hands deep inside his pockets and makes his way now towards the gate. A passing car douses the cemetery wall with dank puddle-water. Turning his face towards the town, those words come to him again (*Come on, luvvy!*), lodging close by his tonsils like the coldest nuggets of ice, orchestrating the familiar tableau that played before him each and every night, threading their eloquence through the days that had been hers with Patsy Traynor, but denied to Pat McNab.

*

There was no one in the playground now and the swing was his alone. Neither was there snow, simply the relentless hiss of the rain and the almost infantile gurgling of the gutters. A sweetpaper blew across the grass, fought with a litter bin for some moments and flew on. Pat clutched the chains of the swing and tried not to think of her face the way it would come when he tormented himself; the lights glittering above the ballroom door, Traynor emerging out from behind the cars, her small sculpted hand in his. As a soft but eerily cheeky voice cried: 'Poor old innocent Pat's gone home at last, Patsy! Now we can have ourselves a decent coort!'

There was a lump in Pat's throat now as he made his way home. There could be no denying it. Just as there had been on that first night – when he had hovered beneath the window (three weeks after Bridie had married Traynor) in the hope of catching a glimpse of her. A wave of revulsion had swept through him as his eyes assimilated the sight that met them. There had been blood upon that gentle face of alabaster as 'The Brute' Traynor raised the melodeon anew and spared her not once with it, its horrible, undulating cacophony seeming to articulate Pat's inner pain as once again its weight bore down upon her, the ogre – for what else was he! – snarling, 'Where's my dinner? I told you to have it! Didn't I tell you to have it?' as his boot caught her plumb in the stomach and his wife collapsed at his feet in a state of exhaustion.

*

Pat turned from the window and made his way to the kitchen to prepare himself some supper. Soon it would be time to retire to bed – alone. As he spooned the cocoa into his mug, he reflected how it had, in the end, been merciful. It hadn't lasted long. With bitter irony, raising the striped mug to his lips, he murmured: 'Probably as long as our love.'

Before sleep came to Pat that night, he construed a marble statue standing all alone in the middle of a cemetery. A statue that reminded him of pale white sculpted hands. And then he saw a frail, hunted creature bruised black and blue as a shadow stood above it, a tattered, would-be musical instrument cast aside, blood-spattered. And there can be no denying that in that instant, Pat McNab harboured hatred in his heart. But, as the soft fingers of sleep eventually stroked him towards its peaceful boudoir, another thought came into his mind. And with it, soft flakes of snow as gentle as thought itself on green and rolling parkland now silently floating down. Until the world seemed covered in it. And it is as if there is no one there but him, until he looks again and sees her, emerging from the pale pure haze, the words she whispers clear now in his ears: 'It's not true, Pat – about our love. For what we had will last for ever, no matter what – I know it will find us again. Just like, one day, you'll find me.'

Pat cried out but when he looked she had gone and there

was nothing remaining but the snow, pale and unbroken and stretching to infinity. But when he awoke, Pat McNab knew for certain in his heart that one day when he closed his eyes he would look up and there she'd be again. In her knitted woollen cap, as large as life, and when he'd say: 'How long this time then, Bridie Cunningham?' she'd smile and reply: 'For ever, Pat, for ever,' and that there they'd stand, with lacy flakes gathering on their shoulders, the softest touch of their lips bringing tinkling notes, like the tiniest drops of falling milk, as if by magic from the air.

CHAPTER ELEVEN

The Garden Where the Praties Grow

The Garden Where the Praties Grow

Have you ever been in love, me boys, have you ever felt the pain
I'd sooner be in jail, me boys, than be in love again.
For the girl I loved was beautiful and I want you all to know
That I met her in the garden where the praties grow

Chorus
She was just the sort of creature, boys, that nature did intend
To walk right through the world, me boys, without the Grecian bend
Nor did she wear a chignon I'd have you all to know
And I met her in the garden where the praties grow

Says I 'My pretty Kathleen,
I'm tired of single life
And if you've no objection sure
I'll make you my sweet wife.'
She answered me right modestly
And curtsied very low,
'O you're welcome to the garden where the praties grow.'

THERE ARE, as is the case with many of the aspects of the life of he who might be termed 'Our hero Pat', two schools of thought concerning his 'thespian ambitions'. Or what Dr Toss Hamblyn (a long-standing patron of Sullivan's Select Bar) often referred to as his 'adventures in the screen trade' – one view being that it was the very pursuit of these which eventually put him 'astray in the head altogether', the other insisting that they had in effect opened up 'a whole new world for Pat'. One which contained within it, indeed, the very seeds of his salvation. His transportation 'over the edge', they continued to attest, being the sole responsibility of one man, the schoolmaster Butty Halpin, whose small-minded egomania resulted, they insisted, not in Pat's reformation or amelioration as a human being but in the planting of further laurel bushes for the purposes of disguising 'grim secrets', a superfluity of which the earth in the garden belonging to Pat McNab now concealed. At this point, in terms of numbers, approaching, thanks to the hauteur and self-aggrandisement of this diminutive, rotund pedagogue, double figures.

*

'Whenever this is all over,' declared Alo McGilly one night in Sullivan's, 'history will see that one citizen of Gullytown and one alone bears the greater share of responsibility for these dreadful, dreadful tragedies – and that man is Butty Halpin.'

Whether true or not, there can be no denying the fact that the Pat McNab who opened the door to Butty Halpin was a considerably brighter and breezier version than that which had been pottering about the murky interior of the McNab household for some several months now. And for this there was a single reason – the fact that only some days before he had descended the stairs to discover in the hallway a letter from the Dublin School of Acting (a response which he had never dreamed of receiving!) inviting him to attend for interview. Which explained the myriad series of voices ('Don't make me laugh, Chan!' and 'Good evening, Miss de Soto!') which he had now begun to spend hours perfecting and the sanguine expression in his eyes as he extended his hand and proclaimed to the small, onion-shaped man who now stood on the step before him with a large briar chomped between his jaws: 'Mr Halpin! How good to see you!'

Admittedly, Pat was somewhat taken aback when he heard his former teacher explain that the reason for his call was that he was, in effect, searching for a place of residence (for it was Pat's intention to devote all his spare time now to his 'travels in fantasy', 'thespian artificing' or however else his cerebral peregrinations might be described, and to eschew all domestic pursuits) – but when 'the Master' (as he was often referred to) explained that he would be 'billeting' for a 'mere three weeks or so', he found himself relieved – somewhat honoured, indeed, that the renowned educator had seen fit to choose his establishment.

*

'So that's the way of it, Pat,' continued Mr Halpin, wiping the remains of his fish fingers from his lips. 'Now that Dots is gone, I'm all on my lonesome below and I thought sure I might as well stop with yourself until the new bungalow is built.'

'And why wouldn't you, Master? Will you have another drop of tea there?'

'I will indeed, Pat – to be sure,' replied the master, extending his blue-striped mug.

There are those who would contend that the fatal moment, i.e. that which was the genesis of the reactivation of the resentment which Pat, despite himself, began to harbour towards his former teacher, occurred directly after this exchange. When Pat, in his excitement, blurted out all the details of his new-found good fortune. There was nothing which could have prepared him for the cold taciturnity of the master's response. Nor for the cruel unwinding smile which followed hot on its heels as he picked his teeth with a match (how well Pat recalled that grating mannerism!) and murmured, in a low, barely audible tone: 'Acting school? But sure you couldn't act your way out of a paper bag, Pat!'

Pat attempted to deliver a frivolous response but only succeeded in flushing to the roots as he stammered: 'I have to go up for my audition. I have nearly all my parts learnt.'

Butty Halpin smiled and played with the few crumbs of marble cake which remained on the plate. Then he looked at Pat, twanged his braces (they were the very same ones he had worn when his host was in fourth class) and said: 'Well, all I can say is that I hope you make a better fist of it than you did the football. Lord bless us and save us when I think of it!'

Pat could feel the words shrinking in his throat but he rallied valiantly and replied, with convincing good humour: 'Oh now! I was an awful case, Master! Wasn't I?'

Butty shook his head as his left brace went: 'Snap!'

'An awful case?' he continued. 'Ah for God's sake, Pat! Sure you could hardly tie your bucking laces never mind kick a ball!'

Pat twisted a thread which was hanging out of the pocket of his black trousers and, hoarsely, replied: 'Do you remember the day Mattie Skutch kicked the ball and it hit me in the face?'

'Hit you in the face is right!' confirmed Butty. 'Hit you in the face—'

'And went straight into the goal!!'

Butty shook his hairless domed head in despair.

'Lost the bloody cup on us! After all my hard work! The whole season wasted!'

Pat gulped and his nostrils gave an involuntary twitch.

'Oh now, Master,' he said, still twisting the thread, 'it was some day all right!'

Butty wiped his mouth one last time with a corner of the napkin and pushed the table away from him as he rose to his feet. He gazed at Pat as you would at an alcoholic whose spouse and dependants have deserted him, and said: 'Well, all I can say is, Pat – I hope you're better at this acting business than you ever were at the football!'

*

Something valiant sporadically arose in Pat as he lay there pondering over these events throughout the small hours – but it was not enough, and when morning finally came and Butty grabbed his briefcase to dash off to school, calling back: 'Thanks, Pat! See you at half-three,' very little of it remained, in its place (where evidence of it had shone in Pat's eyes) two ominously grey, semicircular shadows. A stranger would surely have found his smile deceptive now as he continued to repeat, to no one in particular – for the house was entirely empty – the words: 'Thank you very much for your kind words of encouragement. However, at least I never claimed to be a teacher! At least I never did that, fucking human sausage, effing potato man!'

There was no mistaking the spiderwork of cracks which interwove upon the glass of the mirror as Pat rubbed his bruised knuckles and withdrew, ramrod-stiff, to the sombre confines of the library. As the day wore on, however, Pat, fortunately, began to see the lighter side of events, eventually – at approximately three o'clock – drawing the curtains to admit the daylight and repeating gaily – a new buoyancy in his eyes – for the benefit of his mother's portrait: 'What do I care about an auld baldy dwarf! For that's all he is! Thinks he's fucking Clark Gable, for the love of Jasus!'

He was continuing to chuckle when the jaunty, self-assured echo of the Master's whistling came drifting down the hallway.

*

It was some days later that the dicky bow arrived in the post, meticulously wrapped in cellophane. 'Yes – that's for me, Pat,' the Master announced, smartly removing it from his hands. 'Or hadn't you heard about me entering the Spot the Talent show below in Sullivan's?'

'Spot the Talent?' croaked Pat, quite taken aback.

'Yes! Come Thursday night I'll be up there with the best – giving them what for, eh, Pat? Yes sir, indeed!'

'What for . . .' repeated Pat abstractedly to himself, as the Master continued:

'But then – you won't be here, will you? You'll be off to Dublin to audition for your – ahem! – acting school!!'

It was as though Pat had momentarily contracted amnesia.

'That's right!' he suddenly cried aloud. 'Of course!'

'Of course!' sniffed the Master. 'You're the boy will leave them standing, eh, Pat?'

An acidic sickliness took hold of Pat's abdomen.

*

But it was a happy Pat McNab who arrived home from Dublin the following Friday evening. Butty Halpin, fresh from a hard day's work in St Cashie's Boys' N.S., was there to greet him on the doorstep. 'Well, Pat! How did it go? The audition, I mean?' he asked urgently.

Pat beamed in his box-pleated coat.

'I did it, Master!' he cried proudly. 'They say it's only a matter of official notification now!'

'Fair play to you, Pat! Able to say the big words all by yourself! Official notification! Ha ha!'

Pat blinked uncertainly, unsure of an appropriate response. But he had no need of it for a pudgy hand had already settled on his shoulder.

'Pat! Come in at once!' demanded the Master. 'I want to show you the prize I won!'

The Spot the Talent Waterford Crystal decanter gleamed like diamonds on the sideboard in the late evening sunlight.

'What do you think of that, Pat?' said the Master.

'It's lovely, Master,' Pat replied, gawping in admiration.

Have you ever been in love, me boys

Have you ever felt the pain

I'd rather be in jail I would

Than be in love again . . .' sang the schoolteacher tunefully, adding, 'That's what won it for me – the bold John McCormack, Pat!'

'I had better go to bed now, Master,' said Pat, rubbing his brow.

'Yes, Pat!' replied Butty. 'You must be tired after all your hard "acting" work – ha ha!'

'What, Master?' said Pat, not thinking straight, his mind cluttered with a bewildering variety of 'accents' and 'pieces of dialogue'.

'Goodnight so, Pat,' responded the Master, bemusedly shaking his globed head, as if mystified by the world and its absurdly unrealizable ambitions.

*

It was approximately fifteen minutes past eight the following morning when Pat, lying in bed, heard the plaintive whistling of Tommy Noble the postman as he came sauntering up the lane, followed by the tantalizing flap of the letter box. Within seconds, he found himself bounding down the stairs, falling upon his knees in the hallway and opening up letters in what can only be described as a 'near-frenzy'. His heart sank as *Reader's Digest* fliers, electricity bills and HP hoover offers followed assorted tax communications in their horrid brown envelopes and the realization slowly dawned on him that there was in fact nothing from the 'acting school'. This procedure was repeated, with startling exactitude, the following morning – indeed the one after that, also – with Pat on broken knees in the hallway surrounded by 'scrunched-up' balls of unwanted missives, but nowhere near him the one his heart so urgently desired.

A pall of gloom settled over him as he sat at the kitchen table the following Friday afternoon, alerting a little as he heard the front door close and the sound of his tenant's footsteps coming along the hall. Within seconds, the school-master was standing in the doorway with his nostrils twitching, remarking:

'There you are, Pat! What's that I smell, I wonder? Turnips? God bless us, Pat, but you're a topper, do you know that!'

The bulbous pedagogue pulled a chair out from beneath the table and seated himself by his host. Withdrawing a large white handkerchief from the pocket of his cavalry twills, he blew thunderously into it and, his cheeks flushing bright-red, said: 'You'll never guess who I met coming up the lane, Pat!'

Pat felt a huge tidal wave of possibility swelling within him.

'Tommy Noble!' he cried, with all the excitement of a young child.

'No! Timmy Sullivan!' replied the Master. 'He has me entered for the All-Ireland Spot the Talent this coming Monday!'

He gave his full attention to the steaming meal before him as he busily tucked his napkin into his shirt collar.

'Boys!' he said, rubbing his hands. 'Boys, but them turnips smell bucking powerful!'

There was no mistaking the ghastly pallor of Pat McNab's countenance as he endeavoured to clasp his hands together on his lap, the better to contain their tremulous vibrations.

*

The following morning found Pat poised on the landing awaiting the arrival of Tommy Noble. But it was not to be. And when 'the tenant' came sauntering gaily up the lane at approximately three thirty that evening, it might have been to the 'place of eternal night' he was returning, for the spirit of Pat McNab was as close now to being 'utterly crushed' as it might be possible for a human to endure. Which made the Master's brusqueness all the more insensitive and, without a doubt, indiscreet, as he complained: 'Ah for the love of God, not turnips again today, Pat!'

Pat paused over the cooker and genuinely made an effort to be civil and considerate.

'I thought you liked turnips, Master,' was his reply.

The circular pedagogue stiffened and left down his briefcase.

'Well, I do. But not every day God sends. Japers, man, sure any lug would know that!'

There was an undoubted edge to Pat's response as he said: 'Well that's all there is, I'm sorry to have to tell you!'

The Master was clearly taken aback but good-humouredly made light of it.

'God bless us Pat but you're in good humour today, aren't you? I suppose no sign of Tommy Noble today again, eh? Would I be right, Pat, in making that assumption? Right, would I be, do you think?'

The saucepan Pat held in his right hand made harsh music on the cluttered counter.

'What do I care about Tommy Noble?' he replied, with a hint of iron.

The Master hooked his thumb in his braces and extended his stomach, grinning widely.

'Sure don't I know, Pat!' he said. 'Which is why I suppose you don't want to hear who I happened to meet coming up the lane!'

Pat whirled, simultaneously wiping his hands on his apron.

'Tommy Noble!' he gasped, incredulously.

'No! Timmy Sullivan!' chuckled the Master.

Pat's heart sank anew and he was about to turn away when he felt a thick-fingered hand on his shoulder, the triumphant cry ringing out: 'No! Tommy Noble!'

Pat could not believe his eyes. He gasped as it appeared before him, the plain spotless white envelope expertly poised on the improvised tray of Butty Halpin's upraised fingers.

Moments later, they found themselves together in the quiet confines of the library, Butty's head almost completely enshrouded in blue smoke from his pipe, fragments of paper from the envelope fluttering all about Pat as he endeavoured to make his way inside the communication he had just received.

'Oh, Master,' he cried, 'I can't do it! I'm all butterfingers!'

Butty Halpin puffed on his briar and advised, avuncularly: 'Patience, Pat. Take your time, dear boy.'

Pat gasped, a nerve tapping furiously over his right eye, as if being worked upon by the shoemaking implement of an infinitesimal, painstaking elf.

'That's right!' he said. 'That's right, Master! Patience!'

There was not a sound to be heard – save the distant lowing of a cow – as Pat ran his eyes across the letter which he now held, quiveringly, in his hand. It would not be an exaggeration to say that his entire countenance was then consumed by an expression of 'pure horror'.

Butty Halpin frowned, removing his pipe from his mouth.

'What's wrong, Pat?' he enquired, scratching the upper part of his cheek with his index finger.

'It—' began Pat, hoarsely.

'What? What are you trying to say, Pat? Come on, man!' continued the Master.

'It—' repeated Pat, his lower lip trembling.

'Here! Give me a look at that!' Butty Halpin demanded, a sudden and unexpected peremptoriness in his voice.

Pat might have been a marble statue erected in the centre of the library as the Master digested its contents.

'Well man, dear oh dear. Isn't that a pity now?' he said, running his soft hand along the shining runway of his head.

'Maybe it's a mistake. Maybe it's a mistake, Master!' exclaimed Pat hopefully.

Butty lowered his head and folded the letter in a manner that was strangely tender. It might have been the regretful denial of an official pardon.

'I'm afraid not, Pat. These people don't make mistakes, I'm sorry to have to tell you!'

Pat lowered his head.

'No, Master,' he compliantly replied. 'They wouldn't, would they? They wouldn't make a mistake.'

The schoolteacher handed the folded white square to his landlord.

'Who knows, Pat,' he said, 'please God – maybe next year. Hmm?'

Pat nodded, shamefully.

'Yes, Master. Please God.'

'Well, good luck now,' went on the Master, with a sudden breeziness, 'I have to rehearse below in Sullivan's this evening so I'll be home late. Not long now before the big day is upon us!'

'That's right, Master. Not long now. It won't be long now!'

'As the monkey said when it got its tail cut off! Ha ha! Well – good luck now, Pat, me auld son!' replied the Master.

*

Throughout the entire evening, Pat endeavoured to avert his eyes from the sparkling edifice of crystal that was the decanter reclining on the sideboard and when, the following afternoon, his tenant remarked: 'God Pat but I had to laugh yesterday when I seen your face! You really thought you had it, didn't you?' it required all the resources he harboured within him to brightly smile and respond, as though he hadn't a care in the world, by saying:

'Oh now, Master! Don't be talking! Doesn't it just show you the class of a cod I really am!'

The Master shook his head.

'And the two wee eyes of you – dancing away with un-bridled hope!'

Now it was Pat's turn to shake his head.

'It was nearly as bad as the days when I used to think I was going to get my place on the school team!'

'Aye! Do you mind that!' replied Butty, lighting his pipe.

'Some hope of me ever being able to kick a ball, eh, Master?'

'Oh now, Pat – would you quit!' was the renowned peda-gogue's reply, elevating himself in his chair as he mused: 'Do you know what I was thinking there, Pat? I wouldn't mind a wee dram of the you-know-what?'

'The you-know-what?' replied Pat, taken slightly by surprise.

'Yes,' his tenant responded, rubbing his hands expectantly, 'after all – we should put to some use my beautifully engraved Waterford Crystal decanter which I won only recently in the intensely competitive Spot the Talent competition, don't you think? Don't you think so, Pat, you great big famous actor, you!'

Pat's mouth went dry as he responded.

'Yes, Master. Why yes, of course.'

The Master's proud grin stretched from ear to empurpled ear as he tentatively poured the amber liquid.

'Ah!' he murmured as he ran his nose along the rim of the glass. 'There's no doubt about it, Pat. A drink is not the same until you sip it from an aristocratic receptacle such as this.'

'Yes,' agreed Pat. 'How was it you described it on another occasion? Elo-elo-ocky something?'

'Eloquence, Pat. Eloquence in glass.'

Pat shook his head in admiration and stared into the life-giving waters below.

'You know, Master,' he continued, 'of all the people who ever stayed in this house, you're the brainiest.'

It was as though a small transformation had taken place, the sun suddenly shining out of Butty Halpin's entire being.

'Do you really mean that, Pat?' he replied humbly.

'No! I'm only making it up!' laughed Pat unexpectedly giving him a firm little push on the shoulder.

The Master laughed uneasily and then said:

'Oh, Pat! You always were a cad!'

'Ha ha!' laughed Pat as the amber liquid touched his lips once more.

They remained sipping for another hour or so and then eventually, the Master stretched and said: 'Well, Pat – it's the wooden hill for me. I have the inspector coming in tomorrow.'

'I hope everything goes well, Master,' said Pat, leaving down his glass.

'Oh indeed and it will,' the Master assured him, 'I know what to expect.'

'Of course you do! Sure you know everything!'

'Ha ha!' laughed the Master, a little uncertainly.

Pat did not reply, simply staring at him with nimble, purposeful eyes.

*

It was approximately 3 a.m. when the sinister figure on the stairs mutely crossed the landing, suddenly shaking the old dark house to its foundations with a furious, almost intolerable pounding on the door of the bedroom where Butty Halpin up until then had been sleeping soundly as a child. Out of his dream of Dots (he and his beloved wife had been waltzing in a field of daisies) he awoke sharply crying: 'Aagh!' only to find himself covered in a clammy sweat as a blood-curdling scream issued from the very bowels of the house. Then – nothing, only silence.

*

'Pat,' queried Butty as he advanced upon a crispy rasher the following morning at the breakfast table, 'did you happen to hear anything unusual last night about three o'clock?'

Pat moved a plate with some bread on it and said, coolly: 'About three? Three o'clock, Master?'

'Yes,' replied Butty, buttering a potato cake (with some effort, it has to be said, his knife skidding haphazardly across his plate a number of times).

'Like what?' replied Pat.

'Like a knock on my door?' the Master said, adding: 'A hammering, in fact. Loud hammering.'

Pat shook his head decisively.

'No, Master. I was asleep around that time,' he said.

The Master frowned, the bubbled triangular cake suspended directly in front of his lips.

'It's the strangest thing,' he said, pouting his lips until they formed a round, crinkly 'o'.

Pat stiffened and suddenly turned, pressing his open palms to his cheeks.

'Gosh!' he said. 'I hope the house doesn't turn out to be haunted!'

There was the tiniest echo of anxiety in the Master's response, despite his somewhat forced 'cheeriness'.

'Haunted! Hah! Would you go away out of that, Pat!'

Pat smiled and shook his head, rubbing his hands on his apron.

'Aye, Master!' he said. 'Do you hear me! I'm at it again! Am I ever going to learn? Cripes, I'm getting to be a bigger eejit every day!'

*

That evening Butty arrived home, 'exhausted', he claimed, and looking forward to nothing more than a nice 'wee dram' from the interior of the eloquent receptacle. 'Isn't that right, Pat?' he said to his landlord as he poured it, not having time to hear Pat's reply before spewing the contents of his mouth across the flowers which decorated the wallpaper directly opposite him.

'Jesus, Mary and Joseph!' he squealed, frantically running his sports-coated sleeve across his mouth.

'What's wrong, Master?' Pat cried, running to his assistance.

'The whisky! Why, it tastes like—'

'What, Master? It tastes like what?'

'*Pish!*' exclaimed the shocked pedagogue, who rarely employed such coarse vernacular.

Pat placed his open palm on his lips and paled. Beyond the library window, it seemed, the entire village was throwing up its hands in horror.

*

There was some consternation in the hallway the following morning as Pat knotted his apron and set about doing the breakfast dishes. 'Cursagod!' and 'Cripes!' and 'Mother of Divine—!' are some examples of the irate ejaculations reaching his ears. At once he repaired hallward where he found the Master in a state of some confusion.

'Master—' he began.

'Pat,' said the Master, 'you didn't by any chance see any of my books around the place, did you?'

'Books, Master?' frowned Pat.

'Aye. Sums books. And writing ones,' the schoolteacher continued.

Pat's brow became knitted.

'No, Master,' he said, 'I didn't see any books at all, I'm sorry to have to say.'

The Master scratched his head and pondered.

'I don't know what the hell is wrong with me these days at all.'

'Make sure you mind yourself for Monday anyhow,' advised Pat.

'Monday?' replied the Master. 'What's on on Monday?'

'Isn't the inspector coming in?' said Pat. 'Isn't that what you said?'

'Jesus, Mary and Joseph, Pat, you're right! I completely forgot!'

Pat smiled as a slight tremor announced itself on the upper part of the Master's right cheek.

*

There were seven books all together arranged before Pat on the polished mahogany table of the library as he good-humouredly applied the scissors to them. They included a Hall and Knight's *Algebra*, *Adventures In English* and *My Friend Matso*. Soon, however, to be no books at all, nothing so much, in fact, as a loose arrangement of sliced-up tragedy which Pat was to happily confine to the dustbin. But not before stopping in front of the framed oval portrait of his mother to remark: 'We'll soon show him! We'll soon show Mr Fatarse Bossy Boots. I really do think we will, Mammy.'

The remainder of that day was used up by Pat to clean the kitchen and complete the one hundred and one tasks which were the stuff of the everyday. And which included preparing a nice hot cup of Complan for the tired 'post-inspector' Master who would doubtless be home soon. It amused Pat emptying the contents of the packet – a fine white powder – into the thick depths of the energy-giving food drink, for he had never perpetrated anything quite like that before.

*

The Master proclaimed himself delighted by Pat's thoughtfulness.

'The nicest cup of Complan I ever drank, Pat,' he declared. 'Thank you, Master,' replied Pat, an almost girlish blush tingeing his cheek.

'Pat, I don't know what I'd do without you.'

'Drink up now, Master,' Pat said, 'like Mammy used to say, it'll put a bone in you.'

'A bone in you! Is that what she used to say? Your mother, God rest her?'

'Yes, Master. That was one of her "old sayings".'

'Boys oh boys. Pat – do you mind me asking you something? Pat – you wouldn't mind?'

'No, Master. Of course not. Go right ahead, for God's sake!'

'It's just that – do you think I've been acting a little strange lately, by any chance?'

'Strange? Lately? Not at all, Master! It's just the pressure of next Monday night! The Spot the Talent Final and all! That's what it is, I'm sure you'll find!'

The Master frowned and cupped his hand around the Complan mug.

'It's just that . . .' he began. 'It's just that, this morning I lost my keys. And yesterday – do you know what I did? I went the wrong way to school!'

'The wrong way to school?' replied Pat incredulously.

'Yes, Pat. It's true. I went down by the Candy Box instead of up by Higginses.'

Pat smiled, bent one of his fingers back and straightened it again.

'God but aren't you the desperate man now to go and do that! Japers, if you keep that up, soon you'll be getting as bad as me!'

The Master swallowed and replaced his mug on the table.

'I think I'd best get myself an early night, Pat.'

Pat nodded understandingly and rose to his feet.

'I think you'd better, Master – if you're to win the prize next Monday!'

The Master smiled – an odd, almost sickly smile – as he bade Pat goodnight and left the room. Behind him, Pat's eyes and those of his mother's painted image seemed to fuse as one. 'He's doing it again,' her soft voice appeared to say, curling like a white smoke from her white, impassive lips. 'After all the pain he's caused us he's gone and done it all over again. Hasn't he, Pat?'

Pat wished it were not thus. For well he remembered that day so long ago when to his horror he had glanced out the window of 'fourth class' to perceive his mother advancing furiously on the school building in her large-buttoned coat and pillbox hat. Before appearing, taut with fury in the doorway of the classroom, rasping: 'Oh yes, Halpin! You'd make a laugh of him all right but you wouldn't teach him his sums like you're supposed to! Sending him home to me with the hands slapped off him every day of the week! My little Pat! Look at you, you turnip – for what else are you – you couldn't teach a spelling to save your life!'

*

What is perhaps tragic is that the following morning the old familiar 'Butty Halpin' had returned with a vengeance. It was as though the 'flawed, humane characteristics' which had lately become a feature of the man's personality had been nothing more than a temporary, ephemeral aberration, of no lasting

295

consequence whatsoever. Which made Pat sad as he watched him now, marching down the lane – confidently – brashly! – swinging his briefcase and singing: '*Have you ever been in love, me boys, have you ever felt the pain?*' in practice for the contest that evening. For the truth is that Pat had – to his exquisite surprise – been developing something of an affection for what might be called the 'New Butty'. But soon, he felt – a thesis eventually – heartbreakingly, perhaps – proven correct – such emotions would be destined to belong only in the dungeons of the past.

With an alacrity, indeed, that not even Pat – an atavistic caution where Butty Halpin was concerned notwithstanding – could have begun to anticipate!

*

It was well after midnight that evening when Pat, immersed in a book – *The Actor's Craft* – was startled by the crunch of gravel beneath heavy boots and the intermittent bursts of heavy coughing and loud, triumphant singing of a by now very familiar song. A glutinous unease took hold of Pat's stomach as he heard: '*For the girl I loved was beautiful and I want you all to know, That I met her in the garden where the praties grow – yeehoo!*' Pat stiffened as the key turned in the lock, instantaneously the room reeking of repellent body odours and stale whisky. If Pat had had any doubts, it was now clear that the 'New' Butty Halpin had vanished and the 'Old' made its brash, triumphant reappearance. The teacher's eyes seemed as two insanely burning beads set back in a pulping ball of incandescent pink flesh as he stumbled forward and jabbed the air pointlessly with his Yale front door key.

'What are you reading there, McNab? Give me that!'

'It's a book about acting. Mammy got me a subscription, you see!'

'Her! That flaming lunatic! We were just talking about her down in the pub! Well, the effing trouble I had with that gawshkogue!'

'Gawshkogue, Master?'

Pat went cold from head to toe.

'Aye! Gawshkogue! Isn't that what I said? Storming into my classroom giving me orders! The gamey auld haybag! Small wonder you grew up half-queer! Ha ha – sorry, Pat!'

A nerve flickered beneath Pat's eye.

'It's all right, Master.'

The round teacher stood backwards as he proceeded to open the boxlike brown-paper package he carried beneath his left arm.

'Well, Pat! I got it! I won the biggest prize of all! Eloquence beyond eloquence this time, Pat, I have to say! A beautiful quill pen made entirely of Waterford Crystal – to symbolize all my learning, you see!'

The sharp spear of the quill pen as it caught the light was truly beautiful. Any number of cities might have collapsed to nothingness within the landscape of Pat's mind at the sight of it.

'Well, Pat. I'd best be off up the wooden hill. I think I'm entitled to a snooze after achieving my life's ambitions. Wouldn't you think so, Pat?'

There was a long pause. Before the old Butty – very much so the old Butty – caustically rasped, raising his voice as of yore:

'Wouldn't you think so, McNab?'

'Yes. Yes, Master,' came the instinctive reply, Pat automatically raising his bottom as though from the seat of an old pine desk in the long ago.

*

There is a dream – as though an Eastmancolored reverie, a psychedelic minuet danced in a garden of fantasy – which comes to those whose inner peace is that born of triumph in the field of private, long-held aspirations; of planets bursting in a firmament glowing with a light which is hardly bearable to one's eyes; of towering sunflowers sprouting as from nowhere; of flower-filled fragrances drifting past on a breeze that is for ever summer. But, always, there will reveal itself an aspect which to that ethereal landscape must belong and to no other, as if all private endeavour had been striving towards that moment when the mundane transforms itself, miraculously, into something which is truly celestial; and the sight of Butty Halpin, unremarkable schoolmaster in a small two-room establishment in a barely known hamlet on the side of a windswept road, for well nigh forty years, bore all the hallmarks of the apotheosis of such qualities; declamatory, elegant beyond words as he stood by the bar, the sparrow-taunting notes of 'The Garden Where The Praties Grow' trilling wantonly from his lips as – absurdly! – and without the slightest warning of any kind, upon this warmly glowing landscape of achievement began to perambulate none other than Mrs McNab, mother of Pat, attired now from head to foot in a bridal gown of white, hand-woven lace, smiling from ear to ear as through the air, elegantly cast from her carved, vein-blue hands, floated a magnificently floral bouquet, her voice, he noted, oddly huskier than he remembered it as she intoned: 'Hello there, Master.'

There is a tentativeness within the world of masquerade, of chimera, a fragility intrinsic to its essence that can be shocking in its rawest manifestation; a darkness encircling those crimson planets which burst, a sinister supplication about the heads of sunflowers now which well may threaten to droop if not expire; a heart-stopping bluntness about the crack of lightning which darts across the sky – as it does now, at this very moment – revealing in an instant none other than – Maimie McNab! – no longer about her gowned and lace-clad form the shimmering perimeter of light that is the signature of poesy, fancy and imagination, but cold and poker-stiff, her face a mask of chalk-white flesh from which feeling has been long since banished. His dream crumbling as a window by a propelled stone shattered, a paper bag by a closed fist crushed, Butty Halpin shot awake, a Niagara of sweat upon his back.

'Mrs McNab!' he cried, astonished, pulling the striped collar of his pyjamas about his neck.

There was a long pause as Mrs McNab, in a voice unexpectedly low and sonorous yet resonant throughout the entire room, replied: 'Master – I'm sorry about Pat. He's giving you trouble again, isn't he?'

Butty Halpin gulped. Mrs McNab threw a huge, startlingly vast shadow on the wall.

'No, Mrs McNab. He's not!' he replied unconvincingly.

'Ah, Mr Halpin, he is,' replied Mrs McNab. 'He can't do his sums. And he's no good at the football.'

Butty felt his lips go dry – but the clack of the stickiness inside his mouth was almost deafening.

'No good at the football? ' he replied, weakly. 'No, Mrs McNab, he's powerful at it. He's a great trier. A great trier altogether.'

Mrs McNab moved a little step closer and lowered her head. Then she looked up sadly and said: 'I know, Master. But trying's not good enough, is it? You've always said that. It's simply not enough to try!'

Butty Halpin tried to wet his lips with his tongue as he said:

'Mrs – would you mind if I went? I've been in the house annoying Pat long enough. I'll be off so—'

As if unaware of his own actions, he noticed his feet fall to the floor and his pipe-smoke-stained fingers reach for his trousers which lay draped across the back of a chair. He felt Mrs McNab's presence. Her deep and steady breathing had the effect of unnerving him to a terrible degree. He could feel individual beads of perspiration breaking out on his forehead with a rhythmic precision as if each one was announcing: 'I'm here! Present and correct!'

'Why did you have to call him names?' he heard her say. 'He was only a boy, Mr Halpin!'

'Mrs McNab,' he croaked as he raised one leg to insert into his trousers, 'I have to go now. I really would like to stay but I have no choice, I'm afraid!'

'He was only a boy but you had to call him names! Why did you have to do that, Mr Halpin?'

It was unfortunately at that moment – one foot becoming entangled in the leg of his trousers – that the blood rushed to the schoolteacher's head, leading him to involuntarily ejaculate:

'Ah for the love of God, woman, can you blame me! It was you did it! You and your mad carry-on!'

Almost instantly he placed his hand over his lips and cried: 'No!' his trousers ballooning about his ankles as he did so, the sudden arrow of blue lightning outside disorientating him as the huge shadow loomed above him, its tenebrous texture of glimmering – glimmering? yes! – immaculately blown glass all the way from Waterford, a sinuously curving quill, the plinth of which dealt him a glancing blow to the side of the head as his flailing arm drew wild arcs of both shadow and light from the oscillating lampshade, the screeches of his assailant seeming to issue from an abyss far beyond before coalescing to form the words: 'What with the way you had him, you and your carry-on!'

There could be only one response from Butty Halpin, schoolmaster, in the face of the ferocity of such an onslaught and it was thus: 'Aaargh!' as a rapid succession of large, poppy-red blotches broke in lakes against the window, before becoming thin irregular rivers coursing downward along the sporadically illuminated, blue-lit glass.

*

A figure alone in a field, elbow angled on the wooden shaft of a spade, his soul weighed down by melancholy as he ponders and murmurs quietly in the midge-ridden quiet of the gloaming: 'Even if only one time you'd said it, Master. Just said:

"I don't want to be the big fellow any more. Tonight I don't want to be the big fellow. Instead let's just you and me go down to Sullivan's and have ourselves a little chat about the future and the way things are going to be."

'From now on, not the past, not the old days. Nothing but the future, Master. The future and you and Pat McNab. But you couldn't do it, could you, Halpin? Couldn't do it, could you, you scuttering great tub of mouldy shite!'

*

A solitary figure in a kitchen, softly closing a drawer which contains a wig both sad and lifeless and a once-vivacious bouquet of flowers from a wedding long since faded to the land of sepia. The flicker of melancholy still lingering in his eyes as he whispers: 'No. Had to be all the big fellow and that's all there is to it. Scuttering tubs of guts who have to have it all their own way and abandon the rest of us to melancholy.'

A melancholy hardly evident to stray passers-by on the nights when the moon transmits its ghostly rays and sends them spilling out across the slates of the house which is the residence of Pat McNab, former pupil of Bernard 'Butty' Halpin, Bachelor of Arts (by night), Gullytown. Although, it has to be said, there were occasions upon which even the most casually interested observers might have paused and, cupping a hand around one ear, remarked: 'Why, I do believe it sounds as if there is a party of some description going on, right here in the McNab place!'

As indeed, perhaps there might well have been. But such is not how Pat McNab might have described it, no such words came leaping to his lips as he – some part of him finally having expired as a consequence of the behaviour of his former educator – raised the teapot and enquired of his 'sleeping' mother (utterly oblivious of the assortment of 'mini-beasts' which had clearly been utilizing her eye sockets as some sort of 'mini-beast hotel', long before he had ever ferried her inside from her prone resting place beneath the laurel bush) as to whether she might 'like some more tea at all?' before allowing himself a private little smile and retiring to the library, where, dimming the lights to his satisfaction, he took up his pen and, beginning to hum softly to himself, inscribed, in the most copperplate of hands: 'They're all germs, Mammy. You know that, don't you? That's what they are, you know. Each and every one of them – germs who have to die!', a heart-warming feeling of well-being overcoming him as his pen assumed a life of its own, the contentment he now felt effortlessly forming itself into the words which trembled for a moment upon his lips before – triumphantly, exultantly – soaring from them and disappearing through the window:

'Have you ever been in love, me boys, have you ever felt the pain
I'd rather be in jail, me boys, than be in love again.
For the girl I loved was beautiful and I want you all to know
That I met her in the garden where the praties grow!'

as though for all the world some living, breathing fireflies of song.

CHAPTER TWELVE

Island of Dreams

Island of Dreams

I wander the streets and the gay crowded places
Trying to forget you but somehow it seems
My thoughts ever stray to our last sweet embraces
Over the sea on the island of dreams.

High in the sky is a bird on the wing
Please carry me with you
Far, far away from the mad rushing crowd
Please carry me with you

Again I would wander where memories enfold me
There on the beautiful island of dreams.

High in the sky is a bird on the wing
Please carry me with you
Far, far away from the mad rushing crowd
Please carry me with you.

Again I would wander where memories enfold me
There on the beautiful island of dreams.
Far, far away on the island of dreams.

A COMMON REMARK as time proceeded in the tranquil hamlet of Gullytown and the surrounding district began to be: 'I think McNab's getting worse, do you know that.' And there were few reasonable observers who would venture to disagree with such assertions whenever they'd encounter Pat strolling through the village with bottles of Double Diamond and Macardles Ale clinking in his pocket, biting at his thumbnail and erupting into what can only be described as edgy yelps of laughter for no apparent reason at all. In Sullivan's Select Bar, the plain facts were that they had more or less given him up for lost. Even Timmy Sullivan, when he was approached about matters concerning his customer, merely tossed back his head – in the manner of one who, after months of stoic and almost heroic patience, has finally given up the ghost. 'He was in here again last night,' he would remark, wiping a glass with his teacloth, 'talking about showbiz engagements on the moon, no less! What did I say? Huh! The night before it was some kung fu expert tailing him! Ah look here – I give up.' At which the sober patrons (and there were a few) would just shake their heads and sigh. For it was clear as day to them and to anyone who had come into the slightest contact with him that if he continued in this fashion, Pat would soon be beyond redemption. 'A complete and utter bucking headcase!' was Josh Mulrooney's verdict. 'Not that it's any surprise, mind you, what with him having that for a mother! If anything, she was worse than him!' Insensitive as it may seem, it would have been very difficult to find anyone in the hamlet of Gullytown and district who would demur. 'I mind her coming down the street one day wearing a hat with a plastic budgie!' recalled Tom O'Halloran.

'A plastic budgie? Sure that's nothing! Didn't she come down to the school and bate poor Butty Halpin over the head and the whole school laughing at him! Jasus, Butty was no angel but he didn't deserve that!'

'She slapped me across the face one day – in this very pub!' said someone else.

No, Mrs McNab did not possess many 'fans' in the small community collectively known as Gullytown. As neither indeed did her late husband, 'the Army Man, McNab' as he was known (the news of whose demise, after getting 'blown up' in the war, was greeted with cheers in Sullivan's and other establishments). And in a sense because of which there had always been a lingering sort of sympathy, however unspoken, for Pat and the way he was. 'Ah sure, God help him' was a commonly employed platitude. But even in their very worst imaginings, there were very few – if any – who believed Pat capable of the most heinous crime of all, in all likelihood vouchsafing:

'Pshaw! McNab! Sure that eejit'd run a mile before he'd do the like of that! He's afraid of his own shadow, for God's sake!'

Indeed, had Pat burst through the doors of Sullivan's and glassily declared: 'I've done it! At last I've done it!' he would more than likely have been greeted with an assortment of derisive whoops. For the simple truth is that they would not have been able to bring themselves to believe it. Any more than they would have been capable of envisaging him lifting a finger to his old schoolteacher Butty Halpin! But oh how wrong they were in that particular case, as in so many others! For now that Pat had sipped a number of times from that most exciting, pungent of chalices, the prospect of its vivifying liquid again reaching his lips made his heart beat at a pace heretofore unknown! By the lone resident of the McNab house, at least! 'Take that!' he had howled at poor Butty as he brought the crystal instrument of death down again and again! Chuckling wildly as he swooshed handfuls of clear, cool water about his features to cleanse them, crying with abandon: 'Free! Yes, free at last!' After which, of course, his adversaries were as nothing but perambulating sacks of human compost placed upon this earth for the sole purpose of the fertilization of Pat McNab's back garden. There were those who, phlegmatically, on occasion might mutter: 'Mrs McNab – I wonder where does she be these times at all?' Finding themselves smartly silenced by such implacable responses as 'Oh! She's in America! Away this good while, I believe!'

Similar deductions applied in the case of Butty Halpin. To the query 'Where the hell is Butty at all? He never seems to come in now!' would come the reply: 'Ah since his poor Missus died he hasn't been so well at all. Gone to the sister in Dublin, so they say!'

As all returned to silence.

Unlike the clamour continuing inside the mind of Pat McNab at this time, which might be more accurately described as 'disjointed' and 'cacophonous', particularly since the beating with sticks administered circa the 'moon episode' and subsequent indulgence in more 'roots' enthusiastically advanced to him by one Honky McCool. Not to mention his recent conversion to the world of the 'video nasty', one in which indeed he now passed a great proportion of his waking hours, settling himself in his chair with Taytos and red lemonade, flicking the button with his toe as the cathode-ray tube disseminated its all-enfolding light along with the raucous cries of Chuck Norris, Jackie Chan and Jean-Claude Van Damme. As for ninety minutes' duration, a feeling of peace, bliss and utter contentment would assume residence in the soul of Pat McNab. But, being in such a fragile state (post-moon episode, there was still a lump on his head the size of a balloon) it was perhaps unwise for Pat to dedicate such a generous portion of his time to indulgence in 'unreality'. For the links between the world it represented and that of the tangible, temporal one which the rest of us attempt to negotiate daily were – without his knowledge – becoming ever more tenuous.

*

Which might perhaps explain why Pat on his way home from Sullivan's on a perfectly ordinary Tuesday night – dreary, indeed, with not a little drizzle – after one of his sporadic bursts of coughing raised his head to find a significant proportion of the countryside (in the main, the field between Henry's beech and the barnyard gate) suffused with a shimmering silky green light. It disturbed him to observe this and a certain coldness enveloped him as he perceived a razor-sharp wind whistling past, bending his black greasy hair back behind his ears. By the time he attained sanctuary, it is no falsehood to state that Pat McNab was close to tears and as he sank into his library chair, he plunged his head into his hands and cried: 'Why can't you leave me alone? Why do these thoughts come back to haunt me now! Why can't you be still, insistent drum of guilt!'

*

For three hours that night, he remained immobile in the chair, far off the thunder grumbling as though personally dissatisfied, the rain dribbling in tiny, multiplying rivers down the glass. At once Pat construed himself on fire and abandoned in the arctic snows. 'When will it be?' he whispered, semi-delirious. 'When will it be that I shall be set free? To feel at last about me silence? What? What did you say? Did someone's beautiful voice at this very moment bring me words of longed-for succour? Please say they did. I beg you now – affirm it for me! Affirm that for me!'

308

Unexpectedly, it was a smile of contentment that suddenly began to play about his lips as the first sound of throbbing bongo drums came drifting from afar. Followed by a voice that was the tiniest of whispers lost inside the blunt vastness of the wardrobe.

'Pat?' came the voice. 'Pat, pet?'

Pat's heavy-lidded eyes flickered ever so slightly as he smiled weakly and said: 'That such a word it could be whispered and in this world be real would be to me as a balm in Gilead. But it could not. Alas it can but be my fevered dreams.'

'Pat, love? Can you hear me?'

It was a twinkling speck in a vast and sweeping cosmos.

'Mammy?' Pat heard himself say, with a feeling of hope that appeared to consume his entire being.

The bird-cries came from afar, from a distant place he could not know.

'Is that you, Mammy?' he repeated tremulously.

The familiar feminine voice became more audible now, as though the birds in unison now deferred.

'It's me, love. I'm over here,' she whispered.

It was as though another Pat, a secret, transparent one from pure light fashioned, now detached itself from his recumbent form and by a pulsating, compelling music led, attended by the wardrobe door, the hypnotic lilt of the macaw magically threaded about his cranium.

'Mammy?' he ventured apprehensively.

'Yes, love,' he heard his mother reply.

'Are you in there?'

It was as though Pat was on the cusp of complete happiness and utter despair.

'Open the door, sweetheart!' his mother urged him.

'The door?' replied Pat, a little confused.

'Yes,' said his mother, 'I'm waiting for you.'

The what only can be described as a 'foxfire flash' which

ensued was instantaneous, but not in the least unpleasant – as neither, indeed, was the sight which now met Pat's eyes, one which came close to bringing tears to them as he beheld his mother, a vision now in a mango and papaya-patterned one-piece swimsuit as she awaited him beneath the tallest of coconut trees. Pat felt slightly awkward and ill-prepared in his long, down-to-the-knee black coat. Behind his smiling parent, the bleached white coast trailed along by a clear, turquoise sea which seemed to stretch to infinity itself, the parakeets within the sprouting tropical palms as so many splashes of brightly coloured paint. Pat felt a lump coming into his throat.

'Mammy! I can't believe it's you!' he heard himself say.

His mother smiled.

'Oh, it's me all right. I've waited so long for you, son,' she replied.

Pat gulped.

'Oh, Mammy,' he said.

'Waited for this day,' his mother repeated, her eyes shimmering.

'Mammy, I can't bear it,' Pat said.

'Come on, love,' said his mother, extending her hand.

*

The waves hushed as though teasing the edge of the strand as they both lay beneath the enormous tree that seemed to curtsey to the blushing sky. Far off a porpoise curved and was swallowed up by the warm waters.

'How many nights I've dreamed of this. You coming to visit me here,' his mother said, passing him a sliver of bread-fruit.

'Me too, Mammy,' came Pat's choked reply.

'You dancing. Me singing. I used to dream about it – and think that it would be the most beautiful thing in the entire world.'

Pat looked shyly at her.

'It is, Mammy,' he replied as she took his hand and began to sing, tapping the rhythm on his palm with her fingers.

I wander the streets and the gay crowded places
Trying to forget you but somehow it seems –'

She smoothed his hair back from his eyes and said: 'Sing it, Pat. Sing it for Mammy, will you love?'

Pat was hesitant but gained courage as she squeezed his hand.

'*My thoughts ever stray,*' he sang, '*to our last sweet embraces . . .*'

'*Over the sea on the Island of Dreams!*' she sang aloud, embracing him as he cried: 'Mammy!'

'Pat!'

'The most beautiful day since the world began!'

*

And it really was. The way he knew they would all be now, the days that spread before them, as, the evening closing in around them now, he watched her setting the table in the hut, carefully laying out the impressively crafted earthenware, the house goat sipping the milk, then masticating quietly in the corner.

'Here, Pat!' she said, passing her son a gourd. 'Have yourself some fruit juice.'

'Thank you, Mammy,' replied Pat, good-manneredly.

'You get that down you now like a good fella – and help yourself to anything you want, won't you? I have this skin to put out!'

His mother hummed softly to herself as she disappeared beneath the rattan door and was swallowed up by the sunshine. Pat stared at the goat's matted beard for a moment and thought: 'How can you be so lucky, Pat McNab? How can you have done such a bad thing on your own mother and then finding yourself waking up one morning having been given a second chance? Not only that but given a life which is so beautiful your mind is close to bursting thinking about it! A

311

life replete with mango, banana, coconut, porpoise, parakeet, and paradise bird! Why, it's fantastic! No wonder then you'd cry: "But this, it cannot be! Surely today this rainbow world will fall apart, everything within it turn to dust!"'

*

'Nothing is either good or bad but thinking makes it so,' the bard would insist. And thus it seemed to Pat McNab as he lay there, his anxieties (thoroughly unnecessarily, and induced, most likely, by the torrid heat) becoming transformed into night sweats of the most hideous kind as he strove for sleep in the straw and mud-baked hut he and his mother now called home. 'No! No!' he cried, springing awake in his rudimentary settle bed to envision the goat lying in a corner on its side – *dead!* And placed directly – clearly significantly! – above its sad, unbreathing body, a talismanic arrangement of exotic fruits – splitting open like flesh! Pat cried out anew as he espied the irregular trail of crimson blood winding its ragged way towards the aperture that was the door – and, firmly nailed by the north-west corner, a human heart on fire – that single, vile and unmistakable prognostication of voodoo! Out of nowhere an unearthly howl instilled fear of an undiluted kind into his bones, beside him now appearing a straw-braceleted figure behind a giant painted mask, uncurling from its pitlike mouth the cry: '*Whoah – hoo – hah – hee – haw!*' then total silence as it vanished as though never having existed.

'Pat! Pat! What is wrong?' he heard his mother cry, his heart beating wildly in his chest. Only then did he realize that the entire hut was in silence. Beside him, he noted, his mother looked quite fetching in her native hair accessories.

'Oh, Mammy! The things I dreamt,' Pat cried out, 'I never want to dream them again!'

It was then that true – *true* terror! – knifed its way into the core of Pat's very being as his mother's expression contorted bitterly and she hissed:

'Then you shouldn't have committed the most vile of all the sins! Matricide!'

'No! No! Mammy! It's not true! I didn't mean it!'

But it had all been nothing save a mere consequence of the fevers deep within him, and his mother's words came soothing once again: 'It's nothing, love. Go back to sleep now, won't you?'

Pat trembled as he replied:

'Oh, Mammy! I'm so glad we're back together again, you and me!'

His mother smiled and nodded.

'Yes. It's been quite a long time. But now – you're here! Ssh now and go to sleep, alanna.'

There was something about his mother's expression that unsettled him not a little, and the faint sound of the pulsating bongoes somewhere in the distance did nothing to alleviate it.

*

That Pat's instinct on this occasion should have proven to be so accurate is tragic, yes, but there can be no denying that only hours later, before the light of dawn had yet touched the rattan door of their home, the woman he knew as his mother was standing above him, displaying upon her countenance – the skin of which was drawn tight as papaya over a crude outline of bones – the coldest and most impassive of expressions, which seemed to echo the unmistakable iciness of her speech. 'No mother ever loved a son as I did you, Pat McNab. Why did you do it? Why did you have to do it? Why?' The taut breathing of the middle-aged woman seemed to fill the small enclosure as from her pocket (she was attired in a crude imitation kitchen smock of animal fur) she produced a ghastly replica of the voodoo lexigram and placed it beneath his pillow. Her lips were thin and uncompromising as she said: 'Maybe if you'd come earlier, I could perhaps have forgiven you. But I've had enough of it in my time – from that father of yours, as you well know! But still you had to go and leave it! Why did you have to leave it so late, Pat?'

*

'Mammy!' squealed Pat as his eyelids shot open, only to be dazzled by the all-engulfing foxfire-flash which consumed the hut, the piercing cry of a phantasmagorical demon-bird teasing across the sky as a spear thudded into the wall of the hut, the goat's terrified bleats as distress flares dispatched by the damned. It was then that the familiar words, but this time intoned as if by a harpy from the further reaches of some pitiless place, reached the ears of Pat McNab: '*I wander the streets and the gay crowded places / Trying to forget you but somehow it seems . . .*' – until an all-consuming nausea, then a blackness, enveloped Pat and he awoke to perceive a distorted dance of gambolling flames and before him a familiar figure which seemed behind its horrendous mask (large whorled eyes, random swishes of colour) to speak with the voice of an animal.

Pat squealed as he found himself set upon and stripped *in toto* of his clothes, a single fragment of cloth carelessly arranged about his private parts. The large-breasted native woman retreated in silence as the witch doctor gestured with his spear.

'No! No!' Pat found himself crying helplessly as he was borne aloft by three warriors whose greasy bronzed skin shone brightly in the moonlight, his wrists expertly shackled to the skeleton of a bamboo trellis, as, hopelessly cruciform, he divined before his eyes the coiled shape of a cobra snake – on either side of him placed a steaming cauldron of boiling oil. At once, the bongoes began their complex rhythm, as so many fingers tapping out a solo of torment on his temples.

'No! No!' cried Pat, his heart leaping with hope, incongruously – and as it transpired, foolishly – as he discerned the words of the pith-helmeted white hunter who had abruptly emerged from the damp undergrowth.

314

'I'm afraid you'll find it's a bit late for that, old boy. My understanding is that they have already passed judgement.'

'Who?' Pat, summoning all his resources, choked, 'What are you talking about? *Already passed judgement?* Who are you?'

'Siggerson,' the hunter replied, 'Clifford Siggerson. Cigarette? No, of course not! Silly of me!'

The hunter produced a silver cigarette lighter and fired his tobacco with a flourish. 'No,' he continued, 'I'm afraid it's not looking good for you, old bean. You see – they take a dim view of that sort of thing here. Kill brothers, sisters, uncles, aunts, fathers even. But mothers? 'Fraid not, old fruit. Mother is sacred. As I'm sure you've gathered. Ha ha!'

The hunter's casual gesture led Pat's terrified eyes in the direction of the carved ikon which was clearly a homage to the revered state of motherhood – a smiling, middle-aged face gazing looking down upon her many children. The awesomeness of his predicament dawned on Pat.

'You've got to help me! Please – you've got to help me!'

The helmeted animal pursuer gravely shook his head, proceeding towards the towering foliage.

'Stop!' shrieked Pat. 'Where are you going? Come back, you English bastard! You can't leave me here like this! Go on then, you miserable fool – with your stupid hat! Ha ha! I don't care! O God! Why did I have to do it! It could have been so beautiful! We could have ruled the whole island, me and Mammy!'

With that, the manacled Gullytown man fell in a dead faint. In his sleep, an almost imperceptible smile of happiness played upon his lips. For, in that slumber, he saw what might have been. His mother clapping at a table as he, attired in a colourful 'South Seas' style T-shirt and espadrilles, swiftly disposed of his mint julep and authoritatively shushed the appreciative crowd.

'Thank you, ladies and gentlemen,' he began, 'may I say how wonderful it is to be here tonight at the Club Tropicana.

We'd like to continue with another song for you now and with your permission I'd like to ask someone special to join me onstage – Mrs McNab? If you would be so kind?'

It was a very shy but nonetheless enthusiastic Mrs Maimie McNab who negotiated her way stageward through the tables, her son taking her hand as he pecked her on the cheek and they began – as one! – to sing their favourite song:

'An Irish boy was leaving
Leaving his native home
Crossing the broad Atlantic
To foreign lands to roam
And as he was leaving his mother
While waiting on the quay
He threw his arms around her waist
And this to her he did say:
A mother's love's a blessing
No matter where you roam
Keep her while she's living
You'll miss her when she's gone
Love her as in childhood
Though feeble old and grey
For you'll never miss your mother's love
Till she's buried beneath the clay!'

'Oh, Mammy!' Pat heard himself cry as he drew his mother to his bosom, about to peck her tenderly on the cheek when – *foxfire flash!* – a poison dart shot from a blowpipe protruding through the trees went fleetingly past his cheek, the native would-be assailant tearing back into the undergrowth.

'Come back, you bastard!' Pat heard himself cry. 'You can't leave me tied up here! I'll murder you!' The voodoo mask looming, approaching now as from behind it, a confident, familiar voice growled: 'Oh yes! You'd do that all right!'

'What?' Pat gasped.

'But you won't, you see. For your murdering days are over.'

'Who's that? Who's that?' Pat squealed.

With agonizing slowness, the mask was removed and Pat found himself staring into the face of the woman who had carried him for nine months – his own mother!

'Mammy!' he cried aloud – for no reason that he could determine, illogically consumed by a feeling of wellbeing – 'It's you! Thank God!'

His mother smiled.

'That's right, son. It's me. I came at last.'

Pat smiled broadly, his heart pounding furiously within his chest.

'That's right, Mammy,' he smiled, 'you did.'

There was a sickly, acidic quality to his mother's smile as she continued: 'Yes I did. I didn't leave it until it was too late. Like some people.'

Pat's cheek jerked nervously.

'What, Mammy? Ha ha, Mammy! You're a gas, woman! Mammy, will you take these knots out? They're hurting my wrists!'

'Yes, I will, Pat,' agreed his mother. 'After all – you don't have too long left, do you?'

Pat's eyes widened.

'What, Mammy? Ha ha – oh now! What, Mammy? Mammy, what do you mean?'

His mother clicked her fingers and instantaneously, two warriors were at Pat's side. Within seconds, they had her son released from his bondage. Despite himself, Pat was in quite a jittery state as he presented himself before his mother, towering rigidly above him. (Or so it seemed, although she was actually smaller than him!)

'Phew!' he gasped. 'Thank God for that! Mammy – would you look at the state of this place! The sooner we're out of here the better, if you ask me!'

There was something troublingly wry about Mrs McNab's expression as she contemplated the nails of her right hand.

'Isn't that funny now? ' she replied. 'And you only a couple of days ago saying it was just about the most fantastic place on earth!'

The corners of Pat's mouth expanded and contracted almost simultaneously.

'Aye, I know, Mammy but that was a couple of days ago – look at me now!'

Mrs McNab folded her arms.

'That's you all over, isn't it, Pat?' she said. 'No matter how beautiful something is, you always spoil it in the end. Somehow you always manage to spoil it, don't you?'

Pat swallowed, a Niagara of saliva glutinously making its way past his tonsils.

'No, Mammy. I don't,' he replied, hopefully but without the conviction demanded by the circumstances.

His mother lowered her voice, strangely impassive now.

'Ah you do, Pat. You do. No doubt you'd do the same here if you were let. You'd do exactly the same here if you thought you'd get away with it.'

Pat cried out, unable to help himself.

'No, Mammy! I would not! Now, Mammy, that's not fair!'

'Turn all our dreams to dust, that's what you'd do!' went on his mother. 'Every wonderful day we'd have on this island – you'd go and destroy it, just like you did all the other ones.'

Such was his emotional state that Pat's voice was virtually a croak.

'Mammy, I didn't mean that!' he pleaded. 'That wasn't meant to happen!'

There was a heartbreaking wistfulness in his mother's eyes.

'Went and took your own mother's life! Robbed her of her living breath and left lying there as cold as stone.'

In Pat's eyes tears were gleaming now.

'It's not my fault!' he erupted. 'You wouldn't leave me alone! Why couldn't you leave me alone?'

Suddenly his mother – quite unexpectedly – extended her hand and whispered softly:

'Do you know something, Pat? I love you. Will you dance with me? One last time – will you dance with me?'

Pat's cheek spasmed abruptly.

'One last time? Please, Mammy. Please don't say that,' he said.

His mother studied her crossed hands. Together they fashioned the shape of a flesh-eagle.

'I'm sorry, Pat,' she said, 'it's the law. You know the law.'

Pat brought his brows together with a tension that was almost painful.

'The law, Mammy,' he croaked, 'what are you talking about?'

Before Pat's mother had a chance to reply, the voodoo man appeared out of nowhere, from behind his fearsome mask brandishing a steamy wooden beaker, which he aggressively shoved at Pat.

'What is it, Mammy?' Mrs McNab's son called out – near-terror evident now in his voice. 'What is it he's giving me? Mammy, what is in this mug? Please!'

His mother looked away, impassively.

'I'm sorry, Pat,' she responded, 'you must, I fear. It is the law, you see.'

The voodoo man jabbed Pat on the shoulder with his spear, manoeuvring him towards the proffered receptacle. Tearfully, he felt his lips tentatively make contact with the rim.

'That's it, love,' he heard his mother say, 'for those you have deprived of life by both callous hand and kitchen implement, retribution you must now make. With the life you call your own.'

'Please, Mammy,' begged Pat.

His mother tilted the beaker upwards his lips with a hand that was unmistakably gentle but firm.

'That's it, love! Come on now!' she entreated. 'Soon it will be all over.'

Splashes of the foul, repellent liquid cascaded across Pat's chest. It was as some vile combination of Creamola Foam and whisky, with a tincture of Jeyes Fluid.

'Come on, love,' he heard his mother repeat, 'drink up. The law must be obeyed.'

Pat forced the thick liquid down his scorched, raw throat.

'That's it,' said his mother, 'another little drop now, love.'

Pat spluttered awkwardly as he downed the remainder of the vessel's contents.

'Very good,' said Mrs McNab. 'Come on now, sweetheart. Give me your hand like a good boy.'

With great trepidation, Pat succumbed to her warm embrace as they began to slowly waltz in the firelight, fiercely observed by the voodoo man from a circle of bronzed, statuesque native warriors. Pat felt his mother's hot breath on his cheek as she whispered into his ear:

'You know what's sad? You know what's sad, love?'

A lump the size of a large thumb began to form itself in Pat's throat.

'What, Mammy?' he asked. 'What is it that's sad?'

'That it had to end this way,' went on his mother. 'For you know what? If it hadn't, we could have lived every word of our song. Every single word of it!'

All Pat's nerves seemed to go on alert at once.

'Mammy! Please! Don't! Don't say it!'

But Mrs McNab gave no indication of having heard her son.

'Around this fire – perhaps for all eternity, we could have sung – together we could have sung our song!'

Her eyes slowly closed as out into the hot tropical night floated familiar words:

'*I wander the streets and the gay crowded places*
Trying to forget you but somehow it seems . . .'

She paused and squeezed his shoulder.

'Come on, Pat,' she coaxed him, 'that's my boy!' as, stumblingly, his cheeks on fire, he began:

'*My thoughts ever stray to our last real embraces –*'

But before he could complete the phrase, a wave of intense nausea swept over him and the trees began to metamorphose before his eyes, capering now as if rendered alive!

'Agh!' cried Pat.

'It's going to be all right, I tell you!' his mother reassured him.

'Help me, Ma!' Pat wailed as the mountains melted into liquid.

'It's going to be all right,' a soft voice insisted from far away, as though from the heart of the deepest valley. 'Soon it will be all over.'

'My stomach,' Pat groaned. 'My insides are in flames!'

'Come to me, love. Come to Mammy,' coaxed Mrs McNab, putting her arm around Pat's shoulders.

'O Mammy! The pain! It's like a thousand vipers!'

'Come on, love,' said his mother. 'That's it! Lie down here!'

It was clear to Pat that he was now close to death as palm frond-bearing natives swept towards him in a wave, a new-found kindness in their eyes, robust bass voices delivering a semi-calypso version of his mother's favourite song in a style reminiscent of Paul Robeson, '*Again I will wander where memory enfolds me, over the sea on the Island of Dreams.*'

A blanket of moss served as a pillow for Pat's heavy head.

'Are you comfortable now, love?' he heard his mother say. 'Drink this last hot drop like a good boy. Go on now, there!'

Terrified, Pat complied with his mother's wishes.

'That's better,' he heard her say, his lids weighty as those of dustbins beginning at last to close, her voice merging with that of the islanders as they sang – so beautifully! – before she rose, and, weaving in the firelight, began what might be called a strange, finger-extending 'Britt Ekland' type of dance, her face at last contorting in what can only be described as a series of elastic, wilful and gratified expressions as her mouth became lopsided and she hissed (so like a snake!) close to his ear: '*Over the sea on the island of dreams*' before slithering away once more, chuckling: 'Ha ha ha!' horribly, out of each of her sides a leathery, bone-bisected wing unfurling as she became as a screeching demon-creature swallowed up by the living, palpitating darkness of the undergrowth.

*

The dawn light as it broke was as a brilliantly polished sword which remorselessly cleaved the soul of Pat McNab as he stood bent above the bowl of his bathroom toilet, discharging the contents of his stomach into the opaque waters below. 'Oh Jesus! Oh Jesus Christ!' were the only words which could be heard as the first starlings and thrushes prepared themselves for a day of song.

There was something forlorn about the discarded aluminium container which lay abandoned on the kitchen floor with its skull-and-crossboned label PARAQUAT – POISON prominently displayed. From the bathroom, the heartbreaking cries – punctuated by intermittently raucous evacuations – resonated until the entire house seemed to become nothing so much as an enormous sob. It was all Pat could do to wipe his stained mouth with his sleeve and tumble down the hall when he heard the sound of the front-door bell.

*

Outside on the step, Tommy Noble the postman was reaching in his sack and removing a letter as he whistled a tune.

'There you are, Pat,' he said brightly. 'Grand morning now, thank God. I have a letter for you here.'

Pat endeavoured as best he could to hide from view the lengthy, wing-shaped, already drying mark of regurgitated sick that stained his lapel, preparing to engage Tommy in good-humoured badinage as best he could when the startlingly bright colours of the hexagonal stamp that shone across the white expanse of the letter first of all startled then disorientated him, displaying as they did a bird bearing truly stunning, decorative plumage. 'A bird of paradise!' gasped Pat, feeling a bead of sweat form (as large as a gooseberry) in the region of the base of his spine.

'What's that, Pat?' he heard the postman say, from what might have been a distance of thousands of miles across the sea.

'Come a long way has it, then, Pat? From your mother, Pat, is it? I knew she was away on holidays, all right! Whereabouts, Pat, if you don't mind me asking?'

But there was to be no answer from Pat, a diminutive representation of the smiling postman reflected in his eyes as glassy-eyed he remained immobile, already an assembly of starlings beginning to gather upon the telegraph wires, valiantly trying to reach him with a song he'd never hear.

For What It's Worth (Stop! Hey, what's that sound?)

For What It's Worth (Stop! Hey, what's that sound?)

There's something happening here
What it is ain't exactly clear
There's a man with a gun over there
Telling me I got to beware
I think it's time hey what's that sound
Everybody look what's going round!

There's battle lines being drawn
Nobody's right if everybody's wrong
Young people speaking their minds
Getting so much resistance from behind.
I think it's time hey what's that sound
Everybody look what's going round.

Paranoia strikes deep
Into your life it will creep
Starts when you're always afraid
Step outa line the man come and take you away
I think it's time hey what's that sound
Everybody look what's going round.

IT WAS MANY MONTHS LATER that Pat found himself once more seated at the counter in Sullivan's (ironically, sipping a lemonade – he had consumed twenty-three and a half glasses of Macardles Ale the previous evening), looking up to see a world-weary Timmy approaching him, settling his elbows on the counter and saying: 'Ah, I don't know any more, Pat. I give up.' Pat, a little concerned, raised himself up on the high stool and, scratching an elevated eyebrow, replied: 'What's that, Timmy?' Timmy produced a newspaper from his back pocket, unrolled it and placed it flat down on the counter in front of his customer. His tone was one of utter exasperation: 'Take a look at that,' he said, 'Pat, I mean – for the love of God.'

Pat shook his head wearily as he stared at the words displayed before him in large bold type. They read: HUGE DRUG RAID – BIGGEST YET.

'Now I ask you,' said Timmy Sullivan.

'Dublin's gone mad, Timmy,' said Pat, his fingers doing a little dance along the edge of the paper. Which was the *Daily Mirror*.

'A young one standing out on the ledge in her pelt, Pat! Tweet – tweet – I'm a bird. For the love and honour of Christ!'

Pat's expression turned suddenly grim.

'What if she fell?' he offered.

Timmy frowned. His tone was reasonable now – generous. As that of an experienced, understanding parent.

'I'm not saying they can't have a bit of fun,' he went on, 'but turn a blind eye and where does it all end? '

'You have to nip it in the bud,' affirmed Pat.

Timmy agreed wholeheartedly. His bunched fist came down on the marble-topped counter, softly but with conviction.

'You do! Exactly the same as was done here!'

'That's what has to be done!' agreed Pat. 'There's no other way!'

'Sergeant Foley knew what to do. Straight in – no prisoners!'

'You have to know what you're doing!'

Pat gingerly sipped his lemonade as he spoke.

'Of course you do!' cried Timmy, quite animated now, 'and no hanging back! Cocaine, opium, Dexedrine, Benzedrine, uppers, downers – they all get the same treatment. Go in full throttle! With six-guns blazing, Pat! Otherwise you're just wasting your time.'

Pat nodded vigorously.

'You might as well not bother going in at all,' he said.

A nostalgic smile appeared then on Timmy Sullivan's face.

'Ah, but Sergeant Foley was a good one,' he said, 'and the abuse he got! They used to call him such names! He could hardly walk up the street without them shouting after him.'

'Shouting? Would they? What would they shout after him?'

'Oh, come on now, Pat,' continued Timmy, 'don't be at that old tricking about now. You know very well what they were calling him. For unless my memory is mistaken you could be a dab hand at it yourself from time to time. Would I be right there, Pat, do you think?'

Pat straightened as he felt the colour draining from his face.

'Me?' he retorted stiffly, directing his index finger chestwards. 'I'm afraid I think you have a very good imagination, maybe a bit too good sometimes, Timmy.'

Timmy lowered his head and looked at his shoes.

'Ha ha, well maybe so, Pat,' he went on, 'but unless

someone has put a few of them drugs in my tea when I didn't happen to be looking, it seems to me that I distinctly remember Sergeant Foley walking down the street and someone not a million miles from the other side of this counter shouting after him. Something which sounded very much like "pig" unless my memory is deceiving me!'

Hesitancy or forbearance played no part in the reaction of Pat McNab. He slapped his hand on the counter.

'Take that back!' he snapped.

A broad grin unwound itself between the barman's ears, as though a skipping rope of flesh.

'Ah, would you go on out of that, Pat – sure I'm only joking! Weren't you only a bit of a gossoon! What harm were you doing?'

There was a slight tinge of redness in Pat's cheeks.

'It was all a bit of clean, innocent fun!' he asserted. 'That's all it was!'

'Of course it was!' agreed Timmy, describing an arc on the marble with his teacloth. 'God bless us, Pat, would you take it easy!'

'You know me, Timmy,' insisted Pat – was there a slight quiver in his voice? – 'I'm not the sort who goes around calling people pigs. Until *they* came around, I never called anybody anything!'

'Sure don't I know that, Pat,' murmured Timmy in a conciliatory tone.

'It was *them* did it. They should have stayed away!'

Timmy nodded and pressed his lips together.

'They should have stayed in England, Pat.'

'And then no one would have gone bad or called the sergeant "pig".'

'Or anything else,' said Timmy.

'Think they can come around here acting like they're in London, acting like they own the place, hey man it's the sixties! *Drrng! Drrng!*'

Timmy was quite taken aback as Pat pretended he had an old-fashioned sixties guitar and played some electric notes on it. When the echo of the imaginary melody had abated, Timmy sighed and said: 'They could be a right lippy crowd, some of them – there's no mistaking it!'

'My mother and Sergeant Foley were good friends,' went on Pat, 'I never meant to call him that.'

Timmy tossed back his head dismissively.

'I know that only too well, Pat,' he said. 'Nobody knows it better than me.'

Pat frowned and clenched his fist on the counter as he said: 'They should have stayed where they were!'

He paused for a moment and said: 'Especially – *him!*'

Timmy sucked his teeth.

'He used to come in here and look at me. He'd stare at you up and down like you were a pile of dung you'd see dumped on that road.'

'Peace and love!' blurted Pat unexpectedly. 'Ha ha! I gave him peace and love!'

A chill wind appeared to course through the bar at that precise moment. There was a darkness in Timmy's tone now.

'What's that, Pat? ' he said.

'I said – the town's better off without him.'

Timmy lifted a glass and began to clean it thoughtfully.

'Mm. You know – I often wondered what became of him. He used to drive around with The Beatles, they say!'

'He drove around with no Beatles! He was a liar!' cried Pat.

Timmy Sullivan visibly paled as he held the polished glass.

'Japers, Pat, will you take it easy!' he said. 'There's no need to get so excited! Sure what do I care what he did!'

Pat inhaled and steadied himself against the counter with his fingers.

'Yeah – well why does everyone believe him and not believe

me!' he demanded. 'Why couldn't he mind his own business and leave people's girlfriends alone? '

Timmy paused.

'What, Pat? How's that? You had a girlfriend, did you?'

'No I did not!' Pat exclaimed. 'What – Pat McNab have a girlfriend? Yes – and pigs fly aeroplanes! No I didn't! No I didn't, Mr Timmy Sullivan! Of course not! But Scott Buglass did! Oh yes! Mr Big Scott Buglass all the way from England! 'Ello, dahlin'!'

Timmy scratched the back of his ear absent-mindedly.

'Ah, come on now, Pat,' he pleaded reasonably, 'stop it. Have a pint of something there and forget all about it like a good fellow, will you?'

Pat's reply squeezed itself through a sturdy fencing of firmly clenched teeth.

'Oh yes! Have a pint of something and forget all about it! Forget that it ever happened! Forget that Mr Big-Time Scott Buglass ever came walking down the street in his stupid hipsters and Beatle boots – get out of my way! Well, I won't, you see, Timmy! Just because you thought he was all it! And I know you did – don't deny it, Timmy!! Just like the rest of them around here – oh look, he's from England! Ha ha – well I showed him! I showed him! Why, all of a sudden Mr Smart Alec London Town didn't seem to be Top of the Pops any more!'

Timmy rubbed his eye directly above his left eyebrow. His expression seemed pained.

'Pat – would you not have that pint? I'll pull you a fresh one. That's what I'll do, pull you a fresh one right here and now. You and your lemonades!'

'A pint! What would you do that for? What would you want to go and do a thing like that for? After all, Timmy – I'm the big-time major criminal! Public Enemy No. 1 who called Sergeant Foley – *the fuzz*! Woo, like I mean – wow! How about giving me the electric chair!'

'The fuzz?' gasped Timmy, paling again. 'Sure you never called him that in your life, Pat. Pat – where are you going? Come back here out of that and have this pint, for the love of God! Who cares what happened back in the sixties! That's all over and done with, Pat!'

Timmy shook his head exasperatedly. 'Pat!' he called.

But it was too late. All Timmy heard as he settled the pint on the counter were the uncompromising, icy words: 'Goodnight, barman.' To which the only response he could think of making as he sighed wearily was: 'Ah! I just don't get it! Sometimes I feel like giving up and that's a fact!'

*

It was a Pat McNab in a supreme state of agitation who found himself rooting about in various drawers some hours later in the library, repeating hotly to himself: 'Oh yes! People come to your town! They come all the way from London and say: "Sorry! From now on this is our town! Goodbye now! Have a good time!"'

It was at that moment the photograph he had been searching for magically appeared in his hand. It depicted a group of mop-haired youths arrayed in paisley shirts and assorted necklaces, thumbs arrogantly hooked in the waistbands of velvet trousers. A single figure, the sight of which had the effect of making Pat tremble violently, attained prominence in the foreground, as if by sheer force of will. The entire town seemed to be reflected in the lenses of this person's sunglasses. Pat found himself hissing with a bitterness he would scarcely have believed possible.

'No! London isn't good enough for some people!' he bawled. 'They want you to give them your town as well! Isn't that right, Mr Buglass? Right, Mr Scott? O but of course it is – after all, you're Top of the Pops! You're the Six-Five Special! You always were! Mr C-C-C-Carnaby Street – yeah! Yeah!'

Pat's voice was very loud as he snapped the framed photograph across his knee. But there was no mistaking the sorrow-ful tremor in it as he cried: 'Why couldn't you stay in London? If you had stayed in London, everything would have been all right!'

*

The torn fragments of the photo seemed to magically piece themselves together now before him as the pain in his head beat like a hammer on an anvil. 'Ha ha!' he found himself laughing as he wiped his moist eyes with his sleeve. 'Ha ha, Mr Buglass Clicky Clicky Big Club King!' And it was as though, right there in the modest surroundings of his own kitchen, he found himself magically transported to the Psyche-delic Shack (the town youth club in reality) where the Scott Buglass Four had just taken the stage in glorious living techni-colour! 'It's absurd!' he laughed, adding, 'But then it always has been!'

What a load of rubbish Buglass the idiot was blathering along with clanging guitar! (It was a red one.) It went some-thing like:

> 'If you said to me
> That you'd rather be free
> If you had stayed all night
> And not gone outa sight
> Darlin' what it would have meant to me-ee-ee! To me! Oo – ee!'

Pat felt like throwing himself to the floor and pounding the lino with his fists, howling uncontrollably with laughter. But he couldn't, could he, no because it was the sixties, wasn't it, and he was there dressed up in his clodhopper country trousers and Scott was sporting his candy-striped Brian Jones-style jacket. 'Oo excuse me!' Pat felt like shouting. But if he had, of course, Scott wouldn't have heard him. How could he? He was much too busy nodding and filling five – five! – stupid women with lies and more lies about London and all the clubs he had played in there. Which was why Pat slunk off home.

Not that it made any difference what he did, for what might be called 'The Scott Buglass Saga' was only beginning.

*

A lot of people might say – indeed *did* – that Pat McNab had wanted to *be* Scott Buglass all along, and that this explained why he spent long hours outside the Genoa Café staring in at the English visitor who amused himself by drawing deep on a striped straw and animatedly relating a story to yet another assembly of female admirers. Some even went further to suggest that he was 'in love' with him. And at that time, if he had overheard or otherwise become aware of such assertions, it would not have bothered Pat, not in the slightest would it have bothered him, for he knew in his heart the absurdity of such a claim. He would just lie back on the bed – a gaily coloured silk scarf knotted about his head and in his hands a beautifully sculpted Fender Stratocaster completely fashioned from air. Its feedback howling as the young aspirant guitar player from Gullytown squealed: '*If you had said to me that you wanted to be free . . .*'

A stanza which rarely reached completion, the bedroom door, as a rule, bursting open and his mother – literally trembling with fury – standing before him.

'I thought I heard something!' she would snap. 'What in the name of all that's Christian do you think you're doing? And is that my scarf?'

In an instant it would be torn from his head.

'Standing in front of the mirror like you did jobbies in your trousers! Did you? I hope you didn't!'

'No, Mammy!' would be Pat's weak reply.

'For it's time that quit! You're old enough now for me not to be running after you with the likes of that! Now go on out of there and get your compositions done!'

*

But Pat, despite his best intentions, completed no compositions on such occasions. All he succeeded in doing on those beautiful summer's evenings as the golden light came spilling onto his blue-lined jotter was inscribing the name Scott Buglass close on eight hundred times into his jotter. And thinking to himself how his mother, despite being the most beautiful mother in the world, just didn't understand. Not in the way Scott Buglass's mother would have, he thought, and at once was ashamed. But could not prevent himself visualizing the scene, Scott working out a tune on the piano in the fragrant parlour, his mummy standing in the doorway whispering mischievously:

'Scotty! I hope you haven't done jobbies in your trousers!' as they both chuckled and chortled more like two old friends than son and mother. A black cloud of melancholy settled on Pat that night after he thought that thought.

*

As it did the afternoon he stood, on the far side of McConkey's hedge, staring at a pair of hipsters suspended from the line. Hipsters that belonged to Scott Buglass. Knowing in his heart that Scott's, even if he had done jobbies – such a consideration being in fact laughable, as he well knew – would inevitably have been so much better than his, jobbies which slid snootily down cool snug hipsters as opposed to tumbling haplessly down baggy frieze britches born for bockedy country legs.

For the truth is that even from his earliest years Pat had always *thought* too much – in a hopeless endeavour, perhaps, to create some alternative realities: luxuriating in them to such an extent that he could not see that they might eventually prove harmful, if not effectively engineer his undoing. Which was why he made not the slightest reply of surprise when the 'chick' – who did not exist, of course! – appraised her autograph book and, to her delight, found his name inscribed in copperplate within.

'Oh, Pat!' she cried. 'This is fantastic! When are you and the band playing again? I can't wait!'

Pat raised his shades and smiled.

'I think we're playing tomorrow night, actually!'

'Eek! Fabbo! I can't wait!' squealed his 'biggest fan', which she assured him now she was.

The sad truth being that Pat was not playing tomorrow night or any other night, come to that, and would, in fact, be found, dragging out a zinc bucket from underneath the stairs to wash down the dirty old stairs for his mother. Whose bulky shadow was never far away as she tapped him on the shoulder and 'reassuringly' remarked: 'There's a good fella. Do you think you could give the windows a rub when you're finished?'

*

Throughout those long evenings, when his mother would go 'Ho!' and he would go 'Hum!' it seemed to Pat that all the colour that had ever existed had literally been drained away and all that now remained was a world the colour of stone.

'Do you think it's going to rain?' his mother would say, as he replied: 'I don't know, Mammy.'

'I think it is,' she would say, another page of her book, as though with great effort, being turned, 'I think it is.'

If Pat McNab looked put-upon and weary, at times indeed about to cry, it was because he knew that within minutes of his home existed a world of flashing lights and neon tubes where guitars would squeal and fingers click till dawn. Deep in his heart, of course, he knew that where he truly belonged was in that sucked universe of miserable grey, a place of perennial rain and sighs. The carnival-swirl of possibility was not intended for the likes of him. He knew that. Why, of course he did! Hadn't his mother told him often enough?

'Look at you!' she'd said. 'Wanting this! Wanting that! You'll take what you get! And be glad to have it!'

But Pat wasn't glad to have it. He wanted to open those

curtains and admit strobe lights so strong that there was a danger they might blind you right there and then on the spot! And the more he denied it to himself the more he craved it until it became as a drug he longed to have coursing wildly through his veins.

*

It was on a Saturday afternoon in the middle of that long hot summer (throughout which the temperature had rarely dropped beneath eighty-five degrees) that Pat found himself sitting in the Genoa Café when Scott and some of his friends entered. They considered Pat for a while (he was attired in his customary black suit-coat and his grey frieze trousers) before Scott, staring at his nails (they were beautifully manicured), locked his thumb in his hipster pocket and then, smiling, said:

'So – what type of music do you like, Pat?'

Pat's cheeks flushed a deep red.

'I like pop,' he stammered, 'and rock and roll.'

Scott smiled with a hint of tolerance.

'I know, Pat,' he went on, 'we all like pop and rock and roll. But, like, man – who? Who do you dig, you know?'

Pat gulped.

'Dig?' he replied, the flesh of his cheeks feeling extremely burnt and soft.

Scott's hands were outspread. His companions chortled a little.

'Yeah!' he said. 'Like who in your head is the mostest?'

Pat perceived his eyebrows elevating.

'Mostest?' he said.

'Yeah! Like, hit me!' went on Scott, clicking his fingers.

There was a long pause and then Pat replied:

'I like the ones on the jukebox.'

Scott covered his mouth with his candy-striped sleeve. There was an eager light in his eyes as he leaned forward.

'The what? What did you say?'

Pat swallowed.

'I really don't know their names. The jukebox ones!'

Scott tossed back his head and clicked the fingers of both hands loudly.

'Hey, guys,' he cried, putting his arms around the shoulders of his companions, 'can you dig what's happening? He doesn't know, like! Hey! What about the Walker Brothers! Manfred Mann! The Beatles, man! Surely you've heard of the Beatles! *Help me if you can I'm feeling down!* Oo-ee! Yeah! You've heard of them, Pat – haven't you? John, Paul, George, and Ringo?'

There are no words to describe the depth of Pat's humiliation as he crossed his thumbs in the comforting dark beneath the vinegar-stained formica.

'Yes. Yes I have,' he croaked.

'Sure you have!' cried Scott Buglass, slapping him on the back. 'We drive around with them in London. John Lennon – why he's our best mate, actually. Right, guys?'

It was clear – even to Pat, in his confused state – that this came as something of a surprise to Scott's colleagues but nonetheless they succeeding in rising to the occasion with enthusiastic cries of:

'Yeah!' and 'Right on!' and 'Wot a geezer!'

'Tell you what, Pat,' continued Scott, 'you stick with us. You stick with us and we'll set you straight, if you know what I'm saying. You want it, we got it, all you got to do is ask. You like the Stones, Pat? Here . . .'

Despite himself, and the deep-rooted instincts within him, Pat became aware of a huge feeling of warmth consuming him as Scott pinned an *I Love The Stones* badge on his lapel. Mick Jagger was wearing black and white striped trousers on it.

They left Pat in a daze, fingering his badge, waving to him

as they wiggled their hips and strode off down the main street of Gullytown.

*

The following day, Pat was doing some shopping for his mother when to his surprise he heard Scott's voice calling to him from across the street. He was sitting on the wall with his friends. 'Hey Pat, man! Choogle on over, yeah?' he cried. It was perhaps the proudest day of Pat's life as he sat there with them on the wall, now sporting Scott's own shades. Scott who clapped him on the back and said: 'Hey, fabbo! Sing it for us again!' as Pat gathered all the air in his lungs and began: '*Oh Lord, please don't let me be misunderstood!*', the Animals song which Scott had just taught him.

The following day he found himself with them, having donned a Monkees-style beanie which Scott purchased specially for him. 'What do you think of this?' the dark-sunglassed popster called to some passing girls. 'The most, you reckon?' The girls giggled into their hands and replied: 'Wow! Just about the mostest of the most, Scottie!' before literally exploding, unable any longer to restrain their laughter.

*

It is no exaggeration to say that those midge-ridden summer days were among the happiest of Pat's life. And the Psychedelic Shack nights when he would 'bop' in the middle of the floor, sporting his ever-present 'beanie', windmilling his arms to the twanging music and the thumbs-up approval of Scott and associates, who whispered: 'Wow! Like a stoned scarecrow!' To Pat's face, declaring proudly: 'Hey! Be bop a lula! It's the Pat McNab Show!' and joining him in an untamed 'Woolly Bully' dance that had them all landing in a heap beside the loudspeakers as Pat, to his dismay, found himself overhearing the words: 'Let's hear it for Pat McNab! Hepcat King of

Bumpkin City!' It was the first arrow of pain to find its way into Pat's heart that summer and, as he made his way home that night (it had begun to rain) he felt as if he had been fitted out with lead-reinforced boots. It was the first indication (although, truth be told, he had harboured secret fears) that his desire to *be* Scott Buglass had indeed been seriously misplaced. He was soon to find out that this was indeed the truth, and that all the dreams which had sustained him throughout that time were now about to dribble away like once beautifully painted watercolours carelessly abandoned in the monsoon rains.

*

But what dreams they had been! What dreams they had been, as Roman candles which had burnt so bright and brief! Pat grinned in the dark of his bedroom as he visualized himself in a bead-hung bedsit, all about him Toulouse Lautrec art prints, *Easy Rider* motorbikes and a bronzed tennis player abstractedly scratching her left buttock, his distorted reflection shining (all twisty) from the lens of Scott's shades as the muso looked at him and smiled. 'Pat,' he said benignly, 'you know this vibe?'

Sleepily, Pat heard himself reply: 'What – huh?'

He took the long tapered cigarette between his fingers and inhaled a soothing drag as Scott began to tentatively pluck some Eastern melodies from the sitar. '*I am talking about the space between us all, between you and me and he and she,*' he sang waveringly.

'Scott?' Pat said, a cloud of purplish smoke gathering turbanlike above his head.

'Huh?' Scott replied without raising his head.

'You're quare and good on the guitar!' Pat said.

At this the entire bedsit seemed ringed around with laughter. There was a soapstone Buddha squatting on the table.

'Oh, Pat! Oh, man!' wept Scott, rubbing his eyes. 'You

really are something else! You're two thousand light-years from home!'

'Oh wow!' laughed Pat, clicking his fingers (he had become quite adept at it now) and sucking long and hard on the thin, drooping cigarette, the consequence of which was that the entire room now seemed bendy as a pipe-cleaner house of straws pushed rudely to one side.

'Hey, Pat?' said Scott unexpectedly as he let down his instrument. 'How about you do a number for us?'

'Huh?' replied Pat, some ash falling onto the grey trousers which protruded from beneath his kaftan.

'Yeah, sure!' cried Scott, clicking expertly. 'Come on, man!'

To raucous approbation, Pat found himself in the centre of the floor clutching the sitar. Initially, he hesitated but the coaxing eyes presented him with all the encouragement he needed as out into the night now he watched his voice sailing like some exultant bird of hope.

'*Yeah! Say that you'll be true!*' he sang, all the while twanging (inexpertly, perhaps) the sitar, mostly with his thumb, continuing, '*You said to me! That you'd rather be free! And that then you could love me! Oo – ee! Ee – oo – ee! Really love me – ee! Oo – ee – oo – ee – ee!*'

The whoops of delight and approval that followed his performance were unanimous and unrestrained. As then – coalescing as though to form a living, breathing entity of sound – glided the one they called 'Astra', a tall angel of unfathomable beauty attired in a maxi-length print skirt, clutched in her hand and extended towards Pat, a tall, startlingly colourful sunflower.

'I want you to have this, Pat,' she said softly.

Her voice seemed redolent of crushed petals. Pat found his mouth going dry as he lowered his head.

'No. I couldn't,' he responded shyly.

'No, Pat,' insisted Astra, 'it's for you.'

He felt Scott laying a tender hand on his shoulder.

'Take it, Pat,' he heard him say. 'It's a gift.'

Pat was so overwhelmed that he almost felt part of his head swooping away, never to return.

'Thank you very much,' he said.

The sunflower stood in his hand, noble and perpendicular.

'It's because you're one of us now,' said Scott. 'We're going to travel the world together.'

Pat gulped.

'Travel the world together?' he gasped.

Astra nodded.

'That's right,' she murmured softly.

In that instant, Pat found himself giddily overcome as he saw the kaleidoscopically patterned Volkswagen bus (the curly words: *We are the we* painted on its side in intense blues and reds and purples) zooming off down some endless interstate. 'That's San Francisco up ahead!' he heard Scott say as Pat clicked and sang: '*If you're going to San Francisco! Be sure to wear some flowers in your hair! La la! Ha ha ha!*'

'Cool, Pat!' Scott said. 'You keep hitting that beat!'

'I love you, Pat,' said Astra, to which Pat ecstatically responded: 'Whee – hoo!' as the bus pulled into a canyon where it was their intention to spend the night. Sitting around a campfire as Scott strummed the sitar, Astra looking into Pat's eyes as she softly whispered the words, 'Tomorrow we oughta make it to Sausalito,' fingers of campfire light playing rhythmically on her face. To which Pat – coming back to earth as the uninspiring surroundings and the old dark house once more asserted themselves – longed to reply: 'Of course we should! Why not, youse lying pack of bastards!' But never actually did, for to do so would have irrevocably destroyed his dreams.

*

Not that he need have worried about that – ha ha, as he said himself – for very shortly that was about to happen anyway, without the slightest assistance whatever from Pat McNab or anyone else! As events in the Genoa Café a mere two days later indicated with Scott Buglass puffing a cigarette (an innocent Gold Flake) and wryly suggesting as he inspected his fingernails:

'Tell you what! Let's have one of the chicks make a play for him and see what happens! What about you, Nikki?' (Nikki was attired in a cheesecloth maxi, two long pigtails extending to her waist.)

'No! It isn't fair!' interjected Carole, turning a chip. 'It isn't – really, Scott.'

'Oh, come on,' chortled Scott. 'It's just a bit of a laugh! We'll do it after the gig tomorrow night! What do you say, Nikki? '

Nikki flung her arms in the air and gave Carole – who shrugged – an encouraging push.

'Oh what the hell, Scott!' yelped Nikki. 'It's the sixties, I guess!'

*

Yeah, it was the sixties all right, Pat was often to reflect many years later. The dirty rotten miserable sixties that turned out to be the most hateful time of his life. The effing cunting hooring bastarding sixties when all the things that you ever wanted to do should have been possible but walked away from you as though each of them was but a private in some vomit-inducing army of nothingness. Not that he blamed Nikki, for he knew that in her heart she had been forced into it. Deep down he knew that and had forgiven her for it, suspecting from time to time that they might well have compelled her to proceed with the dastardly plan while under the influence of drugs.

*

It was quite an ordinary night in the Psychedelic Shack with 'Everybody Loves a Clown' by Gary Lewis and the Playboys jauntily playing and Nikki looking into Pat's eyes as she slowly circled her arms about his neck. Her eyes seemed to melt like small marbles of ice. 'I love you, Pat,' she said, in the most beautifully husky voice Pat had ever heard. 'Let's go to San Fran and get married. What do you say?'

'I wish I could, Nikki,' Pat replied, trembling ever so slightly, 'I only wish that I could.'

'Oh, Pat,' whispered Nikki, stroking his neck with one of her nails, 'you're such a sexy man, do you know that? '

It is to Pat's eternal credit that never once after he overheard Scott and his highly amused colleagues discussing the hilarious 'setup' as they called it (they had been surreptitiously ensconced behind some chairs close by the gents' toilets) did he blame Nikki. Never once occurring to him to do so. Indeed, the truth being that, deep in his heart, he knew who he blamed. Particularly when that very day he encountered him outside the Step-Down Inn, Scott clicking perkily as he winked: 'Wo! Pat! Nikki got the hots for you then, has she? Nice!'

*

The effect on him was catastrophic, however – Pat, that is, for in the days that followed sleep became a thing of the past and it might be an accurate enough description to say that he resembled at this time an extremely tightly wound spring or crackling, perambulating time bomb. A state which only his mother was capable of understanding, especially now that she had become aware (Pat having sobbed his heart out to her one particularly bleak evening) of the events which had led up to it. 'Yes!' she repeated, as Pat paced – almost ran around, in fact! – the floor of the kitchen. 'He thinks I want to wear his glasses! I never wanted to wear his stupid old glasses! I didn't, did I, Mammy? I only pretended to! I'd see them sitting on the wall and I'd think – I want to *be* him! But it was only pretending! It was only pretending, Mammy!'

His mother shook her head and poked something out of the inside of her furry grey slipper.

'God, but weren't you the right eejit all the same,' she said. 'You're an even bigger eejit than I took you for.' Her voice fizzed with disdain.

'Me thinking I could go off around the world in a coloured bus! And me only auld Pat McNab! Imagine Pat McNab doing that, Mammy! Doesn't it just show you!'

His mother nodded and her lips went quite thin.

'It does,' she replied, 'it shows you the kind of gobalooka I reared! Letting himself be led up the garden path by every drug addict and Antichrist that comes about the place.'

'Oh now, Ma! And them laughing at me the whole time!'

'Oh, they'd laugh. They'd laugh at you all right!'

'Aye – laughing at me all along! Saying: "This McNab – what an eejit!" God, when I think of what I let them away with I can hardly believe how big an eejit I am myself!'

'You're an eejit, are you? You're no eejit. No son of Maimie McNab should ever call or let himself be called the like of that!'

'What, Ma?' Pat choked.

His mother stopped by the radio. Her voice was hoarse now, and tense.

'I said – you're no eejit. We'll soon see who's the eejit.'

Pat's eyes lit up and his voice seemed to leapfrog into life.

'That's right, Ma!' he cried. 'It's him's the eejit! Buglass! Thinking he could cod me with Nikki! Sure I knew well what she was up to!'

Mrs McNab's face was suffused with a troubling greyness.

'It's him's the eejit! For only an eejit would risk making a cod of the McNabs!'

Pat nodded vigorously and laced his fingers tightly.

'That's right, Ma!' he cried. 'Only an eejit would do it. An eejit from England into the bargain!'

'Yes,' replied his mother, 'an eejit who'll have the best going-away party ever! Isn't that right, Pat?'

Pat had never before smiled so broadly.

'That's right, Ma!' he retorted excitedly. 'He's going away on Monday!'

His mother's expression was impassive. She looked at the clothes pegs in her pocket and replied in a monotone: 'Yes, Pat. I knew that.'

Outside a car drove past on the road and someone whistled far away off in the town. Ironically, and with eerie precision, the melody from the TV series *The Invaders*.

*

'Why Pat, that's fantastic!' ejaculated Scott when Pat told him the news. 'Thanks a lot, mate! You're a real pal!'

'I want it to be the best party you ever had, Scott! Because I know you've been to lots of parties!'

The expressions on all their faces had to be seen to be believed. 'It's going to be the fabbo party of all time!' they cried in unison. 'It really is!'

'Four more coffees, man!' exclaimed Scott as he flicked his ash into the tray. 'We've just had some fantastic news!'

*

It was not common in the town to see decorations such as SCOTT'S GOING-AWAY PARTY, which the banner draped over the entrance to the McNab house proclaimed in vivid red, or lightbulbs strung along the privet hedge at the end of the lane so that they gave the impression of being even more spectacular than perhaps they actually were. Neither was it particularly common for Pat to greet visitors attired in a flower-specked headband (his mother's scarf in reality) with eyeballs so wide they would have suggested *he* was under the influence, greeting, as he did, visitors with the words: 'Mammy wants to know if youse have any drugs on youse? Ha ha!'

346

Ordinarily, this might have been taken as a rather odd statement but such was the level of abandon and frivolity that very little attention at all was paid to it.

Although it might have been a lot better if it had, considering that a mere one hour and a half later, Scott Buglass was lying in a rumpled heap beneath the Sacred Heart picture in the library, with his shades more than a little askew as Pat's mother shook her head vehemently, uncorking another bottle of wine as she cried:

'No, Scott! Have another drop now out of that! Sure you'll never find till you're back in England and neither Pat nor me will ever see you again!'

Scott's grin was lopsided and there was ash all over his candy-striped blazer.

'Somehow, Mrs McNab, I think if I keep this up I'm not going to make it.'

'I know what you mean, love,' said Mrs McNab, rather oddly, as she splashed some more Double Diamond into the muso's glass.

'Mind your hipsters now!' she continued as the liquid wobbled precariously over the brim, continuing: 'Now who's for another little drinkie!' as she made her way towards a bleary-eyed groupie in the corner who gave all the impression of being a bell-sleeved, gamine-haired octopus.

*

It was approaching 3 a.m. when a rather unsteady Nikki sought for her hessian bag behind some bottles, stumbled a little and put her hand to her forehead as she edgily enquired: 'Have any of you seen Scott?'

'No,' hiccuped Carole, sucking hopelessly on a long-since spent roll-up cigarette, 'I guess he must have gone home. He has an early start in the morning.'

'Goodbye,' waved Mrs McNab as they departed into the night, their shoulder bags swinging as they negotiated the squelching mud which the heavy rain had now begun to soften and churn up, 'goodbye – ee!'

They waved and were gone, as into the heaving maw of a sodden, velvet-black beast.

*

Pat was often to reflect, years later, on how it had been the best party ever. The best in his wildest dreams, especially when it had been held – thrown! – by clodhopping idiots who were more than faintly redolent of cowdung smells and ragwort! Namely Pat and his mother, of course! Oh yes!

*

What amused Pat more than anything, however, when sitting by the fire staring into the wavy flames and looking back upon that night, was how nobody had ever bothered – perhaps did not see the need to, considering Scott was due to return to England the following morning – to enquire after him or his welfare – not so much as a single, inquisitive knock upon the door or even a meek: 'I wonder – have you seen Scott Buglass at all?' in the days following the party.

It was as though poor old Bugie had disappeared in a single puff of incense!

*

Pat shook his head and raked the fire. Outside there was a bit of a wind blowing. It had all been so simple, he thought. Scott rooting around in a drawer – their *private* drawer! – and Pat's Mammy just standing there, for *ages*! – looking at him before he even noticed.

'You're a very cheeky fellow,' she said to him. 'You know you really shouldn't talk to people like that.'

'Like what?' Scott said, continuing – unbelievably! – to fumble around in the drawer!

'Like the way you talk to my Pat.'

'Oh yeah – that!' he replied – at least admitting it. 'Yeah, but it was just a joke!'

Mrs McNab did not betray any hint of emotion in her voice as she, quite reasonably, said:

'Yes, but of course what's a joke to one person might not be a joke to someone else.'

Scott – having found the matches he was searching for – lit the cigarette awkwardly and said:

'Oh yeah – but come on, Mumsy . . .'

He was about to cheekily extend this response (he was becoming impatient now and his artificial attempts at 'manners' were at an end) when he heard Mrs McNab say: 'For example – would you call this a joke?'

The single glimpse of the maraca permitted to Scott Buglass was that of a flickering red blur as Mrs McNab produced it from behind her back and deftly brought same into contact with his forehead. Neither did he entirely, clearly hear her next words which were: 'Or this?' as its twin surfaced in her left hand, his forehead receiving an equally fierce 'twin' blow which effectively terminated his conscious state. There can be no describing the state of – perhaps inexcusable! – utter glee in which Pat and his mother (Pat had slipped in unnoticed and gently closed the door behind him) reduced the tormented musician to a helpless mass of unrecognizable pulp in what might be described as an orgy of bloody, frenzied, alternative 'bebop' improvisation.

*

There were the occasional references to Scott Buglass throughout the district afterwards, along the lines of (advanced by perplexed members of Scott's 'crew'): 'We've never heard from him since' or 'Now that he's in England, he's forgotten all about us!' But in the end these too began to wilt as flowers might at the onset of winter or those once eagerly inserted into the barrels of military firearms; and when the rumours of

349

'drugs' – initially advanced in the grocer's by Mrs McNab – began, all talk of Scott Buglass and the so-called 'Fabulous Groovers of the 1960s' began to disappear, eventually, like the sad protagonist, fading without leaving so much as a single trace.

*

Sometimes, for years afterwards, late at night in the library, Pat would place his only remaining talisman of that time (a record by Alan Price, 'I Put A Spell On You', which Nikki had given him – 'I want you to have this') and sit with his chin in his hand wistfully reflecting upon those days. And as the flames in the fire danced once more, he would fancy he heard the voice of a poor deluded musician, a sunglassed sex-bomb in a candy-striped blazer, crying out from where he was trying to reach him. And, you know, sometimes, the strangest thing of all is, it would be as though he were saying: 'Pat! Pat, I'm sorry for what happened – and, if we ever meet again, this time I know that we'll be the best of friends. The way it should have been all along!' small coals shifting as outside the huge night turned towards sleep, the thin sound of a plangent guitar seeming to issue from a jasmine-scented bedsit a thousand continents away.

Twenty-One Years

Twenty-One Years

The judge said, stand up lad and dry up your tears
You're sentenced to Dartmoor for twenty-one years,
So dry up your tears, love, and kiss me goodbye
The best friends must part, love, and so must you and I.

I hear the train coming, 'twill be here at nine
To take me to Dartmoor to serve up my time.
I look down the railway and plainly I see
You standing there waving your goodbyes to me.

Six months have gone by, love, I wish I was dead
This dark dreary dungeon has gone to my head
It's hailing, it's raining, the moon gives no light.
Now won't you tell me, love, why you never write?

I've waited, I've trusted, I've longed for the day
A lifetime so lonely, now my hair's turning grey.
My thoughts are for you, love, till I'm out of mind
For twenty-one years is a mighty long time.

IT IS A FINE FRESH DAY in the garden and there can be no doubt but that Pat McNab is feeling happy and contented with himself as he digs away at his drills beneath the hot burning sun, thinking to himself: 'As soon as I have this done, I'll move on up above there to my turnips and who knows, perhaps the lettuces too if I have time.' Whistling away (a familiar tune, and one which was a favourite of his Mammy's: Cliff Richard's top ten hit 'Bachelor Boy'), he turns over a clod with the edge of his spade, fancying he sees something glittering in it and is bending down to examine it more closely when he receives a large resounding slap to the middle of his back and turns to see what can only be described as the 'colossal' figure of Sergeant Foley towering above him with a broad smile, exclaiming: 'Pat!'

'Jesus, Mary and Joseph, Sergeant, you put the heart crossways in me!' was Pat's reply as he struggled to his feet.

The sergeant doffed his cap and stared morosely into the small amphitheatre of its darkness.

'Pat,' he sighed, placing both hands on his hips, 'you'll never guess what's after happening.'

Pat knitted his brow and touched his chin with the fingers of his right hand.

'What, Sergeant?' he ventured querulously. 'Someone shot? The bank! The bank's been robbed! That's it, isn't it, Sergeant? Oh my God! How much? Everything in the safe taken!'

The sergeant shook his head and drummed a little tune on the circumference of the cap as he continued:

'No, Pat! I only wish to God it had! I could be doing with something like that on my CV, to be honest with you! No, I'll tell you what it is, Pat – the station's been burnt down!'

Pat gulped as he felt the colour drain from his face.

'Ah no, Sergeant!' he chokingly replied. 'Not the lovely station where you've spent God knows how many years toiling away in the service of the community!'

'Burnt to a crisp, Pat,' the sergeant confirmed wearily, 'the Ganger told me this very minute. She'll have to be built from the ground up.'

'Jesus, Mary and Joseph, Sergeant!' gasped Pat.

The sergeant's face grew tense.

'You can say that again, Pat. I'd say you're looking at the guts of half a million.'

Pat could not believe his ears.

'Half a million!' he croaked.

'At the very least,' nodded the sergeant, continuing: 'Well – I wouldn't like to be in Guard Timmoney's shoes, that's all I can say.'

Pat was puzzled.

'Guard Timmoney?' he asked.

The sergeant drew a long, deep breath.

'Him and his deep-fat fryers,' he said. 'Well – you know what this means, don't you, Pat? '

'Yes, Sergeant,' agreed Pat, before diffidently adding: 'What, Sergeant?'

'I'll have to stop with you for a while. That's the best way out of it. I can do my investigating from here.'

Pat felt the skin above his eyes tightening.

'Investigating,' he wondered, 'what investigating?'

Without warning, the sergeant drew himself up to his full height and became stiff as a plank, delivering himself of the following sentence in a tone that was unmistakably frosty, officious and uncompromising.

'I would appreciate it if you would account for your

movements between the hours of three a.m. and seven a.m. on Thursday the 17th of September last.'

He paused and went on:

'Well?'

Waspishly, Pat replied:

'I was *here*!'

There was no mistaking the officer of the law's wide grin: 'Sure don't I know you were, Pat, you auld cod you! I'm only pretending to be investigating! Slagging you, like!'

Pat felt such a fool, his downcast eyes as small reconnaissance spaceships endeavouring to decode the complexity of his situation as he raised his head and, crimson-cheeked, replied: 'Of course, Sergeant! Oh, aye! Of course! Sergeant – do you hear the old carry-on I'm going on with!'

The sergeant sank his right hand deep in his pocket and said: 'Indeed and I do surely, Pat! Sure don't I know you from when you were a nipper! And your father!'

'That's right, Sergeant!' replied Pat, a warm feeling beginning to assert itself in the region of his abdomen.

'And your mother!' continued Sergeant Foley.

'Yes!' affirmed Pat, touching some crumbly clay with the toe of his wellington.

'And all belonging to you!'

'All belonging to me!' grinned Pat. 'Like they say in the films – *yes sir*!'

'*Yes sir*!' beamed the sergeant.

'*Yes sir*!' grinned Pat, perspiring a little uncomfortably.

The sergeant shook his head.

'Oh now,' he went on, 'don't be talking! Pat, do you know what I was just thinking? You must be tired from all that digging you're doing there. Are you not exhausted?'

Pat was a little taken aback by the sergeant's sudden concern and hastened to reassure him.

'Exhausted?' he replied. 'No, Sergeant! Sure, what would have me exhausted?'

'Digging, Pat!' came the sergeant's brusque reply. 'Digging a hole for the body!'

A sickening taste came into Pat's mouth.

'For the body?' he replied weakly.

'Aye!' the sergeant replied. 'The latest one, I mean!'

The corners of Pat's mouth jerked like the flick of whip.

'Oh, aye!' he laughed. 'The latest one!'

The sergeant nodded.

'Sure that would have anyone exhausted! Not to mention the poor fellow that has to go and prove it!'

A muscle leaped in Pat's right cheek – just under his eye.

'Oh, aye!' he said. 'Sure it'd be nearly as hard on him in the long run! Having to gather up all the evidence and everything!'

'And then go and convince the bloody judge! And you know what they're like! Think it was us was on trial or something! I say, you know what they're like, my old friend!'

Pat threw back his head.

'What they're like?' he guffawed. 'Oh, now, Sergeant, don't be talking!'

Pat frowned and grasped the shaft of the spade tightly. His fingers left sweat marks, he noted.

'Don't be talking to me now!' he chortled, although less laconically than he might have preferred.

'I will not!' declared the sergeant abruptly. 'I'll say nothing more to you now only maybe yourself and myself go right up there to the old McNab Hotel and have ourselves a great big hot mug of tay this very second! What do you say, Pat?'

A huge sense of relief seemed to sweep over Pat McNab as he released his grip on the spade and smiled, saying:

'You know what I'd say to that, Sergeant? I'd say there's nothing now on God's earth would taste as sweet!'

The sergeant placed a large, oar-shaped hand on his shoulder.

'Come on out of that so,' he said, 'you great big digging man you, Pat McNab!'

*

It is the following morning and Pat and his new-found lodger (the sergeant having made it clear in no uncertain terms that it was his intention to remain) are reclining in the sun-filled kitchen eating a hearty breakfast which has been prepared by the proprietor of the house. They both seem in exceptionally high spirits.

'I saw you last night, Sergeant!' says Pat then, expertly spearing a sausage, 'and it was great! It was like the FBI or something!'

'Saw me, did you then?' is the sergeant's response. 'And how would that be now?'

'I saw you when I was going by your room. Your room was full of pipe smoke and you were bashing out a report on the typewriter! Clack clack! The noise of it!'

The sergeant nodded as a thin river of yolk was released from the unsteady Table Mountain of egg. He smiled as he masticated.

'Up half the night I was with it too, Pat. But it's all over now, thank God. And before too long, with the help of God, that'll be another fellow whistling his twenty-one years.'

The circle of black pudding paused before it attained Pat's lips.

'Whistling twenty-one years?' asked Pat, perplexed.

The sergeant placed his fork on his plate and, extricating a small portion of food from the canyon of his back tooth, explained:

'Aye, Pat! That's what I used to say to the Missus, God rest her! Every time I put another gangster behind bars, Mary, I'd say: "Mary, there's another go-boy'll soon be whistling his twenty-one years!" Did you never hear it, Pat? The song, I mean!'

'I think Mammy used to know it!' Pat said, enjoying some tomato.

'Indeed and she did surely! And she'd be the woman to sing it for us – if she was here now, Pat! Which she isn't, of course! Mysteriously!'

The sergeant's head was a red ball placed upon his shoulders facing Pat across the table. It disquieted him.

'Ha ha!' he laughed uneasily as the sergeant, good-humouredly, proceeded.

'Oh, indeed she'd be the woman to give us a verse of it, all right! For there was no better woman about this town for a bar of a song – would I be right there, Pat?'

Pat felt his cheeks reddening a little.

'Oh now, Sergeant!' he responded.

'Oh now nothing, Pat! If she was here now she'd shift that table yonder and away she'd go on twinkletoes, round the house and mind the dresser! Wouldn't she, Pat?'

'Yes! I think she would, Sergeant!' Pat found himself replying, a spot of grease bisecting itself and dribbling down his chin.

'*Think* she would?' the sergeant said. 'No thinking about it, Pat! "Come here to me, Pat," is what she'd say. "Before we go off to work, what better way to start the day than a few bars of a song!" Isn't that what she'd say, Pat? Look at me now and tell me that it isn't!'

'It is, Sergeant!' said Pat, quietly.

The sergeant's fork clanged on his plate.

'It is indeed!' he cried. '"Give me your hand!" she'd say. "Give me that paw, me jewel and darlin', and away the pair of us will go!" Oh boys ah-dear, would she not say that or what!'

'Sergeant! Stop!' Pat suddenly heard himself cry as the officer's large fingers curled about his arm and he found himself manoeuvred if not propelled in a semicircular motion across the linoleum-covered floor of the kitchen as the lawman, in full flight, cleared his throat and, fixing Pat with what might be accurately described as a piercing, menacing gaze, began to sing:

'*The judge said, Stand up dear and dry up your tears*
You're sentenced to Dartmoor for twenty-one years.
So dry up your tears, love, and kiss me goodbye
The best friends must part, love, so must you and I.'

Pat endeavoured to unlock his fingers from the officer's vicelike grip.

'Sergeant! Sergeant! I don't like dancing!' he pleaded. 'I'm tired!'

The sergeant squeezed his fingers and pooh-poohed such an idea.

'Ah, Pat, would you go away out of that now!' he laughed, and clearing his throat once more he began:

'*I hear the train coming it'll be here at nine*
To take me to Dartmoor to serve up my time.
I look down the railway and plainly I see
They're standing there waving their goodbyes to me.'

Pat grimaced and cried:

'Sergeant! Please! You're hurting my hand!'

'Oh, am I?' the sergeant replied. 'Right you be, Pat! It's time I was at work anyway! In the prefab! Ha ha!'

'Of course! I'll get you your topcoat, Sergeant!' replied Pat, eagerly, hurtling toward the hallway.

*

The officer thanked Pat for the proffered mantle.

'Sergeant,' Pat said, 'what exactly did he do, this Mc-Clarkey fellow you mentioned earlier?'

'Something he won't be doing for another twenty-one years,' replied the sergeant as he slipped into the heavy blue garment, continuing:

'I can tell you that, Pat. Smashed his mother over the head with a spade and buried her in the front garden! The front bucking garden!'

Pat gave a little shiver.

'The front garden?' he gasped incredulously.

The sergeant nodded.

'Aye. Her and God knows how many others. And maybe a donkey.'

'A donkey?' gulped Pat.

The sergeant examined his nails.

'That bit I'm not sure about yet. But one thing I am sure about – he's going down. Did you ever hear them say that on the telly, Pat? *Going down!*'

'I think I might have,' Pat replied, his mind a little preoccupied.

'"Going down for twenty-one years!" they say. And so he would – if it was true! But sure poor old McClarkey never hurt a fly in his life! All he ever did was rob the poorbox, the big fool!'

'The poorbox?'

Pat scratched his leg with his index finger.

'Aye!' the sergeant nodded. 'Didn't he rob the poorbox out of Father McGivney's Volkswagen! The dirty lug! Well, Pat – I'd best be off! Duty calls!'

In the doorway, a wan Pat stared after him, perplexed, already perceiving himself to be not a little troubled.

*

Which was why some half an hour later he found himself in the privacy of his new lodger's bedroom, pinpricks of sweat breaking out on his palms as the corners of his mouth jerked perpendicularly and he repeated to himself, all the while investigating scraps of typescript discarded by the machine: 'You see what happened is that once we had a sergeant you see, and a very good sergeant he was, except he wasn't happy

360

being a sergeant, was he? No – he wanted to be something else. He wanted to be a big-time investigator, coming around planting things in people's heads to make them say things they didn't want to say and to look at them in funny ways so they'd get all nervous and drop things and make fools of themselves!'

With that, the heavy, cut-glass ashtray fell to the floor, disgorging its contents and breaking into two neat halves. As he abstractedly gathered up the scattered ash with the aid of a cigarette packet, Pat repeated to himself: 'But most of all – telling lies. Most of all, coming round to a person's house and telling *lies*, Sergeant!'

*

A light rain had begun to fall as Pat positioned himself behind some whinbushes, at a distance from the squat concrete bunker that was the police station – perplexingly, totally intact. The words of the sergeant echoing anew in Pat's ears. 'Burnt to a cinder, I'm afraid. An absolute cinder.' A clamminess like a second skin wrapped itself tautly about Pat, as a few pearly drops of rain landed musically on a tin in front of him. It was a tin – or once had been – of Bachelor's processed peas.

*

Quite how many whiskies Pat had consumed some hours later as he reclined in the library armchair beneath the sergeant's cap which was placed precariously upon his head it is difficult to calculate. In any case, for him it was irrelevant, the passage of time being of no importance whatever in the world of the imagination which he now decided to permit himself to inhabit as he chuckled into his hands: 'Yeah! That's right! I got McClarkey twenty-one years for robbing the poorbox! Sure I did! Because I'm all the big fellow! Oh yes, Sergeant! Sure I am!'

But Pat never completed the sentence, for just then there came a crunching of boots on the gravel outside as he feverishly endeavoured to return the officer's cap to its rightful place – squashed in behind the lavatory cistern, invisible to the naked eye. Unlike the pimples of perspiration on Pat's forehead which were very visible as he arrived back in time to greet the sergeant who announced that he would 'do jail' for a 'smidgeen of toast'.

'Coming right up,' Pat had replied, generously.

*

It was some hours later that the sergeant declared that it was his intention to 'retire to Sullivan's' for a bit, spending some moments searching fruitlessly about the kitchen and library. Before, at something of a loss announcing to Pat, who was now busy with the following day's dinner (peeling potatoes): 'Pat, do you know what it is, I can't seem to find my cap – my good Sunday police cap, that is.'

'Your good Sunday cap?' replied Pat.

'Aye,' the sergeant nodded, 'my good Sunday cap that I wear on special occasions. Like when the superintendent comes, for example.'

Pat shook his head and scratched his chin.

'God, that's funny,' he replied. 'But wait – let me have a look!'

Within moments he had arrived back, exclaiming: 'There! I knew I'd seen it behind the chair.'

The sergeant dusted down his hat of harp-badged blue and settled it on his head, remarking:

'Sometimes I think you should be the guard, Pat, not me. Sometimes I don't seem to know whether I'm coming or going.'

Pat smiled and did his best to reassure his policeman-lodger.

'Ah, sure, anyone can forget where they put things, Sergeant. We're all only human, after all.'

The sergeant, gratified, replied:

'We are surely! And I suppose you're more likely to forget it if someone goes and hides it on you, the way a rascal of a youngster might!'

Pat, swallowing, jerked his head back and smiled, a little uncomfortably.

'Oh now, Sergeant!' he laughed.

'Sure a fellow'd do the like of that, stuff a man's cap in behind a cistern – who knows where the hell he'd stop?'

'Aye, Sergeant!' Pat fulsomely agreed. 'Who's to know!'

'A fellow'd do that – sure he'd as quick turn around and kill all belonging to him!'

Pat's reply seemed more distant now.

'I suppose he would,' he ventured, 'I expect so, Sergeant.'

'Oh, he would surely!' insisted the sergeant. 'His mother even! Mother, neighbours, strangers! All the same to him! Dispatch them into eternity like they were the shite of fleas! The lowest form of life in the world – a sack of good-for-nothing germs! Lives snuffed out without so much as a by your leave!'

Pat chewed his bottom lip for a moment or two before saying: 'Without even so much as a goodbye, even, Sergeant!'

The sergeant smacked his fist into his palm.

'Goodbye? Ha! You'd be waiting! But then, of course – a fella like that – there'd have to be something wrong with him, wouldn't there? There'd have to be a want in him!'

Pat frowned and shifted his weight from one foot to the other.

'Something wrong with him?' he said. 'A want?'

There was a dryness consuming the back of his throat.

'Aye. A bit of trouble up top. You know? I read a book one time. About a fellow – begod if he didn't go round the house in his mother's apron. Now, I don't know much about these things, Pat. But do you know what it said in the book?'

'What? What did it say?'

Pat unconsciously curled the string of his apron around his index finger.

'It said he wanted to *be* his mother! Can you believe the like of that? I mean for the love of God – his own mother! There's only one thing you could say about a fellow that would do the like of that. And do you know what that is?'

Pat found himself swallowing again.

'What, Sergeant?' he said.

There was no mistaking the sergeant's buoyant grin.

'He has his trousers on the wrong way round!'

The words seemed to leapfrog from Pat's lips.

'*Shut up!*' he cried abruptly.

It was as though the sergeant hadn't heard a word as he proceeded.

'A fellow'd do the like of that, I know how many years he'd spend cooling his heels in the chokey! And it wouldn't be just twenty-one either! Twenty-one'd be nothing for that!'

'Shut up!' snapped Pat again, with renewed venom. 'What do I care how many years he'd spend in the chokey! I don't care! What do I care how many years he'd spend in the ch—'

'Forty! Or fifty years maybe!' the sergeant cried, almost triumphantly.

'No!' snapped Pat.

'Not twenty-one!' cried the sergeant. 'Not twenty-one! Forty! Or fifty! Sixty at the least!'

'Stop saying that! Stop it!' demanded Pat.

The sergeant placed his large hand on his shoulder and said: 'Ah, sure, I'm only joking! I'm not that bad, really! A fellow that wants to be his mammy – what he'd want is pity. It's no good locking a specimen like him away in chokey. It's a complete waste of time!'

'Yes,' Pat murmured, awkwardly, 'I expect it is.'

'For he wouldn't be worth it!' cried the sergeant. 'Far better off giving him a few wee dolls to play with and letting him get on with it!'

The sergeant sighed and said:

'Well – I'd best get back. I have a report to write. There was a break-in down at Higginse's sweetshop this morning. Oh, by the way—'

His large hand disappeared into his jacket pocket. When it reappeared, it was clutching a small, foot-high female doll. 'I found this behind the chair this morning.'

Before Pat had time to reply, it had landed, as though high-kicking, in his lap, the tail of the sergeant's coat already disappearing out the front door.

*

The large hand upon the clock approaching twelve, at any moment now it will be nine o'clock but within the parlour a world which seems timelessly grey pertains. The only audible sound that of the chair which intermittently rocks as Pat in his apron slowly draws a comb through the long smooth and sparkly tresses of the small doll's hair, repeating hypnotically to himself: 'What does he know, Mammy? Sure he knows nothing! Hello! I'm Columbo! Everybody freeze! After all – Sergeant Foley is in town!'

A silence slowly descending then as Pat whispers: 'All I wanted was some peace, Mammy. That was all I wanted. To be allowed sit here with you. But he couldn't let me do it. They wouldn't let me do it, Mammy.'

It is as if the tiny figure's head and jet-black eyelashes are about to droop in affirmation.

*

It is late evening now and the sergeant is humming merrily as he knots his tie in the mirror.

'Are you going out, Sergeant?' asks Pat good-humouredly.

'Aye, Pat,' the sergeant replies, 'I was thinking of going down to Sullivan's for a few. Would you like to come? There's karaoke tonight, unless I'm mistaken!'

Pat was slightly taken aback.

'There's what?' he asked.

'Karaoke, Pat,' the sergeant replied. 'Lord, but you're not with the times at all. You get up and they have the words and all written out for you. All you have to do is lift out the microphone and—'

Without warning, the sergeant whirled – surprisingly nimble on his toes – and, spreading his hands, began to sing: '*I've counted the raindrops, I've counted the stars! I've counted a million of these prison bars!*'

The effect on Pat was instantaneous.

'Shut up! Shut up! Don't start that again! Go on to Sullivan's, then! Go on to hell!' he rasped.

The sergeant took a step backwards and raised his outspread palms in mock defence.

'Jeekers, Pat,' he said, 'you don't have to attack me! Just because you never heard of karaoke, you know! That's no shame!'

There was no mistaking Pat's high colour and the vibrations of his right hand.

'It's nothing to do with karaoke!'

The sergeant tossed back his head, removed his cap and said: 'Ah, to hell with it! I think I'll stay in. Sure I'm far too old for karaoke!'

'What—' began Pat, puzzled.

But the sergeant had already vanished into the library.

*

The open log fire dispatched large, irregular-shaped shadows onto the walls and ceiling of the library. Pat, fidgeting and seemingly very uncomfortable in his large, wingbacked armchair, appeared as someone bearing a great weight, regarding the composed, thumb-tapping sergeant from beneath heavy lidded, almost sullen eyes. The sergeant turned the pages of *Gardener's Monthly* and continued to whistle a very familiar tune softly before saying: 'Sure that auld karaoke's only for the young ones, eh, Pat?'

His low euphonious ejaculations were resumed once more.

'Will you stop that, please!' demanded Pat smartly.

The sergeant raised his head and said, quite taken aback: 'Stop what?'

Pat's knees slid together and his back became poker-stiff. 'Whistling!'

The sergeant smiled and returned to his magazine.

'Sure, Pat,' he replied, with just the tiniest hint of a smirk.

*

The slow, heavy ticks of the grandfather clock seemed to issue from some forgotten, entombed and cobwebbed basement. In the grate, the flames flapped like flags afire on ships of oak. The filigree of music as it left the sergeant's lips and came drifting through the silence might have been borne upon the wings of moths as yet so very far away.

'Will you shut up!' cried Pat, leaping up in his chair.

The sergeant slapped his knees with his large, foot-sized hands.

'Jesus, Mary and Joseph, Pat! You gave me a fright! God bless us sure it's only a little bit of a song!'

'Well, I don't like it, you hear? I don't like it!'

The sergeant lowered his head and said softly:

'Ah, Pat, but that'd make your mother sad. She used to love dancing to it below in The—'

'Leave my mother out of it!' snapped Pat.

The sergeant approached with outstretched arms.

'Jeekers, Pat,' he went on, 'sure I'm only saying. All the boys used to be saying: "Would you look at Mrs McNab! Boys, but wouldn't you like to—"'

Without realizing it, Pat had risen to his feet.

'Who said that?' he demanded. 'Who said it? They did not say it!'

The sergeant lowered his head, his voice a mere whisper now.

'They did, Pat. Sure didn't I hear them myself?'

Pat moved quite close to the sergeant.

'Who said it!' he demanded to know. 'Who did?'

The sergeant tossed back his head, dismissively.

'Och, sure don't you know! The same boys who said you have your trousers on the wrong way round! Pat – would you let go of my cardigan, please?'

Pat was in fact horrified to realize he had been holding the sergeant's cardigan for quite some time. He brushed the oatmeal-coloured arm gently and slowly moved backwards, a trifle lightheaded.

The sergeant gave him a big, unexpected smile.

'It's not that I mind, Pat, but you see – it was a present from my mother.'

The muscle in Pat's cheek jerked as he replied:

'Yes, Sergeant.'

'Who's still alive, thank God! Still walking the roads of Gullytown and not so much as a bother on her!'

Dusting down his trousers, he rose and stretched, adding blithely: 'Which is more than I can say for some mothers! Or other innocent folk who once upon a time were free to take the air about our little town! Well – good luck now, Pat!'

The sergeant did not turn as he crossed the road to see the orange flames in the grate performing a strange sort of Japanese Kabuki-type dance on Pat's whitemask face where he stood alone in the gloom, as if about to cry out or hurl himself into the fire but actually doing neither.

*

There can be little doubt but that the effect of this small 'contretemps' between the sergeant and Pat, plus, indubitably, the intense heat of the open log fire – and such was the level of his preoccupation that it never occurred to Pat to dampen it even slightly – was to elicit within him a sense of great unease, of feverish uncertainty and unreasonable sensitivity, such as might be experienced in the tropics. Evident now as he stood by the window of his bedroom, attired only in his pyjamas, clamping his hands over his ears in order that he might not hear the constant, piercingly taut strains of 'Twenty-One Years', its indomitable melody persisting, as though whistled from afar.

'Stop it!' Pat cried, stumbling as his eyes snapped shut and in that very instant he was no longer in a room complete with sideboard, bedside locker and portrait of Mother but there beneath a rotating mirrorball – God it was so hot! – in a dancehall of the 1950s ('Welcome To the Merryland!' ran the neon) as he watched spellbound while his mother – the young Mrs McNab! – glided along in a wide-skirted floral dress, smiling as she mimed the words of a familiar song – 'Twenty-One Years'!! And, standing close by, dredging her flesh hungrily, the red-cheeked figure that was Sergeant Foley, sinking his hands deep in his pockets as he moaned lasciviously: 'Would you look at that! Boys, wouldn't you like to slip that the budgeen one dark night or another!'

It seemed as if no time had passed at all, Pat having been returned to his bedroom with 'Foley' lying beneath him on the bed (he had just arrived back only moments before, having forgotten his keys), Pat's hands suddenly clutching the police-man's neck as he throttled the life out of him. There could be no denying the lack of restraint behind Pat's eyes – unshamed, vindicated.

'You're a liar!' he cried. 'You don't know what you're talking about! How dare you insult my mother!'

'Pat! Pat, you're strangling me!' the sergeant gasped, a little intoxicated, only now becoming aware of the gravity of the situation in which he now found himself.

As he composed himself, already sensing the first pigments of discolouring on his throat, he looked up to see Pat rummaging frantically in the wardrobe. A holdall was discharged, landing with a thud at his feet.

'Pack all your things and get out, Foley!' he heard his landlord cry. 'I know what you're doing! You think I don't know? Making all that stuff up to drive me mad! To get me to confess! That's what it's all about, isn't it? Oh yes! Oho but you're the smart fellow!'

'Confess? But confess to what, Pat?'

'The donkey man! The Bannion women! What? I don't know! The germs! Ha ha! The germs – what else?'

'Pat – are you on drugs?'

'No! I'm not on drugs! And well you know it! Maybe you are! Coming in here with your cock and bull stories!'

'Cock and bull stories?' gasped the sergeant, stroking his throat.

'About the station being burnt down. What kind of an eejit do you take me for?'

'Pat – before you go any further might I remind you that anything you say may be taken down in evidence—'

Pat's eyes leaped.

'Evidence! Ha! Prove it! Just prove I laid a finger on Mammy! Or that eejit from Ardee either! Or Tubridy! Old fatarse! Prove it! Go on – prove it about any of them, effing germs!'

The sergeant sighed.

'Pat – I'm not talking about eejits or their donkeys,' he said, 'I'm talking about assaulting an officer of the law. Which you have just done, Pat. Do you know what sentence you might expect from even the most lenient of judges for that?'

A number of fingers encircled themselves about Pat's wrist.

'I—' Pat began.

'You've made a big mistake, Pat!' the sergeant said. 'A *big* mistake!'

'It's your fault!' cried Pat shrilly. 'You didn't have to whistle! If you hadn't started whistling it would never have happened!'

The sergeant shook his head.

'I wasn't whistling, Pat,' he said in calm, measured tones, 'Pat – I was below in Sullivan's – remember?'

Pat's eyes narrowed as did his lips until they were as a looped piece of three-inch-long string drawn tightly across his face.

'You did!' he hissed resentfully. 'I heard you! I *know* I heard you!'

The policeman's countenance wore a sad and pained expression.

'Pat – are you sure you're OK?' he pleaded. 'Look at me, Pat. Tell me, what sort of whistling did you hear?'

There was no reply and no immediate indication that one was forthcoming. This was because the very moment the sergeant had ended his question, Pat's perception of him had begun to dramatically alter, to the extent that the features of 'the sergeant' or 'policeman' effectively now no longer existed, having been supplanted by those of '*Pat's mother*', whose pallid, slightly hirsute face now seemed to melt across the sergeant's and become seamlessly interwoven with it, her frail voice issuing now through faintly lipsticked lips as she said: '*Don't tell him, Pat. Don't tell him a single thing.*' Then, almost imperceptibly, the sergeant's face returned, his hand placed his hand on the back of his neck as he said: 'What sort of whistling, do you mind me asking, Pat?' The tone of voice this time was unmistakably authoritative, stentorian.

'*He's just like them all, Pat,*' Pat McNab was then shocked to hear – his mother's voice quite vivid now – '*just out for himself! Don't tell him a single thing or you know what will happen!*'

In that instant, Pat heard the clang of cell bars and beheld himself in a coarse cotton suit festooned with the heads of arrows.

His mother continued:

'They'll just take you away and you and I'll never see you again. We'll never be able to have our little chats like we used to. Maybe I could have brought you up better, Pat. But I loved you. You know that, don't you?'

A large knot formed in the base of Pat's throat.

'Yes, Mammy,' he said, swallowing hard.

'Pat!' the sergeant's bass voice demanded. 'Do you hear me talking to you? '

But, to Pat, there was only one voice audible, that of a sixty-five-year-old woman, who, through false teeth, continued:

'With horrible people coming around here to say those awful things about me. You heard what they said, didn't you, Pat? Pat, they're not true, those things. It's just so they can get you and me separated, you know that, don't you? Because that's all they want. All he wants. Pat, do you remember when you had something hard to do, I used to say: "Petals, darling, it'll be all right," when something was really hard?'

Pat intertwined his thumbs.

'Yes, Mammy,' he replied.

'Pat! Are you listening to me?' the sergeant's voice boomed – it seemed to emerge from the darkness of an oil drum.

'I love you, Mammy,' Pat said.

'Pat!' rasped the sergeant, shocked, as an odd, thin, sergeant-like smile appeared on Pat's lips.

'Pat,' rasped the sergeant, bunching his fist unconsciously, 'if you don't listen to me, I'll . . .'

Without warning he found himself staring at the tears which were coursing copiously down Pat's cheeks.

'Why can't you leave us alone!' erupted Pat. 'Why couldn't you just arrest me if you think I'm a bad man! Why couldn't you just come and say: "Come with me!" instead of going on and on until you drove me – it wasn't my fault they all ended up in the garden! They were germs! Every one of them, filthy, taunting, humming, singing, sickening-green-maggot germs! They made me! And I'd do it all again, if—'

Within seconds, the crimson-headed sergeant had Pat locked in a half-nelson. His captive squealed:

'And you! Why did you have to say that about the dance-hall! You had to say it, didn't you? You all have to say things!'

'Jesus, Mary and Joseph, Pat McNab, the things you've done! You know what's going to happen now, don't you?'

There was a faint clicking of indeterminate bone as Pat, sniffling, replied, 'Yes, Sergeant,' before adding, 'Sergeant – may I have one last request?'

*

The car park was overgrown and the old sign was more or less gone now, part of it flapping loosely above the drab, paint-flecked double doors, that had once opened on so many star-bright nights in the summers of long ago to admit the throngs of optimistic, apple-cheeked, jitterbugging innocents, Pat's mother among them. 'The Merryland,' sighed Pat to himself, turning to the older man and saying in a voice shot through with deep melancholy: 'Can we go in, Sergeant? Just for old times' sake.'

The sergeant stiffened.

'Oh, very well, then,' he said. 'But if we do – I want a full confession from you below at the station. You hear?'

Pat nodded meekly.

'Yes, Sergeant,' he agreed, adding: 'I'll sing like a lark.'

*

The interior was equally desolate. Slumped forward in despair from the walls hung a torn poster displaying the lost, and yet somehow hopelessly optimistic expression of a scallop-collared combo called Gerry and the Black Dots. Angled precariously above their heads, a splintered, gap-toothed mirrorball. There was a faint smell of urine long swept away and dried. Pat extended his index finger in the direction of the north-western corner.

'That's where she used to dance, Sergeant – isn't it? Right up there by yon corner.'

The sergeant replied, little emotion evident in his voice:

'Aye. That'd be it,' he phlegmatically replied.

'With the boys all saying: "Would you look at that. Would you look at that! I wouldn't mind—"'

The sergeant jerked his charge firmly.

'Come on now – hurry up!' he instructed firmly.

But Pat continued.

'The same boys who said I'd my trousers on the wrong way round and that you could tell by the way I walked I was—'

Suddenly Pat's eyes lit up. Animation is a word which perhaps approaches a description of his quite unexpected emotional transformation as he exultantly cried: 'Look! Look there, Sergeant! It's a guitar! Just like the old ones! It's like the bands never went away!'

Without warning, Pat had leaped up onto the stage, the sergeant gazing in near disbelief as his captive, positioned himself behind an old-fashioned microphone which for many years had stood sentinel in the abandoned palace of dreams long faded, crying:

'Oh, Sergeant! Look at it! Look at it! Isn't it fabulous?'

Pat's booming voice ricocheted from wall to perspiring wall.

'*Ladies and gentlemen! Welcome to the Merryland Ballroom!*'

The sergeant cupped his hand over his mouth and called out:

'Come on now! That's enough!'

'Oh wait, Sergeant! Please!' continued Pat – there was a slight whistling sound – 'And look! There's spotlights! I wonder do they still work? And would you believe it! An old-fashioned

Grundig tape recorder! It's fantastic! Oh, Sergeant! Just one song before we go, I beg you!'

The click of the switch was considerably amplified as Pat's thumb found its mark and the first familiar, crackling strains swam out into the hall – inevitably! –

The judge said, Stand up dear and dry up your tears
You're sentenced to Dartmoor for twenty-one years!

The lights which filled the hall then might have been from the eyes of Pat McNab as breathlessly he cried: 'Oh, Sergeant! If only my mother was here now! Ladies and gentlemen, welcome here tonight! Pat McNab is going to sing a special little song for you! Called: "I Wore My trousers On the Wrong Way Round"! Ahem! "*I wore my trousers on the wrong way round / I wore them in the country and I wore them in the town / And all the boys would say: 'Yes, here he comes again / Here's trousers-on-the-wrong-way-round walking down the lane!'*"'

The sergeant's patience by now was at an end and he leaped forward and gruffly set about Pat.

'OK! That's enough!' he snapped. 'Let's get going.'

Pat seemed to go limp in his arms.

'Yes, Sergeant,' he said, adding, 'Sergeant?'

'What?' the policeman responded.

'Just for old times' sake – can I sing one last little song? Just for Mam?'

'No!' the sergeant firmly replied.

Once again, tears began to appear in Pat's eyes.

'Sergeant! Please!' he pleaded. 'Please! Just one last number!'

The sergeant's cheeks seemed inflamed.

'Oh, for Christ's sake! Go on, then!'

Pat gingerly approached the microphone stand and wet his lips, coughing slightly as he brought his knees together, crossed his hands over his groin and began:

'*The judge said, Stand up dear and dry up your tears*

You're sentenced to Dartmoor for twenty-one years —'

The sergeant's eyes twinkled slightly, despite himself.

'And here was me thinking you didn't like that song, Pat!' he called.

'I don't, actually, Sergeant!' Pat replied – in a surprisingly chirpy tone – before curling his hand about the cold metal of the mike stand, suspending it for some brief seconds before delivering a steady, measured blow to the side of the sergeant's head, an action which he continued to firmly and insistently repeat, all the while shrilly crying:

'That's right! I told you I didn't like it! But you had to whistle it! You had to come along and whistle it! And say bad things about Mam! Why! Why, germ! Tell me, guard germ! Tell, policeman of emerald-green rottenness!'

A *thupp* sound was the consequence of yet another firm blow, this time to the further temple. It was only a matter of time before the now considerably bloodied officer of the law fell to the floor of the stage, issuing only the slightest of moans, as Pat clutched the scarlet-stained microphone stand, wiped his eye and pleaded: 'Why couldn't you just stay in the station and sing ordinary songs? Why? Why did it have to be an Emerald Germ?'

*

There is a smile on Pat's face as he opens the curtains and admits the sun's rays to the morning kitchen, placing a bowl of pot-pourri on the window ledge. Tying his apron string at the back just as he hears the doorbell. 'Hmm! I wonder who that could be now!' he muses to himself, placing an index finger upon his lips. Quite unaware that he is humming '*I've counted the raindrops / I've counted the stars / I've counted a million of these prison bars!*', he opens the door, and there to his amazement sees standing before him the most dashing looking man he has ever laid eyes on, resplendent in brown camelhair coat and silk scarf, his beautiful Italian shoes spotlessly polished.

'Hi! I'm Dexy McGann!' the stranger declared. 'I've been down London way – wo! This past twenty-one years now! I was wondering could I come in? I'm an old boyfriend of your mother's, you see! Herself and me danced a few steps – back in the old days, guess!'

That a gust of arctic wind passed between them in that very instant would be very difficult to prove empirically – the assertion even futile, perhaps. But there can be no denying the dramatic altering of Pat's features and the sudden departure from the region of his eyes of what is commonly known as '*human feeling*' or '*sympathy*'. Something which, sadly, perhaps due to a corrosive 'urbaneness' which had over the years seen off his natural rustic qualities of instinct and alertness, the returned expatriate failed utterly to discern, blithely striding in as Pat smiled and held the door open. Blissfully unaware of the word 'germ' which issued almost inaudibly from the side of his host's mouth, behind him swinging shut an outwardly unremarkable, old-fashioned wooden door which, had the insouciant Dexy McGann but known it, might equally have been fashioned of the most ungiving, Hyperborean steel ever struck in the flaming deepest furnaces of the blackest pits of hell.

Permissions

'The Turfman From Ardee' trad. arr. Margaret Barry, publ. Matchbox Music. Reproduced by kind permission of Saydisc Records.

'Seth Davey (Whiskey on a Sunday)' by Glyn Hughes copyright © 1966 Spin publications assigned to TRO Music Ltd. London SW10 0SZ. International copyright secured. All rights reserved. Used by permission.

'Fly Me to the Moon (In Other Words)' words and music by Bart Howard copyright © 1954 Almanac Music Inc., New York, N.Y. International copyright secured. All rights reserved.

'Old Flames (Can't Hold A Candle to You)' words and music by Hugh Moffatt and Pebe Sebert copyright © 1978 Rightsong Music Inc., USA. Warner/Chappell Music Ltd, London W6 8BS. Reproduced by permission of International Music Publications Ltd.

'Island of Dreams' words and music by Tom Springfield copyright © 1962 Chappell Music Ltd. Warner/Chappell Music Ltd, London W6 8BS. Reproduced by permission of International Music Publications Ltd.

'Little Drummer Boy' words and music by Harry Simeone, Henry Onorati and Katherine K. Davis copyright © 1958 Mills Music Inc. and International Korwin Corp, USA. Worldwide print rights controlled by Warner Bros Publications